FIONA LOWE

Picture Perfect Wedding

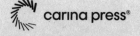

carina press®

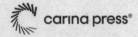 carina press®

ISBN-13: 978-0-373-00240-5

Picture Perfect Wedding

Copyright © 2013 by Fiona Lowe

Recycling programs for this product may not exist in your area.

www.CarinaPress.com

Printed in U.S.A.

Dear Reader,

Welcome back to Whitetail, Wisconsin, and Weddings that Wow! I had so much fun writing this second book in the series, and I even visited a Wisconsin dairy to see the cows in action! So what's been happening in Whitetail since Saved by the Bride (Book One of the Wedding Fever trilogy)? Well, Whitetail is experiencing its second summer as a destination wedding town and the business is growing. It's summer, and the grass is lush and green, the covered bridges cross burbling streams, and farmer Luke Anderson's sunflower field is the perfect place for amazing wedding photos. At least that's what Erin Davis, the wedding photographer from Minneapolis, thinks. She has a very strong reason for wanting to take the perfect wedding photograph in the picture-perfect sunflower field, and she's driven to Whitetail to convince the recalcitrant farmer to give his permission. Luke Anderson, the farmer in question, isn't so sure.

I did a lot of research for this story and learned a lot about family farms. They're both a business and a heritage, and this can make handing them over to the next generation very difficult and fraught. Of course, I like to give my characters a really hard time, so having read an article about the "quarter life crisis" I decided to throw that into the mix, as well. I hope you fall in love with my sexy dairyman, who is gorgeous, conflicted and utterly confused. All his life, Luke has only ever wanted to farm, but these past nine months, he's been questioning what he wants out of life. And for the first time ever he's unsettled and lacking direction. The last thing he needs in his life is a geographically challenged wedding photographer from the city who arrives with crazy ideas, a purse dog and a determination that makes concrete look soft.

There are lots of animals in this book, and I had a blast pairing up a country dog with a city dog. Maggie-May, Erin's pup, is based on a real dog I know...a Maltese Shih Tzu cross terrier who believes she is a cow dog! For photos, visit my website.

All the townsfolk you met in Saved by the Bride are back, and it was my pleasure to be able to tell Nicole's story. She is now the wedding planner for Weddings that Wow, and although she loves the support of the townsfolk, she's also finding it claustrophobic. How does a woman move on with her life when an entire town is grieving for her dead husband?

For photos, the book trailer and more information about the Wedding Fever trilogy please visit my website at www.fionalowe.com. I love hearing from my readers, and you can contact me at fiona@fionalowe.com, or hang out with me on Facebook (FionaLoweRomanceAuthor) and on Twitter (@fionalowe).

Happy reading!

Love,

Fiona x

Acknowledgments

Writing a book wouldn't be possible without the generous help of so many people. Special thanks to Amanda and Swaney for introducing me to Maggie-May, cow-dog extraordinaire. Please forgive the liberty of exchanging the echidna bark for an American coon bark.

A thousand thanks to Dairy Carrie and to Jessica, The Modern Farmwife. Not only have I enjoyed your entertaining blogs about life on a dairy, I've appreciated very much the time you took to patiently answer my emails. Any mistakes I've made about AI, calving and milking are solely mine.

Thanks also to Kari Lynn, who introduced me to Tim and the other fabulous dairymen and dairywomen on Twitter who tweet from their tractors! And to Mark for his invaluable advice about sunflowers. I would have been lost without you all. Go #Agchat!

Special thanks to my good friend Doris from Wisconsin, who took me out to visit a family farm. Poor Farmer Doug had no clue he was going to be quizzed to within an inch of his life by an Aussie who calls four-wheelers quad bikes, and Holstein cows Friesians. Thanks, Doug,

for allowing me to witness a herd health check, for answering all my questions in such detail and for the special opportunity to tour your farm.

Thanks to the entire team at Carina Press and with special mention of my wonderful editor, Charlotte. Carrie and Stephanie, who answer all my queries so cheerfully, Tara and team for the gorgeous cover, and Angela for her enthusiastic support of digital-first.

Last but not least, I give thanks to my family, whose love, support and belief in me keeps me going.

Whitetail Bugle: Online Edition
Positions Vacant/Wanted
Relief milker required at Lakeview Farm. Call Luke
Anderson (715-555-8391) or stop by the farm.
Relief cleaner for Lakeview B&B and cottages. Call
Wade Anderson NOT Luke.
(715-555-8399)

Chicago Daily News
Business opportunity! Weary of fast-paced city life?
Move your photography business to Whitetail,
Wisconsin, land of lakes, glorious sunsets and
brides. Call Nicole at Affairs With Hair at
715-555-4351

Twitter
@ErinDavis. You captured our wedding day perfectly.
Thank you!

ONE

AT DEE END of dee road, turn left.

"Right you are, Patrick." Erin Davis answered her GPS with a grin. She might be in the heart of the dairy state and surrounded by cornfields and cows, but inside the car with her playlist blaring, she was having an Irish day. *Anything* to make the time pass quicker on this unexpected country dash across state lines.

The Cranberries started singing about dreams. Personally, Erin thought dreams were overrated having lived through the fallout of ten too many of her father's ill-conceived ideas. No, she was more of a risk-free planner. She had a gut filled with determination, a goal in sight and, most importantly, a step-by-step chart of objectives, which she was ticking off one by one. The brides she'd photographed were thrilled with her work and recommended her to their friends and family, but as great as word of mouth was, it was all slower than she'd hoped. Bottom line? She could do with more bridal bookings so she could give up her loathsome part-time waitressing job.

A memory of accompanying her mother to a pawn shop and watching the pain as she parted with her own mother's watch quickly reminded her that a slow and steady build of a business was better than a fast rise and a spectacular bust. Things were going okay and if she had anything to do with it, all her hard work would lead to her becoming *the* wedding photographer that brides all over the Midwest and beyond would book the moment the sparkly ring was slipped on their finger.

"I make everyone look happy no matter what and I do it good, hey, Maggie-May."

Her Maltese–Shih Tzu terrier cross and fluffy-white sidekick yapped her *You know it, girl* approval.

The only dark cloud right now was the fact that her current bride wasn't happy, hence the reason Erin was driving from Minneapolis, through lands filled with lakes, to a dot on the map called Whitetail, Wisconsin. It was Erin's mantra to do everything she could to keep her brides happy and with Constance Littlejohn, she was doing that and then some. Unlike her name, Connie was far from constant but she had an open checkbook, shared a great idea and she was Erin's ticket to winning the prestigious "Memories" photo competition for bridal photographers. Winning the Memmy, as it was affectionately known in the industry, would be a pinnacle career point and one Erin wanted not just for the professional accolades but for the security it would give her business. The security she craved so she could sleep at night.

The Welcome to Whitetail—Weddings That Wow sign announced she'd arrived at the town. She'd never heard of it until Connie had dropped a copy of *US Bride* on her desk open at the article about Chicago heiress Bridget Callahan's wedding. Connie had said, "I want the same only bigger, better and with a twist." Erin had enthusiastically accepted the challenge.

She smiled as she passed under a banner announcing a wedding tomorrow and she immediately had to slow for a horse pulling an empty, white carriage. Used to photographing couples in a carriage amid the tall buildings of Minneapolis, she instantly thought of the pretty lake and covered bridge she'd driven past earlier. It would make the perfect backdrop with the early evening light. A fizz of excitement bubbled through her and she made a mental note to discuss it with Connie.

She pressed the GPS to check on her instructions again because she had the world's worst sense of direction and routinely got lost in her hometown. Out here in the boonies, she had no hope without support.

In one quarter mile, take the second left.

She groaned. "Patrick, my lovely, that's all very well but exactly how far is one quarter mile?"

As a photographer she could visualize setups, solve the problems of large group poses, deal with light and depth like a puzzle, but tell her something was fifty feet away and she had no clue and winged it every time. She glanced in her rearview mirror. Unlike the city, at least she didn't have a line of traffic behind her and she doubted the orange tractor would catch up to her. She'd crawl along until the red arrow on the GPS actually showed her the turn and that way she'd avoid her usual mistake of turning too early.

The bridal march ring tone on her cell phone chirped, cutting across U2 and telling her it was a client. Her old station wagon had been built long before cell phones were *de rigueur* and Bluetooth was mandatory so she used the cutting-edge technology of yelling at her phone, which rested in a designated bracket on the dash. "Hi, it's Erin."

"Have you spoken to him yet?" Connie's high-pitched voice demanded.

Erin was used to Connie's direct approach. "I haven't

quite reached the farm, but according to Patrick, I'm not far away."

"Who?"

"Patrick. He's the gorgeous Irish voice on my GPS."

A puff of breath came down the phone. "Concentrate, Erin. I'm talking about Farmer Joe or whatever his name is."

Erin mentally slapped herself. Connie was a busy woman who rarely had time for jokes. The soon-to-be bride was engaged to a man who wanted to marry her and, by default, she had no understanding or need of imaginary chats with a sexy, lilting Irish accent. Nor would she understand that those conversations were as close as Erin had come to a date in months. Working every weekend, whether it be photography or waitressing, made it hard to meet people.

That and the fact you put the business ahead of everything.

She did and she had no problem. She was investing in a secure future and that meant pleasing her clients. She gave herself a shake. "Sorry. Yes, I'm totally concentrating. I know how important this is to you." *How important it is to me.*

"Good, because *you* have to make this happen for me."

When Connie had outlined her ideas for her wedding photos, she'd assured Erin that everything in Whitetail was organized. She'd told her that the bride and groom got the keys to the town for their day and there'd be no problem with the photo shoot because Connie had a friend of a friend whose cousin had married a man who knew a farmer in the county. Erin—perhaps naively—had believed her right up until the mercy phone call she'd received at four yesterday afternoon.

People often commented on Erin's people skills so she had no doubt that making personal contact with the farmer and getting him to agree to the use of his field would all be a walk in the park. "I promise you, it's all going to work out just fine."

"It better. I've left him thirteen messages this week and he hasn't returned a single one of them."

Thirteen seemed a lot. Erin slowed, signaled, turned left and automatically put on her soothing voice. "Connie, I'm sure you have a ton of other wedding things that need your attention and I have this. I'm almost at the farm and by suppertime everything will be just fine."

"Farmers are always crying poor, right, so if you need to, double the money," Connie instructed. "Offer him a few nights at Daddy's hotel so he can get out of the country and live a little in the city. Do what you have to do, just get me that sunflower field."

The line went dead just as Patrick said, *Go straight.*

The minor county road wound through rolling green pastureland dotted with red-and-white barns and tall, blue silos. In the distance, she could see stands of birch, beech and aspen trees as well as her favorite Christmas tree, the white spruce, which up until now she'd only seen growing on a Christmas tree farm. Raised in a series of cities, she was struck by the mix of light and dark green leaves that contrasted so beautifully with the clear, blue sky. Beyond the trees lay the shimmering water of a large lake, which she assumed must be the one the many signs in Whitetail had pointed to promising "the perfect vacation." The vibrant colors of nature combined with such clarity and vividness that she pulled over.

"We have to shoot this, Maggie-May, it's truly beautiful." Grabbing her dog and her camera, she jumped out of the car and took some long shots to help satisfy the urge she had to go exploring rather than keeping on task.

Ten minutes later she was back in the car, following Patrick's instructions, although the last *turn right* had her worried. The farmland seemed to have disappeared and she was driving through dappled light cast by a thousand trees, and there wasn't a cow in sight. She consulted her backup map but it only showed the main county roads and, given this road was unpaved and she'd passed a brown sign a mile ago that had proclaimed Rustic Road, she was pretty certain she needed to go back. There wasn't a lot of room to do a U-turn and the edges of the road looked decidedly soft. She felt every inch a city girl in a foreign place. "Patrick, my gorgeous hunk, where are we?"

At dee end of dee road turn right.

She bit her lip and weighed up her options. If she took the bend she might find somewhere safe to turn around and if she drove slowly she'd avoid ending up in a precarious situation like the people who put all their trust in a GPS. People who drove into a lake or ran out of fuel stranded in the desert. People who ended up on the news, lampooned on websites and, worse still, recipients of a Darwin Award.

Maggie-May barked and pawed the window.

Erin glanced up, gasped and grabbed her camera as a deer leaped and pranced across the road, quickly disappearing into the trees until even its white tail had been absorbed by the dense foliage. Minneapolis seemed a world away from this. With a tug of disappointment that she'd missed capturing the beautiful creature, she set her camera down. "Next time, Maggie-May."

She threw the car into gear and continued down the rough road, which turned sharply. The gravel changed to flattened grass and she bumped along a bit farther until the trees gave way to wide, open spaces. She pressed the brakes hard. Black-and-white cows, with green grass hanging from their big, pink tongues, lifted their heads and turned to gaze at the car with interest. They started walking toward her, their gait increasing with each step. The closest she'd ever been to a cow before was the label on the plastic gallon of milk that graced her breakfast table. Her heart leaped into her throat as one cow licked her window. "Patrick!"

You have reached your destination.

LUKE ANDERSON SAT on the small, sandy beach with his border collie, Mac, resting his head on his thigh. He gazed out at the blue lake, letting the warmth of the sand, the haunting wail-call of the loon and the gray-white colors of the rocks seep through him. No one had ever asked him if he had a favorite part of the farm, but should they, he'd immediately answer, "the lake beach."

Not that he didn't have strong ties to all of the farm; he did. He'd grown up exploring every inch of it and loving it all but this beach was extra special. He'd been coming here for as long as he could remember. He'd run here to lie low the first time he'd gotten into serious trouble from his father. At ten he'd committed a dairyman's cardinal sin by leaving a gate open and inadvertently allowed the bull to escape into a pasture of top milkers. He still remembered the shock that had torn through him as his usually mild-mannered father let rip with a string of curses he'd rarely heard him use before or since—words Luke hadn't even known his father knew.

He scooped up a handful of sand, letting the grains fall through his fingers. This beach had been the site of his first solo campout at nine and much later, at fifteen, it had been the place he'd first kissed a girl. Brandy Peterson. He smiled, recalling the inauspicious start to acquiring a skill he was now told he was very good at. Back then, having no clue what he was supposed to do, his tongue had been frayed by her braces but it had been worth it for the quick touch of his hand against the warm curve of her breast. At that moment, Luke had known for certain that unlike his older brother Wade, he loved the touch, taste and scent of women.

And over the years, he'd fully explored that realization many times with many women, taking full advantage of his college years. Later, he'd built on that experience during the five years he'd worked for an artificial insemination company where the job had taken him across the country and as far away as Australia and New Zealand. He idly wondered what Brandy was doing now. Like him, she'd left town for college, only she hadn't returned. Most of the young women who left Whitetail didn't return, which left the northwoods town with a higher than the state average of single men. He was part of that statistic. Not that he minded the single part—he was more than happy with that.

He shielded his eyes as the thrum of a vacationer's boat engine reverberated across the lake, reminding him of the reason he was on the beach today. The future of the farm. He pulled his phone out of his pocket and reread the email from his high school buddy Axel Jacobson, who was now a real estate agent in Milwaukee. "Parcel of land valued @ 1.3m." He abruptly shut it down, blocking out the number, which made his gut churn every time he read it.

Earlier in the summer, Axel had been in Whitetail, visiting his sister, Annika, who'd both surprised and thrilled the town when she'd married Finn Callahan last winter. Axel had stopped by for a beer and they'd come down to the lake for a cookout and some reminiscing.

"So your mom finally got your dad to go to Arizona?" Axel had asked.

"Yep." Luke shook his head slowly. "I didn't believe it until I saw the truck pull out through the gate. Even then, I expected the old man to be back by milking time because in thirty years I can count on one hand how many times he's left the farm for more than two days."

"And?"

"He promised Mom he'd give Arizona a trial run. His emails make it sound like he loves it down there. I expected him to be on the phone ten times a day giving me instructions and asking about the cows, but when he does call he can only talk about his golf game. I think he's officially retired."

Axel pushed his aviator glasses onto the top of his head and gave him a long look. "So you're really going to take it on? Be a dairyman like your father?"

Luke took a long pull on his beer. The answer to the question should have been an instant and emphatic "Yes." "It's what I always said I wanted. An Anderson has owned this land for six generations."

"Land can be sold. It's how I make my living." Axel had leaned back and taken in the view. "People want simpler times and they don't mind paying for them. Lake frontage like this would give you a pocket full of

Benjamins and then you'd have the cash to do whatever you want, wherever you want it."

And that was part of the problem. He didn't know what the hell he wanted. "It's not just mine to sell, Ax. A family farm is exactly that, and Keri and Wade have a stake in this too."

"So talk to them about it."

Those six simple words had been spoken a month ago and the conversation still remained buried in his to-do list, under the heading of *way too hard*. Now, with the email from Axel, it had suddenly become more real. He ran his hand across the back of his neck, his skin hot from the sun, and he tried to shrug off the unsettled feelings that had arrived with the spring and had been making the long and busy summer days a chore rather than a pleasure.

Mac lifted his head and a moment later Luke heard the low, mellow bellow of "the girls." He glanced at his watch. Usually at this point in the afternoon the heifers were so busy eating their way through the pasture that they didn't have time for mooing.

Mac was already standing, his ears cocked and tilted in the direction of the sound. Luke sighed, feeling weary after spending a large chunk of the previous night bringing in hay. The farm was calling again, as it always did, breaking in on his brief respite. Unlike Mac, he wasn't feeling the thrill of discovering what was probably another problem he had to solve.

Mac barked accusingly.

Luke reluctantly pushed to his feet. "Guess we better go see what's up." He followed his trotting dog away from the lake and back through the thick grove of birches and as he broke clear of the foliage, he blinked.

Twice. An old station wagon was parked in the middle of his field and ringed by confused Holsteins. No wonder the girls were making so much noise. To them, a vehicle meant food but somehow he didn't think this car was going to start heaving silage out of its tailgate any time soon.

Mac gave a low growl.

"Steady."

Mac stayed put but the hairs on his back rose and he quivered all over, every muscle desperate to be unleashed so he could race to the car. He was a friendly dog so this reaction was unexpected but then Luke heard a high-pitched yapping. Now he understood Mac's imploring brown-eyed gaze. There was more than one imposter in their midst.

An automatic groan crossed his lips. It might be a lost tourist looking for Wade's cottages and B and B, although it was probably the new but unreliable cleaner who'd promised to arrive yesterday but hadn't turned up. Either way, with Wade in Chicago for the night, it was a mess he'd have to fix. Hell, he hoped the car didn't sink after yesterday's rain.

As if exactly on cue, the car engine roared, the wheels spun and mud flew everywhere. Thirty seconds later, it sank.

No such luck.

A bangle-adorned, slender arm extended out through the sunroof, frantically waving back and forth.

"Walk up," he instructed Mac who made a beeline for the cows and started moving them away from the car. "Come on," he called out to the girls, backing up Mac, and he cut straight through the newly created gap, put his hand on the car door and yanked it open.

A pair of tanned, shapely legs swung out, followed by a flash of white denim shorts and a watermelon-pink sun top. "Thank you! I thought I was going to be stuck here forever. Oh…" The young woman gazed down at her sandal-clad feet as mud oozed into them and through her toes.

Her head jerked up and chestnut hair—which Luke assumed under normal circumstances probably fell in a smooth, sleek bob—flew everywhere. "Tell me it's just mud?" Wide, green eyes the same vivid green of his freshly mowed meadow implored him to tell her what she wanted to hear. "Please."

He shrugged and a perverse part of him took delight in telling this clothes horse with a lousy sense of direction the truth. "It's a mud and manure combo."

Horror streaked across her cheeks and she wrinkled her nose in disgust, making her diamond nose-stud glint in the sunshine. Her license plates, her clothes and her hairstyle all strongly hinted that she came from the city, but it was the scrunching up of her nose which confirmed it. On someone with a cute, button nose, the action might have been forgiven, but on her honker, the wrinkle screamed pure disgust.

"This is a farm. What do you expect?" A spurt of irritation fizzed through him, gaining hold only to stall abruptly the moment he caught her horror hitting her mouth. It pulled plump lips into a perfect red and glossy O. It was a mouth at complete odds with the rest of her put-together look of Miss-perfectly-matched-and-accessorized. It was a mouth that promised pure, adult pleasure.

"Of course it had to be manure," she wailed. "I'm wearing brand-new suede sandals."

It took Luke a moment to realize he was staring at her lush mouth and he hauled his gaze up to her eyes. "Rubber boots are the footwear of choice around here."

She grimaced as if the thought would summon the fashion police. "I'll be sure to remember that for next time and pack a pair in my trunk."

"Sounds like a plan although I don't recommend you make a habit of driving through pastureland."

Her shoulders rose and fell. "Sorry about that. My GPS let me down. I'm looking for Lakeview Farm."

"You've found it." She must be Wade's missing cleaner although her French nails were at complete odds with that notion. She didn't look like the sort of woman who'd clean for a living but then again, women frequently told him that he didn't look like a farmer, so who was he to judge.

"You should have turned left at the fork in the road to get to the cottages and the B and B." He fished the key Wade had left him out of his pocket. "Seeing as you're late arriving, Wade's not here to greet you but he's left a list of cleaning jobs and he'll be back tomorrow. If you turn around and go the way you came you can't miss the sign."

"I'm not looking for a B and B. I'm looking for…" She turned and opened the car door before bending over and reaching across the driver's seat.

Luke's eyes automatically followed the curve of her ass, which was unexpectedly sweet, and without being aware of moving he found he'd taken two steps forward. It was like being pulled by an invisible force and he didn't like it one bit but before he had time to step back, she straightened up and turned to face him. The scent of crushed mint and lemon rushed his nostrils. It instantly reminded him of the delicious and refreshing sensations of drinking summer lemonade under the cool of a tree on a hot day.

She stopped abruptly as she realized he was standing quite close to her and he felt the breeze against his face created by the piece of paper she was waving at him. "Luke Anderson. I'm looking for Luke Anderson."

Surprise rocked through him and he opened his mouth to reply when a yapping streak of white flew out the open car door.

Mac barked furiously, his hackles rising fast in defense of his master and his property.

"Steady, Mac," Luke growled, not wanting Mac to eat the terrier.

A second later, Luke yelped as the needle-sharp jab of teeth tore through his jeans and clamped around his calf. The damn thing was biting him. He thrust out his right leg, shaking it hard, trying to dislodge the mutt.

Mac leaped.

The woman yelled, "Maggie-May," and threw herself between Mac and her dog. Her chest knocked into Luke's hip and with one of his legs already in the air, the momentum overbalanced him. He fell to the ground taking her with him.

The wind left his lungs, stunning him for a moment but as cold mud lined his back and oozed through his shirt before trickling down into the gap at the top of his jeans, he slowly became aware of hands gripping his upper arms and a delicious heat seeping into him from chest to toe. Her breasts pressed hard against his chest. Her legs tangled with his, and one knee was pushed up against his crotch.

Air whooshed back into his lungs as his entire body

tensed and his testicles tightened protectively against the possibility of being firmly kneed. Then he went hard.

Shit.

Her eyes did that startled wide-eyed thing again, only this time it wasn't caused by mud and he knew she'd just felt his hard-on against her belly. *Double shit.* He'd always prided himself on his control with women and this reaction to her made no sense because apart from that hooker mouth and a sweet behind, she looked exactly like the sort of high-maintenance woman he deliberately gave a wide berth. He dated women who were relaxed, uncomplicated and out for a good time.

Correction, used to date.

Since coming home to the farm a year ago, he hadn't dated anyone because casual was too hard in a town the size of Whitetail. No guy wanted to meet their fling at the grocery store or the bar every day for the next decade. So he'd hardly dated much lately but even so, he had more restraint than this. It was time to take charge and wrench back control.

To the high-pitched yapping of the terrier and the full-fledged barks of Mac, Luke gripped her arms and rolled her off him. Wiping mud out of his eyes, he managed to grind out, "I'm Luke Anderson."

Amidst the noise from the dogs and the cows, he thought he heard her groan.

TWO

UTTERLY STUNNED, ERIN stared at the mud-soaked man in front of her and died a thousand deaths. She'd just knocked the one man she needed to make a favorable impression on into a pile of mud and manure. Then she'd lain on top of him like a dog in heat. Her cheeks burned hot and her breasts tingled at the memory of being pressed against his rock-solid chest and caressed by the faint but firm beat of his heart.

God, he'd felt good. Amazing. Solid. She'd clutched his arms but her fingers had barely dented the firm muscles that lay under all that golden skin. Still, no matter how gorgeous, he was a stranger and she didn't make a habit of lying on top of men she didn't know. She couldn't quite work out why she hadn't scrambled off him the moment they'd hit the ground.

Because this is as close as you've been to a real, live man in far too long.

Well, yes, there was that. To her acute embarrassment, a moment before he'd summarily rolled her off him, he'd given her a look that said, totally *inappropriate behavior.* He knew she'd lingered. Why, oh why, was this man Connie's obstreperous farmer? It wasn't fair that he hadn't given her a single clue to his occupation. After all, where was the flannel shirt? The farm supplies baseball cap? A man in his fifties?

Nothing about Luke Anderson said farmer or even

hinted at the profession. In fact, everything said, *cover model for Calvin Klein.* Messy-cut, sun-kissed blond hair glinted in the sunshine and his cheeks had matching dark gold stubble. His square, broad shoulders supported a royal-blue cutoff shirt, which did nothing to hide solid and tantalizingly rounded biceps, and butt-hugging straight-leg jeans lay against narrow hips and a washboard-flat stomach. He was, without a doubt, one of the most handsome men she'd ever seen.

Piercing blue eyes now tinged with shards of ice burned her. "Get that *thing* of yours under control."

Maggie-May had released his leg but she was now hunkered down facing off the much bigger border collie. Even though Erin knew it was her dog who had caused this mess, she took umbrage at Mr. Luke Anderson calling her precious a *thing.* "That thing is a dog, thank you very much."

He scowled at her and his skin tightened over prominent cheekbones, making his previously handsome face suddenly stark and hard. "No." He pointed to the dog he'd called Mac. "That's a dog. Yours is just a damn nuisance."

"Look, I'm really sorry she tried to bite you but she was just protecting me."

In one fluid movement he rose to his feet and well over six feet of pure, unadulterated maleness stared down at her. A sweep of heat rushed through her, darting directly to the apex of her thighs, making it glow deliciously hot. It hadn't done that in a very long time and she fought hard not to press her legs together and gulp at all that gorgeousness.

Incredulity crawled across chiseled cheeks. "Protecting you from what exactly?"

This time she swallowed and said quietly, "You."

"Me?" His arms flew out in front of him. "What the hell did I do?"

Maggie-May growled and moved toward him. Erin grabbed her diamante-studded collar and tucked the wriggling and barking dog firmly under her arm. "You got a bit close to me at the car."

His jaw tightened and then indecently long eyelashes—the length and thickness women paid a lot of money to have created for them—brushed against his cheeks for an instant before he hooked his gaze to hers and seemed to take in a deep breath. "I apologize for invading your personal space."

Anytime, the frustrated woman inside her called out loudly. Erin instantly stomped on her inner slut and nodded her acceptance of his terse apology, which really didn't sound much like one at all. Taciturn and brusque. Hmm, he was a farmer after all.

"Shh, Maggie-May." She stroked her dog, who gave her a confused look and finally stopped barking, but kept her eyes fixed firmly on Farmer Anderson. Meanwhile, Erin struggled against the morass of mud that slurped around her, feeling her feet slipping inside her completely inappropriate and now ruined footwear. Her wickedly expensive sandals, whose purchase she'd justified as an investment in her business because they gave her the air of a successful photographer, which impressed potential clients.

As much as she wanted to get up out of the mud on her own, the fact she was holding Maggie-May meant she couldn't get her balance. Meanwhile, Luke Anderson hadn't moved a muscle and she was starting to wonder if Connie had been right about him deliberately ignoring her calls. Cross with herself for having to ask for help, cross with him for not offering any, she blurted out, "Would it be asking too much for you to give me a hand?"

Blue eyes narrowed. "Is that useless fluff ball of yours going to bite me?"

She wanted to growl at him just like Maggie-May. "Put it this way. If I let her go so I can get up on my own, she just might. If you help me up while I hold her, she won't."

Without a word, he extended his hand. She slid her palm against his and as she gripped his hand, he wrapped long, work-hardened fingers firmly around her wrist. A vortex of tingling shimmers spun up her arm and then exploded like fireworks in her chest before raining down and spreading through her like the warmth of mulled wine, and stripping her limbs of their strength.

Damn it. As lovely as it was to have a man make her feel like this, Luke Anderson wasn't the guy of choice. She locked her knees against the boneless feeling. It wouldn't be a good look to rise to her feet only to fall. The feminist in her definitely didn't want that to happen.

"Brace yourself against me," he said.

Yes, please. She shook her head against the wanton hoe the mud seemed to have released.

Luke sighed and frustration played over his lips. "Just do as I say or we'll both end up back in the mud."

She quickly preempted and stomped on any outrageous comments her girly parts might make on that visual and said, "Ready when you are."

He pulled and with a departing slurping sound from

the bog, she found herself nose to shoulder with him.
"Thank you."

"You're welcome." The perfunctory words sounded
weary and lacked the backup of their true meaning. It
was more along the lines of, *You're a complete pain
in the ass.*

She gazed down at her new-season but now mud-
stained silk top, horrified to see it was not only see-
through but clung to her like a second skin. She hastily
brought Maggie-May up against her chest to cover her
black lace demi-bra, which this morning had seemed
the perfect choice but was now hiding absolutely nothing. She bit her lip, hating what she knew she had to
ask. "Is it at all possible for me to use your shower?"

Luke Anderson seemed to be staring so intently at
her shoulder that she glanced to her left but all she could
see was more mud.

"It's possible, Miss…?"

Oh, God, she hadn't even introduced herself. "Erin.
Erin Davis." She wasn't prepared to volunteer anything
more until she was clean and wearing clothes that didn't
expose her breasts to the world.

"Well, Erin Davis, it doesn't look like your car is
going anywhere without the help of my tractor." Res-
ignation clung to his words. "I suppose you can take a
shower at the house while I pull it out."

An image of him naked with water sluicing down his
body slammed into her so hard she swayed. Oh man,
who knew falling in mud messed with hormones.

This guy is business not recreation, she told herself
firmly. Besides, the hostile way he was looking at her—as
if she was one giant problem that had to be solved—
left her in no doubt that even if they'd met under better
circumstances, he wouldn't be interested in her at all.

"Thank you, Mr. Anderson."

He quirked a brow but it wasn't accompanied by even the hint of a smile hovering on his wide mouth. "My father's Mr. Anderson."

She waited for the *call me Luke*, which would be the logical progression of his sentence, but it didn't come. It left her unable to read him and that in itself was unsettling because she normally had no problem doing that with people. Using her "keep everyone happy" voice, she said, "A shower sounds wonderful," and she grabbed her overnight bag from the backseat and locked the car.

"Seriously? You think someone's going to go to the effort of pulling your aging vehicle out of the quagmire and stealing it?" Luke's face wore the bemused expression of someone who thought he was dealing with a fool.

"I've got a lot of valuable—" She stopped herself milliseconds before mentioning her cameras. "My laptop's in there." She adjusted the overnight bag in her hand so it didn't rub up against her muddy legs. "Ready to go?"

He didn't offer to carry her bag. "Almost. Leave your dog in the car."

She hugged her precious close. "I'm not leaving Maggie-May here all on her own surrounded by scary cows."

He folded his arms across his sizeable chest and they rested there, implacable and fixed. "I think she's proven that she's more than capable of looking after herself. Besides, she can guard your laptop."

She ignored his sarcasm and played it straight. "Surely out in the country, locking the car is enough?"

"You're missing the point. I'm not having that *thing* anywhere near my house or what's left of my mother's garden."

"But she needs a bath too and—"

He shook his head, his firm and square jaw slicing through the air. "You can leave the dog and have a shower or you can stay here with the dog and I'll return with the tractor after I've cleaned up. It's your choice."

She stared at his resolute stance but he didn't budge an inch. It was Hobson's choice—no choice at all. She loved her dog but she desperately needed a shower and without it she'd contaminate her car with manure and mud. Given the conversation she was yet to have with him about the sunflower field, she couldn't afford to alienate Luke Anderson, who was now looking and sounding exactly like a farmer—grouchy, pessimistic and intransigent. She was tempted to make a comment about the weather just to test her theory.

Accepting the inevitable, she quickly wiped the mud off her dog's feet before dropping a kiss on her muddy head and placing her on her blanket in the car. "You stay, Maggie-May. Sit. We won't let that mean old farmer be our buzz-kill," she muttered into soft doggy hair. "I won't be long."

"Can you hurry it up?" Irritation flattened all the melodic qualities of Luke's deep voice. "I've got cows to milk tonight as well as rescuing *your* car."

Maggie-May put her paws endearingly on her arms as if to say, *He's a butt-head.*

Erin agreed.

LUKE AND HIS relief milker, Brett, had finished the milking and the cleaning of the milking parlor in just under two hours. The Erin Davis fiasco—she'd finally left just before five—had meant he'd started late so to be done by seven had him feeling pretty pleased. It was proof that the alterations he'd made to the parlor last winter—alterations his father had refused to make—were paying off and saving him valuable time each day. It wasn't so vital in winter but in summer when he was cropping as well, he needed to maximize every precious minute. He found himself whistling the last tune he'd heard on the parlor radio as he rode the four-wheeler with Mac sitting behind him, back to the house. The tune died on his lips when he came through the home gate and saw a familiar and now-clean station wagon parked next to his truck.

Erin Davis, chaos personified. He killed the engine and jumped down. He'd said goodbye to her in the top pasture three hours ago. Before she'd left, he'd finally asked her why she'd been looking for him because after the debacle of the mud and the bogged car, she'd never actually said. Her response to his question had been unexpected. She'd looked a little leery, smiled apologetically, mumbled something about a miscommunication and had then started up the car.

Despite the fact her reaction seemed very strange—especially as she'd told him when they'd first met she was specifically looking for him—he hadn't pursued it further. He really didn't want to know. Hell, he was still smarting from overhearing her telling her dog he was mean and old. Just lately he might have been dragging himself through the day, but damn it, he was only thirty. And where did she get off calling him mean? Damn it, he'd been the one inconvenienced. He'd been the one who'd gone out of his way to help her by hauling out the car she'd put into the bog. As far as he was concerned, the sooner a woman like her, with her clichéd views of farms and farmers and her ridiculous excuse of a dog, left the property, the better.

So why the hell was she back now?

Not that she'd left his head in the past three hours. He'd tried hard to shift the image out of his head that her wet and translucent top had branded on his brain, but attaching milking cups to cows' udders for two hours had made it impossible *not* to think about breasts. The visual of her cold nipples standing to attention behind seductive black lace and saying *look at me*, refused to be banished. As did the fact that, of course, he'd looked. Hell, he was male and what guy wasn't going to sneak a peek at the gift of virtually naked breasts?

Still, breasts or no breasts, Erin Davis and her mutt were a royal pain in the ass and he'd been pleased to see the back of them. Mac growled and then Luke heard the yapping of her dog. He instantly spun around, planning to protect his ankles. To his surprise, the thing was inside the car, alone, and clawing at the partially open windows. *Interesting.* So where was its owner?

He strode up onto the porch, telling Mac to lie down on the dog bed that now lived there, having been moved into its current position when his parents had left. Using the old "hands-free" boot remover his great-grandfather had fashioned from an old piece of wood by whittling out a deep V, he tugged off his mucky boots. As he pulled open the screen door and stepped into the wet area, the aroma of onions and garlic drifted out from the kitchen, hitting his nostrils. What the—?

Luke lived alone and tonight's meal was going to be a reheat of last night's leftovers—a meal he'd cooked and it hadn't tasted or smelled like this the first time. Someone was cooking in his kitchen. Only the entrenched routine drilled into him by his parents of entering the house and leaving the farm behind had him washing his hands before he marched into the kitchen. Erin Davis was moving methodically around the old farmhouse table laying silverware, the pattern on her bold, black-and-white polka-dot Capri pants making his eyes spin.

"What the hell are you doing in my house?"

She looked up and smiled brightly. "Country hospitality."

He scrubbed his hands through his hair. "You're from the city."

"How do you know that?"

He couldn't stop himself from rolling his eyes. "Your clothes, your fear of cows and general aversion to mud."

Her chin shot up. "No woman, city or country, is ever going to enjoy a manure bath."

He stifled a desire to smile at her indignation and the way it made her eyes sparkle. "True, but then there's that white fluff you insist on calling a dog. No self-respecting country woman would be seen dead with something like that in her purse. But more to the point, nowhere in the hostess handbook does it say coming uninvited into someone's kitchen is the definition of country hospitality."

Her smile faltered slightly but she extended her arm in a ta-da flourish. "I've cooked you a 'thank-you' meal."

His stomach betrayed his chagrin at her being here, by rumbling in response to the delicious smell of roasting meat emanating from the oven. Every other part of him thought she shouldn't be here at all.

Why? How is this any different from Mrs. Norell stopping by with a cake or a casserole and staying for coffee?

It was plenty different. He'd never once tried to picture the sprightly sixty-five-year-old woman naked, whereas he was having trouble thinking about Erin any other way. *Shit.* He hadn't realized that by not dating, it had put him seriously off his game. It had to stop. Visions of black lace and creamy breasts had to go. Erin Davis was annoying, had a useless excuse of a dog and, in the classic sense of the word, she wasn't even pretty.

Harnessing his determination to get his body back on an even keel, he fixed his gaze on her large nose. "You thanked me by leaving after I towed your car."

Her teeth snagged her bottom lip and his gaze slipped momentarily. He hauled it back.

"Words weren't enough. Supper is the least I could do."

"Hmm."

Her smile looked forced. "Farmers really are men of few words."

Actually, Luke enjoyed a good discussion over either a beer on a hot night or a fine wine with a special meal, but he had no plans to disabuse her of her preconceived ideas.

The tip of her tongue briefly touched the peak of her lip and then she cleared her throat. "Despite what you think about me, I do realize I caused you unnecessary work today and I feel bad that Maggie-May ripped your jeans."

The bruise on his leg throbbed. "Keeping that *thing* away from me is more than enough thanks."

Her eyes flashed like sunlit shards of jade and with a jerk, she gripped the back of the nearest chair, her knuckles turning white. As she straightened the chair, the legs scraped loudly against the floor, but she remained silent.

The fact she hadn't rushed to defend her dog both surprised and disappointed him in an odd sort of way. He couldn't work her out. When she'd knocked him into the mud, she'd had no qualms telling him exactly what she thought but now she said nothing? He surreptitiously studied her face and detected a tension around the edges of her mouth hovering under the smile.

Something was definitely up. He'd bet his bottom dollar there was more to this "thank-you" supper than just gratitude for towing her car. Exactly what though, he had no clue, but he felt sure it was connected with the reason that had initially brought her to the farm this afternoon. The fact she was now being so polite indicated that she wanted to keep on his good side.

His stomach rumbled again. Although his first reaction to finding her in the house had been to ask her to leave, needs won out. Lunch had been a very long time ago. He was very hungry, and the food smelled delicious. An idea started to form. He could enjoy a home-cooked meal *and* get her not only to leave the house and farm, but more importantly guarantee that she'd never want to return again. Given she had him pegged as a stereotypical farmer, why not behave like every cliché rolled into one? This was going to be fun.

Regretting he didn't have a piece of straw to chew and that he'd done the right thing by hanging up his hat before entering the kitchen, he now sat down at the table. Overriding years of exceptional table manners along with the fact he'd always treated women as equals, he picked up the knife and fork, balanced them on their ends and brought them down onto the table with a clunk. "I'm starving. Bring it."

Her finely shaped chestnut brows hit her hairline but again she didn't rise to the bait. "Certainly."

She walked into the kitchen and dished up roasted vegetables and succulent prime rib and he caught a flash of pastry in the oven. Pie? His mouth watered and he had to silence the admiration he always voiced for anyone who could put together a meal. Sadly Wade had inherited the cooking gene from his talented mother, leaving Keri and himself struggling to fry eggs.

Erin returned to the table holding a gravy boat and expertly balancing two plates on her arm, waitress style. She slid one plate in front of him and positioned the boat before circling the table to sit opposite him.

As she started to lower herself into the chair he said, "The Anderson men have always eaten alone."

She stalled, her body hovering just above the chair. "Excuse me?"

He pointed with his knife. "My mother served us and then ate her meal at the counter standing up in case we needed anything extra."

Her eyes widened into huge discs of green similar to the waters off the coast of Australia and he had the distinct urge to lean forward and dive in. Instead he shoveled a large piece of meat into his mouth and said, "Get me some water."

If she'd been standing in the woods on a hot day, the sparks from her eyes would have started a forest fire, but still she didn't light into him with the expected verbal attack. Instead, her body coiled with tension and she rose, picked up her plate and returned to the kitchen. With her back to him he allowed himself a smile at the massive effort she was putting into not stomping or throwing her meal at him. Meltdown was only a matter of time.

"Would that be iced water from the filter or bottled water?" Her voice was pure, excessively polite waitress but she hadn't quite managed to school her face into a bland, non-judgmental expression.

"Filtered."

The clink of the ice dispensing from the door of the fridge filled the room along with his deliberately loud chewing.

"Here you are." Her voice was as cool as the ice in the glass she put down in front of him. "Anything else I can get you?"

"A beer and more of those potatoes."

"Right away." She turned and he thought he heard her mumble, "I hope you choke on them."

He grinned. The meat was sublimely tender and melted in his mouth. The potatoes were crunchy on the outside and oh so creamy on the inside, and the beans—cooked to perfection—snapped in his mouth. Apart from the times Wade invited him over to the B and B, he hadn't eaten this well or had this much entertainment in a very long time.

Erin wanted more than anything to shove a roast potato up Luke Anderson's left nostril, but she doubted that would help her cause. The idea of cooking him a meal had come to her like manna from heaven when she'd been standing in the Whitetail Market and the gregarious owner, John Ackerman, had proudly told her about his locally supplied organic meat and fruit and vegetables. She'd always thought there was a kernel of truth in the old saying of "The way to a man's heart is through his stomach," and although there was no way she wanted Luke's heart, she did want his sunflower field. No, she needed his sunflower field—her future was predicated on it.

Prior to her brilliant idea, she'd been racking her brains about the best way to approach the topic, given she'd caused so much chaos on arrival and Luke was so grouchy. She'd been absolutely certain that if she'd floated her request at any time between knocking him into the mud and him towing her car, it would have resulted in an instant "no" and she planned to do everything possible to avoid that answer. After her shower, she'd done a quick explore of the bathroom vanity and had been pleased to find an absence of scented soaps, boxes of tampons and women's moisturizing razors. That, combined with the house being empty of people, made her conclude that Luke lived alone. Sure, it was brash coming back and using his kitchen uninvited, but farmers did a lot of physical work, right, so she'd been confident that once *hungry Luke* tasted her food, he'd forgive her that one teeny-tiny indiscretion.

She'd expected him to be his usual grumpy self when he returned from the dairy, but she'd pictured herself apologizing and him accepting it before they sat down together to enjoy the meal with a glass of Wisconsin Domaine du Sac, which was a perfect match for the meat. The food and wine would mellow him and take the edge off his irritable demeanor, and only then, after he was filled to the brim with two servings of her cherry pie, would she serve coffee and introduce the subject of the sunflower field.

That had been the plan.

The plan hadn't even got to first base before it imploded. The reality was that, despite Luke Anderson's gorgeous work-toned and tanned body, golden stubble and sky-blue eyes that would make a Hollywood talent scout take a second look, he was not only farmer-grumpy, he was also Neanderthal Man and a misogynist rolled into one. No wonder he'd hardly given Connie the time of day. She tried not to shudder as she recalled the half-masticated meat she'd glimpsed when he spoke to her with his mouth full. As for his "women belong in the kitchen" thing, she wanted to take off her shoes and hurl them at his sun-bleached head.

"Seeing you've been slow coming over with those extra potatoes, you can add some more meat too."

She turned to see him holding out his plate toward her while he wiped his mouth against the sleeve of his shirt.

Every part of her wanted to scream in horror.

Chill. Remember the reason you're here.

She served the extra meat and potatoes and then ate her meal at the counter, trying to work out her next move. Her gaze roved over the kitchen. The wallpaper was slightly faded but it was still a warm and cozy room—the heart of a home—and it was well stocked with cooking equipment and very clean. It didn't match up with the man in front of her who was inhaling her carefully prepared meal as if it was merely fuel, and not to be savored for flavor or enjoyment. Perhaps he paid someone to come in and clean? She recalled he'd thought she was a cleaner when she first arrived.

She heard the scrape of his chair and looked up to see him walking toward the door carrying his plate.

Panic made her blurt out, "Where are you going?"

"Mac can finish this up."

"You're giving your dog USADA prime rib?" She couldn't stop the rising inflection in her voice.

He shrugged. "Real dogs eat real meat, but then you wouldn't know about that."

Yet another crack at her dog had her best intentions fraying fast. "I suppose he'll lick the plate clean and save you washing it?"

The corner of Luke's mouth twitched. "Oh, I don't wash up, Erin. That's women's work, but if you want Mac's help, I'm sure he'll oblige."

She knew he was serious about the washing up but she wasn't certain if he was yanking her chain about the dog licking the plate or not. After he'd gone through the door she peeked out the window onto the porch and saw him rub the dog's black-and-white ears. She thought farm dogs were always chained up because they were working dogs but this one wasn't leashed and he seemed to have a comfy bed in a sheltered position. Although she could see Luke's mouth moving, she couldn't hear what he was saying to the dog. With a final pat on the head, he set the good china plate in front of Mac, totally bypassing scraping the meat into the blue dog bowl.

Holy crap. She really was dealing with the most uncouth guy she'd ever met. How was she going to explain the aesthetic value of art and photography to someone like that and have a hope in hell he'd understand?

The screen door slammed and she jumped back guiltily from the window as he returned to the kitchen. His questioning eyes flickered over her face and she felt her cheeks flame at being caught. Then to her horror, a tingle of attraction shimmered deep down inside her. *No! No way. Not now I've seen him eat.* God, she really was completely losing it. Sure, in the past, she'd had a bit of a thing for guys a bit rough around the edges but she'd grown out of it because none of those guys would fit into the new world she was creating for herself. Besides, Farmer Anderson wasn't a bit rough, he was positively unhewn.

Angry with herself and her reaction, she stomped to the freezer and hauled out the very expensive tub of decadently creamy Vermont vanilla ice cream she'd bought and then she pulled her steaming pie out of the oven. Dumping both in the center of the table with a spoon, she said, "Shall I just call the dog in to eat with you?"

"Sure, but set a place first because he prefers his own bowl."

The mildly spoken words held a trace of something new but was it laughter or affection for the dog? She had no clue. All she knew was that her meal hadn't primed him for her request in any shape or form and she'd run out of time. She had to ask him straight out and she had to do it now. Shoving the spoon into the ice cream for fortification, she dug out a scoop and popped it in her mouth.

"Hey! That's my ice cream."

So the farmer liked ice cream. Good. Taking her time, she licked the cold sweetness off the spoon and then held it out to him. "Help yourself."

The spoon hovered between them but although he seemed to be staring straight at it, he didn't move to take it from her. "Suit yourself." She put it down next to the cardboard tub and sucked in a deep breath. "I'm a photographer."

He snapped out of whatever momentary daze he'd been in, wiped the spoon on his shirt and plunged it into the ice cream. "And you're telling me this why?"

There was no point avoiding the reply. "Because I'm a wedding photographer and I'm here today representing my client. When she gets married, your sunflower field will be in full bloom and I wish to shoot some of her wedding photos there."

The ice-cream-filled spoon stalled at the peak of his full lips. "No."

She couldn't say she was shocked at his reply but she was pissed at the fact he hadn't even taken a minute or even a second to consider it. "Just like that?"

He put the spoon in his mouth and closed his lips firmly around it before pulling it out clean. "Just like that."

For an insane nanosecond she wondered what it would be like to have those lips closing around her mouth and then her common sense screeched *ewwwww*. Given his lack of table manners who knew what went into his mouth or when he'd last cleaned his teeth.

He didn't have bad breath when you were lying on top of him earlier.

Shutting out the off-topic nonsense, she said, "Believe me, the photos will be stunning. The golden light of early evening will blaze against the vibrant heads of the flowers."

"Yeah?" He scratched his head.

"Yes." A ray of optimism had her leaning forward. "The photos will not only capture the magic of the moment but they'd be enduring art passed from generation to generation."

"I don't think so."

The man was a philistine. "Granted, you may not be able to picture or appreciate how artistic and stunning these photos will be, but I can assure you that you'll be well compensated for the use of your field."

"I will."

For a moment she wasn't sure if he'd asked a question or if he'd made a statement. She decided to plow on rather than let herself panic that he was about to name a dollar amount beyond the exorbitant fee Connie had approved for the field. "You most certainly will."

His eyes flashed a thousand shades of blue. "I'm glad you agree that my crop of high-energy sunflowers will increase my cows' milk production and as a result, earn me more money."

For the first time since he'd sat down at the table, a keen intelligence shone through. Along with his words, it completely disarmed her. "Um, that's great for you and the cows I guess, certainly, but why not maximize the field's full potential by letting my client and me pay for two hours of its time? I'd shoot at the covered bridge first and then come to your field."

"I don't need the aggravation of a wedding party tramping through my pasture and—" he raised a brow "—squealing when cow dung stains their shoes."

It was a direct shot at her reaction to the loss of her suede sandals earlier in the day and her chin shot up defensively. "Now that I know about the conditions, the wedding party will be well-prepared with appropriate footwear."

He snorted. "I'll bet my last dollar your bride has never stepped out of the concrete-and-glass jungle she lives in or worn rubber boots."

Bingo. So he did know about Connie, which meant he must have listened to all her messages on his phone. Irritation at his snap judgment about people who lived in the city spilled over. "Is that why you won't take her calls? Because she lives in a city? How very rural of you."

He leaned forward, the golden stubble on his face glinting in the rays of the setting sun that streamed through the window. "No." He spoke softly, his breath fanning her face.

Her focused mind started to fog around the edges.

He leaned back. "I didn't return her calls because she's batshit crazy."

She shook her head quickly, knowing exactly how to play this. "No, she isn't. She's just a bride who wants the best. I've worked with a lot of brides and sure, they can get a bit jittery a few weeks before the wedding, but that's expected. When Connie didn't receive a return call from you, that may have contributed to her becoming a little angsty."

He looked at her with razor-sharp astuteness. "A *little* angsty? Is that what you're calling the hysterical rants she left on my phone?"

Hysterical seemed overly dramatic even for a pragmatic farmer. She knew Connie could be demanding but she wasn't hysterical. "Which is why *I'm* here as a voice of reason and to appeal to your sense of…um…" *What?* She searched her brain wildly, looking for the right thing to say. *Appeal to good breeding?* Nah, that wasn't going to work.

As she stuttered and struggled, he watched her and this time he raised both brows. Again his eyes gleamed with an intelligence she might have underestimated.

He pulled your car out of the mud. "…sense of community," she finished triumphantly.

He slowly tilted back in his chair and the front legs left the floor. "Only Miz—" he elongated the title "—Littlejohn isn't part of *my* community and to be honest, she's the sort of nightmare I can live without."

The field was slipping out of her reach and along with it her shot at the Memmy and a secure future to banish her worst fears. "Would it help if I promised you categorically that we wouldn't cause a fuss or get in the way or—"

"Just like you didn't get in the way this afternoon?" The front legs of his chair hit the floor as his rumbling-bass laughter filled the room. "Oh, yeah, I can see that working here...or not!" He stood up as if the conversation was finished.

Desperate, she shot to her feet. "Two thousand dollars will go a long way toward something on the farm."

He stiffened. "Money isn't going to make this fall your way, Erin Davis. A sunflower field is food for my stock and covered bridges are for preventing the formation of black ice. It's that simple."

Utter frustration wrapped around disappointment and she slapped her hands against her hips. "And silly me. Here I was thinking Whitetail was all about weddings and giving the bride what she wanted."

"It is, but that's the town and this is *my* farm."

So much for a sense of community. She threw down her last card—the one she hated playing because no one ever cared about other people's dreams except the person involved, but desperate times meant desperate measures. Pressing her hands together in supplication, she said, "Haven't you ever wanted something so much it ached inside you? For me, this is exactly like that."

For a moment he gave her such a long look she got the oddest feeling he wasn't actually seeing her at all but gazing right through her and glimpsing something else entirely. It took all of her self-control not to look over her shoulder to see what he was staring at.

A new tension ringed him and his mouth firmed into a straight line. "Wash up before you leave."

Despair curdled her stomach. "Is there *anything* I can say or do that will change your mind?"

"No." He grabbed his hat and walked out into the night.

The slamming of the door behind him rammed home how badly she'd failed. She'd let down Connie and herself, and their brilliant idea had taken a mortal blow. It wasn't just a sunflower field and a picture of a bride; it was her insurance policy for the future. She sank into the chair and let her head fall onto the table, trying very hard not to cry.

Memories assailed her of the time she was fifteen and her world had been turned upside down by her father. Back then, in the space of a few hours, she'd lost everything she'd known to be her life. The horror and dread that it could happen all over again clawed at her, pulling her back to a dark place she'd vowed long ago she'd never visit again. Tonight, she barely had the energy to resist and when her phone played the bridal march she did the unthinkable and let it go through to voice mail. She hated how one man could stand between her and her dream. One very ill-bred, uncivilized, close-minded, country hick!

So much for country hospitality and friendliness— obviously that was just a rumor propagated by the tourism board. She stood up feeling raw and vulnerable, needing a cuddle from her precious dog, which would make things slightly less dismal, but when her fingers closed around the door handle, she stopped and turned slowly around.

A large, greasy roasting pan along with an array of other cookware sat waiting to be cleaned. Every part of her wanted to turn her back on the mess that represented her current problems, but that would be exactly what Luke Anderson would expect of someone from the city. No, she wouldn't give him the satisfaction and besides, burning bridges had never been her style. The only thing of any use that her father had taught her was that you never know what's around the corner and yesterday's enemy may well be tomorrow's friend. Although not in a million years could she ever picture Luke Anderson being a friend.

The low moos of the cows in the barn drifted in through the open window and she remembered the pretty view she'd photographed and all the farms dotted over the countryside that she'd driven past today. *That's it!* The idea slammed into her, buying her hope.

Luke Anderson might have just said no, but she was in rural Wisconsin and his wasn't the only farm in the district. She smiled at the thought.

THREE

THE FOLLOWING MORNING the sun was shining, buoying Erin's spirits. The clerk at the motel on the edge of town hadn't been able to answer her questions but he'd suggested she go to the Whitetail Market and Video early because the townsfolk started their day by stopping there to buy coffee, doughnuts and the paper, and to generally chew the fat. "It's the unofficial version of the town meeting," he said. "If someone doesn't know the answer, they'll know someone who does."

The moment she crossed the threshold of the shop, John Ackerman boomed, "You're back! And how did that meat roast up for you?"

She smiled. "As you promised, it was perfection. Do you make coffee as perfect?"

"I have a breakfast blend freshly brewed. Cream and sugar?"

"Just cream, thank you. I imagine you know most everybody in town?"

The grocer beamed. "And the district. The Ackermans have been in town almost as long as the Andersons."

She tried not to shudder at the memory of last night. "As in Luke Anderson?"

"Yes, ma'am. They beat us here by a few months, but we're both considered founding families."

He was taking her proffered money when a rushed

voice called out, "Have the strawberries been delivered for the wedding?"

"Fresh picked this morning, Nicole, and so sweet I was tempted to keep some for the store."

"Great. I was worried that Lindsay and Keith might have been distracted given everything that's happening today."

The woman sounded stressed and Erin stepped back to allow her to move forward to the coffee counter.

As she brushed past she said, "I'm so sorry, that was very rude of me."

Dressed in a black pencil skirt, white blouse and a cinch-waisted jacket, she gave Erin an apologetic smile as her shoulders drew up and rolled back.

Erin got the distinct impression the similarly aged woman was putting herself back together to present a different face entirely. Despite her perfectly blow-dried hair and tailored suit, there was something about her that seemed almost sad.

"Please, let me pay for your coffee," said the woman.

Erin shook her head. "It's fine, really, but it sounds like you need more than just breakfast blend."

She laughed tightly and extended her hand. "I'm Nicole Lindquist and I'm always a little strung out when we've got a wedding on."

"Nicole's Whitetail's wedding planner," John said proudly, "and my niece by marriage. Are you in town for the wedding, Erin?"

"For a wedding, yes, but not today's. I'm a photographer and—"

"You saw my advertisement?"

Nicole's squeal of delight made Erin jump. "Ah, no, should I have?"

"We need to talk." The pervading air of sadness vanished. "Can you spare me a minute?"

The request intrigued her. "Sure, and perhaps you can help me with my problem too?"

"I'll give it my best shot." Nicole motioned her over to a table by the window, tucked away from the counter and the rest of the busy store. A vase of summer daises gave it a homey touch and a copy of the *Whitetail Bugle* sat next to it, neatly folded.

As they seated themselves, John arrived with two apple Danishes, gave Nicole a wink and said, "My treat."

"Thanks, John." Nicole gave Erin a guilty smile. "John knows my sweet tooth goes into overdrive on the morning of a wedding. I always make a vow that I'll get through on almonds, carrots and celery sticks but—"

"Coffee and pastries are so much more satisfying." Erin understood completely, knowing how much physical energy she burned up on a shoot lugging her equipment, not to mention nervous and creative energy. "Tell me about this advertisement I haven't seen."

Nicole wrapped both hands around her coffee mug. "A year ago, Whitetail hosted the Callahan-Neiquest society wedding and from that moment we've had a steady stream of bookings. Not only can we provide the chapel and the reception, we can also provide everything a bride needs from invitations to transport. The only thing stopping us from being full-service is a photographer. As a stop-gap measure, if brides don't have their own photographer, we've been using Eric from *The Bugle* but weddings are not his strong suit and we really need a resident wedding photographer."

Erin shook her head, not wanting Nicole to get her

hopes up any further. "I'm sorry, but I live in Minne-apolis."

"But you travel anywhere the bride wants to get mar-ried right?"

"I do, but I'm building my business in the Twin Cit-ies."

Nicole nodded and sipped her coffee. "So you have a studio and everything there?"

"I wish." She sighed thinking how after the debacle with Luke Anderson, her big plans for a secure future seemed almost unobtainable. "I rent studio space if I absolutely have to, but for engagement shots, I find the best photos are often the ones taken in locations famil-iar to the couple. Where they're most relaxed."

She smiled, picturing the set of prints she always showed prospective clients. "My favorite engagement shoot took place in and around a tree house. The couple had been childhood sweethearts and the tree not only relaxed them but it represented the solid love they had for each other."

Nicole's eyes lit up. "That sounds amazing. So are you heavily booked?"

Erin pictured her planner, which had sporadic book-ings scattered over it, but was empty for the next few weeks until Connie's wedding. She shrugged, not want-ing to be too specific. "You know what the wedding business is like. Feast or famine. How do you keep going over winter?"

"It's quieter for sure, but in a small town everyone has more than one job. I run the hairdressing salon so I have work all year round but it's the weddings I love best. This year, we've got four winter weddings booked already because Annika, our invitation designer, married Finn Callahan. They had the most amazing winter wedding complete with a sleigh." She sighed dreamily before giving a wry smile. "And because Finn had been considered the Chicago bachelor no woman could ever land, the wedding got a *lot* of publicity."

Nicole sipped her coffee. "Summer's a different story, though. Every weekend is booked through until the leaves fall."

Erin stared at her not quite believing her ears. "Every weekend?"

Nicole nodded. "It gets frantic, that's for sure, and I have someone doing most of the salon work. Not every bride wants me to be their wedding planner and some bring their own team in with them, but most use me because I know everyone in town and where their strengths lie and what they can offer." She glanced at her watch before looking back at Erin. "You said you needed some help?"

She pulled her mind back from the fact that White-tail was such a popular wedding destination and said, "Has a Connie Littlejohn ever contacted you?"

"The name's familiar." Two lines appeared at the bridge of Nicole's nose as she thumbed through her notebook. "Oh, yes, I remember. I took a phone meeting with her to book the chapel and the supper club but she was brusquely insistent that she was doing everything else herself."

That sounded like Connie. "We've run into a snag with the photos and I need a sunflower field in full bloom in three weeks' time."

"Too easy." Nicole smiled. "Lakeview Farm is perfect and the farmer's name is—"

"Luke Anderson, I know." She tried to sound bright

and cheery because she never did sad. "I met him yesterday, but he's the grouchiest, most disagreeable guy I've ever had to deal with. And he said a categorical no."

"Luke said no?" Nicole sounded stunned.

"Yes. So can you give me the names of five other farmers around here who grow sunflowers and I'll contact them."

For the first time, Nicole frowned. "I don't think there are any others. This far north it's not a commonly grown crop."

Erin's gut churned with rising panic that an alternative sunflower field was unobtainable. "Are you sure there are no others?"

"Pretty sure. Most of the local farmers think Luke's crazy giving up a field to sunflowers."

"That makes sense," she said, relieved at least that her gut reaction about Luke Anderson had been spot on. "He sure seems crazy to me."

"Luke graduated summa cum laude from CALS."

"What does that stand for? Crazy as a Loon School?" Erin gave a tight laugh before taking a sip of coffee.

"No." Nicole's brow furrowed as if she didn't understand the joke. "It's the College of Agriculture and Life Science at UW Madison."

Coffee spurted out of Erin's nose and she grabbed a napkin. UW was no community college. It was a widely respected school and known internationally. She took a closer look at Nicole. Her expression held no guile, which matched the fact that her voice had been firm and matter-of-fact. She thought of the moments last night when a sharp intelligence had pierced Luke's backwoods persona. "You're serious, aren't you?"

"Of course I am. I'm sure the only reason some of

the older farmers think he's crazy is because he's innovative and it unsettles them."

The picture Nicole was drawing wasn't sitting at all well against the man she'd spent the previous evening with. "So Luke Anderson's eccentric as well as being ridiculously grumpy and letting his dog eat off his good china?"

This time Nicole laughed. "Are you sure you actually met Luke? I think I've only ever seen him angry twice in his life. Mind you, it's hay season and every farmer's grumpy from a lack of sleep."

"Six foot two, blond, blue eyes and a misogynist?"

You forgot ripped body.

"The height, hair and eye color are definitely Luke."

A niggling feeling that she'd been played by Mr. "Women belong in the kitchen" Anderson started to grow.

Nicole continued, "I can't understand why he'd say no to you. His family is very civic-minded and have always hosted Breakfast on the Farm. Do you want me to talk to him?"

No. What she really wanted was a totally different farmer. One who didn't look like he'd been touched by the gods of gorgeousness, one who didn't make her lurch from desire to repulsion in a heartbeat, leaving her totally unsettled, and especially one who hadn't spun her along, all the while laughing at her expense. "All I need is *one* other farmer with a sunflower field within a twenty-mile radius of Whitetail."

Nicole got a scheming glint in her eye. "I tell you what. If you can be the photographer for today's wedding, I'll put out the word that you're looking for a sunflower field."

Erin didn't mind the barter exchange but she had some professional concerns, knowing from acute experience that brides didn't cope well with last-minute changes. "Usually I've photographed the bride and groom at an engagement shoot and built up a rapport. Won't it stress the bride that she's never met me?"

"Not Lindsay. She's lived in Whitetail all her life and is the most laid-back woman I've ever met, which is why she was happy to use Eric. Truth be told, I've done more stressing about her wedding than she has." Nicole stood up. "How about we go meet her now and she can tell you what she wants. I promise you it won't be sunflowers."

Erin's phone bleated out the wedding march and Connie's number came up. A streak of guilt caught her under the ribs and she clicked on Decline Call, sending it to voice mail. She'd texted Connie earlier saying, *things looking up.* She hadn't told Connie that Luke had said no and she didn't plan on doing that until she had an alternative to offer the bride. Why unduly upset her when in a few hours' time she'd hopefully have another field to use and a much more cooperative farmer to work with?

Besides, the fee for the wedding shoot would more than cover another night's accommodation and the waitressing tips she was giving up by staying in Whitetail. In fact, it would cover a lot more.

"It all sounds like a plan." With a smile she stood up and followed Nicole out of the store.

LUKE ARRIVED LATE to Lindsay and Keith's reception, having been held up by a difficult calving. At least he wouldn't need to explain. Lindsay and Keith were longtime time family friends, and their picnic wedding reception in the park was in full swing with the three-piece band belting out tunes from the eighties. The couple had been married quietly with just their immediate family in attendance, but they'd invited most of the county to the party, which doubled as Lindsay's fortieth birthday celebration. He grinned as the tall and willowy bride in a simple, white sheath dress strode across the grass to greet him. Even in bare feet she was taller than her new husband.

"Congratulations, Lins." He kissed her cheek. "After all those years of living together, you finally made an honest man out of Keith."

She laughed. "I always intended to but life gets busy. Now you're running the farm, you know exactly what it's like. Have you finished your hay?"

The groom, an organic vegetable farmer whose stocky build, chrome-dome and earring made him look more like a biker, joined them. He slid his arm around his new wife's waist. "No shop talk today, honey. No talk of the weather, fertilizer or strawberry-eating gophers. Come dance with me."

He spun her away and Luke looked around for something to eat and drink. A group of women gave him a "come join us" wave as they sipped on champagne and bit into enormous chocolate-coated strawberries. From the accompanying giggles he figured they'd been doing it for quite some time. He gave them a friendly wave before looking beyond the bar to a long line of trestle tables he assumed had groaned with food earlier in the afternoon. Lindsay and Keith grew the best produce in the county and he saw the remains of platters of crudités, as well as marinated mushrooms and sundried tomatoes along with fresh, green salads. Luke had nothing against salads or vegetables, per se, as long as they were decorating meat.

The thought of meat reminded him of last night's supper. Erin Davis's only redeeming quality was that she could cook and the meal had even eclipsed Wade's roasts, which was saying something. Even so, he'd been relieved when he'd got back to the house at midnight to find it empty and her car gone. After his little performance last night, he was certain she wouldn't be making a return visit to Lakeview Farm; in fact she was probably back in Minneapolis by now. Not that his "no" to the sunflower field had been acting. He'd only ever listened to one of the thirteen messages Connie Littlejohn had left on his machine and even then, that had been one too many. The tone and content of the message had been enough to tell him that he wouldn't want her anywhere near his farm no matter how much money she was offering.

As his gaze came to the end of the row of salads, he saw the pig on the spit. Now that was more like it. He picked up a plate and was making a beeline for the chef when he heard someone call his name. He spun around to find Nicole hurrying toward him.

"You're here," she said, looking relieved.

"Hey, Nicole. This looks like it's all going well."

She smiled, taking in the scene with a practiced eye. "A lot of work goes into making something like this feel casual and effortless while at the same time providing food and drink for two hundred people."

"You've done it well. It suits Lindsay and Keith perfectly and—" he tilted his head to the twirling couple

on the temporary dance floor "—they're having a fabulous time."

"Thanks." Nicole's face flushed with pleasure. "It's
great to be able to give people exactly what they want
for their wedding. You know, to make it a special day
they'll remember forever."

It wasn't something he'd ever given much thought.
"I imagine it is."

"Do you remember how the whole town pulled together to put on Bridey Callahan's wedding at such
short notice because we knew it would put Whitetail
on the map?"

"Hmm." He nodded, agreeing automatically because
most of his mind was on the fact that the staff looked
like they were starting to clear the food away for des-
serts and he didn't want to miss out on the spit roast.

Nicole kept talking. "Here we are a year later and
things are going well but we can't rest on our laurels,
Luke. We need brides in three states to know we're here
and we can offer them something unique. You've always
been supportive, right from the start and…"

Something in her voice pulled his concentration
away from the thought of succulent pork and back to
her. "And?"

She gave her hesitant smile. "We've had a request
from a bride to use your sunflower field for photos."

He stilled, half irritated and half impressed at the
photographer's doggedness. "Did Erin Davis ask you
to ask me?"

Nicole's smile became wry. "No, not at all. In fact
she asked me for the names of other farmers with sunflower fields, but we both know you're the only one.
I don't understand why you told her no when you and

your family have always been so supportive of the town. Is there any way you could change your mind?"

He opened his mouth to say *when hell freezes over*. He had enough on his plate with every passing day, making the farm feel more and more like a thankless chore, without adding in a bride who sounded decidedly unhinged, and not to mention that being around Erin Davis made him feel like he had an itch that no amount of scratching would ease. That on its own made absolutely no sense to him and added even more to his current sense of disconnection to his life. Only he couldn't say any of that to Nicole without sounding like a jerk. Her husband, Bradley, had died in active duty, killed serving his country and defending the rights of freedom. Now the sacrifice was borne by Nicole as she raised their little boy alone.

Luke's sigh came up from his feet, dragging through him and leaving him in no doubt that he couldn't refuse Nicole. Her life had been turned upside down and somehow she managed to get up each morning and put one foot in front of the other despite her grief. As much as he hated the idea, he knew he could put up with *one* bride.

That means Erin too.

Crap. He'd make sure he wasn't anywhere near the sunflower field that day. In fact, he might just go fishing.

"Luke?" Expectation shone on Nicole's face.

He ran his hands through his hair and went for damage control. "Only if I deal direct with you. I don't want to have anything to do with crazy brides or photographers with purse dogs who bite."

A startled expression crossed her face. "A purse dog?"

He shook his head. "Don't ask."

"I'm sure both the bride and Erin will be more than happy to liaise through me. Thank you, Luke. It means a lot."

And he knew it did, because even he'd noticed that when Nicole was working on a wedding she looked less drawn and sad, and the town could breathe again.

She consulted her watch and went straight into wedding planner mode. "Now it's time for your speech. There's a microphone on the table next to the cakes, along with a glass of champagne for you to use when you give the toast. Are you ready?"

He threw a longing glance at the chef who was closing the spit-roast lid over the remains of the pig and he realized he'd just missed his chance at lunch. "Point me in the right direction."

Although Lindsay had wanted the day to be informal, Keith had insisted on one speech and he'd asked Luke to give it. As he picked up the microphone, the trumpeter in the band played a long, loud riff, which silenced everyone and expectant faces turned to him.

"I think it's safe to say that everyone here today had given up on this day ever happening. We know that Keith lost all his hair waiting for Lindsay to say yes."

Loud cheers erupted.

"In typical Lindsay and Keith style they've chosen to share their day with us all, just as they share their produce and their time. Whitetail wouldn't be the same without their theme movie nights—"

Keith leaned into the microphone. "The next one's a fifties night on Saturday the tenth so put it on your schedule now."

More cheers went up and Luke laughed. "You're supposed to be concentrating on your wife."

"Have you seen the zucchini groom's cake?" a slightly slurred voice called out. "She's gonna be the one concentrating."

Lindsay peered into the crowd. "Douglas Peterson, it's time to start drinking water because I expect you to be on the farm tomorrow at dawn, fresh and ready to pick the beans."

The young man hung his head slightly. "Yes, ma'am."

Luke decided at that point to ditch the bulk of his speech and move onto the toast. He raised his glass to the crowd. "Please join me in wishing Lindsay and Keith all the very best. May their lives together be fruitful—" he paused for the expected collective groan at the play on words and was rewarded "—and may they find joy and peace as they move forward together united by their love and shared goals for the future. To Lindsay and Keith."

"To Lindsay and Keith."

Wolf whistles pierced the air as Keith dipped Lindsay in his arms and gave her an enthusiastic kiss on the lips.

Luke found himself taking a long gulp of champagne as he noticed lots of couples in the crowd sharing a kiss. Nothing like a wedding to remind people of the vows they'd made to each other or were going to make. For five years, Luke had been giving speeches at weddings as his friends had one by one settled down and usually at this point he sat back filled with relief that it wasn't him and absolutely content with his single status. Only today, he couldn't quite shake the feeling that he was the one missing out on something—something he couldn't even put his finger on.

Lindsay and Keith made their way to the table to cut the simple wedding cake, which was decorated with

their luscious strawberries. At first he thought sunshine was reflecting off the ornate silver knife but as
they plunged it into the cake and Lindsay bent her head
down to kiss Keith, he heard a very familiar voice say,
"Perfect."

His head jerked around so fast it hurt. Erin Davis
was kneeling on the ground with her camera tilted upward, capturing the traditionally iconic moment at a
very untraditional wedding.

Dressed remarkably unobtrusively given her usual
explosion of color, she wore black pants, a black silk
blouse and ballet flats. She could have easily been mis-
taken for one of the waitstaff from the Silver Birch
Supper Club, which is probably why he hadn't noticed
her. But he was noticing her now. His mind instantly
pictured black lace. Lace he knew nestled under a de-
ceptively simple black camisole, which the sheer silk
skated over. Every movement of the material teased the
eye, and there was a lot of movement as she continu-
ously adjusted her position and her camera to capture
the moment. Every part of her was completely focused
on the bride and groom.

He realized he was staring and tore his gaze away.
What the hell was wrong with him? He was at a wedding, surrounded by women so there was absolutely no
reason for him to be mentally undressing Erin Davis, especially when she was wearing more clothes than most
of the female guests. He turned toward the champagne-
and-strawberries group of women who were well primed
and ready for a good time. Surely one of them was from
out of town and ready to be physically undressed. The
time had come for him to get his game on and douse this
crazy reaction to an equally crazy photographer.

He stopped a waiter, relieved him of his tray of drinks and then strode over to the group with a wide smile on his face. "Ladies, so sorry to have kept you waiting."

FOUR

"THANKS FOR STARTING, Wade." Buzzed with champagne and wedding cake, along with the promise of an evening with Marlene from Madison, who he had plans to meet at the Udder Bar, Luke was seriously late for afternoon milking. He'd given Brett the night off milking so he could enjoy the after-wedding party, which had already started and would probably continue until midnight.

"No problem," Wade said. "It's good to keep my hand in but I can only stay an hour because the B and B's full tonight. I'm loving this wedding-business idea and my business is benefiting." He deftly attached the milking machine to a cow's udder. "I'm guessing my cleaner didn't show?"

"No." Luke blocked the recalcitrant memory of Erin, which instantly popped into his head at the mention of the cleaner and he immediately changed the subject to block the thought. "How was the antiques fair?"

Wade's eyes lit up. "I bought a beautiful Victorian chair for the honeymoon suite."

Luke smiled. Wade loved antique furniture and cooking, but with his beefy build and utilitarian clothing, people often thought at first glance that he was the farmer. Luke enjoyed the incongruity. "Are you sure you want a valuable chair in a honeymoon suite? It might get used for more than sitting in."

"Furniture should be used and it's good to know that

at least there are people out there getting some, unlike the two Anderson brothers." Wade gave a wry smile. "Did you meet anyone at the wedding?"

"A Marlene," he said quickly against the image of Erin's compact body in black silk and lace, which hovered on the edge of his mind. "I'm going to meet her later." It had taken Luke a few years to feel comfortable asking Wade about his love life, but with maturity came perspective and as long as Wade didn't give him any details or ask him to match-make, he could cope. "What about you? Did you meet any like-minded guys at the fair?"

Wade sighed. "Only gay couples and women, and then it was time to come home."

"Do you ever think of leaving Whitetail?"

Wade paused, his hand on the release bar of the gate. The front cow mooed indignantly, cross at being held up from leaving the parlor and reentering the barn where more food waited. He pulled the gate open with a laugh. "Only if I win the lottery."

Luke thought of Axel's text. He opened his mouth to say, "What if the farm was the lottery?" but closed it again because this discussion needed to happen with both his siblings present. He'd call Keri tonight and ask her to come up next weekend.

The radio blared with Lady Gaga, and to the tune of Wade's off-key singing, they fell into a companionable rhythm of milking. Luke joined in when the golden oldie "Blueberry Hill" came on, singing the bass to Wade's wobbly tenor and generally hamming it up. He hit the low note at the same time he was slapping the rump of the most stubborn Holstein of the herd, trying to get her to move forward.

Wade stopped singing midline. "Luke." He tilted his head to the door.

Luke turned and caught a glimpse of black rubber boots decorated with hot-pink umbrellas—boots the likes of which the milking parlor had never seen. Boots so bright they made him squint. He raised his gaze, running it over the pink-rimmed top of the boot, along bare knees and smooth, tanned thighs to the cuffs of black denim cutoffs, until it met a pair of manicured hands pressed firmly on hips. Hands he recognized instantly because they'd gripped his yesterday.

Erin stood on the top step that led down into the milking parlor and she didn't look happy. In fact, Ms. "Country Hospitality" looked decidedly pissed. Given that he'd said yes to the sunflower field, and Nicole as the go-between would have told her that, she should have been smiling all the way.

"Nice boots. Why are they here?" He gave Gertie another push. "I told Nicole I'd allow the photos but everything has to go through her."

"I'm not here about the photos." Erin stomped forward, her shiny new boots hitting the first trace of muck but it didn't stall her progress any as she bore down on him with her green eyes flashing.

Her index finger sliced the air. "You! You know how to use a napkin. Your dog doesn't eat off fine bone china and your mother never ate her meals at the kitchen counter, did she?"

Damn. Of course she'd heard him speak at the wedding. One small speech had blown last night's stellar performance into a thousand pieces. He shrugged. "I'm sure there were times when she did."

Wade looked between the two of them and burst into

laughter. "Mom eating at the kitchen counter? Now there's a sight I can't imagine. The only person I remember eating there was Luke when he was asked to leave the table due to some table manner infractions."

Erin hit Luke with a sarcastic glare. "So that would be last week, then."

"Why use a napkin when you've got a sleeve?" he said, attempting to salvage something from last night's performance.

"As you so ably demonstrated last night when you were eating *my* beautiful meal and making a fool out of me." Her arms shot across her chest, pushing her breasts forward.

Luke overrode the slither of guilt that caught him under his ribs that he'd played her, and tried not to look at her breasts. Instead he reminded himself exactly how annoying she really was and how he didn't have anything to feel guilty about. "I recall the meal was both an apology for your mutt's bad manners and a thank-you to me for pulling your car out of the bog. Your little escapade derailed my entire afternoon and if you felt like a fool, then the onus lies at your feet, not mine."

"Oh, that's rich." Her arms flew up into the air and her bobbed hair swung around her face. "You took advantage of my good nature and you know it."

He was having none of that. "It was the other way around. You used food and wine to soften me up so I'd say yes to the sunflower field."

Her chin shot up but not before he caught a flicker of something close to the guilt he'd experienced himself. "I was being nice." Her voice rose with indignation.

"Lady, you were playing me, so don't come here acting all hurt and innocent and chew me out."

Confusion worried at Wade's forehead. "A guy takes one night off and it seems a lot happens here, little brother? Fill me in."

Luke loved Wade dearly but sometimes family didn't help his cause. With a sigh he said, "Erin Davis, this is my brother, Wade. Erin's a wedding photographer." *And as aggravating as hell.*

Erin immediately extended her hand toward Wade and then tensed. Luke caught the moment she realized exactly where Wade's hands had been, but to his surprise, she didn't pull back.

"It's a pleasure to meet you," Erin said.

Wade waved at her. "I'll shake your hand after I've washed mine."

Erin gave Wade a wide and grateful smile. "Are you the brother who owns the B and B?"

"And cottages. That's me." He shot a questioning look at Luke as if to say, *and she knows this how?*

He grudgingly admitted, "I mistook Erin for your cleaner."

Wade's wide shoulders rocked as he hooted with laughter.

Luke blew out a frustrated breath. "What's so funny? She could have been."

Erin nodded. "He's right, I could have been."

Luke instantly stilled and studied her face. Two minutes ago Erin Davis had been ready to take his head off and now she was agreeing with him? Something was very wrong with this picture.

Her hands opened in front of her. "Apparently, Whitetail is short a wedding photographer. Today I shot the Leiderman wedding and tomorrow Nicole's set up appointments with other brides who may wish to use my services. As it's a six-hour round trip from Minneapolis, I was wondering—"

"The cottages and B and B are booked solid this time of year," Luke interjected loudly, shooting his brother a look he hoped Wade would read as *not in this lifetime are you letting her stay*. The last thing he needed was Erin Davis on the farm, even if the cottages were a good mile away from the farmhouse.

Wade frowned at him before asking Erin, "Do you need accommodation?"

She shook her head. "No. I've got a room at the motel."

Relief dribbled through Luke. *Lucky save*. She'd come to the farm to yell at him and redeem her pride—end of story. He had to admit that on one level he'd got some entertainment from sparring with her so he'd let her yell some more and then she'd happily leave.

"Has your cleaner arrived yet?" Erin's entire focus was centered on Wade, but there was something about the turn of her mouth that made Luke tense.

"No, and she isn't coming." Wade rubbed his chin and sighed. "Apparently, on the four-hour drive from La Crosse she met a guy in a diner and decided to take the waitressing job on offer. I need someone local but during summer wedding season, most everyone's working in town."

Erin tucked her hair behind her ears, which unlike her nose were small with a delectable curve. Luke hated that he'd even noticed.

She smiled again. "I might be interested in the job."

"No." The word shot out of Luke's mouth hard and fast as his general unease morphed into panic. "You're a photographer, not a cleaner."

Her shoulders rolled back and she seemed to stand a little taller than her five feet four inches. "Right now I'm a photographer and a waitress. I could just as easily be a photographer and a cleaner."

"With those nails?" he muttered.

Her nostrils flared and she hooked his gaze with a withering look. "I'll do anything when I'm wearing rubber gloves, including burying dead bodies."

An image of her wearing a skimpy black-and-white French maid's outfit complete with pink rubber gloves socked into him, making him hot, bothered and hard.

Shit. What was it about this woman that had him acting like a horny seventeen-year-old? He didn't like it and he wanted it to stop.

"Thanks so much for stopping by," he said sarcastically. "Don't bother doing it again." He turned back to the milking, rescuing a set of cups that a cow had just kicked off before she trampled them.

He heard Wade's voice behind him. "Erin, do you want a part-time cleaning job while you're in town?"

"Wade!" Luke swung around, not able to believe his brother had just offered her a job.

"What?" Wade looked defensive. "You know how hard it is to find staff and if Erin's offering, I'll take it, even if it is only for a few days."

He knew how stubborn Wade could be, so short of saying *I don't want her on the farm*, which he knew would sound deranged and would prompt even more questions, he tried another approach. "Don't let looks deceive you. She travels with a killer dog that bites so think of your guests."

"Really?" For the first time Wade looked uneasy. "You have a pit bull?"

Luke couldn't stop his snort.

Erin rolled her eyes. "I have a very friendly Maltese–Shih Tzu cross, which your brother believes doesn't qualify as a dog."

Wade's face brightened immediately. "Oh, ignore him. Farmers have this thing about dogs being all about work, not pets."

Who needs enemies when you have family? "Mac is both," he ground out. "He earns his place unlike that pampered inbred."

Erin gave him a sweet smile similar to that of a crocodile. "So Mac's a working dog who isn't pampered even though he has a bed on the sunniest side of the porch rather than being chained up in the yard?"

Damn it, the woman had eagle eyes and a memory like an elephant. "He works hard. He earns that."

Wade grinned at Erin as if he wanted to give her a high five. "I'm looking forward to meeting your little guy."

"Her name's Maggie-May. She's a good judge of character and can detect sincerity at fifty feet." She threw a derisive look at Luke before turning back to Wade. "I'm sure she'll lick *you* to death."

Wade said, "Oh, sweet. Actually, I've been thinking of getting a little dog for some company but you can see what I'm up against."

Erin nodded sympathetically. "Maggie-May's fabulous company. Spend as much time with her as you like over the next few days so you can get a feel for the breed."

"Wear steel-cap boots and gaiters," Luke said caustically, incensed that his brother had just cast him as the bad guy when he never commented on Wade's life choices. Hell, he'd only given his opinion on a lap dog because Wade had asked.

"Erin, I feel bad that you're staying at the motel," Wade said. "The job does come with a small two-room cottage. It isn't anything fancy and it needs some work but it's functional."

"There's no point in her moving into the cottage for a few days," Luke countered, feeling himself being sucked into quicksand and the situation fast spinning out of his control.

Wade waved away Luke's words. "How about we agree to this? As long as you clean the cottage when you leave, it's yours for as long as you stay?"

Luke groaned.

Erin leaned in and gave Wade a hug. "*You're* lovely, thank you."

The pointed reference wasn't lost on Luke but as he couldn't care less what she thought of him, he put his general feeling of resentment down to the fact that despite his best efforts, Erin Davis was going to be staying on the farm. "Just keep your dog away from my cows."

Bertha, one of his best milkers, chose that moment to drop a load and Erin shuddered. "Believe me, neither Maggie-May or I will be coming within a bull's roar of you or your cows."

Perfect. "Good to know." He glanced at the clock. "Now, as neither of you are any help to me, go talk about your business arrangement elsewhere and let me finish up."

Wade slipped his arm under Erin's elbow and said conspiratorially, "He's got a date. First one in a while."

What the...? So help him, he was going to kill Wade. Erin nodded slowly as her face filled with thoughtful consideration although her eyes danced with fun. "Dating can be scary, Luke, and no one likes being rejected. Given how we both know you have a serious problem with general etiquette, I recommend you shower off the cow manure, use deodorant and remember to chew with your mouth closed."

He'd had enough. "Out! Now!"

Only she didn't jump at his loud and booming yell, nor did she look remotely offended. Instead of throwing him a scalding look or shooting back a snarky response, she threw her head back and laughed. Not a tinkling, modest laugh that fitted her styled hair and coordinated pink-and-black clothes and accessories, but a loud, deep belly laugh that made the cows look up from their feed trough. The rich sound reverberated round him, pulling at the strands of discontent that had been rumbling inside him for months and tempting him to follow the sound to the source. To that wide, pink mouth. To those plump and luscious lips. To—

God, he wasn't losing it. No, he'd lost it. Totally and utterly. Somehow in the past six months not only had everything he'd always loved about the farm changed, but he'd lost the ability to differentiate between the type of women he enjoyed and the type he loathed. The sooner he got into town, met up with Marlene, got drunk and got laid, the better.

NICOLE SAT BACK and sipped her coffee while watching Erin, who was intently listening to Jenna Ambrose. The bride's wedding was a week away and Nicole had her fingers crossed that Erin's portfolio and friendly manner would wow her, because Jenna had already fired two photographers and Eric's style wouldn't suit her. Nicole had a plan which involved connecting Erin to as many brides as possible either in person or over the phone and hopefully the brides would sign with the bright and cheery photographer. The longer Nicole could keep Erin working in Whitetail, the bigger the chance she'd relocate her business.

Nicole had seen the first rush of photos Erin had taken at Lindsay and Keith's wedding and she'd been blown away by how well Erin had captured the essence of their day. It wasn't just the way Lindsay and Keith's joy radiated from the pictures, it was also the photos of the little things that defined them as a couple—the white bowls filled with bulging strawberries, their rings resting together on freshly turned dirt, Lindsay's bare feet on the grass with her fire-engine-red painted toes, and Keith's loving gaze. They'd wanted a casual celebration and Erin had given them the perfect pictorial memory of their day. Every time they opened the album they'd be instantly taken back to their special time in the park, and they'd remember the wonder.

At least, that's what should happen. Nicole wasn't naive and she knew that often photos lay in their album and the album in its beautiful linen box—both rarely opened because those revisits came with regret.

She bit her lip and thought about her own wedding album. The last time she'd looked at it was the night of Bradley's funeral. That one look had brought back in a rush all the memories of her hopes and dreams for their future together. A future that had turned out to be so very different from how she'd imagined.

"I want a casual feel to my photos," Jenna said, spinning her ring on her finger. "No lining up like a school photograph."

Erin leaned forward, her smile bright and friendly. "How many in your wedding party?"

"Fourteen adults, a page boy, a flower girl and Greg's dog." She gave a half grimace. "There's been a lot of family pressure so I had to include my cousins as well."

Erin nodded as if she understood. "Your mom sees your wedding as a big family event?"

"That's exactly it. It's like it's her special day and Greg and I just have supporting roles." Jenna's lips thinned. "Well, I won't let her dictate the photos!"

"It must be so frustrating for you," Erin agreed. "Can I share something with you that I've learned from photographing weddings?"

Surprise flitted across Jenna's face. "I guess."

Erin flicked the pages of her portfolio until she came to the photo of a large wedding party and extended family. Twenty-two faces smiled at the camera. "This bride felt exactly like you but she gave her mom one formal photo. Believe me, you want to enjoy your day and having a grumpy mom will take the gloss off of it. So, early on, soon after the service, I can organize everyone into position and at the very last minute, you and Greg will put down your champagne glasses and just slot into the center of the group. I'll take the photo and then it's over. Painless. No memories of school photos and waiting in line."

She turned another page showing photos of the same wedding where everyone looked to be having so much fun. "You see? This bride got the feel you want and her mom got the mantelpiece picture and everyone was happy."

Jenna peered closely at the other photos, turning the

pages slowly and then without looking up said, "You know, that might work."

Erin was good. Nicole was giving her a grateful smile and a thumbs-up over the bride's bent head when she felt her phone vibrate. With Jenna still distracted, she glanced at the text from Maddi, a high school senior.

at park max hurt come

Her mouth dried as her heart leaped into the back of her throat. She'd left Max in Maddi's care to take this meeting and now... She shot to her feet. "I'm really sorry but my son's hurt and I..."

"Go," Erin said before the bride had even looked up. "Jenna and I are fine to keep chatting and getting to know each other, aren't we, Jenna?"

The bride nodded. "Sure."

"I hope he's okay," Erin said, picking up Nicole's purse and shoving it into her hands.

Nicole nodded and ran to her car. Five minutes later she pulled up at the park and her breath stilled in her lungs. The Whitetail fire department's rescue truck was here.

Oh God, first Bradley, now Max. Flying out of the car, she frantically scanned the park for the bright blue shirts of firemen kneeling down around her prostrate and unconscious child, but apart from a toddler on the swings with his father, she couldn't see anyone. She ran directly to the truck.

"Mommy! Look." Her eight-year-old son was sitting in the truck wearing a red fireman's helmet on his head and beaming widely.

"Max?" Her heart still raced, even though her eyes clearly told her that he was obviously not seriously injured. In fact he looked happier than he had in a long time. "What are you doing up there?"

"Tony said I could."

Tony? She sucked in some slow, deep breaths trying to get rid of the feeling that she'd just been hit upside the head. Not a lot was making sense. "Who's Tony? Where's Maddi?"

"I'm Tony Lascio."

A fireman with short, cropped black hair and tanned skin that gleamed like bronze, smiled at her and she realized that in her panicked state she hadn't noticed him standing there. His name badge clearly said Fire Chief.

So this was the new chief everyone had been talking about at the town meeting last week? She swallowed at his sheer masculinity. With a wide neck, solid, broad shoulders and sculptured forearms with veins that bulged, he looked like he could take on a freight truck and win. Now she understood why Melissa and Emily had been so animated when they were talking about his appointment. Whitetail, with its Swedish heritage, was not used to dark and husky men like Chief Lascio.

He continued to smile at her and she got the oddest sensation in her stomach—like a squad of butterflies doing gymnastics—which rode in on top of her previous adrenaline surge, making her feel hot, flustered and confused. Her cheeks burned under the intense gaze of his chocolate-noir stare.

"Um…I'm…a…" Her mind blanked. *Name!* She closed her eyes for a moment to think.

"Are you okay? Do you need to sit down?" A slightly rough hand slid under her arm with reassuring warmth.

Warmth that flowed into her and then eddied in the

most delicious way, calling up distant memories of being touched. Stroked. Caressed.

Her stomach flipped. Her eyes shot open and she managed to splutter out, "I'm fine. Just a bit wobbly after the text I just got." She stepped back from his touch, remembering who she was and how that defined her. "I'm Nicole Lindquist, Max's mom." She glanced around looking for the sitter. "What's happened? Where's Maddi?"

"Maddi hurt her head," Max said. "She's in the bed with the legs that go up and down."

"What?" Nicole jerked her head back to Chief Lascio who was nodding his affirmation of Max's report.

"It seems Maddi misjudged the timing of the swing and she took a nasty knock to the head from Max's feet."

"Oh, no. Is she alright?" Nicole's concern instantly shifted.

"She's conscious but a bit dazed. We're doing head injury checks on her and she needs to go to the hospital for observation."

"But I don't understand." Nicole held up her phone. "She sent me a text saying Max was hurt."

The chief smiled again, his faced wreathed with sympathy and understanding. She found herself wondering if his smile would be different if it was bestowed upon someone in a non-professional capacity and instantly gave herself a mental shake. She did *not* need to wonder that.

"I think you'll find it was Max who used Maddi's phone to send you the text. He told me he did that after he'd called 911. You've got a smart little guy there," the chief said, his voice full of approval.

Max called 911? When Bradley had died, Max had

started waking up in the middle of the night, asking her over and over what he should do if someone was hurt bad like Daddy. She'd taught him 911 to reassure him so he could sleep again. She'd never thought he'd use it.

"Good job, Max." She tried to kiss him but he squirmed away, too busy having fun sitting in the truck.

"Tony, can I turn on the siren? Please," Max pleaded.

"Sorry, Champ, Maddi's got a headache so we don't want to make it worse. Tell you what, you can keep the hat."

"Awesome." Max's eyes were as round as saucers.

"What do you say, Max?" Nicole demanded gently of her son.

"Thank you." The little boy suddenly leaned out of the truck and threw his arms around Tony's neck.

The fireman's wide, firm stance didn't move despite the fact a child's weight had been hurled at him, but surprise streaked across his face. "Whoa there, little guy."

"Max. Get down," Nicole snapped, her heart sinking as she disengaged her son from the fireman's chest. Since Bradley's death he'd taken to hugging people but this was the first time he'd hugged a perfect stranger. Desperate to ease the uncomfortable moment she said, "May I speak with Maddi?"

"Sure." He extended his arm, indicating she walk the length of the truck to the back.

Joe, the second fireman-cum-EMT who Nicole knew well, was sitting inside checking Maddi's IV and writing on a chart. Maddi was propped up on the stretcher looking almost as white as the sheet that was tucked around her.

"I'm really sorry, Mrs. Lindquist," she wailed.

"Don't be silly, Maddi," Nicole soothed. "I'm just sorry you're hurt. Is your mom on her way?"

The teenager shook her head, her eyes filling with tears. "She and Dad are in Duluth and they won't be back until tonight. I'm scared, Mrs. Lindquist."

"Sweetie, there's nothing to be scared about. The nurses at the hospital will look after you."

"She needs an adult with her at the hospital," Tony said, expectation clear in his eyes that she should be the one to sort this out.

He moved past her and the scent of male cologne tickled her nostrils. A whoosh of wondrous goose bumps rose on her arms and a half second later the searing pain of guilt doused them. She rubbed her forearm. "Yes, of course. I'll make some calls."

Her mind raced. Max at the hospital wasn't a good idea. Her parents were busy and Bradley's were on a vacation in Canada. Could she ask Dana Callahan if she could mind Max again so soon after he'd had a sleepover with Logan? Nicole had been so busy she hadn't had time to reciprocate and although the Callahans always said "anytime" she didn't like to impose on their vacation.

She hated asking for help but asking came with the territory of being a single mom and over the past year necessity had given her a diploma in it.

Max tugged on her hand. "Did Daddy go in an ambulance like this?"

She thought of the squat, mine-resistant-ambush-protected ATVs that were used as ambulances in Afghanistan. The only thing that the two vehicles had in common was the medical equipment. "Sort of."

"Did he have a Tony or Joe?"

Nicole nodded, having spoken to the two men who'd been with her husband when he'd died. "He had a Dan and a Kevin."

Tony started to close the doors and Nicole called out, "I'll meet you at the hospital, Maddi."

The girl gave a wan wave as the doors shut completely.

The chief squatted down so he was at eye level with Max. "Bye, Champ. Thanks for all your help."

"My daddy was in an ambulance," Max said. "He had a Dan and a Kevin look after him."

Dark eyes looked up, scanning Nicole's face with an intensity that made her shiver. "Shh, Max. Chief Lascio doesn't want to hear about that." *Doesn't need to hear about that. I don't want to tell him about that.*

The fireman's gaze returned to Max. "I'm glad he had Dan and Kevin." Then he pulled Max's helmet over the little boy's eyes.

Max laughed.

The sound of pure, giggling delight should have brought joy to her, but for some reason it only added to Nicole's jangled nerves. She gripped her hands together. "Thank you very much for looking after Maddi and Max, and for the hat and—"

He rose to his feet. "No problem, Nicole. It's my job. It's what I'm paid to do." With a quick wave he strode to the front of the truck and in one fluid movement, he swung up into the driver's seat.

Nicole stood and watched him drive away.

FIVE

"I WANT TO come and see it." Connie's strident tones crackled over speakerphone.

Erin silenced today's GPS accent of choice—the hunky Aussie Ken with his distinctive diphthong—as he told her to "turn roight."

She pulled over. "Connie, Luke Anderson is…"

How did she describe him? Difficult? *Gorgeous.* Pigheaded? *Funny.* Rude. *Eloquent.* Graceless? *Sexy as hell.* "…adamant that he doesn't want people traipsing over his farm before the day. We don't want to tick him off and risk him pulling the plug on the idea now we've finally got him to say yes."

Now that Nicole had gotten him to say yes.

"I need to know it's going to work." Connie's voice ratcheted up a notch.

"It's going to work," Erin said firmly. "I'll go check out the field, study the light and shoot a bunch of angles so you can see that it's all going to be perfect. Then you can relax. How does that sound?"

Erin crossed her fingers and rode out the long silence.

"Okay," Connie finally replied. "But do it today."

"Um…" Erin thought about her schedule. "I'll do my best."

"I always expect that, Erin."

The line went dead and Erin pressed the message

icon on her phone and texted Nicole. She'd been planning on starting the editing process to give the "Erin Davis" touch to Lindsay and Keith's wedding photos as soon as she'd finished putting together the package outlining all their album options. She could picture a rustic album complete with photos mounted on handmade paper and using a bark cover to pull the entire package together. It would perfectly reflect the couple's connection with the land and she was excited about discussing it with them after their short honeymoon. All too often, she fell in love with the final albums and found it a wrench to part with them.

Usually she discussed the package details with the couple at their engagement shoot or when they signed the contract to employ her as their wedding photographer. She smiled at the thought of the two newly signed contracts she had tucked safely in her leather satchel. Counting Connie's, she now had three weddings to shoot and Nicole had hinted at another two.

Her phone beeped with Nicole's reply. *Sorry. Am at the hospital. Can't meet you at farm today.*

Fabulous. Erin groaned, remembering the last time she'd seen Luke and how she'd let her usually restrained temper get the better of her. During Lindsay and Keith's wedding, when she'd been mingling in the crowd and taking photos, she hadn't seen Luke. She'd almost dropped her camera when she'd heard his richly timbered voice over the PA system. His speech had been pitch-perfect for a crowd that had been partying for a few hours and yet it still honored the bride and groom. It totally reinforced Nicole's opinion of Luke and had decimated hers. At that moment, her growing suspicions that he'd played her for a fool became an absolute belief.

She hated being played for a fool. Her father had done it to her with false promises she'd believed and she refused to allow any man or woman to do it to her again. Her fury at Luke had simmered from the moment she'd heard his speech and by the time she was free to leave the wedding she'd been so livid, she'd stormed into his milking parlor, guns blazing. He, in turn, had called her on her own behavior, laughed at her and made it clear he still didn't want her around.

Why couldn't his brother, Wade, be the guy she had to deal with? He was a total sweetie. She rested her head against the steering wheel feeling like she was between a rock and a hard place. Nicole believed Luke Anderson was the most reasonable of men and Erin wanted to believe her, given she'd been the one to convince him to allow the use of his field. The only problem was, other than his begrudging towing of her car, she'd never glimpsed "reasonable" in any of his dealings with her. In return, she'd lurched between friendly and fuming, only making things harder for herself.

Dumb, dumb, dumb. She banged her forehead against the top of the steering wheel, welcoming the physical pain because it was easier than the emotional turmoil she went through every time she came face-to-face with Luke Anderson. He didn't like her, and she would have been fine with that if he wasn't the owner of the sunflower field she really needed for Connie and her Memmy entry. He was adamant he wanted to deal with Nicole in regards to the photos and no one else. In a perfect world she'd have followed those instructions to a T but she was an expert on the fact that the world was far from perfect, having learned that particular lesson at fifteen.

What she did know was that if she didn't send Connie some photos tonight, she'd be hosing down anxious bride fires all day tomorrow. She had no choice. Sucking in a deep breath, she called Luke's cell.

"Luke Anderson." His warm and self-assured voice came down the line, sounding business-friendly.

He doesn't know it's me.

Just be polite and professional. "Hi, Luke, it's Erin. Erin Davis." She quickly added, "The photographer."

He gave a resigned sigh. "I know who you are, Erin. Given the drama you've managed to create on your three visits to the farm, I'm unlikely to forget you any time soon."

Just keep going. She bit her lip. "I'm sorry to bother you—"

"Seriously?" This time he laughed as if she'd cracked an incredibly funny joke. "You've been bothering me for two days without apologizing so why start now? What is it this time? Are you lost or bogged? Do I need to bring the tractor or will the truck do? Better yet, is there some other hapless farmer you can call on?"

His laughter was sending delicious and heady shimmers through her, which wasn't right given they didn't like each other, not to mention the fact that they reacted like oil and water every time they met. She tossed her hair for reinforcement and thought about the sunflower field. "I'm sure the truck will do fine."

"Erin? Are you okay?"

She shivered at the way his voice had dropped to a deep and serious bass as if he was actually concerned about her. "I'm fine, but I need to sight the sunflower field today for light levels and to take some photos."

There was a moment's silence—one that roared loud

in her ears, deafening her. He was going to say *no*. She knew it. She could hear it in that mellow, no-nonsense voice of his and—

"Okay—"

And there was the no. "I know you'd prefer to deal with Nicole," her words rushed out, running into each other, "but she's stuck at the hospital and I prom—"

"Erin."

The firmness of the tone stopped her yammering. "Yes."

"I said okay."

Okay? "Really?" Her voice came out as a squeak.

"Really." His amusement poured down the line. "I can say no if you'd prefer."

"Ah, no, great, thanks." Relief made her chest relax and she savored the scent of sweet, late-afternoon air sweeping into her lungs.

"Where are you now?"

She reached over, grabbing the GPS, and her fingers brushed the screen. As she told Luke she was on County Hill Road, Ken said loudly and nasally, "Turrrrn around when possible."

"Is someone with you?" Luke asked.

"Ken, from Australia. I thought he might give me better directions than Patrick from Ireland. It was Patrick's fault I ended up in your pasture."

"Be very careful, Erin." Luke's voice vibrated in a way that seemed to roll her name in a caress. "I've spent time in Australia and those Aussie men will lead you astray every single time."

Will you? The thought slammed into her, making her body hot and heavy and her head dizzy. Was she losing her mind or was Luke Anderson actually flirting with her?

She thought about the last time she'd seen him, when he'd tried his best to make sure she didn't stay at Wade's cottage.

You are so totally losing your mind.

"Erin, are you there?"

"Yes." It came out all breathy and she cleared her throat.

"You need to keep driving west—"

"How do I know which way is west?"

She heard him take a breath but at least he didn't sigh. "The road runs east-west so keep the town behind you and you're heading west, into the sun. You'll come to a four-way stop with corn on every side. Take a left at the scarecrow."

Having seen quite a few scarecrows over the past few days and being very aware that she could easily turn at the wrong one and get horribly lost, she asked, "What's it wearing?"

"A straw hat and a black bird," he said sharply. "How the hell should I know? Does it matter?"

His smooth liqueur voice, the one which had wrapped her in wondrous warmth, had vanished, and the abrasive Luke she knew all too well was back. *This* Luke she'd met. With this Luke she knew exactly where she stood. "Actually, I've seen quite a few fashion-conscious scarecrows in fields so I take it you dressed this one in flannel and overalls," she teased him a bit unfairly because she'd never seen him wear either of those things.

"Do you want the rest of the instructions or not?"

"Yes, please." She grinned happily as she wrote them down.

* * *

LUKE SAW ERIN'S car parked in the space between the gate and the road and he pulled up behind it. He'd driven down to the field because despite giving her detailed instructions on how to get here, he was convinced he'd be getting an "I'm lost" phone call. He'd decided he may as well just come to the field now rather than start something only to be interrupted. Besides, he wanted to make sure she'd closed the gate.

Admit it. You just want to see her.

He wasn't anywhere close to ready to concede that. It had been forty-eight hours since he'd last seen Erin and had watched her leave the milking parlor with her laughter ringing in his ears. Forty-six hours since he'd disengaged Marlene's arms from his neck and her tongue from his ear, tucked her into her motel room bed and come home sober and celibate. It wasn't supposed to have turned out quite like that, especially given how agreeable Marlene had been to doing exactly what he'd wanted—a fun evening ending in mindless sex, and all for one night only.

However, as the evening with Marlene had progressed, instead of her general agreeableness making him feel like a king, he'd found himself making increasingly outrageous political, social and religious pronouncements to see what it would take for her to disagree with him. The more she continued to say, "You're so right," the more he found himself thinking how Erin, with her brilliant green eyes flashing indignantly, would have jabbed him in the sternum with one of her manicured fingers and called him on it.

It made absolutely no sense to walk away from Marlene who stroked his ego just because he was thinking about a woman who didn't, but that's what he'd done. It still stunned him and his frustrated libido wasn't at all happy that his brain had overruled it. He couldn't believe that even when Erin wasn't anywhere near him, she was still getting in the way and interrupting his life.

You're the one interrupting your life. You're the one who doesn't know what he wants.

He whistled Mac from the truck to shut up the rogue thought and then he walked to the gate, checking the chain. "Well, Mac, it looks like she's in the field and she's shut the gate behind her." His palm slapped the top of the fence post. "Job done. Guess we can leave now."

Mac's big, brown eyes gave him a quizzical look when he leaned over and unlooped the chain from its anchoring stump, opened the gate and passed through, closing it behind them. Row upon row of sunflower stalks taller than Erin faced him, their large heads bursting, almost ready to flower. Mac trotted happily next to him for a bit and then started barking.

Luke ruffled his ears. "Stay, Mac."

A white ball of fluff appeared at the end of a row, straining to move forward but going nowhere, and then Erin came into view, holding a leash in one hand and her camera in the other. Her dog yapped and bounced at her feet, desperate to meet Mac nose to nose, but was unhappily restrained by the leash.

"Sit, Maggie-May," Erin instructed firmly.

Surprisingly, the dog did just that. He and Mac walked up.

Erin checked her watch and astonishment raced across her cheeks. "Don't tell me you've delayed milking just to come check I closed the gate?"

She's too smart by half. In her bright yellow, plastic

clogs, white skirt and canary-yellow top with black trim, she looked like a happy sunflower in bloom rather than a perceptive woman. "Gates are important."

She smiled and her nose suddenly fell into perfect proportion to her wide mouth. "I know. You told me *three* times on the phone."

"It's farming 101 and I can't emphasize it enough." He shoved his hands in his pockets feeling caught out, and his reaction ran parallel to the general discontent that pervaded his life at the moment—like the constant feeling that the farm was controlling him instead of the other way around.

She tilted her head, studying him, and the tips of her hair caressed her chin. "Do you and gates have a history? Did one chase you with a whip and traumatize you as a child?"

He grinned at the image. "Something like that. All I'll say is that it involved a gate, a happy bull, some surprised cows and a furious father."

Her eyes lit up with interest. "That sounds like a story worth hearing."

And oddly he wanted to tell her, only that wasn't how he was supposed to be feeling because she was everything in a woman he didn't want. "Put it this way, I've never left a gate open since. Now you're fully briefed on all things gates, you'll avoid a similar trauma so I'll leave you to it." He turned to go and Mac rose to his feet.

"Actually," her voice cajoled, "seeing as you're here, can you be my model?"

He spun back, not sure he'd heard right. "What?"

Her smooth hair swung as her mouth formed a wry smile. "It would really help me if you stood in a few different places so I can check the shadows and the light. If I have a person in the photo, Connie will be able to picture it all a lot better."

"I'm not a bride."

"So be the groom."

He wasn't planning on being either of those things. "Use Mac to stand in for the bride." He deliberately palmed his forehead. "Oh, sorry, that won't work, he's not batshit crazy."

Erin shook her head emphatically. "Connie isn't crazy either. She just knows what she wants, which in a lot of ways is easier than a bride who constantly changes her mind."

Luke wasn't convinced about the crazy part.

"This is going to be the most fabulous setting when the flowers open and the photos will be stunning." She threw her arms out and spun around, her face filling with a dreamy look.

A heavy feeling dragged at Luke, as if he was missing something.

The spinning stopped abruptly as her feet stilled and the dreamy look vanished. She hit him with an intense stare. "The flowers *will* open in time, right?"

He rocked back on his boots, surveying the bulging heads that were so very close to opening. "They should, unless we get an unexpected cold snap or a hail storm that decimates the entire field."

She blanched, her features looking stark and pinched. "Is that likely to happen?"

He shrugged. "In farming, anything can happen. In a lot of ways it's an inexact science because there's only so much you can control."

Her whole body jerked as if she'd just been shocked.

"The weather *must* be perfect because this shoot has to work."

Her reaction and forceful tone surprised him because as a photographer she must be used to dealing with brides and inclement weather. "If it's a complete disaster there are other places you can use for your difficult bride, like the covered bridge and Mrs. Norell's garden." He rubbed his neck. "Although if hail flattens this, it'll probably take out those gardens too."

"And that's you trying to reassure me?" She shook her head slowly as if she couldn't quite believe her ears. "For a moment there, I'd forgotten farmers are pessimists."

"Hey!" He took offense at being cast as a naysayer. "I'm not being negative. I'm just being a realist. You asked would the field flower on time, and I gave you the facts."

"The facts…" She stared at him for a long, contemplative moment. "You're a guy so of course you gave me all the facts because facts are important."

"Damn straight, they are."

Her face creased in a genuine smile. "My brother's always giving me the facts. Sorry, it's just this shoot is really important to me."

Me? He raised a brow. "Isn't it supposed to be important to the bride?"

"Yes. I meant the bride." She sounded defensive and her body seemed to bustle with exaggerated movement as her hands tied the leash around a fence post. "So, is your dog going to play nice with Maggie-May while we do this?"

He got the distinct impression she wanted to change the subject. "Mac will stand with me."

"Great. I need you both to stand—" her fingers closed around his forearm and she tugged him into the middle of the dirt strip that ran down the center of the field "—here. Now if you can just turn around…"

Her hands were suddenly on his shoulder, her fingers pressing firmly into the bare skin at the tops of his arms. There was nothing gentle or tentative about the touch—it was all business—a photographer used to putting her hands on people to position them exactly where they were needed for the shot. Only it was making him think Swedish massage, hot oil, naked skin and her hands pummeling every part of him.

When she finally stepped back from him and he was left alone facing down the field with his back to her, he gave up a silent thank-you. At least the time it took her to take the photos would give him a few moments to get his body back under control and give his erection time to deflate.

He heard the sounds of the camera behind him and grabbed on to an innocuous topic to help the process along. "I've never understood why digital cameras make shutter sounds?"

"This one's a top-end SLR and it's got both an electronic and a mechanical shutter. It means a sharper picture. Even if it only had an electronic one, I'd have the shutter sound turned on for my clients because when they hear the click, they know I've taken the photo. Can you walk over to the sunflowers, please?"

He did and Mac followed him. Maggie-May bounced on her leash, yapping, as if saying to Mac, *It's so not fair you're walking free.* This time Erin wanted Luke to face the camera and he crossed his arms, feeling uncomfortable. "What do you want me to do?"

"Just stand." She squatted down and angled her camera.

He found himself studying the way her hair fell from her part, which ran perfectly straight until the last quarter where it snaked crookedly. It was at odds with the neat bob that fell effortlessly in a shining waterfall of hair. He instantly remembered the silky feel of it against his chin when she'd fallen on top of him and the delectable scent of fresh fruit.

Don't go there, buddy.

It was too late.

The memory made way for the one he'd tried to forget—the one where her body had wriggled against his, sending her heat scudding through him and making his blood pound hard and fast. Sweat broke out on his top lip as he tried to keep his blood supply north of his groin. Frantic for a distraction, he looked up at the sky and was instantly mocked. There wasn't a cloud in sight to watch or wonder about.

One twelve is twelve, two twelves are twenty-four, three twelves—

"Actually, Luke, you're taller than the groom. Can you bend your knees?"

He wanted out before she noticed he was hornier than a teenager watching porn. "I can hear the cows getting angsty."

"Five more minutes. Please."

She flashed him a quick "all business" appreciative smile, and despite the assault of color from her clothes, the slightly ditzy and chaos-causing woman he'd first met was nowhere to be seen. Neither was the overly polite or the pointedly snarky one. Instead he was faced with focused professionalism and gratitude.

Shit. It meant he really couldn't walk away without looking like he was a grumpy and difficult farmer.

Why worry? Two nights ago you wanted her to think exactly that.

For some unfathomable reason it now bothered him and that ticked him off. He found himself missing the general animosity that usually swirled between them. That he understood and it had kept him from acting on the fact his body wanted her. With a sigh, he bent down. "I feel ridiculous."

"You're really helping. You probably could have been a model if you hadn't gone into farming."

He snorted. "Yeah, right." He'd been raised on a farm and was a country boy through and through. He had no time for fripperies and false images. He fingered the soil as he often did, but the excitement he usually got from feeling the perfect mix of moisture and organic matter didn't come.

The camera clicked rapidly. "Can you walk into the actual field and then do a peekaboo from behind the stalks?"

He rose to his feet. "You're kidding me, right?"

"No." She looked taken aback and came and stood next to him. "I want to see if the shot will work or if the shadows are too long."

The request hit the limit of his patience. Everything he believed about being a man was suddenly at stake. "Not even a whipped groom is going to pop out from behind sunflower stalks."

Her chestnut brows quirked knowingly. "Believe me, a groom will do pretty much anything his bride asks, especially if she's invoked the 'no sex' rule for the previous seven days."

Her lush lips had formed a perfect red O when she said "no," and when it combined with the smoky way her voice rolled over the word *sex*, he let his throbbing body take control. He stepped in close. The fruity scent of her hair and the crisp fresh aroma of her perfume flooded him and he looked straight into those upward-slanting eyes rimmed with thick, cocoa lashes. "A groom will do pretty much anything the bride wants, you say?"

Her eyes widened at his softly spoken words but she didn't back away. "So I've been told."

"Then he's not much of a man." He slid his hand under the bob of her hair, his fingers cupping the soft skin of her neck. Her warmth caressed his palm and her pulse bounded against it.

She shuddered at his touch, the delicious movement flowing into him like a heat-seeking missile with its target fully in its sights. He groaned and stroked her bottom lip with his thumb, gently easing the damp fullness down.

For a long moment time stood still—his thumb suspended against delicious softness. Then she flicked out her tongue, its pink tip circling the pad of his thumb, around and around and around. His blood roared, shattering his pretense at restraint and he lowered his mouth to hers.

Erin shut her mind to all the reasons why kissing Luke Anderson was a hugely dumb idea. Instead she focused on the fact that he was real rather than a disembodied, sexy GPS voice, and she closed her eyes on a blissful sigh. Who knew the gorgeous to look at yet often irritable, difficult and confusing guy was a kissing god. How could that be?

But answering that question was beyond her as his mouth trailed over hers. The slight scratch of his work-hardened hands was as rough as he got. There was no saliva-loaded attack, no tongue lashing at her teeth trying to gain entry before being plunged down her throat. No, this kiss was soft, enticing and divine—a slow exploration of her lips as if they were some precious parcel to be unwrapped slowly and carefully, layer upon layer upon layer.

Her arm lost strength and dropped to her side, her grip on her camera barely holding, and she leaned into him. Pliant and sighing against his mouth, she lost herself in the wonder of the moment, hoping it would never end. She could stay here all day being kissed like this, pressed up against his broad, solid chest, and still be left wanting more.

His fingers toyed with her hair, gently rubbing her scalp as his mouth moved slowly off her lips and reached her jaw. Her body turned liquid as pleasure streamed through her, slowly waking her up cell by cell and stripping her muscles and bones of their form. Her head tilted back of its own accord, giving him access to more skin, wanting more of the same, and as his mouth roamed, her body floated. It was like lying in a warm, fragrant bath surrounded by candles and listening to the lulling sounds of Vivaldi. He plied her skin with featherlight kisses as if she were fragile porcelain and any more pressure might make her shatter.

Oh, yes, please.

She gloried in it all and was just hoping that he'd start nuzzling her neck, especially the dip at the base, when he reached her earlobe. He kissed it tenderly. She sighed again.

He nipped it with his teeth and sucked it.

Her eyes flew open as her blood burst into flames.

Delicious lethargy vanished. She wanted to taste him. She wanted to feel him inside her. She needed his tongue to plunder her mouth, to brand her with his heat, and she wanted to do exactly the same to him. And more. Forgetting she was holding her camera, she threw her arms around his neck and it banged him on the bony scapula.

"Ouch."

"Sorry."

"Put it down."

"No, it's worth a fortune."

"Keep the damn thing still then."

"Shut up." Her free hand pulled his head down to hers, and she opened her mouth and invaded his.

Stars exploded in the back of Luke's head. Erin tasted of vanilla coffee, mint and a hot and desperate need that matched his own. There was nothing delicate or tentative about her kiss. She was exploring his mouth exactly how he liked it—taking what he offered and leaving her own mark.

He felt her breasts tighten against his chest, firming into two hard balls of arousal and if he wasn't already totally hard, he would have matched her. He slid his hand under her tank top, his fingers sliding against smooth, warm skin until they met the clasp of her bra. With one deft flick, the back opened.

She broke the kiss, looking up at him with a grin on her face. "You've done that before."

His hand snuck around and cupped her left breast. "Once or twice. I'm pretty good."

She half gasped, half moaned and he ached for her.

"I'm better," she said as her free hand whipped down

from his neck. A second later, she was gently cupping his testicles through his jeans.

Game on. He stroked her nipple.

She shuddered, hooked his gaze and stroked him, her fingers gently sliding over the bulge of his erection.

He shuddered.

They matched stroke for stroke, gasp for gasp and moan for moan until she fell against him and he lifted her off her feet, not caring that the damn camera was now digging into his back. All he knew was that he had to feel her legs wrapped around him and the pressure of her body pressed hard against him.

The yapping sounds of her dog floated on the air but he ignored them as he buried his mouth against those pillow-soft lips and felt them yield to him. God, she was so responsive, he could barely see straight.

Mac's insistent bark joined the yapping and Erin's tongue paused in its delicious assault. He flicked his tongue against hers to kick-start the kiss.

"Luu-ke."

Erin unwrapped her legs so fast he almost lost his balance.

"Luu-ke."

He realized someone was calling his name. "Shit."

"Let me go!" Erin pushed at his arms, which were supporting her thighs.

He half lowered her, half dropped her as some of his blood managed to reach his brain. He saw Erin fumbling with her bra. "Do you need a hand?"

She shook her head as Mac's barks sounded closer. "Should you go meet him?"

"Mac?" He wasn't sure he could actually walk.

"Not Mac." She half pushed him toward the end of the row. "The guy who's calling you."

"Luu-ke! Mac, go find him, boy." The booming voice sounded really close now.

What the... Shock thundered through him so fast he swayed as lust was replaced with utter astonishment. He shoved his shirt into his jeans and with a throbbing pain in his groin, he stepped out onto the dirt road.

"Dad?"

SIX

THE DOGS HAD stopped barking and Erin could hear the rumble of male voices. The longer she stayed hidden in the sunflower row, the more difficult it would be to appear without drawing attention to the fact she'd been there for two minutes. That she'd had her tongue stuck down Luke Anderson's throat, had been rubbing herself hard against him like a dog in heat and mere moments from an orgasm.

Her cheeks burned so hot that eggs could be fried on them. Dear God, she'd thrown herself at the man, letting her sex-starved body call all the shots. Instead of spending her time flirting with Ken and Patrick, she should have been taking practical care of her libido with a little bit of self-love every now and then. That way, she might have had some control over her inner slut. But no, she'd happily pushed her sex drive onto the back burner, thinking she was the one in control, only to find herself dry-humping the first man who'd kissed her in months. She had to buy herself a vibrator. Now.

Yeah, but he can so totally kiss.

She couldn't argue with that. He was an awesome kisser, but that didn't mean kissing him again was going to be the best idea in the world. The man didn't operate within any normal social boundaries. Well, not with her anyway. She found it so much easier when he was being his grudgingly polite self with lapses of rudeness—that she could deal with because it was expected. Luke being obliging—like when he'd allowed her to use him as a model—was unexpected and not only did those cooperative moments confuse the hell out of her, it made him even more sexy and oh so hard to resist.

But sexy or not, she didn't have time in her life for confusing. She had a business to establish and a photography competition to win and those two things took priority.

Time to face real life. Finger-smoothing her hair, she gulped in some breaths and then proceeded to back out of the row of sunflowers with her camera up at her face. The visitor wasn't to know she was shooting clear, blue sky.

As she came clear of the plants, she turned and called out casually, "Thanks, Luke. I'm done."

Luke was standing next to an older, slightly shorter version of himself. Unlike his son, who specialized in wearing jeans teamed with cutoff shirts that showed off his wonderfully work-sculptured arms, his father wore a baseball cap, a golf polo shirt with a club logo and long shorts. He had Maggie-May tucked firmly under his arm and Mac lying at his feet. Was he a dog whisperer?

As she approached, Luke didn't flash her the expected conspiratorial-partners-in-crime look that said, *Phew, that was a close call. We almost got caught in flagrante.* No, he gave her a curt nod as if he hadn't moments ago had one of his fingers inside her panties.

"Erin, meet my father, Vernon Anderson."

She shot out her hand and then realized it was holding her camera. With a laugh that sounded slightly more anxious than she'd hoped, she quickly passed it to her other hand. Remembering what Luke had said the first time she'd met him, she said, "Pleased to meet you, Mr. Anderson. Unlike your son, you seem to have bewitched my dog."

He smiled broadly. "She's a friendly little thing…"

Erin threw Luke an "I told you" look just as Vernon said, "…only don't let her near the cows."

"Which is exactly what I told her." Luke's divine mouth tweaked up on one side as if to say, *score one*.

"Talking about cows, son, are you operating on Arizona time too?"

Erin heard a thread of criticism in Vernon's voice and for some reason she found herself saying, "It's my fault. I held Luke up, sorry."

Luke ignored her defense. "Brett will have started, Dad, and I'm on my way now."

"I always started at four."

"You did." Luke ran his hand across the back of his neck. "Where's Mom?"

"Back at the house starting supper." Vernon handed Erin a now struggling Maggie-May who was desperately trying to get to her. "I'll let Martha know there'll be an extra, shall I?"

Luke didn't even look at her. "Erin won't be staying, Dad."

I won't? Okay then. Good to know we both regret those few minutes of complete craziness. "Thank you very much for the invitation, but I've got turn-down duty at the B and B and photos to edit."

"Another time, then. Martha and I are going to be here for a few weeks."

Luke made an odd sort of choking sound and then coughed. "Summer cold," he said, quickly clearing his throat. "What about the golf tournament you were telling me about? Isn't that next week?"

The bellows of cows floated over to them.

Vernon slung his arm around Luke's shoulder. "Come on, I'll give you a hand with the milking."

Erin watched them walk away, struck by the set of their shoulders as Vernon's arm fell back by his side. Surrounded by acres of beautiful countryside and bucolic fresh air, neither father nor son looked remotely relaxed.

"MORE LEMON MERINGUE pie?"

Luke smiled at his mother and shook his head. "No, thanks, Mom."

Disappointment scudded across her cheeks. "It's your favorite."

"Actually, it's my favorite, Mom. Mine and Wade's," his sister, Keri, said, serving up another two portions and handing one off to Wade. "Luke's favorite is cherry pie à la mode."

Martha laughed. "Of course it is. I should have remembered that, especially as there's a slice of cherry pie in the refrigerator."

"Poor Luke," Keri said with mock concern. "Reduced to buying frozen pie."

"I believe poor Luke had it baked for him," Wade said, his eyes twinkling as he scooped up a mouthful of the decadently rich lemon custard.

"Really, you made him a pie?" Keri asked.

Wade grinned and rolled his eyes. "I'm a caring brother but I'm not that good. No, I believe Erin not only baked him his favorite pie but cooked him prime rib."

Suddenly three sets of questioning eyes swung to Luke and locked on to him.

Thanks, bro.

"A woman who can cook? Luke, way to go." Keri slapped him on the back approvingly. "Keep this one. It's why I married Phil."

"Erin?" Vernon asked. "The unusual-looking girl in the sunflower field with the enormous eyes?" He nodded his head slowly as realization dawned across his gray-whiskered face. "Now I understand why you were late starting the milking."

His mother's face lit up with a combination of hope that he might finally be thinking of settling down and chagrin that Vernon had met her first. "Invite her over, Luke, so we can meet her."

Luke silently groaned, knowing he had to stomp on this fast or he'd find himself sitting down to supper next to Erin while his loving, well-intentioned but extremely misguided family subjected them to the third degree, including the expected date of their fourth-born.

"Erin only cooked me a meal because she wanted to discuss using the sunflower field for one of her client's wedding photos. We're not a couple. We're not even dating."

Just almost having sex on the dirt in a field.

"It's just business," he said loudly and instantly regretted the volume. He dropped his voice. "Lakeview Farm is doing its bit for Whitetail's wedding business, is all."

"I think it's a good idea," Wade said approvingly.

Sometimes he couldn't figure Wade out at all. His brother had neatly dropped him in it by teasing him about Erin, and now he was changing the subject to protect and smooth over Luke's overemphatic denouncement that nothing was going on between them. And nothing was going on.

Nothing except for the fact she'd kissed him like he was the last man standing and he hadn't been so aroused in—ever.

No, not even close. He fondly remembered Julia from Australia and Lisa from New Zealand, and how both of whom had raised the bar along with Penny from Pepin. All three had firmly established the fact that farm girls were perfect for him.

None of them kissed like Erin.

He had the overwhelming urge to go chop wood. Lots and lots of wood to silence the voice in his head.

Wade kept talking. "The cottages and the B and B are benefiting from Whitetail's new direction and I think we could be more involved in the wedding side of things."

We? Luke's brain snapped on topic, but as he opened his mouth, Vernon spoke first.

"Wade, Lakeview's a farm."

"I'm well aware of that, Dad." Wade wore the look of an adolescent boy who'd struggled to find a place in his father's world and still be true to himself.

"And talking about the farm…" his mother rushed into the conversation, inserting herself between her eldest son and her husband like she'd done so many times in the past twenty years "…is why we're here and why we picked Keri up on the way. We want to talk to you all together. We've had almost a year in Arizona now and your father and I think it's time we formalized things."

Shit. Luke tensed and drained his glass of water. He wasn't ready for this.

Martha looked expectantly at Vernon and nodded as if to say, *I've got their attention, your turn now.*

His father sucked in his cheeks and fiddled with the edge of the place mat.

Martha frowned. "Vern?"

His father sighed. "Your mother thinks it's time to talk about officially transferring the farm over to Luke and involving everyone in the family trust." His gaze sought Luke's and Keri's. "As Luke's the only one of the three of you who wants to farm, this is the fairest way of doing things."

Tell them. "Unless we sell," Luke said, pulling his phone out of his pocket. "The beach acres alone are worth over a million dollars."

Silence greeted him as four jaws dropped and four heads turned sharply in his direction.

Then the yelling started.

"What the hell are you talking about?" His father's fist hit the table, making the remaining silverware bounce.

"How do you even know this?" Wade's expression held the pain of betrayal that Luke hadn't mentioned it to him.

"Oh my God, that's a lot of money." Keri, who was always a ball of energy, sat perfectly still in her chair as if trying to absorb the figure.

"Luke?" His mother's voice was pure anxiety. "What's going on?"

I don't know. The heavy feeling that had been dogging him in months felt like a lead weight on his chest and molten lead in his veins. "Nothing's going on. Axel was over last month and we were down at the beach and he valued the land. I thought you should know how much it's worth. All I'm saying is that it's another option to put into the mix."

"The hell it is," Vernon roared. "This farm's been in my family for five generations and dividing it up has never been part of succession planning and it's not going to start now."

Keri sat forward. "Luke's got a point, Daddy. It's an option worth discussing."

"I can't believe you've been sitting on this for a month," Wade said accusingly.

Luke tried to dismantle some of the tension that encircled them all and he looked directly at his brother. "It could be that lottery you were talking about. A chance to leave Whitetail and meet someone."

Wade glared at him. "I wasn't serious. With the Whitetail wedding business taking off, I'm in a prime position to capitalize on it and have guests discover we're not just any old B and B. My guests use that beach and it's a big draw. When I told you about my plans for the mini nursery-farm for families staying at the cottages, you said it was a good idea and promised me calves. Now, all that time, you've been planning to undermine me. My business is connected to this farm, Luke, and selling isn't an option."

"At least one of my sons understands," Vernon ground out, the veins on his neck bulging. "Pity it isn't the farmer."

"We should never have left you alone on the farm before you were married and settled," Martha said, wringing her hands. "It's too hard living this life on your own."

"Jeez, Mom." Luke shot to his feet as her words vibrated deep down inside him like a chord—a very discordant one. "Being single has *nothing* to do with this. Nothing. God, I'm sorry I brought it up."

"I'm not," Keri said.

"Keri…" The warning tone in Vernon's voice may have silenced his sister when she was fourteen but at thirty-four and a mother of two, it wasn't going to silence her now.

"What, Daddy? Are you telling me that because I married and moved away, I don't get a say in the family farm?"

"Your father isn't saying that at all," Martha said, her face pinched.

"I'm not saying anything else, period. This conversation is over." Vernon pushed back in his chair. "I'm going for a walk."

"I'll join you," Wade said, meeting his father at the door.

Keri flounced off toward her old room. His mother followed, but not before giving Luke a look that begged him to explain why he'd just thrown a grenade into the next step of succession planning for the farm.

Doors slammed.

Silence hung heavily.

The walls of the house bore down on him, filled with condemnation. He didn't know what he hated more— the fact he'd just imploded his family or the fact that all he could think about was Erin.

THE COTTAGE THAT came with the cleaning job was tiny, consisting of two rooms and an en suite bathroom and although it was way too small for a family vacation, it was perfect for Erin. Wade had told her it had originally been built quickly in the twenties for a bachelor farm worker and the sloping floor was testament to its age. Long after the farm worker had moved on and housing expectations had risen, it had become the teenage retreat cum band room for two generations. Now it was careworn and required a lot of work, including repairs to the sagging entrance, which currently made the front door stick shut. Erin entered and exited through the slider glass doors of the bedroom, which was no big deal.

She'd spent the evening doing the jobs that she'd set aside to photograph the sunflower field. She was just about to turn out the light for the night when Maggie-May started barking. A second later the slider doors to her bedroom vibrated from loud knocking and she spun around with a jerk, staring at the drawn curtains she'd closed against the doors to shut out the massive expanse of darkness. Earlier she'd tried to enjoy the starlit night and the silence but after living in the city all her life, the quietness and the inky black had freaked her out a little bit.

She gave herself a shake. *No boogeyman is going to bother driving down a muddy lane to find you. It's probably just Wade telling you which cottage to start with in the morning.*

"Maggie-May, quiet. Sit." When her precious had stopped barking she called out, "Who is it?"

"Luke."

Maggie-May barked and pawed at the curtains with a whine as if saying, *Let me at him.*

Luke? Anticipation and panic collided, leaving her stomach flipping and her head spinning. *Was this a booty call?*

Unlikely, she told her panting inner slut. Given the cool way he'd acknowledged her after what she'd been referring to all evening as *the kiss*, she doubted he was here to continue where they left off.

"Erin, can you call your dog off so I can come in?"

Yes, no, I don't know.

"Just a minute." She stifled a groan at what she was wearing, picked up her dog and locked her in the other room before doubling back, flicking on the deck light and sliding open the door. Mac sat quietly next to his master but her breath caught at the sight of Luke leaning up against the doorjamb. Clean boots, clean chinos, and he wore a pressed, long-sleeved Oxford shirt the color of a summer sky. The blue lit up his eyes and took them to a level beyond piercing.

After throwing herself at him like a wild thing earlier, this time she was determined to be Ms. Civilized and match his previously detached air. "You're all dressed up? Have you been to a party?"

"Family supper. Mom expects clean hands, clean shirt, clean pants and clean shoes."

And he looked divine. Just as he had at the wedding. Not that he didn't look fabulous in his cutoff work shirts, but there was something about a man who took some care in matching his clothes to the occasion. "I like the sound of your mother."

He huffed out a breath. "Yeah."

Given that he'd been the one to stop by, he wasn't exactly full of conversation. "So I take it supper's over?"

"You bet." The words held a sardonic edge.

She searched his face looking for a hint of why he was here but she came up blank. His expression was neutral and his eyes shuttered. "So at ten p.m. you thought you'd stop by and…?"

"And—" his voice dropped to a delicious burr "—see you."

His eyes, which up until that moment had been fixed on her face, proceeded to flick over her—one small brushing glance at a time.

Mini explosions of lust detonated until they coalesced and rushed through her, making her blood thick with hot and heavy need. God, she really should have paid overnight shipping on that vibrator.

As his gaze hovered, reading the writing on her tank top and then dropping to her black-and-white pants, he made a sound that was half laughter and half groan. "Nice pajamas. Do you always dress to suit your location?"

She crossed her arms over the black tank top that had a picture of two cows wearing black fedoras, suits and ties, and said The Moos Brothers. "They were an ironic birthday present from my brother. Who knew I was actually going to end up living next door to cows?"

"Who indeed?" As he stepped past her into the bedroom, he slid his arm around her waist and pulled her in close.

His voice and his touch had her sighing. Quickly forgetting she was supposed to be cool and detached, she relaxed against him, breathing in his clean scent of soap with the undertones of pure masculinity. Running her hands along the soft cotton of his shirt, she reacquainted her body with the hard contours of his. Man, he smelled and felt fantastic.

He nuzzled her neck exactly the way she liked it— the stubble on his cheeks tickling her skin, the gentle pressure of his mouth on hers, the decadent flick of his tongue followed by the erotic suction of his lips. Every part of her started tumbling toward doing anything he desired, because chances were it was exactly what she wanted too.

His mouth cruised down her décolletage and when he reached the top of her tank top, he lifted his head. "You being dressed like a Holstein is slightly disconcerting. I was hoping to forget the farm tonight."

Her totally aroused inner slut called out, *No problem. Strip my pajamas off me now.*

His words, however, had kick-started her brain, which rudely interrupted with, *Why did he say I was hoping to forget the farm?*

Her body tensed. As a come-on line it was very one-sided. Shouldn't it be *we can forget the farm?* No, that wouldn't have made sense because she had no reason to forget the farm or even a reason to remember it. However, it seemed he had a reason to forget it or why would he have said it? Her brain continued to whirr, firing questions at her and slowly her body started to calm as the rational side doused the lust.

If she added in his cool detachment this afternoon, moments after *the kiss* and then combined it with this unexpected evening visit, she suddenly felt like she was being used. "Are you drunk?"

"Nope." He stared down at her with an easy smile and her legs immediately turned to jelly again despite the fact her head was warning her that he'd never smiled at her like that before. From the moment she'd met him, all previous smiles had either been sarcastic grimaces, wry, reluctant or had come with accompanying tension clinging to the edges. His words were at odds with the smile.

"Buzzed, then?"

"Little bit." He stroked her hair behind her ear. "But you have nothing to worry about. I promise you my performance will only be enhanced by a little help from Jack."

She rolled her eyes thinking he was more than just buzzed. "Research doesn't support that theory."

"I'm willing to prove research wrong," he said, still holding her hands and stepping backward. He sat down on the end of the bed, pulling her toward him until she was standing between his legs. He smiled up at her, those blue-on-blue eyes gazing at her as if she were the only woman in the world.

Even a little bit drunk he was good and she needed to harness every ounce of energy to stop herself from pressing her hands to his shoulders, pushing him backward onto the bed and climbing on top of him. *Distance.* She needed distance. Somehow she stammered out, "Would you like a hot beverage?"

"I don't need a drink." His smooth, deep voice wove around her like the promise of cozy heat on a cold night and all she had to do to get it was snuggle up. "All I need is you."

All I want is you. But she knew she had to override her wanton libido and slow everything down. She tugged her hands from his loose hold. "I think some hot chocolate would be a good idea."

His eyes lit up with wicked intent. "Excellent idea. I think you'd look fabulous wearing nothing but chocolate."

The thought of him licking her clean made her gasp as the slow build of fire between her legs roared to life with flames leaping high and fast. Her muscles twitched against nothing, desperate to close around something, and because of the reckless command of her body, she almost agreed to have sex right here, right now. Right this very second. God knows she was ready. Her body was beyond ready, willing and absolutely able, and there was no argument that she wanted him. Handsome, gorgeous, ripped, Luke Anderson. What was not to want?

Except he was more than buzzed and *something* was going on with him. Something she had no clue about but she wasn't fool enough to step into the middle of whatever that something was, no matter how much her body was begging her to have sex with him.

Obviously all talk of chocolate was extremely dangerous. "As hot chocolate is off the menu, I'll go make us chamomile tea then."

He snorted. "Seduction by sleeping? That's a hypothesis not even worth testing."

She wanted to smile. "We can drink tea and talk."

He groaned. "You're killing me, Erin. I didn't come here to talk and you sure as hell weren't interested in talking in the sunflower field."

Embarrassment tinged with guilt burned her cheeks. "True, but tea and talking are all I'm offering now."

Her inner slut flounced off in a stomping huff.

He glared at her. "I'm not drinking any new-age mumbo-jumbo pansy-assed tea."

Somehow she suppressed the urge to laugh. "Instant coffee then?"

He flinched as if the offer was abhorrent. "Hot chocolate," he said with a smile that would have melted stone. "You know you want it."

I do, I really do. "I'll go check on Maggie-May and make the drinks." She fisted her hands to stop them reaching out to him and turned to leave.

"Erin?"

She paused, wondering if she really should risk turning back. "Yes."

"If you have any compassion at all you'll wear this." He threw a hoodie at her.

She pulled it over her head and Luke's eyes scanned the words printed on the front.

"Photographers do it in the dark?" He groaned. "More irony from your brother?"

She sucked in her lips as laughter hit them. "A college friend."

"Do you own anything that doesn't scream sex?"

He looked so forlorn she almost felt sorry for him, but talking about sex would just head them straight back to her being in his arms, which wasn't wise. "I'll go make those drinks."

"Yeah, you do that." He fell backward onto the bed, his moan of frustration echoing loudly behind her.

As she waited for the water to boil she hugged the feeling close that although he wanted her, he respected her right to say no. Despite the fact that her second impression of him as a misogynist had been completely erased, this was the first building block of her new picture of Luke. She wanted to add to that picture. So, after they'd talked and she'd worked out exactly what made Luke Anderson tick, maybe then she could risk kissing him again. After all, they were adults and if they agreed beforehand and limited themselves to just kissing, they could finish the evening in a most delicious way.

With her plan all set and the water boiled, she returned carrying the two steaming mugs along with a packet of chocolate cookies tucked under her arm. "Here we are."

She'd expected Luke to be sitting up watching the sports channel but he was still lying down. "Luke?"

A gentle snore was his only response.

Disappointment streaked through her.

She set down the drinks and grabbed a throw rug, settling it over him. As she tucked it under his chin, she couldn't help but notice the lines of strain around his eyes. She remembered the rigid set of his shoulders earlier in the day. For someone who lived the supposedly carefree country life, he wore strain on him like a cloak. It took one hand holding back the other not to smooth the skin with the tips of her fingers, and it took almost superhuman effort not to crawl in next to him and snuggle up.

With a silent sigh, she picked up the spare quilt and trudged out to the sofa. Sleeping on an old, lumpy sofa with Luke Anderson mere feet away was the perfect definition of an oxymoron.

SEVEN

"AND IT'S GONNA be a perfect day today with clear skies with the temperature hitting eighty-five."

Luke listened to Gary, from Whitetail's Bait, Tackle and Beer, who not only sponsored the local weather on the radio, but also got to write his own copy.

"So get down to the lake early or late, bring the bait and kick back with some beers. Spotted Cow six-packs are today's special and there's a free one to anybody who brings in a walleye weighing over thirteen pounds."

Vernon grunted. "Gary knows his beer is safe."

This was only the second time his father had spoken since Luke had entered the milking parlor. On his arrival, he'd greeted Vernon with a nod. "Dad." Vernon had replied with "Luke" accompanied by a pointed glance at the clock.

Yes, he'd been late but he'd made it to the parlor by 6:09 and he thought that was a fair effort given he'd only woken up at 6:01. By 6:02 he'd known he wasn't in his bed or in his room—the sight of one of Erin's cameras on the bedside table along with the scent of her perfume on his skin from her sheets being big clues. He'd automatically stretched out his arm only to hit crisp, early morning air and stone-cold sheets.

That had jerked him awake fast and then he'd remembered.

The family argument after supper. The company of Jack. Going to Erin's cottage.

You know you want it.

He silently groaned again at the memory of his behavior last night, just as he'd groaned when he'd woken up. *Very smooth, Anderson.*

By 6:04 he'd been on his feet, the ancient floorboards creaking under his weight and the sound had caused Mac, who must have slept on the deck, to bark. Erin's dog had immediately joined in with scratching and whining on the other side of the closed bedroom door and he'd expected Erin to appear, tousle-haired, arms crossed over her pert breasts and with eyes rolling at the fact he'd fallen asleep moments after declaring he wasn't drunk.

Only she hadn't appeared and he'd been the one to open the door to let her dog out. As the white fluff ball had shot between his legs, he'd looked toward the couch and glimpsed the curvaceous line of Erin's hip and her ass. A line he'd badly wanted to trail last night, first with his fingers and then with his mouth. *Just last night?* Who was he kidding? In the dawn light, he'd still wanted to do it, only, unlike last night, he'd had the presence of mind not to even try.

Now, as he attached the milking cups to a docile Holstein's udder, he wished that the routine of work could vanquish the humiliation of last night. *Good luck with that.* So far nothing was working. Not the cross-pasture run to the parlor, not his single-minded focus on the list of today's jobs, which was a mile long, nor the elephant in the room that was milking alongside his father.

As a single man in the dating pool, he prided himself on being charming and entertaining, and all the while focusing solely on the woman he wanted to bed, making her feel unique and special. Which she was. All of the women he'd been with over the years had been unique and special in their own way. The fact he didn't stay with any woman for very long was more to do with him but it didn't make any of them less singular. Over the years, he'd perfected a seduction style and he knew what worked for him and what didn't. As a result he never deviated from it.

Except for last night.

Except for last night when he'd screwed up big-time. With women, timing was everything and he'd let the memory of one kiss upset his timing and lead him down the wrong path. A path that had ended in briars and a sink hole of sucking mud. A hole he had to dig himself out of and still keep his dignity intact. Exactly how, he had yet to work out.

"Why have you got sunflowers growing in the top field?" His father's voice broke into his thoughts.

Luke's hand paused on the trigger hose he was holding to clean the cow's teats. Erin wasn't the only mistake he'd made last night. "To increase milk production."

"Humph."

"You disagree with my decision?"

"You gave up a field of corn to do it. Come winter, you'll miss it."

He breathed in slowly, like he always did when the older farmers in the district questioned him. "Maybe, but then it will be my mistake, Dad, not yours."

His father faced him for the first time. "I might have been okay with that if I wasn't the one who was going to have to step in after you and deal with your mess."

Vernon's words hit him in the chest. Unlike Wade, Luke had always shared a close relationship with his father—one cemented by his decision to follow in his father's farming footsteps. "I'm not asking you to come out of retirement."

"The hell you are." His father twisted the suction hose to release the milking cups, catching them with his other hand. "I don't know what's going on with you, Luke, but right now the cows are more organized. I'm on Arizona time and I managed to get up at five. What's your excuse?"

A picture of chestnut hair, emerald eyes and the lushest mouth he'd ever experienced on any woman formed in his mind.

You forgot attitude.

True, Erin had that in spades. Either way he wasn't telling his father any of it and his carefully controlled temper unraveled. "Jeez, Dad. Nobody held a gun to your head to make you get up early. You were the one who told Brett he could take the mornings off for the next week because you wanted to milk."

His father glared at him as if Luke had asked him to give up his vacation to work on the farm. "Your priority is this farm, Luke. Since you were ten, it's what you've always said you wanted. I waited for you to grow up, go to college, travel and sow your wild oats before you returned to farm. You have no right to walk away from it now."

Before Luke could reply, the milk truck blasted its horn and Vernon stomped off into the dairy.

The lead mass that had been pressing hard against Luke since spring intensified, gaining more weight.

"AND FINALLY, I want to thank you all for the warm welcome to Whitetail."

Tony Lascio gathered up his papers to the sound of polite applause from the town meeting. He was about to step down from the lectern when John Ackerman leaned into the mike and said, "So any questions for our new fire chief?"

An older woman with short gray hair tipped in pink rose to her feet. "I'm not surprised you wanted to come to Whitetail after living on the Jersey Shore. We might not have the ocean but we have a lovely lake and you'll be much better off here."

Tony was a bit taken aback. Surely the senior knew the television show wasn't the real Jersey and yet her expression hinted at a caring pity and a real joy that he'd got out. He spoke into the mike. "Ah, thank you. I'm sure I'll enjoy it."

He glanced around expectantly, encouraging anyone else to step up and ask a question.

"And have you come to Whitetail alone?"

His head swung back as his mind was telling him he must have misheard the blatantly non-PC question. "Excuse me?"

The woman, who looked to be in her late sixties, continued to beam at him. "Are you married?"

Not anymore. "No."

"A bachelor in the wedding town." The woman sighed with delight. "You do know Whitetail's all about weddings, don't you?"

Tony was seriously questioning if he'd moved galaxies rather than just across six states. Back in Jersey, he'd been a fireman for a lot of years and the community had only ever questioned him on protocol and safety. This woman, with her benign looks of a sweet, elderly lady, was more terrifying than fighting a roaring inferno. Next she'd be asking him his jock size.

"Mrs. Norell," a quiet voice spoke from the back of the hall. "I'm sure the chief's well aware of Weddings That Wow."

Tony instantly recognized Nicole's voice. He hadn't seen her since he'd driven away from the park, although he'd thought about her. Thought about her way too much given she had a child and wore a wedding band on her left hand. Two big signs that said *not available, leave well enough alone.*

For a time, his marriage breakdown had totally screwed with his head and his ethics, and he'd done some things he wasn't proud of, but coming out here to Wisconsin was a new start. He wasn't risking that by hooking up with a married woman in a town the size of a pocket handkerchief. Only there was a vulnerability about her that had touched something deep down inside him. Something he'd locked away two years ago.

Nicole stood up, her white-blond hair brushing her shoulders. "If no one else has any questions that are pertinent to Chief Lascio's *job*, perhaps we can wrap this up now? I know a lot of people are keen to try your chocolate beet cake, Ella."

"Oh, yes, good idea, Nicole. I'll make sure you have the first slice, Chief." Mrs. Norell waved at him before hurrying away to the reception room where he knew a scrumptious spread of food lay waiting.

The sound of chair legs scraping against the wooden floor filled the meeting room and chatting people drifted through the now open concertina doors. Tony found himself ushered forward by John, presented with coffee and instantly surrounded by a group of older ladies. They pressed platters of sandwiches and cake on him, and peppered him with questions such as where he grew up, how long he'd served as a firefighter, what was his favorite food and did he want to get married. He was also introduced to a Melissa and an Emily and their single status was emphasized vehemently and often.

He quickly realized that dealing with these women of Swedish descent wasn't any different from how he treated his nonna's friends at the senior center. With some gentle flirting, complimenting each lady on her baking prowess and then shoving food into his mouth, he managed to dodge the super-personal questions, although at this rate he'd be bench-pressing well into the night to burn off the massive calorie load. The words of his ex-chief rang in his ears about firefighters going country and going soft.

"So, Chief," Mrs. Norell said with genuine concern in her voice, "aren't you lonely living out on old creamery lane? I mean it's quite removed from the buzz of the town."

Somehow, he managed not to inhale the moist, rich beet cake as he stifled a laugh. Whitetail was basically six blocks by nine, with scattered housing beyond that and a permanent population of around twelve hundred. Buzz didn't come close to describing it, which was exactly why he was here. He wanted quiet. He needed peace and quiet after the high-octane drama of life with Loretta.

"It's fine, Ella," he said with a wink. "And if I ever get lonely, I can always come into town and visit you."

"Oh, you're a wicked one," she said, giggling like an eighteen-year-old.

When he'd finally tasted something that every senior had made, he managed to excuse himself and as he strode around the table toward the exit, he met Nicole.

"And after that baptism of fire, Chief, I think you've survived your first town meeting."

The smile in her voice made him grin. He put his

arm under hers, propelling her forward another few steps until there was some distance between them and the seniors so their conversation couldn't be overheard. "Is it always like this?"

"An inquisition with a food chaser? Absolutely."

She laughed and the tinkling sound washed over him, making him think of the chimes his *nonna* kept in her trees. Wind chimes? God, next he'd be breaking out into song.

You've only been out of Jersey two weeks. Stay tough, man.

"Exactly how often do I have to attend?"

Still laughing, she patted his arm as if he was a small child needing reassurance. "Once a month."

Her honey-tanned hand looked pale and tiny against his swarthy forearm and he had an overwhelming desire to cover it with his and keep it safe.

She's married, genius. Ask about her kid. "How's Max?"

Her hand instantly fell away. "Except for bed and bath time, he hasn't taken that hat you gave him off of his head."

"Good to hear." Tony loved kids. Loved seeing the enthusiasm and joy on their faces that life hadn't yet crushed out of them. "You should bring him over to the station one day so he can sit in engine seven. It's a real fire truck."

Her laughing eyes instantly sobered and she suddenly looked embarrassed.

Hell. Had he crossed a line talking about her kid?

She tugged at her ear. "Perhaps you can talk to the vacation camp coordinator."

Oh, yeah, he'd crossed the marriage line. "Sure. I'll talk to her and organize it."

"I'm sure the children will love it." She checked her watch and then gave him a brisk nod, as if she was concluding a business meeting. "Enjoy the rest of your day, Chief."

And the moment of connection he'd felt sure they'd shared at the start of the conversation had disappeared and it was as if it had never happened. *Chief.* That's all she'd ever called him, despite the fact he'd introduced himself as Tony the first time they'd met. It was a line in the sand. A place keeper.

As he watched her walk away, hips swinging and her black pencil skirt skimming her sweet behind, he knew he was going to be adding a long run and a cold shower to those bench presses.

"Mommy?"

"Hmm?" Nicole glanced up from studying the seating plan of the Ambrose wedding, wondering what Jenna was thinking sitting her divorced sister at the same table as her now ex-husband and his new girlfriend.

She turned her attention to Max who was looking at the photo album she'd made for him after Bradley died. She'd gathered together as many photos as possible that had been taken of Max and Bradley together, although in the past couple of years, there hadn't been many. "Why isn't there a photo of you and Daddy in here?"

She couldn't stop the flinch of pain that caught her under her ribs. *Because your father stopped loving me.* "Because it's your and daddy's special album."

"You should be here. I want a picture of you with Daddy."

She breathed out. "Okay. What about one on the day we got married or the day you were born?" If he was insisting on a photo of her and Bradley together, then it would be one when they'd been happy together. When they'd fit like two pieces in a puzzle and had shared the same vision of their life together.

Max's forehead creased in thought and then he announced, "The day I was born."

She smiled at the memory of that wonderful and momentous day. "Good idea. Go choose one from your baby album and I'll print you another copy."

As Max ran off to his room, Nicole returned to the seating plan and tried to find a way of seating two acrimonious ex-lovers as far away from each other as possible without destroying twelve other perfectly matched tables. Every attempt to move someone was like dropping a pebble into a pond and watching the ripples radiate outward to impact and upset the next table. She tried a few different permutations and combinations but her mind wasn't up to the task. Tony, with his inky eyes and Italian good looks, kept intruding into her thoughts by seating himself at every table instead of the woman she was trying to move.

She pressed the heels of her hands into her forehead as if that would help remove him from her head. She'd thought if she only ever called him by his title or thought about him as the chief, she'd be able to get over this thing she couldn't quite define. She certainly didn't want to call it a fascination, and an obsession was not only way too far from the mark but way too creepy, so she was sticking with *thing*. Only, somewhere along the line she'd started to think of him as Tony.

And that was bad.

What on earth had possessed her to intervene on his behalf at the meeting? He was a grown man and more than capable of fending for himself—he had to be if he was going to survive the well-intentioned but nosey Whitetail community. Intervening and protecting him from Ella's questioning was one thing and could be passed over as easing him into dealing with the town's citizens. The flirting, not so much. Why had she done that? It wasn't as if she was an expert or that flirting even came naturally to her. It didn't. Far from it, in fact, and if truth be told she hadn't flirted with a man since...

As she thought back, she realized that she hadn't flirted with any man since her senior year of high school. Even then, it had been Bradley flirting with her and her return attempts had been inept at best. She dropped her hands back to the desk with a groan. Nothing had changed. She was still clumsy and inexpert and the image of her hand resting on Tony's deeply tanned, olive-skinned arm—ivory on ebony—was burned on her retinas. Permanently there to remind her of her folly.

Only, it wasn't just the image. Her palm kept tingling with the memory of the tickle of his black hair, the solid feel of the tautness of his arm muscles, and the heat of his skin. She rubbed her palm with her fingers as if it was still resting on his arm and her cheeks burned hot.

Not only was she embarrassed that she'd touched him in an intimate way as if she knew him very well, her ensuing panic at what she'd done ended up making her rude, brusque and officious. Tony had merely been making polite conversation, inquiring about Max and issuing an invitation which would thrill him to the core. An invitation that meant she had a valid excuse to see him again and that would thrill her.

And that was the problem on so many levels it didn't bear thinking about.

"Mommy, what about this one?" Max slammed his baby album onto the table, his finger pressed hard against a photo. It showed Bradley gazing down at a newborn Max with love in his eyes and Nicole gazing up at Bradley with love shinning in hers.

Her heart dropped to her feet and nausea pummeled her. Even then he hadn't loved her. How had she not been able to see it until just now?

"Mommy?"

She stiffened her spine and snapped to attention, just as she always did when she felt herself tumbling backward into the dark and dangerous black hole of grief— a grief everyone who knew her assumed they knew the cause of and yet utterly misunderstood. "It's perfect, buddy. Let's print it now."

EIGHT

LUKE PULLED THE tractor to a halt as he saw the unanticipated sight of Keri waving a picnic basket at him. He and Brett were chopping grass for silage while his father and Wade took over the milking. He glanced at the sun. Scratch that. They'd have finished milking by now. He on the other hand would be working well into the night and returning to the house for a sit-down supper wasn't an option.

He jumped to the ground, leaving the tractor idling, and met his sister at the fence line. She'd spread a rug and arranged a meal of cold chicken and salad subs, fresh apple juice and a cheesecake.

He raised his brows at the unexpected feast and wondered if it came with an agenda. Erin and her meal immediately sprang to mind, although after spending mind-numbing hours driving up and down a field, pretty much every association to anything made that happen. "That's quite a spread you've got there, sis."

Keri handed him some hand wash. "Mom's in her element feeding us."

He bit into the sub, letting the combined flavors of grainy mustard, chives, egg mayonnaise and chicken roll around his mouth. He loved this recipe of his mother's and realized with surprise how much he'd missed it. "I thought you were leaving first thing this morning and heading back to Phil and the kids."

She watched him eat, fiddling with a loose thread on her light sweater. "I'm leaving in the morning but I wanted to talk to you first."

He kept chewing, knowing she'd say what she wanted to say without any encouragement from him.

"Did you get Axel to price the entire farm or just the beach acres?"

And there it was.

He took a long slug of juice, welcoming the coldness against his throat. "I didn't even ask Axel to price the beach acres. He took that upon himself."

Her eyes narrowed. "If you weren't interested in selling, you wouldn't have told us at all."

He shrugged against the complex knot that was his feelings for the farm—a tight and tangled mess he couldn't seem to untie. "The price surprised me."

They both turned at the sound of a four-wheeler. A moment later, Wade jumped off and shot both of them a killing look. "Plotting against me, are we?"

"Don't be ridiculous, Wade," Keri said, her voice tight.

"I think you just answered my question, sister dear."

Wade stood with his hands on his hips, looking like a solid, concrete wall.

Luke offered him a sub, wanting to build bridges with his brother. "Sit down and eat with us."

"Oh, you mean like supper last night, Judas."

Luke lowered the plate. "I thought you might want to hash this out rationally rather than resorting to amateur dramatics."

Wade folded his arms across his chest. "Listen, Luke. You're the one causing the drama. You can't just change your mind about running the farm, because, guess what? You're not the only person affected."

Luke shot to his feet, mad at being told what he couldn't do, twice in one day. "So I have to live my life to suit yours? This is rich coming from the man who played the 'if you're not homophobic, Dad, you'll prove it by giving me Grandpa's house and some land to run my business from' card."

Wade's ears burned red and his arm shot out in a fist that came very close to striking Luke on the shoulder. It fell back to his side. "You got the whole fucking farm!"

Keri scrambled in between them. "I'm the girl in the family and I got sweet fuck all."

Luke stared at them both as their waves of antagonism bashed against him and part of him regretted ever mentioning the land value while another part of him knew that he had to. Even so, he wasn't going to stand for being painted as the bad guy. "Newsflash. Neither of you wanted the farm, and to put things in perspective, it's not like you get nothing. If I stay farming, there are the dividends from the family trust."

"Only in the good years," Keri said. "It's not reliable income."

Luke wanted to yell at her, telling her that inheritance was a privilege, not a right, and that the family trust dividends were income off of *his* hard work. But, after last night's reaction from everyone, he was learning. Swallowing the comment meant Keri couldn't jump on it and tell him to sell the farm, take his share and go. Right now, he didn't know if he really wanted to walk away from the farm or not. All he knew was that as things stood, he wasn't happy.

Sticking to cold, hard facts and avoiding the minefield that was anything to do with emotions, he said, "Due to the size of the herd, the last decade has had more good years than bad. Why do you think Mom and Dad could retire to Arizona?"

Keri ignored him. "The sale of the beach acres would go a long way toward paying Grace and Ethan's college tuition."

"They're eight and ten!" Wade yelled. "You and Phil have the means to earn that money between now and then or, here's an idea, they take out student loans like the rest of us."

Keri's mouth hardened. "That's my point. It would mean they start their life without a debt load."

Wade leaned in like a boxer ready to throw the first punch. "I think you failed to factor in the reality that the money has to be split four ways. Selling the beach acres won't even cover their tuition."

Keri matched his stance. "It will if the farm is sold." She spun around to face Luke. "That's what you want, right, little brother?"

Luke was sucked back in time to when his older siblings fought and then each one tried to get him to side with them against the other. He was all grown up now and he wasn't falling for that old chestnut. "Right now, I want to get back to loading the freshly cut grass into the silage bags."

"See, Keri," Wade said with victory in his voice, "he wants to keep farming. Your money-grabbing power play isn't going to work."

Keri's mouth flattened into a line of sheer determination. "Really, Luke? I can't believe that's what you truly want."

He wasn't prepared to say either yes or no. He wasn't

prepared to admit anything to either of them, especially not the fact that he felt lost. God, he hated the feeling. It swamped him, accompanying him everywhere and tainting everything he did. How had it happened that the life he'd always envisaged with great excitement had suddenly become a chore? Where was the joy he'd always found here as a kid helping out? Where was the enthusiasm that had propelled him through CALS? Where was the drive that had him working outside of the farm to gather a wealth of information so he could bring it back here and implement it? He'd started and then he'd stalled.

He ran his hand through his hair. "I want the farm in tip-top shape no matter what my decision. I'm going back to work."

He swiped the cheesecake off the plate and trudged back to the tractor.

Wade's voice carried over the evening air. "Keri, you haven't brought the kids to the farm since before Mom and Dad retired and I know they want to see you all. I've got a vacancy in a two-bedroom cottage next weekend. Bring Phil and the kids up to visit."

Where the hell had that invitation come from? Sometimes he really didn't understand his siblings at all, but then again, they'd run hot and cold with each other all their lives so why would he expect today to be any different?

THE MOON WAS high as Erin pulled into Lakeview Farm Road on her return journey from Minnesota. With bookings coming in, she'd needed more cameras, her big computer and clothes, so she'd made the long trek there and back in a day. She'd also taken the opportunity to print out Lindsay and Keith's photos.

Many photographers gave their client a DVD, but she believed people responded best to handling the physical photos rather than staring at a screen. She always went one step further by inserting the proofs into a standard white album and mounting her favorite shot of the couple. This gave her clients a real feel for the potential of their final album—an artistic collection representing love, hopes and dreams. A potential heirloom piece that could be handed down to future generations.

She slowed as she rounded the final bend and just before she passed through the open gateway into the grounds of the cottages, she braked. Work lights beamed from the middle of the adjacent field and her eyes scanned the lit area. Even with the distance, she easily spotted Luke. Despite his shoulders being equally as broad as Wade's, his height made him stand above most men and his distinctive shock of hair gleamed golden under the lights.

Her stomach flipped in a good way.

She glanced at the dashboard clock. 11:37 p.m.

Why was he working at this late hour?

Does it matter? You often work late into the night.

She couldn't argue that.

She hadn't seen him since she'd flicked a throw rug over him last night. Now he stood on a machine, which was attached to the back of the tractor, and trailing behind that was the biggest and longest white, plastic "slug" she'd ever seen. The combination of moonlight and artificial light bathed the field in complex shadows but all the energy was centered on Luke. She wanted to capture the moment.

Maggie-May barked and pawed the window, her ears sticking up like eager triangles and then she whimpered her *I need to get out of this car right this minute* whine.

The silky, smooth voice of "Soul Barry" sounded from the GPS. *You have reached your destination, baybee.*

She shivered as a thrill of anticipation shot through her, making her tingle all over. If Barry was telling her in his oh-so-seductive tones that she'd reached her destination at the exact moment she'd been staring at Luke, then who was she to argue? She'd take the photo and then go talk to him. Last night he'd definitely wanted to talk to her.

No, he'd wanted to have sex with you.

She sloughed off the semantics. He'd been a permanent guest in her head all day and she wanted to see him. She wanted to have that "getting to know you" conversation they'd totally bypassed when they'd leaped straight into a *take my clothes off me now* kiss. The conversation he'd fallen asleep before they could have last night.

Throwing the gearshift into Drive, she drove the short distance into the parking lot for the cottages, switched off the ignition and then, having learned her lesson on the very first day on the farm, she tugged on her hot-pink-and-black rubber boots. Who knew rubber boots could be such fabulously fun footwear, or that they came in so many fantastic designs. The choice had been tricky because she'd been torn between buying three pairs—the ones she'd purchased, a pair covered in pictures of handmade chocolates and a black pair with bright red tartan tops.

She leashed a now-frantic Maggie-May and got out

of the car with her camera, tripod and flashlight. Maggie-May darted under Wade's rustic post-and-rail fence, while Erin hefted her gear over and then she followed, gingerly throwing her leg over the rail. Arcing her flashlight back and forth, she hoped there were no badger holes to trip her up and was immediately struck by the thought. How did she even know about badger holes? Obviously, watching local television was more informative than she'd thought. Next she'd be quoting the specifications of farm machinery.

Once she'd found the perfect place to shoot the photo, it didn't take long to attach the camera to the tripod and then quickly set the f-stop for a long exposure. As she lined everything up and pressed the shutter release, she heard a second dog panting by her side. She tousled Mac's soft ears. "Hey, boy, how are you?"

The border collie rubbed his black-and-white head against her thigh and Maggie-May barked indignantly as if to say *forget her, I'm here.* The two dogs sniffed each other in that friendly greeting routine common to all dogs—nose to nose and nose to nether regions. Sometimes Erin wondered if that told them a lot more about each other than humans ever learned from a handshake.

Luke smells like sunshine.

"Mac! Here, boy." Luke's command drifted across the field.

The farm dog hesitated, as if he knew he should respond instantly to his master, but at the same time being tempted to stay with Erin and Maggie-May.

"Come on, Mac. Let's not give him an excuse to be grumpy with either of us."

Slinging her camera bag and tripod over her shoulder, she continued to walk carefully toward the tractors and lights. As she entered the spill of light, she saw there were two other men working alongside Luke.

Luke had his back to her and she heard him say, "You guys call it a night. I'll finish up."

"Are you sure?" asked the man Erin now recognized as Brett.

"You bet. See you at seven to start over."

"Hey, Erin." Brett nodded toward her camera. "Great moon."

"It sure is." She gave him a wave as he departed with the other worker in the truck.

"Erin." Luke faced her and his greeting neither welcomed or rejected her.

His flirting tone, which had been present yesterday, was now absent and she struggled against her disappointment.

She reminded herself there was no need to be disappointed. In fact, it was probably a good thing because she was here to talk, to get to know him and not to get sidetracked just yet by thoughts of his amazing mouth, which could stroke hers as softly as a feather and be as hard and demanding as granite.

Oh, yeah, that's the perfect way not to be sidetracked.

As she tried to shake off the unhelpful voice in her head, she lowered her tripod to the ground. "You're working late."

Go, Erin. What a fascinating conversation starter. Try leading with the weather next.

Luke shrugged as he stepped down and off the machine. "Just normal summer farming hours when we're cutting hay."

She frowned. "I thought hay went into stackable

bales or those big round things I've seen in the fields all around Whitetail."

He stared at her for a moment, his intelligent blue eyes flicking over her face with traces of puzzlement. It was as if she'd just spoken in a language that should be familiar to him but was sounding very foreign.

"Cut grass dries and becomes bailed hay. It's important we cut it during a hot, dry spell and we rake it so it loses all its moisture before we roll it or bale it. Wet bales can smolder and then spontaneously combust." He gave her a teasing smile. "Burning down the barn isn't something any farmer recommends."

Spontaneously combust.

His words and his smile took her instantly back to the sunflower field. To the magical feel of the slow burn of his lips against hers and the exhilarating moment that touch had ignited the pure, insatiable burning lust in both of them. The memory sparked rafts of quivering tingles, which shot through her like a meteor shower. She clenched her thighs together, hard. Very hard, in a desperate attempt to squash the darting and delicious throbbing that was beating a steady tattoo of need deep down inside her.

Did he realize he'd just described their kiss?

"...freshly chopped green grass or haylage gets stored in—" He pointed his thumb over his shoulder "—polyethylene bags."

Possibly not. God, she had it bad.

"...chemistry happens and in a few months we have cow food."

Chemistry. The thing that so often vibrated between them, although tonight it seemed the vibrating was restricted just to her. She fought to get herself under control so she sounded intellectually interested rather than breathy and aroused. After all, she was on a "getting to know Luke" mission.

"Wow." It sounded deep and strangled and she cleared her throat. "I had no idea there was so much science in hay."

He grinned. "There's science in everything. I'll turn the lights off so you can get that shot of the moon."

She didn't follow. "The moon?"

Surprise flitted across his face. "That's what you're out here for, isn't it? The call of the full moon on a clear night and a perfect photo opportunity?"

The call of you.

"Sure, yes, absolutely." She quickly opened the legs of her tripod as if she had come to do just that. "Only don't turn the lights out just for me. I can wait."

He shut down the generator and the light slowly faded. "This job's finished and I'm done."

He sounded weary and she wasn't surprised given she'd heard him leave the cottage around six this morning. "For a few hours anyway. I'm guessing the cows always need milking."

"They do."

A shaft of moonlight put his face in half shadow and half light. It was like looking at a black-and-white photo and she swallowed at the haunted look it gave him. Then he moved and the light shifted, vanquishing the look and she was left wondering if she'd imagined it.

She pulled her gaze away from him and concentrated on setting up the photo he was expecting her to take. The silver rays of the moon bounced off the grove of trees on the far boundary of the now slashed field, creating a thousand tones between the iridescent white of the moon and the inky black of the trees. She wasn't used to a lack of artificial light pollution and she was in awe at the sight. "The moon's a massive LED."

He nodded with a smile. "It's harvesting light."

The long exposure finally came to an end, her camera signaling it with a distinctive click.

"May I see?" he asked.

She hesitated. "It's going to look better on a computer screen where you can see all the nuances."

"You'll have to show me sometime."

I'll show you now.

Only, unlike last night when every statement he'd made had been a double entendre intended to get her naked and horizontal, tonight he sounded genuinely interested in seeing the photo, rather than her. As she unscrewed her camera from the tripod, she felt oddly let down.

He leaned against the enormous wheel of the tractor, his body relaxed and his expression interested. "Do you do much artistic photography?"

His words lifted a scab on a wound which was often inflicted on wedding photographers. "All my photography is artistic," she snapped more sharply than she'd intended.

"Have I hit a sore spot?" he asked mildly.

"No." She collapsed her tripod. "You've only exposed your ignorance."

He didn't bite at her barb. Instead he shifted his weight and said, "So, enlighten me."

Her head jerked up and she scanned his face for derision but found only curiosity. Her hands fluttered out in front of her. "Sorry. It's just I get weary of the jokes like what's the difference between a wedding photographer and a monkey."

His mouth twitched. "I'm assuming you don't want me to try and guess the answer?"

She grimaced. "No, thank you."

He pushed off the tractor and reached in behind the seat, before handing her a chocolate bar. As he pulled down the wrapper he said, "So why do you choose to photograph weddings?"

She thought about how everything could be lost in a heartbeat. How with one decision a bank account could be emptied and a home could cease to exist. How lie upon lie from a father could rip a family apart, destroying everything except poverty, heartache and dislocation. Her laugh sounded tight. "Too easy. They're happy. They're filled with joy and love and I consider it an honor to be allowed to capture those emotions for perpetuity."

A streak of disbelief rode across his cheeks. "There have to be levels of happiness though, right? Some weddings would be happier than others."

She pondered the question. "I suppose so, but I can honestly say my brides always look so happy they glow."

"And the grooms?" he teased. "Do they all look happy?"

A collage of grooms flitted across her mind. "Some have looked a little shell-shocked, but that's part of my job too."

"Making people shell-shocked?" His rich, bass laugh floated around her like the smooth, velvet tones of a mellow red wine. "I can see that. The cows and I were certainly surprised the day you arrived."

She gave a wry smile. "And no doubt you think you're hilarious."

His face creased in a smile. "The cows laugh at my jokes. So back to your job and shell-shocked grooms?"

Again, his genuine interest surprised her but she loved talking about her work to anyone who would listen and right now, Luke was a captive audience. "Relaxing people is part of my job. When you take the time to put people at ease, you're gifted with moments of such honest emotion that it can hurt."

"Hurt?"

"Yeah." She nodded her affirmation. "But in a good way. You know that clutch you get in your chest and you don't know if you're going to laugh or cry? Like that, only it gives me such a rush when I know I've taken a picture that immortalizes that."

"It's obvious you love your job."

He sounded almost wistful, which was unexpected. "I do love it. It's the sort of job you have to love to do it well." She thought about the Memmy and crossed her fingers. "And you know, I dare anyone to argue with me that a bride photographed in a sea of sunflowers isn't artistic."

He pushed off the tractor, his face animated. "So *that's* the deal with the sunflowers. You're after professional recognition."

How could she have ever thought this man was a yokel? His brain whirred so fast she could almost hear it. "More like client recognition. Photos like that attract more customers."

He nodded slowly. "Still, they have to see your photos to know about them."

She loved that he understood and unlike two days

ago, she now felt safe telling him about the Memmy. "True. It's why I have a website and a blog to complement word of mouth, but I'm going to enter the best of Connie's photos into a competition. If it's judged one of the finalists, it will give me national exposure."

His eyes twinkled in the moonlight. "So you do want that photo as much as that crazy bride?"

She gave him a mock punch in the arm. "She's not *crazy.*"

"So you keep telling me." Laughter played on his lips but his eyes remained unconvinced as he captured her hand.

It seemed the most natural thing in the world to move in against him and she let her forehead rest on his chest. Breathing in deeply, she filled her nostrils with the scent of hard, physical work, freshly cut grass and vibrant, pulsating life. All of it was Luke and he made every guy she'd ever been with seem frail and anemic.

She could have stayed there forever but with her face pressing into his chest he couldn't kiss her. Well, sure, he could press kisses into her hair, but she didn't want that. She wanted his lips on hers and more. Very slowly, she tilted her head back.

He stared down at her, meeting her gaze with a quiet, *oh yeah* smile. It was the start of the moment that dictated they both move inexorably toward each other, but the only movement she could perceive from him was the rise and fall of his chest under hers. She paused and waited for him to catch up. Waited for one hand to slide around the back of her neck, for his other to angle her chin while his head inclined closer to hers, and then for his lips to part.

Her blood pounded so hard and fast with eager anticipation that her vision swam. Every part of her screamed *kiss me*.

His hand, which held hers, opened and he slowly laced his fingers between hers.

What? Kiss me. Now!

Frustration poured oil on need. What was he doing? More to the point, what was he *not* doing? Building anticipation was one thing but her body now teetered on the brink of pain-induced withholding and she needed action. With a puff of dissatisfaction that he was so slow to respond, she pulled her hand from his, rose on her toes, slid both her hands against his cheeks, angled his mouth and kissed him.

Her lips pressed against his and the slight scratch of his top lip grazed hers as she coaxed him to open his mouth to her. Chocolate, coffee and heat flowed through her, spinning currents of delight eddying through her, feeding her need for this man like oxygen fuels fire.

His fingers delved into her hair.

Yes. Finally. Now he was part of the kiss and her mind spun off on a promised bliss ride.

His fingers tugged slightly on her head as he pulled back and a shot of evening air zipped between them. Her eyes flew open. *What?* His lips, which a moment ago had been doing wondrous things to her, were now forming words. Words she was having trouble decoding.

"Erin, you're confusing me."

She blinked. Twice. The auto response was all she could manage because her brain was still off partying elsewhere. She'd kissed him. How could that be confusing? Oh, God, was it a bad kiss? Had she done it wrong?

Shut up. "How…why am I confusing you?"

He gave an exaggerated shrug. "You're contradicting yourself."

"I am?" She tried to muster enough functioning synapses to recall what she'd said during their conversation that may have contradicted what she'd just done. She got nothing. "I don't understand."

He sighed as if she was a slow learner and he had to be the one to patiently explain everything. "I didn't think you wanted us to do this."

"This?"

"Yes, this." One of his hands clamped on to her behind and pulled her hard against him—legs lining legs, hips matching and her breasts flattened against his chest. Then his tongue lazily roamed her mouth as if he had all the time in the world.

Her entire body melted into a puddle of need and she sagged against him, knowing that if he stepped away now, she'd fall.

He raised his head and gave her a soulful look as if he was the injured party. "Now I'm sure you can see my confusion about kissing."

No, sorry, seems perfect to me. "It's not totally clear to me but perhaps another kiss will make it clearer." Her fingers slid between the snaps on his shirt. "I'm fine with that."

"That's very generous of you." His breath brushed her face. "The thing is, what's puzzling me is that last night you told me you only wanted to talk."

Chagrin blew through her like a Minnesota blizzard. "You weren't exactly sober."

He had the temerity to grin. "I wasn't exactly drunk either."

She narrowed her gaze, searching his face. "There

was more than just Jack and sex on your mind. You objected to my cow pajamas saying they reminded you of the farm."

A muscle twitched near his eye but he held her gaze. "If they'd had cats on them I would have objected, saying they needed to come off before they upset the dogs. I just wanted you out of them."

She shivered as a tingle of such overwhelming longing rolled through her. He wound a strand of her hair around his finger very, very slowly, and all the while the pad of his finger caressed her cheek. Her mind, halfway to returning to cognizant thought, did a sharp U-turn back to bliss.

He kept talking. "The thing is, I knew exactly what I wanted. Something I'd made clear to you in the sunflower field. You, however, seem to be going back and forth, being undecided and reading stuff into off-the-cuff comments. I don't want to add to your uncertainty." His hands dropped to her upper arms and he gently pushed himself away from her.

Deep down inside her something sobbed. "I—"

"Shh." He raised his forefinger to his lips.

"Yes, but—"

"It's okay." He tilted his head. "I understand. When you know what you want, come find me."

He whistled for Mac and swung up into the tractor. Maggie-May barked.

Erin stood stunned, her mind scrabbling to play catch-up and then, courtesy of the cabin light, she caught Luke's expression—pure, unadulterated mischief.

He winked at her and then the slow chug of the diesel engine filled the air as the tractor drove off.

Maggie-May whined.

With a clunking thud everything fell into place and she buzzed with fury and embarrassment. Luke had wound her up until she was prepared to do just about anything with him and then he'd deliberately walked away.

"Come on, Maggie-May. No man or dog is worth it." She slung her camera bag over her shoulder with so much force it hit her on the ass. Yes, last night, she'd said no but he'd been the one who'd sought her out and she hadn't deliberately enticed him and aroused him to the point of insanity.

Um, you sought him out tonight.

Yes, I did it so I could talk to him!

And oh how he'd let her talk. He'd asked questions, taken an active interest in her job—Oh, God. Her hand flew to her mouth in horror. By making the conversation all about her, he'd basically given her mind an orgasm. How had she been so blind not to recognize such seriously skilled seduction? He'd aligned her brain with her body, had both of them panting in unison for him, and she'd walked straight into his arms, demanding him.

Just like he'd demanded her last night.

And then he'd said a calculated no. Worse than that was he knew she wanted him and this gave him all the power.

Come find me.

Payback was a bastard.

Clutching her gear she stomped back across the field immune to the moon and its glory. She didn't know what she was most aggrieved about—the fact he'd gotten away without apologizing for coming to the cottage buzzed last night, or the fact he'd said no to her, leaving her with a body humming for him along with an accompaniment of agonizing emptiness.

A searing thought pinged into her mind and she stopped walking. Neither one of those things was making her most angry. What galled more than anything was the fact he'd left knowing a hell of a lot more about her than she knew about him. She'd blurted out stuff that gave him a picture of who she was, while he remained the enigma he'd always been. A sexy, gorgeous enigma who'd lead her a merry dance.

She rolled back her shoulders and recommenced walking. She knew this was the second time she'd let him make a fool of her but damn it, it was *never* happening again. If Luke Anderson thought she was going to come calling in the future and just walk into his arms like she did tonight, he could think again.

On the other hand, the idea of making him beg for her and having him come to her held a lot of appeal.

NINE

NICOLE STRETCHED HER back, feeling the strain that came
with a full day on her feet and back-to-back hair clients.
During the busy summer wedding months she sublet her
salon chairs to Donna, who did the bulk of the work at
Affairs with Hair. Although Nicole still did some summer cutting, she worked a lot less hours and her back
got used to an easier life.

She loved that the town understood how important
the wedding business was to everyone and how most
people happily swapped between the two hairdressers
from June to September. On wedding days the salon
was closed, which rarely mattered to their customers
because so many of the townsfolk were working in some
capacity for the wedding. The flip side to this was it
made for busier days on non-wedding days.

Today Nicole was working in the salon alone, filling in for Donna who'd taken her teenage daughter to
a concert in Minneapolis. The latest teen idol was on a
national tour and the Twin Cities was as close to Whitetail as he got. Donna had said, "Believe me, the rest
of my summer won't be worth living if Becky misses
this concert."

Nicole didn't mind being busy. Between mother-
ing Max, managing weddings and her hair clients, she
didn't have time to think, and that had been her aim
ever since she'd opened her front door to find a soldier

in dress uniform, respectfully holding his hat in front of him and wearing an expression of regret. Actually, the need to blot out everything had started a week prior to that fateful visit.

As the clock ticked past four-thirty and she'd said goodbye to her last client, she was now filling in the product order form before closing up. The unexpected tinkle of the bell above the salon door made her automatically glance up. The pen she was holding slipped out of her grip, rolling across the counter before falling with a clatter onto the floor.

Tony Lascio, all stocky, five foot eleven of him, stepped into her salon with a look of surprise crossing his face. It instantly morphed into a warm smile.

A smile that did ridiculously odd things to her. She was glad she was sitting on a stool otherwise her legs might have folded underneath her and she'd have been joining the pen on the floor.

"Hi, Nicole."

"Hello, Tony."

Chief, you're supposed to call him chief. She pushed her glasses up her nose, giving herself a few precious seconds to pull herself together. "May I help you?"

"I'm not sure. I don't need a wedding planner, but I do need a haircut."

He smiled at her again and she realized it was slightly crooked, which made it even more endearing.

"Lucky for you, I'm both."

You're flirting again. Be businesslike.

Clicking the mouse on the computer, she looked up Donna's appointment list. "Donna has an opening tomorrow at noon."

He shook his head. "That won't work. I'm doing fire

extinguisher tagging all day tomorrow. Actually, I was hoping I could get it cut now."

Now? A rush of sensation had her suddenly feeling uncharacteristically hot and her hand fiddled with the top of her blouse as if to fan herself. "I'm not sure that's going to be possible."

He glanced around the empty salon and then back to her with a hopeful look in his inky eyes. "Are you expecting another client?"

Say yes. But honesty had been pummeled into her from the cradle and she couldn't do it. "No, but I have to pick up Max from camp at five and—"

"No problem…"

Thank you. "So I'll just make—"

"Half an hour is plenty of time. My barber in Jersey always cut my hair in fifteen minutes flat. So, which chair?" He gave her an expectant grin.

"I…ah…" Her voice sounded faint and she gave herself a shake. This was ridiculous. She was a hairstylist and he was a client. Cutting his hair would be no different from cutting anybody else's hair. She walked quickly to a chair and rested her hands on the back of it. "This one."

As he sat down, she flicked a black-and-white cape over him and snapped it closed around his wide neck. "What style do you prefer?"

"Short?" He stared at her through the mirror with a perplexed expression. "My barber just cuts it."

She laughed. "Yes, I understand that, but do you have it thinned out here and here or do you wear it longer on top and short on the sides?" Her fingers rifled his thick hair and tight curls sprang around them, capturing them as if they didn't want to let her go. "You have very strong hair."

He grinned. "My *nonna* says my curls are like tentacles and they grip on to anything."

She quickly pulled her fingers out of his hair, horrified that she might have let them remain there too long. She linked her fingers in front of her to keep them under control. "I'll thin out the top, make the rest short and tidy up around your ears and your nape. How does that sound?"

"Perfect."

She pulled her gaze away from his reflected one and said briskly, "If you make your way over to the basin, I'll wash your hair."

"Okay. My barber never did that either." With a bemused smile, he followed her. "I guess this is a perfect example of never being too old for a new experience."

"I take it you've never been to a unisex salon before?"

"Nope." He settled back into the chair, his neck fitting against the curve of the basin. "Giuseppe's been cutting my hair since I was twelve. From eighteen the hair cut came with a shave along with unsolicited opinions on politics, stock advice, religion and sex." His eyes dilated, staring up at her like polished ebony. "Relationships," he said emphatically as if correcting himself. "He gave advice on relationships."

He looked so aghast that he may have offended her that Nicole found herself grinning down at him. "My cut doesn't come with a shave, I'm afraid, but I can try my best to trash talk politics, although I might steer clear of relationship advice if you don't mind."

He closed his eyes as she positioned the nozzle of warm water against the back of his head. "That sounds fine. I'm in a good place right now and I don't need any relationship advice so you're off the hook."

"I'm glad." *Why? Are you in a happy one? Out of one? Looking for one?* Her fingers vigorously scrubbed shampoo into his hair as if the action would empty her brain of unwanted thoughts and questions, which was very hard given the way his heat radiated into her.

With his eyes closed, she took the chance to study his face—the way his hair receded slightly at his temples, the small white scar above his thick jet-black eyebrows, the sexy, dark shadow of afternoon stubble that circled his lips, and the corded muscles in his neck that disappeared under the drape while hinting that there was a lot more of the same below.

A zip of longing seared her, settling in where it didn't belong and making her panties feel wet. *Stop it.*

"Is the water temperature okay?" Her voice strained over the words and she desperately hoped he'd say, *add more cold.* She needed a jolt of icy sanity from all this heat.

"Hmm, perfect."

I guess that's a yes. Pumping the large container of conditioner, she filled her palm with the peppermint-scented lotion and rubbed it into his hair. The mundane task felt anything but. Instead it was filled with an arousing intimacy that spun through her. Her fingers stalled as her lips started to form the standard question she always asked at this point.

He won't know about scalp massages so don't even mention it.

You're a professional and he's a client. Ask him.

Trying not to breathe in any more of his pine-fresh cologne, which already had her blood pounding faster than was probably safe, she said, "At this point I usually offer a scalp massage, but don't feel you have to accept it. Not everyone enjoys them."

One piercing eye popped open, fixed intently on her face. "As everything to do with Whitetail is a new experience, I guess I better try this too."

"Okay, then." Her smile felt so taut she was convinced her face would crack. She cleared her throat against an increasing tightness. "It lasts a few minutes and it may make you feel drowsy. If you start to feel uncomfortable at any time, just say stop."

Her fingers pressed into his scalp with a strength she had to summon up from her toes, desperately needing it to counter the tingling riffs that had now consumed her entire body. In one way, the shimmers made her feel weak and vulnerable, yet in another way they created such a powerful need in her that she was potent with it. It stunned and shocked her. How could she feel like this for a man she barely knew?

Responsible mothers of little boys didn't behave like this. The grieving widow of a war hero who lived in a small town certainly couldn't afford to behave like this.

Besides, despite Emily and Melissa telling her he wasn't married, that didn't necessarily make him single. As she worked his scalp with her fingers moving in firm circles, she bit down hard on the inside of her cheek. It was only the metallic taste of blood, which reminded her of her life and her responsibilities that kept her from embarrassing herself by lowering her lips to his. It wasn't, however, enough to stop the fantasy.

Tony breathed in deeply trying to regain some control over his body, which was in the throes of ecstatic agony. What the hell had possessed him to say yes to a scalp massage? When Nicole had asked the question, he'd been too busy wondering why, with her silver-blond hair, didn't she have bright, blue eyes? Not that he minded one bit because her enormous, milk-chocolate eyes suckered him every time she looked at him. In fact they'd been doing exactly that when he'd agreed far too promptly to the massage.

You didn't think that one through, did you, pal?

Now he was paying for it with a series of tantalizingly torturous touches—every brush of her thigh against his arm as she leaned over him, every lingering atom of her coconut-and-mango scent, which made him think of warm, Caribbean breezes, and with every press of her fingers.

Holy shit, her fingers. The power that came through them shot straight to his groin. Thank God the cape she'd draped over him hid the evidence that would make him look a fool and scare the hell out of her. As her touch reached the base of his skull and his cock ached hard against his workpants, his thoughts drifted to the idea of her fingers on it rather than his head. From a very long way away he heard a moan.

Her fingers stalled. "Am I hurting you?"

Shock drenched him in cold sweat. Had he just groaned in pleasure? *Fuck.* He'd never expected he'd have to invoke a safe word for a head massage. He opened his eyes and met hers—eyes filled with concern and something else he couldn't read but given he could barely see straight, that was no surprise. "You can stop now."

She gave a curt nod and then with jerky movements she flicked on the taps, rinsed his head and then toweled his hair dry, all with brisk strokes. It was probably the same no-nonsense touch she'd used from the start, only his warped mind had read far too much into it.

He moved back to the chair and she started cutting his hair, her scissors flashing silver and clicking fast. Neither of them spoke for a bit and as she raised strands of hair between her fingers, lining them up at ninety degrees to cut, her wedding ring caught the light and sparked in the mirror. It was just what he needed to see. A timely reminder. A safety zone.

"I'm slowly getting to know all the volunteer fire-fighters. Is your husband one of them?"

Her scissors stilled and she appeared to be studying his hair intently as if it was the most fascinating thing she'd ever seen. Slowly, she raised her head and met his gaze in the mirror. "My husband's dead."

Great going, Tony. So much for the safe zone. "I'm so sorry. I—"

"No!" She violently snapped the scissors closed against his hair. "Don't be sorry. I'm so sick of people being sorry."

He stared at the two pink spots of heat on her now pale cheeks and fought the urge to duck against the waves of antagonism that rolled into him. His brain shot straight to some of the difficult domestic situations he'd been called to act on as an EMT. "You wanted him dead?"

Her eyes widened in shock. "God no. Of course I didn't. It's just…" She pulled up more strands of hair between her fingers.

He felt sure she needed to say whatever it was she'd just self-censored. "Just?"

"I assumed you knew." She snipped at his hair in short, jagged cuts. "I'm surprised someone in town didn't sit you down on your first day and tell you Bradley's story."

Grabbing some hair clippers, she abruptly turned on the power and the buzz of the fast-moving combs sounded ominous. He had a sudden urge to protect his neck.

"He died in Afghanistan. A war hero." Her words sounded infinitely weary. "Everyone in Whitetail owns his memory."

It was then he remembered Max telling him that his father had been in an ambulance. *Hell.*

Everyone in Whitetail owns his memory. He didn't know what to say and yet given the complex war of expressions on her face, he needed to say something. "I guess that can be both good and bad for you."

She nodded furiously, waving the clippers above his head. "Exactly, and that's why it's such a relief to meet new people where I can be *just* the wedding planner or *just* the hairdresser or Max's mom."

Not a widow dealing with her own grief as well as the town's. Slowly he understood. She could be those three things, but she wasn't ready to be anyone else. Disappointment cramped his gut.

With dexterous strokes, she used a brush to remove any stray cut hair from the back of his neck and then she held up a mirror so he could see the back of his head. The hairdresser was back in control. "How's that?"

He barely glanced. "Great, thanks."

"Good." Her fingers brushed his neck lightly as she undid the cape and he gripped the arms of the chair to stay immune from the unintentional touch.

He met her at the counter and pulled out his wallet, paying for the cut. "Thanks again, Nicole."

"You're welcome."

"Say hello to Max for me."

"I will."

He knew the score—it was time for him to leave. "I guess I'll see you round town somewhere, sometime."

Her teeth scraped her bottom lip and she nodded slowly.

Okay, then. He raised his hand in farewell before pulling open the door. The tinkle of the bell sounded overly loud in the strained silence. His right foot hit the sidewalk.

"Tony…"

Had he forgotten something? He turned back. "Yes."

She laced her fingers in front of her in the exact same way he'd noticed her do a few other times in the past half hour. "Most mornings I stop by the market for a coffee before starting work."

The bottom of his gut soared, high-fiving the top. *Be cool, man.* He managed to stall the dopey grin that wanted so badly to spread across his face. "That sounds very similar to my routine. You never know, we might run into each other."

Her mouth curved into a shy smile that had his blood pounding. "It's a possibility."

It most certainly was.

LUKE WAS WASHING up after having assisted a cow with a difficult delivery. Thankfully, both mother and calf were now doing well but there'd been a few moments when he doubted a positive outcome. As he dried his hands, he was struck by the thought that right now his life was filled with women causing him grief—the cows, his mother with her disappointed and accusing looks that he was ruining her and his father's retirement, Keri with dollar signs in her eyes, and Erin.

Come to think of it, the cows were looking pretty low-maintenance right now. Erin, on the other hand, with her rainbow-bright clothes and those parodies of rubber boots she wore, was beyond high-maintenance. Last night he'd foolishly played a game that had in essence ended up being a double dare for him. Not that it had started out that way. When he'd seen her in the field silhouetted by the moon, his sole aim for the meeting was to regain his dignity after having fallen asleep on her bed and to reestablish his reputation as a man who was always in total control with all things to do with women.

It had started out well enough with him directing the conversation because there was no way on earth he was falling for any of her *let's talk* crap. Talking wasn't something they needed to do. As far as he was concerned, this thing between them that lived, breathed and grew daily was purely sexual.

Everything had been pitch-perfect right up to the moment after she'd kissed him. That was when the plan—backed up by years of experience—dictated that he walk away, thus leading the play. It guaranteed that when next they met, the game would be over because they both knew they wanted the exact same thing. The cards would be faceup on the table and with nowhere to hide, they'd move straight to sex. It was a simple, foolproof plan.

But had he walked away?

No.

Idiot! Not content with the fact he'd not only gotten back his control but he also had the evidence she still really wanted him, he'd let his ego step forward and get in the way. At the time it had seemed like such a brilliant idea to leave her with his calling card—a kiss that told her exactly what she could have if she came and got it—before nonchalantly walking away. The problem had come immediately after he'd draped her along the length of him and kissed her until she'd made that incredible sound in the back of her throat. He'd been lucky to manage walking.

He jammed his hat onto his head and strode out to the four-wheeler, pissed with himself yet again. He knew the rules and the risks, and none were worth blowing the perfect seduction. Twice. What the hell was wrong with him?

Pressing the accelerator down hard, he sent the bike into top speed, jolting up the farm road toward the top pasture. The lake shone blue and he thought about his small yacht in the boat shed on the beach—the one he hadn't managed to sail yet this season. As he passed the boundary of Wade's place, he saw Erin's dog trot out of a cottage and he unconsciously slowed. A moment later, Erin followed with a bucket of cleaning products on one arm and clutching crumpled sheets under the other.

Mac leaped off the bike, racing toward her with a joyful bark. "Too eager, Mac," Luke muttered under his breath.

A second later he wanted to slam his head hard against something. *Come find me.* Mac had just heralded Luke's arrival and by default made a mockery of his exit words to Erin last night. He'd dropped him right in it.

Maggie-May greeted Mac joyously, bouncing and barking with sheer delight and they raced around Erin's feet chasing each other while at the same time demanding her adoration.

She gave it, sinking to her feet and letting the dogs

lick her face as she scratched under each of their chins and bellies.

A vivid green flash socked into Luke. He shot off the bike, hating he was jealous of his dog. He vaulted the fence. "Mac! Sit!"

Erin's head swung around and her now sun-streaked hair followed, brushing her cheeks. Unlike her usual coordinated style, this morning she wore an old, baggy T-shirt, tattered cutoff jeans and bare feet—her rich cranberry-red painted toenails her sole accessory. As she disentangled herself from the dogs and rose, her oversized T fell forward and he copped an eyeful of soft, creamy breasts threatening to spill from a hot-pink-and-black bra.

Breasts he wanted to bury his head in, touch, taste and adore. His eyes stayed fixed on all that sweet, rounded flesh, flesh which taunted him, making his blood surge with lust so pure it hurt. Every part of him tensed, ready to move and lift her into his arms and take what she offered. Take what he so desperately wanted. His groin ached, his head spun and one booted foot started to move.

With her T-shirt still providing a clear view of her breasts, bra and belly, she tilted her head and hooked her gaze on to his. Her brows rose as if to say, *they're yours if you ask nicely.* Then she straightened up with a coy smile.

"Gosh, Luke, what a surprise seeing you here. And here I was thinking that I was supposed to come find you."

Stay! Hauling on everything he had, he glued his feet to the ground recognizing that her coy smile was actually a siren call to dash him against the rocks. To make him move first. She knew all too well that when she was bent over he could see straight down her front. It was a deliberate ploy, total power play and a bold grab for control.

A lightness swept through him—something he hadn't felt in months and he wanted to laugh with delight. Erin Davis wanted to play delicious, sexy games with him. She wanted to flirt and tease and bring him to his knees. He appreciated the sentiment oh so very much, but she had no clue who she was dealing with. It was going to be fun watching her come. First.

Rocking back on his work boots, he smiled. "Sweetheart, I'm sorry to disappoint you, but I'm here because Wade asked me to fix the door on your cottage."

Technically this was correct. Wade had asked him a month ago and with hay cutting it had fallen down the list.

A flicker of something he liked to think was disappointment flashed in her eyes and as she leaned down to pick up her bucket of cleaning products she stalled. This time he was slightly ahead of her and was prepared for the flash of pink-and-black lace.

She grabbed the bucket and straightened up, her chin tilting skyward. "Wade's taken a family to pet the calves and as much as I'd love to spend time chatting with you, some of us have work to do. I've got to clean their cottage while they're out."

"First rule of business is keep the customer happy." He grinned and shooed her away with his hands. "Don't let me hold you up."

"Or me you."

Her softly spoken words invoked the memory of the way her soft curves had sunk into him last night and how he'd leaned equally into her. It socked him with a scorch of heat, making him question why the hell he was holding out instead of sliding his arm around her waist and pulling her close.

Because you want to win.

"Luke…" Her green eyes sparkled knowingly as her voice huskily rolled over his name, making his blood pump harder and blurring his vision.

He met her gaze with a smile. "Yes, Erin."

She pouted her lips like Marilyn Monroe and slowly ran her index finger around the O before letting it come to rest on her chin. "I'll be in cottage number two."

God, she was hot and he wanted her right now. He hooked his thumbs into the waistband of his shorts to keep his hands from reaching for her. "And I need to know this why?"

She shrugged coquettishly, her shirt falling off one lovely shoulder and exposing her bra strap. "I thought perhaps you might need to come find me."

He grinned at her, loving the game. "That's not how I remember the arrangement."

"Perhaps your memory is playing tricks on you." She started to walk away from him, the bucket swinging in her hand, and then paused, turning slowly. "Just one thing, Luke. Don't linger here too long before coming to the cottage because I'm only changing the sheets once."

The thought of rolling her under him on a bed collided with the thrill of the game. He'd thought her high-maintenance but he'd been wrong. She was turning into the perfect gift—a sexy package with a wicked sense of fun. He buzzed with the heady excitement of anticipation and the sense of feeling alive for the first time in a long time.

He watched her swinging hips and cute behind cross the grass, and as she entered the cottage, she lifted one long, smooth leg in a perfect 1940s kissing style, before completely disappearing inside. He laughed out loud at her blatant flirting and planned his own strategies to bring her running into his arms.

TEN

It was early afternoon when Erin heard the sound of hammering and the noise made her jump. Most everything today was making her jump, especially when it came to Luke. She'd had the jitters from the moment Mac had rushed up to her when she'd finished cleaning cottage six, because wherever Mac went, Luke wasn't far behind. When Luke had vaulted the fence, his sheer athleticism had brought her so close to changing her mind, admitting defeat and saying *take me now, I'm yours* that her plans to taunt him mercilessly until he begged for her had almost come undone.

The challenge in his blue eyes had steadied her. His expectation that she'd be the first to give in had rescued her and steeled her own determination. If anyone was capitulating first, it was him. Although she was no expert at deliberately using her body to entice and the feminist in her was having conniptions, two could play at this game of sexual Mexican standoff. This awesomely wild and wondrous game.

She'd been stunned to discover just how much of a kick it gave her knowing that he wanted her. His gaze on her had been so scorching hot it had fired her skin with a glow that had stayed with her for the rest of the morning. A glow that had her floating through the monotony of cleaning and tidying two cottages, and had lessened the disappointment that he hadn't stormed in and taken her on cottage two's bed. It was probably a wise decision on his part, given that the family could have returned at any moment. Still, as exciting as the anticipation about when "it" was going to happen, the expectation was messing with her concentration. She'd already made three attempts to edit one photo and it still wasn't right.

Maggie-May whined at the door, pressing her nose to the glass where Mac now stood on the other side. "Want to go play with your friend?" *I want to go play with mine.*

She opened the sliding door and her dog shot out and the whirring scream of a drill came in. Luke had switched from hammering to drilling. She intended to distract him from that particular job and get him to focus on what they both wanted. Clicking on her mouse, she saved her most recent photo edits, plucked an apple from her fruit basket and stepped out into the lazy heat of the afternoon.

Wade kept the lawns in immaculate condition and she loved the feel of the thick, lush grass against the soles of her feet. It sure beat the hot concrete sidewalks in Minneapolis. She paused at the edge of the cottage, just out of sight, and adjusted her off-the-shoulder short T so it rested on the tops of her arms and skimmed over her cleavage. She'd chosen it because it finished at her midriff and her skirt started at her hips, leaving an expanse of skin complete with a jeweled belly ring.

Tossing the apple into the air, she caught it with a grin. She was ready and Luke Anderson didn't stand a chance. She gave him less than ten minutes before he caved and they were both horizontal in her bed.

"Hi, Luke…" She stepped into view but the rest

of the sentence stalled as her brain fried from visual overload.

His shirt lay on the ground and his burnished skin glowed with a sheen of sweat that highlighted every work-sculpted muscle on his torso. A tool belt was slung low on his hips—the icing on the beefcake that was Luke. It also screamed *I'm good with my hands.* The idea of his hands skimming over her skin made her sway.

He greeted her with a lazy smile. A smile that said *baby you know you want me now* and it spun through her, leaving her panting.

"Erin, I'm going to have to take off your—"

Yes, please. Everything.

"—door."

Somehow the word managed to penetrate the roaring sound of her blood, which was thundering loudly in her ears as it pumped heady need into every nook, cranny and far-flung crevice of her body. She tried desperately to gather her scattered wits while at the same time trying to sound both coherent and sexy. "No problem." The words came out on a squeak.

Luke's lazy smile morphed into a wicked grin.

I'll raise you. She slowly lifted the apple to her mouth and bit into it, flicking her tongue out to catch the juice that sprayed her.

His eyes instantly zeroed in on her mouth.

Won't you walk into my parlor said the spider to the fly. It was all too easy and she was back on top. "My door? I guess that means you'll need to come inside?"

His blue eyes sparkled like the lake in sunshine. "I guess it does."

He expertly spun the hammer in his hand before de-

positing it neatly into the vacant slot on his tool belt.
He stepped in close, dropped his head so his lips al-
most brushed her ear and his breath caressed her skin.
"Lead the way."

The deep timbre of the words sent an erotic shiver
whooshing through her as his mingled scent of sweat,
musk and something that was intrinsically Luke circled
her. It cast invisible threads, which hooked into her
with tantalizing temptation that immediately drained
her brain. He was so close. He smelled so masculine
and amazing, and all she needed to do was move the
smallest of distances and their bodies would be touching. He'd be hers.

No. It's what he wants.

It's what I want.

She stifled the scream of frustration that her throbbing body sent up, because letting him win when he
expected to—as if it was his right—was just too much
for her. With superhuman effort she spun away from
him, knowing her resistance was barely holding and
the time had come to ramp things up so he capitulated
sooner rather than later.

Channeling her fledging inner seductress, she motioned him forward with her finger. "Follow me."

SOMEHOW LUKE MANAGED to remove, plane and restore
the front door despite the fact his brain wasn't fully
soaked with oxygen-carrying blood and right now it
was thinking more about what Erin was doing behind
her closed bedroom door than concentrating on the job
at hand. When she'd sashayed in there fifteen minutes
earlier, moments after waggling her finger at him and
saying in that throaty voice she used when she flirted,

"follow me," he'd fully expected her arm to reach out, grab his and pull him in after her.

Hell, that had been the whole point of him removing his shirt and risking a sunburn. Of risking the hypnotic pull of her amazing eyes when they'd widened into huge pools of green that shone with an arousal that matched his. It had been the whole point of risking his stake in the game by standing so close to her that he could almost taste her.

He opened and closed the front door, noting with some satisfaction that it now moved freely. One job done. The other job of Erin getting him into bed was taking a lot longer than he'd expected and hoped. He'd underestimated her stubbornness and as much as that excited him, and as much as he was enjoying this cat and mouse game between them, he was so wired for her he didn't know how much longer he could hold out. He sure as hell probably shouldn't be attempting to use power tools.

His mind roved over his next play—one that would bring all of this sexual tension to the delicious détente they both wanted. Desperately wanted. As he opened the door and stepped out onto the porch, he heard Mac's bark, the terrier's yap and Erin's laugh. He spun toward the sound and squinted into the sun. Erin was on the walking track heading toward the beach. Although he assumed she must be wearing a bikini, from this distance he could only see skin and two of the narrowest strings he'd ever seen—one across the middle of her back and one across her hips. Other than that, nothing else touched that glorious expanse of tanned, smooth skin. From this view, she was virtually naked.

Without stopping to close the door he ripped off his tool belt and jumped off the porch. It took everything he had not to break into a run.

THE MOMENT ERIN walked into the privacy of the grove of trees and she knew Luke could no longer see her, she pulled a pair of board shorts out of her bag and stepped into them, instantly covering the bikini thong. She immediately relaxed. Although she was fairly certain all the B and B guests were with Wade on the farm visit, part of her had been worried she might meet someone on the beach. Being virtually naked for Luke was one thing but she didn't want to scar any young children or give any other man the wrong idea.

She'd never worn this bikini before—it was really more like three miniature triangles of material—and she felt ridiculously exposed. It had been an impulse online buy last summer on an evening home alone when she'd drunk too much wine. Since its arrival in her mailbox, it had lain in her drawer reminding her of her folly until a few days ago when she'd gone home to pack for her few weeks in Whitetail. Impulse once again had made her pack it. If she could hold on to her resolve for a little bit longer, the bikini might just earn its keep.

The dogs tore off along the small but pretty beach where the trees came right down to the waterline. A small wooden shed and a picnic table rested in a grassy clearing just above the sandy beach. She wondered if the sand was natural or if it had been brought in. Either way, it was warm against her skin, unlike the water, which was chilly. As she dived under and the cold sucked the air from her lungs, she hoped Luke wouldn't take long to arrive on the beach. She broke the surface and flipped onto her back, sculling through the water and using the warmth of the sunshine to try and even up the temperature disparity.

"Erin!"

Luke stood on the beach with one adoring dog gazing up at him and a cautious Maggie-May hunkered down and ready to respond, as if she expected the worst. Couldn't her dog see Luke was a golden-haired god, glinting and sparkling in the sunshine?

Her body ached for him so badly she struggled to stay afloat. Flicking her wrist in a royal-like wave, she tried to look so much more sophisticated than she felt. "Come on in. The water's as warm as a bath."

He laughed, the rich, melodic sound booming around the cove. "Sweetheart, this far north the water's always cold. I promise that you'll be a lot warmer if you swim back to me."

With goose bumps lining her flesh, she knew this to be true but being in the water was all about winning. "You've come this far to find me, Luke. Just think, another few feet and I'm all yours."

His nostrils flared with the same unmet need that vibrated between them and the movement raced across his shoulders and down his bare chest before disappearing under the band of his work shorts. Yet still he didn't enter the water. Instead, he sat down on the sand and took off his boots before rolling onto his side and resting his weight on one arm so that every muscle bulged. "It's pretty nice here on the sand. Hot even. I'll wait for you here."

Her body both leaped and wept at the sight of him. She plunged her feet onto the bottom of the lake and stood up with the water lapping at her waist, knowing full well the now-wet material was see-through. "That's disappointing."

His strangled moan floated across the air and his hands pulled at his hair. "That's dirty pool, Erin."

"Oh, and you shirtless and in a tool belt isn't?"

"I got hot."

"I imagine you did." She threw her head back, knowing the movement would lift her breasts and she was filled with the sexual power of her body—an intoxicating power she'd never been fully aware of until she'd met Luke.

An expletive hit the air and he rolled to his feet, shucking his work shorts.

Suddenly she was staring at black, low-rise trunks, fully extended forward by his erection. *Thank you, thank you, thank you.* For days the throb of desire had been part of her, intensifying hourly until it consumed her and was all she could think about. She hadn't thought it possible for it to gain any more momentum but sweet wonder, it expanded again, only this time it held an edge of pleasurable pain and it beat out *soon, please God, soon.*

"Mac. Stay!" His voice commanded absolute obedience and then his strong legs were plowing through the water, creating mini waves that washed up against her. As he made his way to her, she fantasized about what he might do when he reached her. Would he pick her up and throw her over his shoulder, claiming her, and then stalk back to the beach with his prize, or would he just haul her against his hard chest and kiss her right here in the lake? Her legs wobbled. Both scenarios sounded fantastic to her.

He halted just short of her, his chest heaving and his blue eyes simmering with equal parts desire and frustration. She was intimate with those feelings—they'd been driving her quietly crazy for days. Now he stood in front of her, so near and yet so far.

"Um, Luke, just a teensy bit farther."

"For you to move, I know." The guttural edge to his voice hinted at fraying control but his wicked smile sizzled, promising everything she'd dreamed about and more.

Her breathing hitched up and she stretched her arm out toward him, letting it rest on the surface of the water in the few feet between them. "I thought men got off on the thrill of the chase."

He stretched out his arm, his third finger a nanometer away from touching hers, and his eyes darkened. "There's nothing hotter than a woman who takes what she wants."

And at that moment winning became semantics. He'd come into the water, virtually to her, and if making that tiny move was his fantasy, she'd gladly oblige so she could have hers. Her fingertip touched his and flames engulfed her. His large, strong hand closed around her wrist. She lunged toward him as his arms lifted her at the hips, and then her legs were wrapped around his waist, and she was burying herself against his chest. She was home. Her body, so taut with ragged need for so long, stilled for a heartbeat, suspended in bliss, and then primal energy thundered through her. Wrapping her arms around his neck, she lowered her mouth to his and kissed him.

His lips met hers—blistering hot—and she took his heat and transferred her own. His mouth was both familiar yet different and she flicked her tongue around it, stealing his flavor so it ran through her veins, branding her and driving her onward. His hands roved her spine—one splayed across her back and the other at the base of her head, clamping her against him as if he couldn't get enough of her body touching his. She understood exactly.

Her tongue met his and she took her time exploring it. She wasn't quite done when he groaned and a moment later, his tongue was lashing hers in delicious strokes. She yielded to him, taking control of the kiss, surrendering to his wickedly divine ministrations and thankful he was holding her up. While his expert mouth stripped her of everything except her burning desire for him, she explored his shoulders and back with her hands, pressing and rubbing the muscles and bone and committing to memory the moments her touch made him moan in pleasure against her mouth.

His hands moved to her buttocks and with ragged breathing to match her own, he released her mouth. "You thought this was a good idea?"

Her mind was incapable of constructing a thought other than she was exactly where she needed to be—wrapped around Luke. "What do you mean?"

His dark and enticing eyes gazed down at her. "You're shivering so hard you're vibrating and in case you didn't know it, water at this temperature isn't complimentary to a guy."

He looked gorgeous to her and she didn't quite understand. "How isn't it complimentary?"

He shook his head as if he couldn't believe she didn't comprehend. "Let me put it this way. Cold water means shrinkage."

She blinked, understanding dawning. "In that case we need to go back to shore. Now."

He laughed, his face creasing in joyous lines. "We finally found something to agree on."

She traced a finger down his sternum. "Carry me in."

He stared down at her. "Isn't that a little too *caveman* or *man knows best* for a modern woman like yourself?"

Her cheeks burned with embarrassment. "I know, right, but…"

One brow quirked up and lust flared bright in his eyes. "But?"

Her embarrassment vanished. He wanted her so why not let him know what turned her on. "When you were striding toward me all powerful and determined, I got excited thinking you were about to throw me over your shoulder and carry me off."

"Like this?"

The next minute she was upside down with her head resting halfway down his back. She squealed with delight. "Totally like this, only don't drop me."

Suddenly she was back upright with disappointment slugging her.

Blue eyes, which held the tiniest hint of being pissed, hooked hers. "If you want me to give you a caveman fantasy, you can't tell me what to do."

She tried her best to look contrite. "You're right. Sorry. Cavemen don't take orders. They give them."

He grinned. "Damn straight. Now we're on the same page."

A skitter of unease ran through her that with all this outrageous flirting she'd perhaps given him the wrong idea about what she liked. "I won't need a safe word, will I, because I really—"

He brushed the gentlest kiss across her mouth. "I'll never intentionally hurt you, Erin, and if you ever feel at all uncomfortable just tell me."

Her heart, which up until now had been totally separate from her lustfest, fluttered for a second. She instantly steadied it by kissing him, thankful for the rush of euphoria that numbed her to anything else.

Luke swung Erin over his shoulder for the second time in two minutes and grinned. Erin totally surprised him. Not only was she sensationally sexy, she wanted to role play, which meant he had permission to channel his inner caveman. As he walked toward the shore, his free hand paddled her gently on the butt. "And what's with the board shorts? Last time I saw you there were two naked buttocks calling out to me."

"I panicked there might be people on the beach."

His chest expanded at the thought she'd done all of this just for him. "You do realize there's going to be a consequence for you teasing me like that. I'm going to have to strip them off you."

He waited for her compliant, *Yes, Master*, response although the thought struck him that he might be mixing up the fantasy with that of stealing a slave girl.

"I see. Well, I think it's only fair then that I…" Her hands slipped under the waistband of his boxers and her palms curved around his buttocks.

His glutes tensed and every part of his body strained to stay in control. "Erin," he managed to grind out, "if you don't want me to drop you, you might want to wait until we get to shore before you do that."

Her hands shot to his back but her heat lingered, promising things to come.

Her dog started barking, unhappy that her mistress was on his shoulder and he feared for his ankles. "I've got bare legs, Erin. Tell your dog to stay."

"Maggie-May, it's okay," she called out. "Sit. Good dog."

The terrier didn't look happy but stayed next to Mac who'd joined in the barking.

When he reached the beach he lowered her to her feet, wrapping his arms around her. "Dizzy?"

She rested her head on his chest. "Just a bit."

The dogs went berserk, wanting both of their attention but he held her close until her eyes cleared. As she picked up her bag, he grabbed his shorts and dug out his keys. Catching her hand, he ran them to the boat shed with the dogs in hot pursuit. "This is the best I can do for a cave at short notice."

She shivered in the shadow cast by the boat shed and her teeth chattered. "The beach is sunnier."

"Really? You, who put board shorts on for fear of public indecency, are thinking of having sex on the beach? Not to mention the added dimension of sand and two dogs who'd either try to bite or lick us?"

She groaned through slightly blue lips. "You were supposed to follow me into my bedroom. This is all your fault. You distracted me."

He grinned as the padlock on the boat shed opened. "I promise to distract you even more."

Her eyes dilated into dark pools and he tugged her into the boat shed, closing the door firmly against the imploring eyes of two dogs. A moment later she was in his arms, her breasts pressing against his chest, and her nipples hard and erect grazing his skin. He kissed her deep and fast and then pulled away, staring at her breasts. Two tiny triangles of blue Lyrca technically covered them but hid nothing. "You're beautiful." He lowered his mouth over the thin material and sucked it into his mouth.

She sank her fingers into his shoulders and cried out.

He pulled back. "Did I hurt you?"

"God no. It's amazing but let's get rid of this." She

reached for the knot at the back of her neck that kept the bikini top in place, but her trembling fingers couldn't seem to untie it. "My fingers are too cold."

He moved backward, taking her with him, and grabbed a bath sheet out of the cupboard. "Wrap yourself in this while I wrangle the knot and then I'll warm you up."

She gave him a grateful smile before she turned around, kicked off the wet board shorts and dried her midriff.

The close-up view of the two perfect orbs of her buttocks touched only by a scrap of blue lace that ran across her hips had his fingers fumbling on the knot. Ironically, the micro-bikini barely covered anything and yet the damn knot was holding fast, making him work harder than he'd ever worked before to free a pair of breasts.

"Just break it, Luke."

"What with? My teeth?"

She gave a strangled laugh. "I'm sure a caveman would have done that."

The knot shifted slightly. "I'm not sure a caveman had to contend with much more than pulling an animal skin over his woman's head." The knot gave way and he easily untied the one across her back. "Gotcha." With a deft pull he held the top aloft before letting it fall from his fingers.

Her gaze followed its descent to the ground. "I guess you should be rewarded for all your hard work, then." She let the towel fall to her feet and stood before him like Aphrodite rising from the water.

If he'd thought he was aroused before it had nothing on this. His blood pounded, every muscle tensed for action and he wanted to lift her up against the wall and take here right now, but he also wanted to explore every inch of her body—every bump, every curve and every imperfection he'd ever noticed, all of which now seemed perfect. "You're a gift."

"So are you." Her eyes drifted to his boxers. "Now can I get to the unwrapping part?"

God, she was amazing and she was going to test every particle of his endurance so that he didn't come just from the sight of her and the sound of her voice. "Come here, now."

He virtually dragged her the length of the boat shed, skirting boxes of sails, engine parts, oars and years of accumulated beach toys, until he reached the old sofa bed. He lowered her onto it and gazed down at her. "Ready?"

Her eyes shone brightly and she trailed a finger down his cheek. "I've been on a state of high alert from the moment I met you." She unfolded her hand to reveal a foil square rested there.

"I love a woman who's all prepared." He lowered his head toward her breasts. "I think I'll start here."

Luke's tongue lazily licked Erin's hypersensitive left nipple and a rainbow of colors streamed through her. Then he dawdled across the gap between the breasts and licked the right one. Her left ached in pain, throbbing and desperate for his touch again. When he suckled her, she cried as her head thrashed back and forth against the mattress. It was as if her body had completely separated from her mind. Nothing existed other than the mass of aching desires and wondrous throbbing pain that swung between quivering desperate need, hot demanding fulfillment and moments of utter bliss. The need for even more surged back stronger than ever.

As his mouth trailed down her stomach pausing for due deference to her belly button and ring, her muscles starting twitched so hard, frantic to grip something, that she thought she'd go insane. She tugged at his head and brought his lips back to hers. "It's not that I don't appreciate the foreplay, seriously I do, it's just—"

"We've been doing foreplay for seventeen hours straight."

"Yes."

The light in his eyes danced like a kaleidoscope. "So you want me to speed things up a bit?"

She pushed the condom into his hand as sheer relief tangoed with the empty feeling inside her, promising that soon the feeling would be one of fullness. "Please."

"Seeing you asked so nicely…"

She heard the foil of the condom being opened and instantly regretted that she hadn't thought to be the one to roll it on him. Rising on her elbow, wanting to watch, he pushed her gently back onto the bed. *Missionary position?* At this point she didn't care how it happened as long as it happened. She shimmied out of the thong and raised her knees to wrap her legs around his waist so she could take him deeply.

His hands pressed gently against her inner thighs and she panted, knowing that any second he would be hers. As she reached down her hand to guide him into her, his stubble grazed her thigh. *What?* But the thought was detonated as his mouth touched the lips of her labia.

No. Her hands pummeled his shoulders and she opened her mouth to protest that she wanted him inside her when his tongue found her clitoris. Two strokes of his tongue was all it took. She fell off the precipice she'd been teetering on for days, exploding into a thousand tiny pieces as wave after wave of release shook her, unfurling ribbons of ecstasy that streamed to every point of her body. Her screams of delight floated back to her and as her breath steadied, she opened her eyes to find Luke's smiling eyes and dimpled cheeks an inch away.

He kissed her. "I take it that worked for you?"

She pursed her lips in thought. "Sort of."

His brows shot up in disbelief. "You screamed so loud that if the roof wasn't hammered down it would have fallen in on us."

She ran her hands along his ribs and found a spot that made him flinch. *Ticklish. Excellent.* "I didn't want to hurt your feelings seeing you were trying so hard to please me but what I really want is—" she dug her fingers into the space between his ribs and as he recoiled slightly she moved, pushing his shoulder back and flinging her leg over him until she was straddling him "—this."

He shook his head slowly from side to side, his cheeks edged with strain. "Erin, we really need to work on your fantasy definition. I thought you wanted to be dragged into my cave where I took you for my pleasure."

As he stretched out his hands toward her breasts, she saw the calculating look in his eyes and instantly clamped her thighs hard against his so he couldn't flip her back under him. "I think I just got a new fantasy."

She gazed at his erection in awe and then tentatively ran her finger along its impressive length. "It's a shame you don't have your hat so I could wear it."

Every inch of his body tensed and the blue of his eyes almost vanished under huge jet discs. "Sweetheart, you're getting your fantasies mixed up. I'm a dairyman not a cowboy."

She leaned forward and whispered, "Never mind. I'm still happy to ride you."

His guttural moan roared through her, filling her with pride that she'd aroused him to this point, but also with some worry that she'd overdone it and he'd come before she could experience him. "Sorry, I'll stop talk—"

"Good idea." His hands gripped her hips and he lifted her over him and then very slowly he lowered her down.

Her body, oh so very ready and desperate for him, opened easily, absorbing him bit by bit until she'd stretched to the limit and he completely filled her. The sensation was indescribable and she experienced the oddest feeling that she was going to cry, which made no sense because her body was on fire for him. Her throbbing muscles, which had ached for him, closed around him and need became fire driving her upward to seize the ultimate prize.

Her panting fell in sync with Luke's as he drove into her and she impaled herself so willingly on him. Whirling awe built and built until the edges of her mind started to blur. She kissed him quickly before throwing her head back, and with his touch and feel completing her, she let go and soared beyond herself into a realm of wonder.

A moment later he followed.

ELEVEN

LUKE CONSIDERED HIMSELF fit but as he lay on his back with his lungs cramping, he realized that perhaps his dry spell had lost him some sex fitness. Not that it had impeded things in any way and he now welcomed the post-orgasm languidness that stole into his bones, filling him with a sense of peace.

A thought pierced the post-coital fog that was his brain. Why the hell hadn't he had sex in months when it was this damn amazing? He was an idiot not to have realized his lack of sex was probably the reason he'd been feeling so out of sorts for so long. *Dr. Luke to the rescue. Problem solved.*

Erin's head rested on his chest for a moment before she rolled off him and lay on her side with her back to him.

He reached out his arm, scooping her close, so her butt nestled warmly into his belly, and he pressed a kiss to her shoulder. "Thank you."

She laughed. "Thank *you*."

He ran his hand down her arm, across the bumps of her ribs and the dip of her waist before tracing the outline of a small tattoo on her hip in the shape of a Chinese symbol. "What does this mean?"

The only sound was her breathing.

"Erin?"

She sighed. "Security."

He'd been expecting something like faith, hope or love because it was his experience with women that they sought all of those three in their lives. "Security?"

"Yep." She abruptly rolled away from him and stood up.

He watched her move across the boat shed and pull a sarong out of her bag before briskly wrapping it around her and tying a knot that rested in her cleavage. All evidence of the flirting temptress was gone.

She threw his shorts at him. "We should really get going."

He frowned as his thoughts of trying for a second helping of sex pie suddenly ran into a brick wall. He patted the space next to him. "There's no hurry."

She started brushing the sand off the sheets where their feet had been. "It's past four. Don't you need to start milking soon?"

He had a vision of his father and a speck of chagrin sneaked in under his euphoria. "The cows can wait another half an hour." He caught her hand in his. "That gives us time to explore another one of your fantasies."

"Sorry. I've got a meeting with Nicole. Apparently there's a space in the wedding warehouse where I can set up a temporary studio for clients who want more formal-type shots."

He smiled the smile he knew made her weak at the knees. "You could text her saying you're running late."

She closed her eyes and sucked in her lips. When she opened her eyes he recognized stubborn resolve. "This is business, Luke. It's my livelihood and my future and I don't ever keep anyone waiting."

The words sliced into him with an emphatic edge and he couldn't help but wonder why they were so sharp.

Remorse crossed her face and she kneeled on the bed, resting her hand lightly on his chest. "Are you working half the night tonight?"

"That depends if any cows need help with labor."

"I'll be back from town by seven. I could grab some supplies and cook supper for us." Her eyes danced and a cheeky smile tugged at her lips. "That's if you promise to eat with your mouth closed."

He tugged her against him, wrapping his arms tightly around her. "I'll bring my exceptional manners and a healthy appetite for you."

Her eyes popped so wide and her skin flushed so pink that he thought he had her and she was coming back to bed. When she kissed him deeply using that tongue of hers in a way he was certain was illegal in many parts of the world, he was utterly convinced. His blood shot to his groin and he was good to go.

With a gasp, she pulled her mouth away and struggled free of him. "Bye, Luke."

As she opened the door to the cacophony of manic barking, she raised her hand in a wave before disappearing from view. He couldn't stop the grin that spread across his face. Sure, he was disappointed she was leaving now, but by her action of leaving first, she'd just told him that this amazing thing between them was all about the sex. Nothing else.

Yes. Absolutely nothing about her demeanor hinted at a woman with unrealistic expectations. There was no hint of high-maintenance or looking for anything more than just good times. He pulled his hands up behind his head and gazed at the dust motes dancing in the sunlight, which streamed in through the cracks in the siding. Life was good. Even milking wasn't looking too shabby.

AFTER MEETING WITH Nicole, Erin switched on her phone and it beeped wildly. She glanced down at the screen.

You have 3 new messages.

Darling, I'd love to see you. It's been too long. Call me. Dad.

Her breath caught in her throat. How did he even have this number? Her father hadn't made contact with her in over three years and she certainly hadn't tried to contact him because she didn't trust herself not to let him back into her life.

She stared at the words, reading them twice. And the chaotic ball of emotions that always rolled through her whenever she thought about her father started turning. She quickly clicked on the next message effectively blocking his out.

The photos look good. Can picture it all. Want to ditch church ceremony and use marquee in front of sunflowers. Also want the dog. Connie.

She swallowed and decided Connie's request wasn't as complicated as her father's but it still wasn't instantly solvable so she'd come back to it. The next message said, *Hey, sis, the band's playing at the Fine Line next Wednesday at 9. See you there? Jesse.*

A strand of guilt ran through her that she hadn't told her brother she was out of town. Not that he always told her when he was away, but still, his level of communication was a bar worth raising. She hit the call button.

"How's it going, sis?"

"Hey, Jesse, I'm good. I'm working in Whitetail, Wisconsin, and—"

"Where?"

She explained it in terms he'd understand. "Ninety minutes from the nearest Starbucks."

"Have you been abducted?"

She thought of how Luke had scooped her over his shoulder as if she weighed less than a sack of potatoes and a rush of heat made her laugh sound oddly deep. "I know, right? It's totally unexpected, but by some serendipitous chance this little town is a wedding mecca without a photographer so I'm stepping in for a bit."

"Careful, sis, you might get stuck in the Wisconsin marsh mud and I'll never see you again."

This time her laugh sounded far more normal. "It's pretty, but me staying here forever isn't something that's going to happen. I've got weddings booked into late August and perhaps beyond so I'm here for a bit. Can you water my houseplants, please?"

"Well…"

She recognized his cagey tone of voice. "What?"

"If I move into your apartment I can talk to them too."

"Why do you need to move in?"

"Rory sublet his couch out from under me."

She rolled her eyes at her brother's unstable housing arrangements. "Okay, but under no circumstances sublet my couch to anyone, understood?"

"Understood." A beat of silence followed. "Ah, Erin, Dad came to the bar the other night. He wants to touch base with you too."

She thought of the out-of-the-blue text and sighed, not liking where this was going. "So it was you who gave him my number?"

"I'm sorry." His voice held regret. "I held out for as long as I could, but he offered me Kobe beef."

Jesse was trying really hard to make it as a musician and money was always tight. She understood how being broke made dangled temptations even harder to resist but she hated that she'd been the fall guy for a thirty-dollar steak.

Jesse ignored her silence and kept talking. "He's changed, Erin. He apologized for all the crap and he wants to do the same for you. I couldn't say no to that."

She closed her eyes but the memories of how her father betrayed her mother, Jesse and herself rushed her, beaming in full color. Not wanting to go back to those bewildering days, she opened her eyes and moved to reassure her baby brother. He'd been too young to remember a lot of the awful stuff that had gone down. "It's okay, Jesse."

"Sure?"

"Well, seeing as you're feeling bad about it you can repay me by keeping my houseplants alive and my apartment clean."

"Consider it done. You want me to mail you some Blonde Roast coffee beans?"

"No, thanks, I'm good. They have a pretty good breakfast blend here at the market."

He gave a mock gasp. "They haven't just kidnapped you, they've brainwashed you as well. Be afraid, sis, be very afraid."

She rang off laughing. As if there was anything to be afraid of in Whitetail. Well, there were cows, only she was getting used to their constant chewing, their big, pink tongues and huge, brown eyes, and as long as they didn't get near her feet they didn't scare her too much. There were no bulls to be afraid of either. Wade had told her that due to AI, bulls on the farm were a thing of the past.

Are you scared of Luke?

He frustrated her and he challenged her to think on her feet to stay one step ahead of him. His smile made her weak at the knees and his deep voice was like the woody smoothness of malt whiskey, complete with the same slow-burn fire that heated her from tip to toe. And the sex was beyond her wildest dreams, but no, he didn't scare her.

Her phone beeped with an incoming text and she ignored it, expecting it to be Connie because she hadn't instantly replied to the previous one. Exactly how she was going to broach the subject of Connie getting married on the farm with Luke, she had no clue. The phone beeped again and she knew it would keep doing that until she'd read the text.

I'm not sure I pressed the right buttons the first time so trying again... I'd love to buy you a meal, darling. It's been too long. Call me soon. Dad xx

The idea of talking to her father? Now *that* scared her.

ERIN LAY WITH her head resting on Luke's chest, feeling and hearing his heart beating solidly and rhythmically under her ear. Maggie-May was whining on the other side of the door.

Luke's hand wound through her hair. "That dog of yours needs to go back to obedience school."

"She's used to being inside with me, is all, and you being all macho about dogs staying outside isn't helping." She traced the delineation of his pectoral muscles, loving their shape and feel. "If she came in she'd sit quietly on the bed and this would be far more relaxing."

He shook his head. "She'd do her level best to get me out of your bed. You and that dog have codependency issues."

"Really? And are you ever seen anywhere without Mac?"

He grinned. "That's different. He's a farm dog."

She elbowed him in the ribs. "He's working really hard out on my deck at the moment. What's he doing? Rounding up ants?"

"He's keeping the raccoons at bay." He kissed her and then wrapped his arm around her. His enthusiasm for cuddling after sex surprised her. Not that she had loads of experience with men but every woman knew that when it was just about the sex—and this thing they had going on between them was purely about the sex—guys tended to avoid the snuggle. In fact she'd been expecting him to up and leave for the past ten minutes.

He gave a contented sigh. "This bed is a hell of a lot more comfortable than the boat shed. I'd forgotten how bad that sofa bed is."

Without thinking she blurted out, "How many women have you had sex with there?"

His gaze found hers. "You make two."

She felt her face betray her surprise.

"You expected more?" He grinned as if she'd given him a compliment. "There've been plenty more only not in the boat shed. If you hadn't put on that barely bikini, I would have made sure we were somewhere less utilitarian."

She'd loved the shed and the way the light streamed in through the cracks in the siding. It had danced across his bladed cheekbones and cast his body in sexy shadows. If she had the chance again, she'd photograph him there. "So Whitetail women expect more than a boat shed?"

He shrugged. "I haven't had sex with a woman from

Whitetail since high school. Life is less complicated that way."

And there it was. Confirmation of what she understood to be happening, which in a way was a relief given they'd had sex before they'd had *the talk* and set out the ground rules. She was from out of town and only here for a short time so this fling suited them both. Even so, she found herself frowning. "But you live here now? Doesn't your personal code of conduct make you lonely?"

"No."

His eyes flashed and his vehement tone made her start. "Okay, then."

He rolled her over so she was under him. "That's enough about me. What about you?"

She laughed, not particularly wanting to admit her experience probably didn't come even close to touching his. Nor did she want to tell him that work was more important to her than anything else because unlike her childhood, she was never going to risk having a zero bank balance. That sort of conversation didn't belong here, especially given his confused tone when she'd told him what her tattoo stood for.

Sinking her hands into his hair she said, "Recently, I've flirted a lot with Irishmen, Australians and Brits. There's something about a man with an accent that makes me go weak at the knees every single time."

His wicked grin reappeared. "To be sure," he said in a fair imitation of an Irish accent, "I'll try and remember that, darlin'."

Her body leaped again, calling out for him and she wrapped her legs around him, pulling him down to her. "Thank you."

"You're welcome." Then in an Irish lilt, he whispered in her ear gloriously indecent things he wanted to do to her and things he wanted her to do to him.

This might just be sex but he was the most amazing and considerate lover she'd ever known, and she happily obliged.

NICOLE PULLED THE car up outside the market and turned to Max who was sitting in the backseat. "I'll just be a few minutes and—"

"Aw, Mom," Max whined. "Why do we have to stop?"

"Because, I'm buying a coffee like I do every morning, only usually you're already at camp." She stomped on the flash of guilt that flared in her chest. Today was her and Max's day off together and yet she didn't want to give up her chance of seeing Tony.

It was pathetic really but she'd come to look forward to their morning ritual of buying coffee. She was addicted to the buzz of receiving his *hello* smile, which made her feel as if it was a smile just for her despite the fact they were always surrounded by several other coffee addicts. They seemed to always stand across from each other in the casual circle of people as the daily conversations discussing town concerns took place. This informal group was where many of the formal agenda items for the town meetings were born.

She was intimate with the feeling of being alone in a crowd but his smile always made her feel like the two of them existed separately from the group. She also knew she was imagining all of it and that this was a ridiculous schoolgirl crush which could go nowhere.

However, knowing all of that wasn't enough to stop her from stopping by each morning.

Max unbuckled his seat belt. "I want a hot chocolate."

He was off and out of the car, running into the grocery store before she could open her mouth to reply.

Grabbing her purse, she followed and by the time the automatic doors had opened for her, John was greeting her with, "Good morning, Nicole. I hear it's a day of fun for you and Max. Coffee coming right up."

"Thanks, John."

As the hissing sound of steam blasting through milk filled the coffee-cart area, she glanced around looking for Max who had a tendency to run straight to the candy section of the store and stare at it longingly. She commenced walking.

"Mom! I'm here!"

She turned to see Max sitting high on Tony's shoulders, his feet dangling against the fireman's broad chest. He looked so happy, she had to blink.

Tony winked at her, a wide smile on his face. "Apparently hot chocolate is on the menu."

She smiled weakly, her body totally confused as maternal love collided with the feelings she always got when she saw Tony. Today it was all gift-wrapped in guilt. "I guess that's only fair given my coffee addiction."

His eyes, already so dark, seemed to deepen. "Neither of us can stand in judgment then."

The words wrapped around her making her pulse jump. This was why she came for coffee. This was why she couldn't miss a morning.

You need a twelve-step program.

"One latte, one espresso and one hot chocolate," John called out the combined order.

Tony set Max down and pulled out his wallet. "I'm paying for them, John."

A slight frown creased the grocer's forehead and he gave Nicole a questioning glance before silently accepting Tony's money. Leaving the fireman's coffee on the counter, John picked up the hot chocolate and Nicole's latte, and handed them directly to her. "You and Max enjoy your picnic. It will good for the both of you to spend some time together."

Mother guilt flared. "I spend a lot of time with him, John."

"It's not a criticism, dear. You're a great mom. You and Bradley were a wonderful team."

Tony silently reached around her, picked up his coffee and walked over to the sugar stand.

No we weren't a great team, John. But blurting that out in the middle of the coffee club wasn't the time or place. She'd learned there was never a time or a place. Stepping back from the cart, she felt her frustration building at the way John inserted Bradley into many of their conversations. It wasn't that she didn't appreciate the way he looked out for her and Max but just lately she was feeling increasingly stifled by her past.

She joined Max, who was now standing next to Tony at the sugar stand busily telling him they were going to the lake for a cookout and a hike. Before she handed him the hot chocolate, she checked the temperature.

"That sounds like fun, champ." Tony stirred his coffee. "What are you going to cook?"

Max gave him an incredulous look. "Brats of course."

Tony looked over Max's head to Nicole as if her son was speaking a different language. "Brats?"

"German sausages cooked in beer. They're a Wisconsin state dish." She could feel John's eyes on them and the accompanying waves of disapproval. Something inside her snapped. "Tony, Max and I would love for you to join us if you have time."

Max jumped up and down, tugging on Tony's arm. "Please, Tony. I've got a football, only Mom's not very good at throwing it."

Nicole rolled her eyes. "Thanks a lot, buddy."

"It's just the truth, Mom."

Sometimes she yearned for the simple concrete world of eight-year-olds rather than the complicated one of adulthood.

A thoughtful expression crossed Tony's face. "I have a few things on this morning but I could certainly join you by three. Is that too late?"

Nicole had planned on making the cookout lunch but as she caught John straining to hear their conversation she decided to shift her day around to accommodate this change. "Three would be just fine. We'll meet you at the fire house and go from there." She grabbed Max's hand, gave a curt nod to John and stalked out of the store.

"I THINK MAX has got some mountain goat in him," Tony said, watching the little boy jump from boulder to boulder with light-footed ease while he and Nicole carefully picked their way down from the cliff-top path, back toward the lake.

Nicole laughed. "I know, right? He whines when we walk along the flat but whenever we hit rocks he's off like a shot."

They'd been hiking for an hour and Tony couldn't remember enjoying himself this much in a very long time. Nicole's invitation to join her and Max had been a bolt from the blue, but as his *nonna* always said, *there was no point arguing with the unexpected*, especially good unexpected. He wanted to shout out to the world how great this all was.

Going slowly and testing the waters with Nicole was driving him quietly around the bend but he knew rushing her would only backfire on him. Hell, he wasn't even certain she was ready to move on from her grief but the signs were optimistically solid. First she'd told him her coffee routine and now the hike. Nothing ambiguous about either of those two things. Both meant she wanted to spend time with him and when he added to that how relaxed she was compared with the other times he'd met her, it was all good.

The tension that usually surrounded her had vanished and their conversation ranged all over from music and books, to touching briefly on local politics, discussions about his job and, of course, the wedding business. All of it flowed easily, punctuated with laughter and numerous interruptions by Max and his contagious enthusiasm for the outing.

Tony rested his hand on the granite before jumping down a boulder that was larger than the length of his stride. He offered his hand to steady Nicole's jump. "Do you hike often?"

She hesitated for a moment and then accepted his help, her hand sliding easily into his. "Not that often. During the summer I try and do an activity of Max's choice with him once a week. It invariably requires negotiation."

"My sisters are experts at that with their kids. Let me guess. You suggested the hike instead of video games?"

She jumped, landing awkwardly in front of him, her breasts brushing his chest and her scent raining down on him. Her startled gaze reminded him of a doe in headlights and all he wanted to do was pull her in closer, tell her she was safe and kiss her until she was leaning against him needing his support.

"Mom! Tony! Hurry up!" Max's voice floated up to them.

"Sorry." Nicole immediately dropped his hand and scrambled backward as if his touch was burning her. "Max chose the hike. He did it with his dad a couple of times."

Her eyes, which had sparkled for the past hour, now filled with shadows and the memorial presence of her husband. The dead solider had inserted himself firmly between them, reestablishing unspoken boundaries.

"I can see why Max would want to repeat the fun things he did with him." *Why you'd want to.* His gut burned from a mess of emotions, none of which he wanted to acknowledge.

Jealous of a dead war hero? Not cool, man.

They'd reached the point where the rugged cliff walk joined the flatter lake path and the edge of the picnic ground was visible in the distance. He could see Max lugging the tabletop grill onto the picnic table. "I think Max is hungry."

"I'm starving." Nicole laughed, rubbing her belly.

His gaze drifted to the healthy feminine roundness that her hiking shirt hinted at and he immediately imagined his mouth against her skin. Beads of sweat broke out on his forehead and he moved his gaze to her face. "It's always good to work up an appetite."

Something flared in her eyes and then she dropped her gaze, her hands fluttering over her shorts as if she was brushing away invisible dirt. When she looked at him again, her expression was schooled into neutral. "Thanks for coming today, Tony. Max really likes you a lot and although I try and do guy things with him, like he told you, I suck at throwing a football."

Her words barreled into him, knocking him sideways as the reason he'd been invited along today glowed with crystal clarity. The invitation wasn't so Nicole could spend more time with him. She didn't need that because she was still in love with her dead husband. No, she'd invited him along because her fatherless son needed a male role model. A mentor.

The sting of disappointment whipped along his veins. It wasn't that he didn't like Max. Hell, he loved kids and he really enjoyed spending time with the little guy, but that wasn't all that he wanted.

"No problem. He's a good kid." He hated the gruffness that snuck into his voice—the tone hinting at his feelings for her.

She frowned. "I'm sorry, that sounded really rude. Of course I'm enjoying our friendship too."

Shit. She'd invoked the *let's be friends* rule. The three words every guy feared and loathed the most because being put in the friend zone was like being benched before the play had even started. Any chance of getting into the game now was virtually nonexistent. She'd drawn the friend line into the sand of their relationship.

He forced a smile. "I guess I better go do the guy thing then and help him grill."

"Oh dear." Mock horror danced across her cheeks. "If that means charcoal-black, burned brats maybe I better cook."

Her dancing eyes and flirty tone—at such stark odds with what she'd said about being friends—hit him in the chest, utterly discombobulating him. For a brief and hopeful second he wondered if he'd misheard, but he knew there was absolutely nothing wrong with his hearing. What he did know was that trying to be friends with Nicole was impossible.

TWELVE

LUKE CAME INTO the house from the morning's milking to the aroma of bacon, eggs, pancakes, syrup and coffee. On one level he knew it was wrong that his mother was cooking for him on her vacation, but there was no doubt that when his stomach was filled with a big breakfast, he coped with the long summer days so much better. Not that he couldn't fry eggs himself, it was just that time was tight and he usually grabbed coffee and toast because it was quick.

"You're lucky there's still food left." His mother handed him a fully loaded plate and a steaming mug of coffee.

"Thanks for this." He took his place at the table and flicked open the napkin.

"You're welcome. Did you get held up?" His mother poured herself a coffee and took a seat across from him.

"Hmm." He sipped his own drink, not wanting to confess to the fact he'd stayed in the dairy longer than was absolutely necessary so he could avoid sitting down to breakfast with his father. It was hard enough milking alongside his disapproving silences and his not-so-silent contempt, without extending that into meal times. At least his mother wouldn't be commenting on why he got in so late last night because the crazy hours farmers kept in summer was the perfect cover for the fact he'd been with Erin until 2:00 a.m. Part of him had wanted to stay until dawn but he'd needed to check on a cow and after that, his own bed had been a lost closer.

"You getting up early to cook and Dad getting up even earlier to milk has to be the oddest vacation the two of you have ever taken."

She wrapped her capable hands around her mug and smiled. "Oh, I don't know. We did that farm vacation when we visited you in Australia, remember? Your dad milked on five different farms and his eyes still light up when he talks about it. Then there was the French cheese tour that the Wisconsin cheese board ran."

He mopped up the yolk of his egg with his toast. "I don't remember you doing that."

"It was when you were all small and your grandparents were still living on the farm."

He couldn't remember much about his grandparents as they'd both died a long time ago in a car accident when their car had skidded on black ice. "Why France and why cheese?"

She sucked in her lips as if the memory wasn't happy. "It was a time when milk prices were particularly low and I think your father was looking for something new and he thought making cheese might be it."

He couldn't imagine his father as a cheese maker. "What happened?"

She shrugged, her expression guarded. "Who knows with farming? It was around the time his parents died and I guess milk prices went up." She drained her coffee. "Can you cope without your dad for a day or two? If I can drag him away from the farm, we're going down to Janesville to visit with Auntie Gwen."

He slid his cutlery together neatly on the plate.

"Mom, I've been running the farm without him for a year."

"Of course you have, dear, but summer's a busy time for you and I'm worried you're not getting any time off."

His mother had the work ethic of an ant so her concern on this surprised him. "Mom, you and Dad didn't have any time off in years. Our family vacations were mostly camping at the lake so Dad could continue to milk."

"I know that and it wasn't perfect either, but the world's a very different place now and your father had me to come home to at the end of the day. I just wonder if you being here on your own without any downtime is good for you."

Again, her words burrowed in uncomfortably like a tick and he moved to throw off the feeling. "Mom, we had this conversation before you left for Arizona and we really don't need to have it again. Getting married is not something I'm interested in."

Her pale blue gaze pinned him. "Why?"

He swallowed a sigh. "Because like you said, it's a different world now and settling for one person isn't the only option."

She stiffened as if he'd just sworn at her. "Neither your father or I settled, thank you very much. There's more to life than casual sex."

He choked on his incoming breath as her words whipped him and images of Erin blared in his brain. When had his mother become such a straight-shooter?

She rolled her eyes at his coughing. "You think your mother doesn't know about sex. Good grief, Luke, I've lived on a farm all my life. I also know the date and day you bought your first packet of condoms from Ackerman's market and although I disapproved that you were having sex at sixteen, I approved of your responsibility. I don't want to know about the number of women since but I can see it isn't making you happy."

His shock at the fact she'd known all this time that he'd lost his virginity at sixteen finally got pierced by anger and he grabbed it with both hands. "I'm an adult, Mom. I don't need your blessing for how I live my life. It suits me and I'm doing just fine."

Sadness filled her face and she shook her head slowly. "I don't understand how you and Keri could grow up in the same household and turn out so different. She's happily married and settled but you—" she sighed as if she was bone weary "—you have the oddest concept of what a mature relationship is all about."

He refused to have his mother turn his life into an object of pity and he quickly diverted the conversation away from him. "While we're analyzing my life, let's not forget Wade."

She glared at him. "Don't you dare turn this around onto your brother. Given the chance, he wants nothing more than to settle down."

Luke threw up his hands. "He needs to leave Whitetail to do that."

"That's nonsense."

"Really, Mom? Is it? He's Whitetail's only resident gay guy. How is he going to meet anyone if he doesn't leave town? The sale of the beach acres would give him that option."

Martha shot to her feet. "You heard Wade tell you that he doesn't want to take that option but I think you do." Her voice cracked. "I really don't understand you anymore, Luke."

He wasn't sure he understood himself either. The eddies of discontent, which had stilled somewhat started to stir again and he found himself wondering if Erin was on the farm right this minute.

ERIN FOUND WADE in the office of the B and B. She loved the cozy and welcoming feel of the old house, which Wade had told her was the original farmhouse. With its teal shutters and white gingerbread fretwork around the gables and porch, it reminded her of the last house her family had lived in before they'd lost it. She hoped the memories pounded into the stairs and walls of this house were a lot happier.

She knocked on the open door and peered around the architrave. "Hi, Wade, have you got a minute?"

He looked up from the computer—one of the few modern pieces of equipment in the room—and rubbed a deep V, which had formed at the bridge of his nose. "Oh dear. The best and most reliable cleaner I've ever had is telling me she's leaving?"

"No, not at all. I'm good for weekday cleaning for three weeks at least, but we might have to juggle things over the next two weekends, which are filled with weddings." She face-palmed herself. "I guess you're full too?"

He nodded. "We are, but my sister's going to be here so it will all work out. Believe me, you taking care of the midweek work is really helping."

"Great." She swung the conversation around to why she was really here. "I've got a problem and I could do with your advice."

He stood up and waved her onto the Queen Anne club chair before crossing to a side table. It was set with teacups, a fine china, rose-covered teapot and an antique cake stand. Her mouth started watering at the idea of tasting one or more of the many tiny cakes and slices.

Wade, a self-confessed Anglophile, gestured to the pot. "I've just served afternoon tea to the B and B guests. Would you like some?"

"I'd love some, thank you." Visiting Wade was like stepping back in time and she sank into the old leather chair, the history of a thousand stories and conversations welcoming her.

He passed her a napkin and a plate of cakes before pouring her tea. When he'd made sure she had everything she needed, he sat down at his wide, walnut desk, propped his chin in his hands and said, "Tell me."

"The bride who's having her photos taken in the sunflower field now wants to get married there too."

Wade's eyes lit up. "That's fantastic news. This could be the start of the farm and the B and B being another venue for weddings. The bridal party could get dressed in the house and using your photos I could add a whole page to the website." He clicked on the mouse and peered at his screen. "What weekend is that again?"

"The fifteenth."

He clapped his hands and grinned at her, his excitement palpable. "I got a cancellation on the honeymoon suite yesterday from a couple who'd wanted it for their anniversary. Some things are meant to be."

She put down her cup and saucer with a rattle, worried he was getting way ahead of himself. "Wade, I don't know if you're aware but when I originally asked Luke to give permission for the photos he said no."

Wade's lips thinned and she thought she heard him mutter *that figures* but she must have misheard because the night she'd met them both in the parlor, the brothers seemed to share a genuine camaraderie.

She blew out a breath. "So, I was thinking, seeing as the wedding could involve the B and B, you could be the one to ask him?"

He shook his head. "No."

No? "But he's more likely to say yes to you than to me."

He sighed. "You know the adage about family and money. Since my parents arrived, some family stuff's happened and right now I'm the last person to ask him." He tapped his chin. "Actually, I'm not certain we even need his permission."

A tremor of unease ratcheted up her spine. "But it's his farm."

"No, it's the family's farm." A steely glint appeared in Wade's usually friendly eyes. "Luke's running it at the moment but that could change."

Really? She bit into a delicious chocolate cake filled with decadent hazelnut cream and remembered the night he was drunk was the same night his parents had arrived.

I was hoping to forget the farm. She realized yet again how little she knew about Luke. They had sex but they never really talked.

One thing she did know was he could be as stubborn as a mule and given Wade's intransigent look maybe that was a familial trait. If Wade bypassed talking to Luke she could see them losing the field completely and with it losing her shot at the Memmy. She shivered at the thought.

It wasn't her job to fix the problem between the two brothers but she didn't like the thought of this wedding driving an even bigger wedge between them. She knew all about families, money and the fallout. Her need to keep everyone happy had her mind spinning, looking for solutions.

Wade tapped a pen against a legal pad. "How did you get Luke to change his mind last time?"

"I didn't. It was Nicole."

"Ah."

"Ah?" Obviously there was some significance attached to that, which she had no clue about. "Does Nicole have magic powers?"

"No, but her husband, who was born and raised in Whitetail, died last year in Afghanistan, serving our country. I think all of us feel guilty about it so we generally do whatever she asks."

So Nicole was Luke's Achilles' heel. Could it work again?

"I've got an idea." She sat forward excitedly. "Given we both think Luke will say no to us, we need to talk to Nicole. If she can get Luke to agree then I'll tell Connie she must use Nicole as the wedding planner and your B and B as her bridal party's dressing rooms along with prewedding drinks and canapés. Everybody wins."

Everybody except Luke.

She blocked out the rogue thought. Business was business and it wasn't like she was being devious. Nicole, as the wedding planner, had the right to ask Luke and he had the right to say no. But she was pretty sure he wouldn't.

Wade beamed at her. "Clever girl. We need to talk to Nicole right away."

TONY HAD DELIBERATELY missed stopping by the grocery store for coffee the past few mornings. Instead, he'd made his own at home, poured it into a traveler cup and had driven directly to the station. Life was busy with training sessions for his mainly volunteer force. He was whipping them into a slick firefighting machine as well as liaising with the Department of Natural Resources about fire permits. Three times his team had been called out to attend brush fires lit by vacationers who had no clue that a hot, windy day was the worst time to light a fire.

He'd spent this morning doing some door knocking and general fire education among the vacationers who owned their properties and he was now on his way back into town. As soon as he got back, he was going directly to the real estate agent's office. Ellery Johnston did most of the holiday rentals and Tony wanted fire-education pamphlets inserted into the display folders in each cottage, along with the more vacation-specific brochures on where to rent a Jet Ski and White-tail Market and Video's home delivery service. Vacationers needed to know the risks and respect the heavily wooded environment.

He slowed for an intersection on the minor county road and was surprised to see a sign saying Del's Diner. It was a run-down-looking establishment, tucked away on a quiet road but the parking lot was full. It was way past lunch so he decided to stop by and see if they could do a decent BLT. It would make a nice change from Sven's Swedish Smörgåsbord.

As he opened the door, a wall of noise rolled out to meet him. The place was packed, and a huge guy dressed top-to-toe in white called out from behind the counter, "What's it gonna be?"

Tony grinned. This reminded him of Jersey. "What's the choice?"

"Burger, burger or burger." A beefy hand waved toward the menu. "They all come with butter."

Of course they did. With butter and cheese, because now he lived in the dairy state. "I'll have a double cheeseburger with everything on and a coffee."

"Good choice. Find a seat and we'll find you," the guy replied, turning back to the grill and whacking two burgers down.

Tony scanned the crowd looking for a busboy working on a table, which might indicate a free seat. A flash of blond hair caught his eye and he paused, automatically looking for Nicole only to realize the head belonged to a guy and the color was more gold than her ash white. Hell, he had it bad. Whitetail was full of Swedish descendants and blond hair was as common here as black hair was in Jersey. He started to move down the narrow line between tables.

"Tony, hi, over here."

He didn't have to turn his head to know who was calling him. Her voice featured nightly in his dreams despite his trying very hard to exile it. He looked left. Nicole was sitting in a booth with the blond-headed guy. Even though Tony was one hundred and ten percent heterosexual, he had to admit the guy was a good-looking bastard. He wanted to storm over and shirtfront him.

He raised his hand, acknowledging he'd seen and heard her.

Her smile—hesitant at first—broke free and he felt three days of good intentions to stay away from her start to crumble.

"Come sit with us," she called out.

He wanted to refuse but their booth looked like it had the only spare seat so he reluctantly made his way over.

"Tony, this is Luke Anderson."

The guy had risen to his feet and towered over him. Tony gave a curt nod and shook his hand. "Tony Lascio, new fire chief."

Luke returned the shake with a genuine smile. "Good to meet you. Sorry I missed your welcome. Summer on the farm's pretty intense."

A woman, wearing fashionable clothes and matching accessories, rushed up to the table. She had a large bag slung over her shoulder and she stopped abruptly, her expression startled. "Nicole? Hi." She turned to Luke. "Sorry I'm late. My GPS battery went flat and I didn't have the charger in the car."

"Did ya turn roight where I told ya?"

Luke suddenly sounded part British with a hint of strangled Australian and Tony gave Nicole a questioning look.

Her shoulders rose as if to say *I have no idea*.

Erin laughed but her eyes stayed firmly fixed on Luke's, sharing the in-joke. "I promise you that I did everything you said."

Luke rolled his eyes but his grin was pure affection. "I swear, you get lost standing still." He extended his arm. "Erin, this is Tony. Erin's an excellent photographer but with a lousy sense of direction."

"Wedding photographer," Nicole added.

Tony shook Erin's hand and noticed that Luke's now rested on the small of her back. *Okay then*. He recognized that signal—the farmer was claiming the photographer. He had no problems with that at all and he took his seat next to Nicole just as his burger arrived.

"How's the sunflower field coming along, Luke?" Nicole asked.

Luke smacked Erin's fingers as she tried to sneak two fries out of his red burger basket. "It will flower when it's ready. Given the forecast, that will be right on time for the damn wedding." He looked at Tony by way of explanation. "Some bat-crazy bride wants her photos taken in my field."

Both women flinched.

Tony gave a noncommittal nod mid-chew. With four sisters and having been married himself, he was a wedding veteran but he could understand the bachelor's take on the whole deal.

Nicole leaned forward. "I've had a new request from the bride."

Luke gave Erin a questioning look but she was intently reading the label on the ketchup bottle and missed it.

Luke sighed. "What is it?"

"She wants to have the ceremony on the farm with the sunflowers as the backdrop."

This time the farmer flinched. "No."

Nicole acted as if she hadn't heard him. "This wouldn't involve you or the farmhouse in any way. Wade's offered the B and B for the bridal party and he tells me that guests can access the field from an external road so there's minimal disruption to you."

Luke took the ketchup bottle out of Erin's hand to get her attention and he pinned her with a gaze, which declared that looking away wasn't an option. "Wade knows about this?"

The photographer's eyes widened into pools of iridescent green but before she said a word, Nicole interrupted with, "Luke, I discussed this with Wade because the farm should benefit in some way from this."

The farmer's gaze swung to Nicole, his face stiff with tension. "The B and B is a totally separate business."

"But Wade uses the farm in his advertising so I thought..." Nicole frowned. "Connie Littlejohn will of course pay for rental of the field and you can ask an outrageous price for it."

"I don't want money."

The words came out through gritted teeth and Tony saw the war of emotions on Luke's face. He'd already said no so why did he look like he was wavering when he was clearly unhappy about it?

Nicole fiddled with her wedding band. "You can always donate the money to the town's support fund."

The farmer's jaw was so tight that Tony thought it would snap. What was going on here?

He glanced between the three of them. The photographer's mouth was closed but her throat was working and Luke's gaze was now fixed on the third finger of Nicole's left hand as she sat quietly waiting for a reply.

The town owns his memory.

His burger stuck in his throat. Her dead husband was every goddamn place he turned.

THIRTEEN

NICOLE WATCHED TONY ball his napkin and toss it into the empty basket before rising to his feet.

"Nice to meet you all but I've got work waiting."

A zip of regret turned the delicious burger in her stomach to stone. She'd hoped he'd stay longer so they could actually talk rather than him having only been a silent observer in a wedding business meeting.

Luke stood up to shake his hand. "Erin and I will walk out with you."

"Sorry, Luke, change of plan," Erin said. "Now you've said yes to the Littlejohn wedding, Nicole and I have a bunch of things to sort out."

Annoyance played around his lips. "I can still change my mind."

Erin laughed but the sound was brittle. "Can we re-schedule our, um…" she bit her lip "…appointment? I'm free from six after I've finished a studio shoot. I could bring some of that chocolate peanut butter ice cream you want to try back with me."

Nicole's gaze swung between the two of them, her interest piqued.

Luke's eyes twinkled. "That might go some way toward easing the inconvenience. Just make sure you don't get lost because it will melt."

Luke walked out with Tony and as soon as the diner

door closed behind them, Nicole blurted out, "Oh my God, you and Luke are having sex. I'm so envious."

Erin blinked and looked worried. "I'm sorry. I didn't know that you had a thing for Luke."

She shook her head. "I don't." She fiddled with her wedding ring, which she had a habit of doing when she was nervous, and then realized what she was doing and sat on her hands. "I like Tony but I'm not sure he feels the same way.

"We've sort of been doing this quiet, slow-burn thing with both of us arriving to buy coffee at the same time every morning, and we spent a fun day together hiking with Max. I thought it went great but since then I haven't seen him anywhere, and you saw right now, how he couldn't leave quick enough."

Erin wriggled her nose. "Did something specific happen that might have made him want to avoid you? Some uncomfortable moment?"

Nicole thought back to the hike and with a groan dropped her head in her hands.

"What?"

She raised her gaze. "I told him how much I appreciated his friendship."

"Oh, dear." Erin gave her an affectionate yet pitying look. "You really are out of practice."

"I was never *in* practice." Her voice rose on a squeak and she sucked in a deep breath. "I married my high school sweetheart and he was the only guy I've ever been with. He died over a year ago."

Erin looked thoughtful. "This might sound blunt, but if you're really ready to move on and you're interested in the chief, it might be time to part with your wedding ring."

She brought her hand back to the table and stared at the gold band that had been there for so long she barely noticed it anymore. Once, she'd ripped it off her finger and sent it spinning across her dresser where it had rolled off the edge to rest with the dust bunnies. A week later, she'd been forced to retrieve it and slide it back on to get through Bradley's funeral. Its absence would have sparked questions she was too shocked and angry to deal with. She'd intended to take it off again immediately after, but that was before she'd been hit with everyone else's grief. It had gotten harder and harder to find the right time to remove it.

Erin was right. It was giving out the wrong message to Tony and she tugged it off, zipping it quickly into her purse. "I'm not sure taking it off is enough. The problem is that the last time I dated, Britney Spears was a young, sweet thing launching her debut album, so basically, I'm clueless."

Erin sipped her milkshake. "What about getting a sitter for Max and inviting him out to supper?"

Nicole's fingers reached to swivel the ring and found only skin. "Won't that look like I'm desperate? I mean I was the one who asked him out on the hike and he's avoided me ever since."

Erin laughed. "He didn't avoid you today."

"He didn't stay long either."

"Women *are* allowed to make the first move you know, Nicole. I have a tiny sidearm to my business called boudoir photography. You'd be surprised how many women want to have tasteful photographs taken of themselves, which show their sexy side. They make the perfect gift for a lover."

Erin got a dreamy look on her face. "Personally, I

love taking these photos in black and white. There's something elemental about the medium and with your hair out and some gorgeous lingerie, the pictures would be amazing."

The idea both appealed and terrified her. "Wouldn't that be rushing things? I mean we're both so restrained and polite around each other that I want to scream."

"Like I said before, the ring was probably seriously getting in the way. Perhaps the chief needs something like a gorgeous photo so he stops seeing the widow Nicole and starts seeing the woman?"

Her mouth dried as quivers of excitement thrummed inside her. Could she really do something like that? Something so bold?

What if he really isn't interested?

Fear instantly doused the excitement. "Maybe I'll start with supper first and see how that goes."

Erin smiled. "Sure. You need to do whatever makes you feel most comfortable, but if you ever change your mind, just call me."

HAVE TUB OF ice cream, two spoons and am naked. E.

Luke read the text and grinned. He'd known for a couple of hours that she was back at the cottage. He'd seen her car when he'd gone down to check on a problematic irrigator but he loved the way she was letting him know. He couldn't deny he'd been ticked off when she'd passed on their planned matinee this afternoon but it looked like she was making it up to him now.

He whistled Mac and drove to the cottage. He found Erin dressed in her cow pajamas staring at her computer screen. A bride with a faraway look in her eyes was gazing across the lake as if that was where her future lay and she couldn't wait to step into it. The raw emotion on her face—happiness, excitement and a belief that this was her path—caught him in the chest. God, he'd love to be that sure of his life again.

He tried to block the envy. "I thought you were naked." The tightness of his throat made the words sound harsh.

Two small lines appeared at the bridge of Erin's nose and her eyes flickered. "Everything okay?"

No. "Everything's fine except for those damn cow pajamas." He gently tugged her to her feet. "Like I said, I thought you were naked."

Her fingers caressed his temple before burying themselves in his hair. "I imagine I will be very soon."

Her husky voice drove him to action. He tugged the offending shirt over her head and called her dog. "Prove your worth, Maggie-May. Go play." He balled the shirt and threw it at the dog.

"Hey, they're my only pajamas," Erin protested, her breasts moving against his chest as she reached for his outstretched arm.

He upended her and amidst her token squeals of protest, he whipped off the pajama bottoms and tossed them to Mac. As the dogs took off, wrestling with the clothing, he pulled her into his lap and gazed at her appreciatively. "Now *this* is so much better."

She wrapped her arms around his neck. "You do realize they're going to play tug-of-war with them and shred them to pieces."

"That's the general idea, yes." He kissed her.

She moved her lips from his and hooked him with a penetrating gaze. "I thought you liked cows."

This thing with Erin was all about forgetting the farm, not talking and thinking about it even more. He nuzzled the hollow in her neck—the place he knew from experience made her stop talking and start panting. Her head fell back, and her breathing quickened.

Now we're talking. This was the only conversation he wanted right now and it didn't involve the language of words.

Using his tongue, he traced a line straight down to his favorite place, the spot that nestled between her two beautiful breasts. He let his face rest there for a moment, savoring the pillow softness that caressed his cheeks. She smelled of vanilla and tasted of salt and he couldn't get enough of the feel of her body. Reverently, he cupped her breasts in his hands, savoring the weight of them against his palm.

She gave a moan of pleasure and he felt her breasts tighten. He grinned. He'd never had a lover this responsive. Very slowly, he moved the pad of his thumbs across her nipples. Her body jerked and her eyes opened as wide as a cat's. In the clear, green depths he clearly read desire—hot, molten need for him.

And God, he wanted her. Sex with Erin—losing himself in her lush body—drove every unsettled thought from his mind. It gave him a break from the farm, from his family, from his life, and it was beyond fun playing these sex games with her. He lowered his mouth planning to draw one dusky, erect nipple into his mouth and tantalize her with his tongue to the point of screaming, when he felt her palms pushing firmly on his chest, sending him tumbling backward onto the bed. A second later she was straddling him.

He stared up at her and shook his head. "You have control issues, Erin Davis."

Her eyes danced. "No, I just know what I like."

Her fingers tweaked his nipples and red-hot blood streaked to his groin, making him ache in the most delicious way. She leaned over him, her breasts caressing his chest, and kissed him hard.

Stars exploded in his head as her tongue both stroked and lashed, giving and taking, making his body burn with a visceral craving. He felt his mind slipping as her hand closed around him and started to move firmly and rhythmically up and down. He fought the feeling. He loved that she was so sexually confident but this time he wanted to call the play. He wanted to feel her muscles gripping him, not her hand. He wanted to watch her shatter as his thrusts sent her over the edge.

His hands found her hips, gripping them, and then he kneaded her buttocks as his mouth wrenched back control of the kiss. He plundered her mouth and swallowed her moans of pleasure. As her body slackened, he flipped her over onto her back and caught her hands in his.

Surprise thundered through Erin as she felt the pressure of the mattress against her back and Luke's fingers loosely around her wrists, pinning them to the bed. She trusted him implicitly but a tiny part of her felt exposed and vulnerable. "Wh…what are you doing?"

He smiled down at her. "I promise you, you're going to like it."

"I liked what we were doing a second ago." *I knew what I was doing. I was in charge.*

"You'll like this just as much."

His hands slid down her body, setting up a delicious shiver from head to toe, and then he was pulling her gently across the bed until her buttocks rested on the edge. He rose to his feet and she was momentarily distracted by the sight of him—thick, erect and beautiful.

"Comfy?" he asked.

She blinked, remembering where she was. "Uh-huh."

"Good." His hands lifted her thighs, raising her legs until they touched his chest.

"Luke, I'm not a gymnast. Are you sure—"

"Do you trust me?" Intense blue eyes hooked hers.

"Yes."

"Then let me show you what can happen if you give up the need to be in charge all the time."

He had no idea what he was asking of her. She hadn't allowed anyone to be in charge of her since she was eighteen because that way no one could let her down. Her hands automatically gripped the sheet as every part of her railed against the fact he was asking her to hand over the reins to him.

"Relax, it's going to be fine."

She wasn't convinced.

He kissed the back of her knee before resting her calves against his shoulders. A moment later his fingers found her slick, wet clitoris and stroked it in small, magic circles.

Her body instantly liquefied, giving in to the pleasure and betraying her mind by overruling the fact she was flat on her back with her legs in the air, not able to move or even reach Luke with her hands.

As the warm, rich ball of heat started to build inside her, Luke gently entered her.

"Oh," she breathed out in wonder. "That feels amazing."

"I promise you," he said huskily, "there's more."

Each thrust sent him deeper and deeper and still his fingers caressed her. Hot, tingling, tempting sensations spiraled inside her, calling her to catch hold and ride with them. She sucked in short, sharp breaths, somehow unable to fill her lungs completely as her body forged its own path and she was swept along in the slipstream.

He moved against her, stretching and filling her completely, each stroke making her gasp. Her muscles convulsed, gripping him, never wanting to let him go and urging him to keep touching the spot that made her both heavy and light all at the same time. She wanted to consume him until he was part of her.

"Oh, God." Her head thrashed against the bed as the sensations met each other, merging into one. She burned for more of the same, yet fought it, too, because with each thrust she lost more and more control over her body.

I need to pee.

She gasped, horrified at the thought, which tried to settle and rule her. "Luke, I— Oh!" Her body rejected all thought with another wave of mind-altering pleasure. It hit her, catching her up in its promise of even better things to come and she followed it willingly, desperately and addictively. "Keep. Doing. That."

"You. Bet."

His breathless voice rained over her as her body started to shake.

Luke's hands tightened on her legs as he plunged into her.

"Yes!" she heard her mouth shout as her mind gave way completely. She was melting and exploding as wave after wave of sublime intensity rocked her unlike anything she'd ever known. Tingling streaked from her toes to her hair and the room vanished in a vortex of bliss as she spun out, separating from Luke and flung far from everything familiar, including herself.

LUKE LAY ON his back next to a boneless Erin and grinned. He'd not only made her beg for him to keep going but he'd sent her flying. Watching her come apart had been almost as amazing as his own orgasm. Usually, he was the one who fell asleep pretty fast after sex but tonight he was too wired. He'd stared at the photo on her computer screen. He didn't particularly want to look at it but it had a hypnotic effect and kept on drawing his gaze. "That's not your average bride photo."

Erin slowly rubbed her foot against his calf and beamed. "Thank you. You're looking at the Erin Davis touch." The pride in her voice was unmistakable.

"You mean you use Photoshop?"

She slapped his chest indignantly. "No, I do not."

He quirked a brow.

"Only to even out skin tones because no one needs acne on their wedding-day photos. What I'm talking about is the inner glow Jenna has. It radiates from her, doesn't it? It's why you keep looking at it."

"She looks hopeful and optimistic." Two things he missed.

"She does, but fifteen minutes before I took that shot, she was in a furious argument with her mother."

He rolled onto his side to face her. "So really, this isn't a true depiction of her day at all."

"You think she wants to be reminded of how her mother tried to control her wedding?" Her voice developed an edge. "My job is to show happiness and to that end I can and will make any bride look happy. Life has enough crap and sadness in it and I refuse to record it."

Show happiness. He stroked her hair as her words blasted into him. Shouldn't that be showing love? "Has your life had crap and sadness in it?"

She stiffened against him. "Oh, you know, divorce, bankruptcy, just the usual stuff."

He knew about manageable debt but he'd not experienced the other things. Had she? The idea that she might have been married surprised him. Drawing back slightly, he looked into her eyes for clues. "You're divorced?"

She shook her head. "God, no. That would mean I was once dumb enough to get married. No, it was my parents who got divorced."

He understood her feelings on marriage as they mirrored his own, but something made him think of her tattoo. "Because of the bankruptcy?"

"Sort of. It was the final straw in a long line of financial indiscretions."

"Want to tell me about it?"

She wriggled her nose. "It's all pretty boring, really."

He doubted that. "Try me."

She met his gaze, her eyes swirling with a thousand thoughts and then she moved into him, resting her forehead on his chest. The hair on the back of her head tickled his nose and he fully expected her to change the subject.

"My father calls himself an entrepreneur." Her voice was muffled against his skin. "My mother calls him a gambler."

He stroked her hair. "Horses? Slots?"

"Nope. Businesses." Her sigh rolled the length of her body and she flipped onto her back but her legs stayed tangled with his. "High risk with big returns. Only, there's a massive downside to businesses like that."

Her fingers fiddled with the top sheet as if she was having an internal argument. Silence played out between them and then, slowly, she started talking again. "Financial highs and lows punctuated our lives. I've only got snapshot memories from when I was young. Stuff like Mom giving me clothes to wear that I knew had belonged to my cousins and the look on her face, which was at odds with her words when she told me I was lucky because they were mine now."

She blew out a breath. "I remember being woken up at night by the sound of raised voices and if I wasn't trying to soothe my crying baby brother, I was cuddling up to my teddy bear to try and block out the sound. They're only vague recollections, though, because when I was in the fourth grade we moved to Highland Park."

"Where's that?"

"A leafy Chicago suburb. We had a big house with a yard and a swing hanging from an old oak tree. I went to private school and I grew up with pretty much everything a preteen and teen girl could want."

He thought about her clothes. "Pink everything?"

She gave a wry smile. "Pink and purple did feature some, yes."

He reached out to trace the length of her arm. "Did everything include a camera?"

"It did." The smile in her voice wrapped around him. "Dad bought me my first camera at ten and it was pretty much love at first sight. There's something about being able to isolate a moment in time and—"

She sat up abruptly, pulled on his T-shirt and padded into the other room.

He tugged on his pants and followed, finding her sitting at the counter eating ice cream. He sat down next to her, accepted the proffered spoon and squeezed her hand. "Sorry. I didn't realize it was a story that needed ice cream."

She grimaced. "It's a story that needs Jack but I don't have any."

Looking at the pain in her eyes he knew he should say *if it's going to upset you, you don't have to tell me*. Only he knew he couldn't say that because he really wanted to know her story.

While he waited for her to start talking again, he sampled the ice cream. He'd always loved ice cream and he savored it with the same concentration that a sommelier tasted wine. It was good but nothing startling and he thought it could have been a lot creamier and the flavor more pronounced.

Erin twirled her spoon in her fingers. "When I was fourteen, the arguments started again. My mother always looked drawn and strained and Dad was away a lot. I retreated. I spent lots of time taking photos of my friends, of people having fun doing crazy things and I spent even more time in my darkroom developing them, even though by then I had a digital camera. I still love using film." She scooped up more ice cream and sighed. "Just after my fifteenth birthday I came home to find a massive moving van parked out front and three burly guys marching all our possessions, including my cameras, out of the house. My father had gone to ground, leaving Mom to deal with the trauma and the embarrassment of losing everything while our neighbors stood on the sidewalk watching."

He knew farmers who'd been forced off their land but he could only imagine the gut-wrenching trauma of losing everything. He didn't know what to say. Sorry sounded lame so he pressed a kiss into her hair.

She blinked three or four times and ate more ice cream. "We had our clothes and that was about it. Without money, I had to change schools and obviously we had to move out of the area. Every connection I'd ever known, the camera club, Girl Scouts, school friends, all got severed. I learned really fast about the differences between true friendship and acquaintants. Tragically, so did my mother. We spent a month with my grandparents and then Dad showed up. I hated what he'd done to us but it took him less than two weeks to convince Mom we needed to be together as a family."

She snorted. "So started three years of constant moving. I went to five high schools as we traipsed across the country with Dad, following the next *surefire thing*."

"And did he find it?"

She nodded. "He did, but by then my mother had collapsed from emotional exhaustion and had spent time in the hospital. She never really recovered and she died crossing the street one day when she stepped out in front of a truck. Jesse and I ended up living with Mom's sister and I went to community college."

"And your dad?"

"He dropped in and out of our lives but I haven't seen him in three years." She bit her lip. "It's better that way. It saves me hoping he's changed and then getting hurt again."

He didn't know what to say. Right now things were rough between him and his father but just the thought of not seeing him hurt. Then again, Vernon hadn't monumentally let him down.

Raising her head she looked straight at him, daring him not to pity her. "So that's my sorry story but I promise you, I am *never* going to be put in a situation like that again. Ever."

In her eyes he glimpsed the hurt, angry and bewildered fifteen-year-old who'd lost everything secure in her life. Now her tattoo and driving work ethic made total sense and so did her lovely clothes. After years of hand-me-downs he understood her need to wear clothes that she'd chosen. He, on the other hand, had grown up surrounded by stability—something he'd never really thought about much until recently when the solidness of the farm had started suffocating him.

He slid off the stool and drew her into his arms. Unlike other times when her body touched his and he instantly went hard and all his thoughts were about burying himself deep inside her, this time he had an irrational need to just hold her. Keep her safe and sheltered.

"Ah, Luke." Her voice was muffled against his shoulder. "Too tight. You're suffocating me."

"Sorry." With a jolt of panic, he realized what he was doing and dropped his arms.

She rubbed her upper arms against the potential bruise from his crushing hug. "No, I'm sorry. This is a perfect example of why I don't tell people that story. That and I can't afford the ice cream calorie consumption." Her laugh held strain. "We need to lift the mood by finding happy and I know exactly where to find it."

Her hands trailed down his chest and slid under the waistband of his pants until she was stroking him and all coherent thought fled. He stumbled backward, pulling her with him to the couch. He fell back but she didn't follow. Instead, she kneeled between his knees.

He'd expected sex but the fact she was suggesting

oral sex both excited and surprised him. She'd always been generous in bed, but she'd not initiated a blowjob before. Something made him say, "I don't expect this. You don't have to."

She pursed her lips. "Maybe I just want to."

With a sharp jerk, she tugged his pants out of the way and then starting using her hands, mouth and teeth in a wicked yet determined combination. Silver spots spun across his vision.

His blood grew thick with pulsing need and he felt himself starting to spiral up into the pleasure whirl. His hands sought her hair, desperate to touch her, to feel her skin under his hands, to connect with her. He hadn't realized how important that was to him until this very second but she shook his hands away and her mouth took him deeper.

Any regret that he wasn't holding her fell away as his body took over, drowning in the rising, exquisite sensations and canceling all coherent thought. As every muscle in his body teetered on the edge of oblivion, she glanced up at him, her eyes overly bright, glittering green and swirling with memories.

He tumbled into the orgasm knowing she'd just used him to block out her past.

WITH THE AFTERNOON sunshine streaming in through the car window, Martha glanced across at the profile of her husband of thirty-six years. His hair, once as golden as ripened wheat, was now white but it was still as thick today as it ever had been. A life spent outdoors gave him a healthy tan and he was as fit as when she'd met him at the state fair all those years ago. She put her hand on his jean-clad thigh. He immediately covered it with his own and smiled before returning his gaze to the road ahead.

She sighed. "It was nice to visit with Gwen and have some time away from the farm."

"You've had eleven months off of the farm," Vern said mildly.

"I know, but these last few weeks haven't quite been the vacation I imagined."

Vern didn't reply but she noticed his jaw stiffen. Since arriving back in Wisconsin, her husband had been tense and irritable. She'd put it down to him missing his golf games. For a man who'd retired, he still rose every morning at dawn like he'd always done, only in Arizona he'd exchanged milking for golf. Now it was the other way around.

She gently squeezed his thigh. "Have you gotten any further with Luke, finding out what his plans are?"

Vernon thumped the steering wheel. "That boy doesn't know his ass from his elbow."

She withdrew her hand. "You know that isn't so. Something's bothering him and we need to find out what it is. I've tried but no luck. I hoped he'd tell you."

"He's not saying squat."

Just like you. Over the years she'd learned to ride out the times when Vern closed down. Early in their marriage she'd believed his distracted silences were the result of something she'd said or done to upset him, but with time and maturity came understanding. Nine times out of ten his silences had nothing to do with her and were usually related to a problem on the farm. It had taken her a long time to work out that those silences meant he was thinking—working his way through issues such as why the tractor wouldn't start, why his best milker was off her feed and, in the early days when money was tight, how he'd manage to pay the vet's bill or the bank. He'd be so busy working out the problem that he'd completely tune out everything else.

"Do you think it's the farm, Vern? Is he losing money?"

He shook his head. "The books look good and his changes to the parlor have made milking easier."

Martha heard the grudging respect in his voice. "Then what can it be?"

"Dunno, but what I do know is, we're gonna have to move back here."

No! Her heart hammered hard against her chest as trepidation settled in. "But this is our time."

He frowned at her. "What were the last thirty years then?"

"Don't be like that. You know what I mean. You've worked hard for years and now it's time to slow down."

"For God's sake, Martha, I'm fifty-seven not seventy." His sharp, critical tone sliced into her. "There's no way I'm allowing the farm to be sold."

"And what happens when you're seventy?"

"Keri's kids can continue the line."

"Oh, Vern, they're city kids. You know that isn't going to happen."

The jut of his jaw was intransigent and she could see her new life in Arizona—one of golf, bridge, volunteering and not an iota of snow—being torn from her. She'd given thirty years of service to the farm—to the family business. She'd served it with care and devotion, shared her husband with it and raised a family on it. Now it was time off for good behavior, to be free of the 24/7 demands that were both the joy and the bind of farm life.

No way was she letting her new life in Arizona slip away from her. Come hell or high water, she was going to find a solution that kept Luke on the farm.

WANT TO TRAVEL *to reception on a hay cart. Arrange it. Connie.*

A hay cart? Erin blinked at the text wondering why it had come to her and not Nicole. Connie, with her stiletto heels and designer clothes, was an urbanite through and through, but if she wanted a hay cart, she'd have a hay cart. Erin almost texted back, *Do you know how scratchy that stuff is?* But instead she typed, *On it.*

She and Luke had rolled in the hay—literally—two nights ago after she'd made a quip about him being boring and always wanting to have sex in a bed. He'd marched her to the barn, chased her up a ladder into the hay loft and pulled her down with him. The sex had been joyous and fun but she'd conceded that the bed was indeed a lot more comfortable than hay, which spiked her in a variety of places. Plus, she was still finding bits of it in her clothes.

Sex with Luke was always an adventure but she bit her lip against the trembling pull of need that she was fast losing control over. He just had to wink at her and she was wet and panting and although on one level it was amazingly erotic, on another it was downright terrifying. She didn't want to need anyone because that way no one could let her down. It was safer that way.

Pulling her mind back to business, she forwarded Connie's message to Nicole who was a magician at sourcing things. The wedding was getting closer and both she and Nicole were dividing up the thousand details that made a wedding memorable. One part of her was pleased Nicole was on board because Connie's requests seemed to be doubling daily and she had no desire to swap photography for wedding planning.

She moved on to the next text.

Picnic in the woods behind the B&B at noon. Have made Caesar salad wraps. Please come and bring Maggie-May. Wade.

She hung up her cleaning bucket and checked her watch. It was 11:50. Perfect timing. She could enjoy a lunch she hadn't made herself and still have time to keep her appointment with Lindsay and Keith who were now back from their honeymoon. She couldn't wait to show them her suggestions for their album.

As she called Maggie-May, her phone beeped two more times.

Erin, your dear old dad is feeling unloved. I miss you.

A throb set up at her temple and her thumb hovered over the call button but she couldn't make herself press it. She opened the other text.

The scarecrow says thank you. L

A picture was attached and she laughed out loud. Her cow pajamas were now gracing the scarecrow near the sunflower field, complete with the large hole Mac and Maggie-May had torn into one of the pant legs.

While she and Maggie-May walked down the trail that led from the cottages into the woods, she texted back, *Tell Scarecrow that theft of pajamas means I only have my rubber boots to wear to bed.*

The reply was instant. *The scarecrow wants pictures.*

Laughter and a melee of voices, including children, floated on the air and Maggie-May strained on the leash, wanting to hurl herself into the middle of the action. Wade had tied a red ribbon around a tree trunk and she cut off the path through the grove of birches following the noise. Just before she cleared the grove, she stopped and brought her camera up to her eye.

In the clearing, a girl and a boy were squealing with delight and chasing Wade who was dodging and weaving to avoid being tagged. Mac was barking and racing around the perimeter, trying to round them up as if they were sheep. A woman, who had the same keen eyes as Luke and the stocky build of Wade, sat watching them, calling out tips and egging them on to *bring Uncle Wade down*. A man she assumed was the woman's husband lay on a picnic rug with one arm slung over his eyes and the other resting gently on the woman's back.

She set her camera to a fast shutter speed to catch the action and took ten shots in quick succession. Then she moved her camera left. Luke squatted at the fence line. Even though he was technically sharing the same space as the other picnickers, he was completely distanced from the group. One hand held soil, which dribbled through his fingers, and his gaze was fixed far in the distance, out across the emerald fields of the farm. He was a man surveying his domain. His land. She reset her camera, zoomed in, focused and captured the moment.

Maggie-May took advantage of her distraction and with much joyous barking, raced into the melee of kids and dog and tag.

Luke immediately stood up and looked beyond Maggie-May, his face creased in a frown until his gaze found her. Then he smiled.

Erin's chest tightened, making it hard to breathe. She gave herself a shake, wondering what on earth was wrong with her. It wasn't like Luke never smiled at her. He did—every time he saw her—and mostly it involved a wicked twinkle in his eyes, which meant he was planning to get her clothes off her as fast as possible. An intent that suited both of them.

He strode toward her, surprise clear on his face but when he met her, he walked her back slightly until the trees screened them from view. He pulled her close, kissing her. "I didn't know you were coming."

"Neither did I until Wade texted me." She scanned his face wondering if her being here crossed the unspoken rule of summer flings. "It looks like a family thing though. I don't have to stay if it's going to make things weird."

A slight frown marred his high forehead. "It's not going to make things weird. My family is that already." He caught her hand, and before she could protest, he walked her into the center of the group. "Keri, Phil, this is Erin."

"The photographer who can cook?" Keri shot to her feet, her face filled with interest. She gave Phil a nudge to get up.

Luke rolled his eyes at his sister and squeezed Erin's hand as if reassuring her. "Yes, but don't even think about putting her in service to bake for you. That's why you have Phil."

Phil wrapped his arms around his wife, pulled her back against him and rested his chin on her head. "I baked her a lemon meringue pie the night I proposed, Erin. It was my guarantee of getting a yes."

Erin quickly disengaged her hand from Luke's, not wanting to give his family the impression they were a real couple. At the same time, she tried to shrug off the odd feeling that Keri knew about her. "I'm really more of a photographer than a cook."

Keri's eyes lit up. "Could you take our photo?"

"Keri." Luke's tone held a warning growl.

"What?" His sister's eyes filled with feigned innocence. "I meant all of us together. It would be a great present for Mom and Dad to take back to Arizona." She fixed her attention on Erin. "Of course, we'll visit you at your studio and pay you for your time."

Erin smiled at Keri. "I'm happy to take a family shot. Let's do it now."

Keri looked askance. "But we're not dressed."

"You look dressed to me and more importantly you look happy and relaxed. Wouldn't your parents want a photo of you all together on the farm? Where you grew up? A place that belongs to you all?"

"Did you hear that, Luke?" Wade asked with an edge to his voice as he joined the group. "The farm belongs to us all."

"You better name your price, Erin." Luke's shoulders stiffened as he tilted his head between his siblings. "These two are known to argue over money."

Keri shot both her brothers a killing look before smiling apologetically at Erin. "Please ignore them."

Erin glanced between them all, knowing she was caught in the middle of something that was making them unhappy. Luke wore the grumpy expression he'd specialized in the first few times she'd met him and she realized with a start that it had been a very long time since she'd seen it. Wade's usually smiling face was set in hard lines and Keri had schooled hers into a neutral expression.

It's the family's farm.

Wade's comment came back to her loud and clear. Did they all want different things from the farm? As she matched up the expressions on their faces with the memory of their father's tension she knew without a doubt something huge was going on and it was eating at all of them.

She hated the old tension that had returned to cloak Luke, draining the sparkle from his eyes, and she respected Wade too much not to feel distressed for him.

You can make them look happy. It's what you do best.

And she could. If they saw a photo of themselves looking happy and relaxed on the farm, then it might open them up to finding a way through whatever the issue was.

"Keri, what are the kids' names?"

"Grace and Ethan."

Erin squatted down. "Hey, Ethan, has your uncle Luke ever told you the story about how he forgot to close the farm gate and some cows decided to take a walk?"

The boy shook his head and glanced up at Luke. "Where did they walk to?"

Keri laughed. "Oh, I remember that. They started walking down the town road and totally blocked it. There were cars backed up in both directions and the cows didn't care. They had new grass to chomp on by the side of the road and they totally ignored the police chief who was jumping up and down. Luke was still finding cows at ten o'clock at night."

Luke grinned. "But that story isn't half as funny as the one where your mom got all dressed up for a date and came into the parlor to say goodbye to Grandpa. She was too busy admiring her reflection in the stainless steel so she missed a cow raising her tail. It dumped all over her and she squealed like a girl when we hosed her down."

"That water was icy." Keri tried to sound indignant but failed as laughter took over. "At least I didn't cause Whitetail's most infamous traffic jam by driving the tractor to school and getting his friends to do the same."

Wade looked sheepish. "The car was out of gas and I didn't want the tractor to look lonely in the school parking lot so I invented drive-the-tractor-to-school day." He grabbed his niece's hand. "Your mom came up with the best idea of how to take a snow day. She—"

"I think Erin wants to take the photo now," Keri said hurriedly as her son's eyes lit up at the hint of his mother breaking the rules.

Luke leaned in toward the children, his grin wide. "If you two come help us with the milking tonight, Wade and I will tell you lots of stories about the things your mom did growing up."

"Awesome." Ethan high-fived Luke.

With a groan, Keri buried her head in Phil's shoulder. "Remind me again why coming to the farm for vacation was a good idea?"

Phil gave her a cuddle. "Sharing your happy childhood memories with the kids."

And Phil was right, Erin mused. The tension between the siblings had taken a backseat just as she'd hoped. "Let's start with everyone over on the rail fence with the corn in the background?"

"Race ya!" Grace called as she took off fast.

All the Andersons sprinted after her.

FOURTEEN

TONY STRODE INTO the foyer of the Silver Birch Supper Club. He'd not eaten here before, although he'd checked and tagged all their fire extinguishers. Now he was here to meet Max and Nicole. Earlier in the day, Max's camp class had come to the fire station for the field trip he'd organized. The kid had positioned himself next to him for the entire tour, asking a zillion questions, and Tony would've had to have been blind not to see how much Max craved some adult male attention. He understood perfectly.

Growing up in a household dominated by women, he'd idolized his father who'd taught him how to be a man, to respect women no matter what and to keep his mouth firmly shut at certain times of the month. Now, after having spent years putting his fatherhood dreams on ice for Loretta, they were now out of cold storage. He wanted to be a dad. He'd always wanted to be a dad and the pleading in Max's eyes made it impossible not to want to be the guy in his life he could rely on and respect.

The only complications were Nicole and the specter of Max's dead father. He already knew that spending time with Nicole and Max together was only going to taunt him with what he couldn't have so he'd decided that spending one-on-one time with Max was the only way to stay sane. His solution was to suggest to Nicole that he spend time once a week with Max when Nicole was tied up with a wedding. He'd been about to suggest this when she arrived to pick up the little guy but before he could open his mouth, the kid had invited him to supper.

He'd laughed it off but later, when Max was out of earshot, Nicole had said, "The supper club has a great menu," and she'd suggested a time to meet. The venue had surprised him as he'd thought Del's or the local pizzeria would have been more suitable for an eight-year-old. He could imagine the damage Max would quickly inflict on the tablecloths.

"Hello, Chief," Mrs. Norell greeted him as he crossed the foyer. "Are you here for the Friday-night fish fry?"

"I guess I am." He smiled at the pink-haired dynamo. "Nicole's introducing me to Wisconsin's culinary traditions. We grilled brats last week."

Her usual friendliness faded and her mouth tightened at the edges. "I heard that you did."

Had he offended her somehow? She'd always been so friendly and had even gone to the trouble of cooking him some casseroles for his freezer. He tried his flirting banter, which usually made her and the other older ladies of the town twitter. "I've yet to try cream puffs, though, and I hear yours rival those of the state fair."

"Oh, they do."

But an invitation to sample them wasn't forthcoming.

She gripped her purse tightly on her shoulder. "I guess I'll be seeing you at the town meeting, Chief. I expect by then you'll have done something about that pile of lumber at the Gundersons'. It's tinder dry and a danger to the town. Goodbye."

Her parting serve torched him like the flames from

an unexpected blaze and he needed to roll his shoulders to physically throw off her unpredicted animosity as she walked away. He pulled open the restaurant door and glanced around the busy room. His Nicole-attuned radar meant he quickly spotted her.

"Evening, Chief."

One of his volunteer firefighters was working as the host. "Hey, Eric. Great work the other day. I'm really proud of how you guys are pulling it all together. Next year we might think about entering the firefighters' games."

"I think the guys would like that." Eric gave him a friendly smile, looked beyond him and picked up a menu. "On your own tonight, then?"

"Actually, I see Nicole Lindquist over there and—"

"Bradley was a good husband to her and a great father to Max."

He nodded silently at the grief on the man's face. Trying hard to overcome his jealousy of a dead man, he gave Eric what he hoped was a sympathetic smile. "So I'm told."

Eric strode across the room to the small table where Nicole was sitting alone. "Are you okay with the chief sitting here?"

Nicole's eyes darted between him and the host. "That will be fine, Eric."

He turned back toward Tony, slapped down the menu, shot him a look that said *hurt her in any way and you're toast*, turned on his heel and walked away.

What the hell?

"Hi, Tony," Nicole said. "You made it."

Despite being dressed far more casually than her work wear, Nicole looked and sounded nervous. She also looked gorgeous. Her hair was loose, just brushing her shoulders and in place of her usual black business suit she wore a floral sundress with skinny straps that exposed her tanned shoulders. His body gave a collective groan and he quickly looked around seeking the distraction of Max. "Have we lost Max to the rec room already?"

The tip of her tongue moistened her top lip and with a massive effort he pulled his gaze away before he got hard in a public place and Eric punched him out. At that moment his brain managed to register what his eyes had been trying to tell him. The table only had two place settings.

"Max is at my parents'."

He was instantly concerned, especially as the station had provided all the camp kids with a drink and a snack. The potential of having given fifteen kids food poisoning made him nauseous. "Is he sick?"

"No. I—"

The waitress arrived, cutting off the conversation. As she filled Nicole's water, she asked her about Max and then said how she was counting nights before school started again and her own children were out of the house. She turned to Tony. "Are you eating?"

He smiled at her. "I think I'll try the fish fry."

"It's finished," she said flatly without offering up any other suggestions.

Nicole laughed. "Wow, that has to be a first in the history of the club."

The waitress, whose name tag said Tina, ignored her and started to tap her foot.

Tony quickly scanned the menu. "Steak then. Medium and I'll have the vegetables."

"There's only salad." The waitress plucked the menu out of his hand and left before asking him what he'd like to drink. He called out, "Excuse me, Miss…" but she continued walking away.

He had the distinct sensation of having entered the Whitetail twilight zone. Everything and everyone looked the same but nothing was normal. "Is she usually so brusque?"

Nicole's cheeks pinked. "Sorry. Tina has some problems at home and sometimes it spills into work. Eric always sits locals in her section and with tomorrow's big wedding, it's especially important the tourists and guests don't get her. Everyone gets a little on edge the night before a big wedding."

At least he was being considered a local. "Now, *that* explains a lot."

Nicole's heart skipped a beat as Tony leaned casually back in the chair, looking relaxed and gorgeous. Dressed in chinos and a red polo shirt that fitted across his shoulders and chest like a second skin, she didn't need any imagination to know just how muscular and ripped he really was.

She pushed her untouched glass of water so it was in front of him and she took a slug of Dutch courage from the old-fashioned she'd ordered earlier. "So you've been here a few weeks now, how are you settling in?"

This is a date, Nicole, not an employee review. Relax. She was jumpy because unlike Erin, who seemed at ease with the idea of asking for whatever she wanted, Nicole had wimped out at being totally up front about this being a date. Obviously, Tony had expected Max to be here. What if he'd only come because of Max?

She pulled in a long, slow breath and let it ride out. Feeling calmer, she wrapped the fingers of her left hand around her glass, hoping Tony might notice what was missing.

Tony's brow was creased in thought. "I think I'm settling in well. I'm surprised at how much I'm enjoying the slower pace and I love waking up in the morning to the dawn chorus. There aren't a lot of birds in Hackensack so it's all new to me. I can now tell the difference between a common grackle and a yellow-bellied sapsucker."

She loved the way his enthusiasm roved all over his face. "You're way ahead of me then. All I can recognize are a hummingbird and an osprey, and I grew up here."

He seemed to hesitate before replying and then leaned forward, looking slightly embarrassed. "I bought a bird book and a bird feeder but please don't mention it to the guys or I'll never live it down."

Not many men would dare admit to something like that and his expression was so endearing that it sparked a warm and fuzzy feeling around her heart. Ruggedly handsome and strong as an ox on the outside and with a soft and gentle middle. God, he was better than chocolate.

She breathed in his cologne and tried not to sigh. "Your secret's safe with me."

"Good to know." His eyes sparkled at her. "As far as I can see, the only thing missing in Whitetail is a place that makes a really good cannelloni or lasagna."

Their conversation reminded her of the easy companionship they'd shared on the hike and she basked in it. "Whitetail's a bit low on Italians. Apart from you, the closest we've got is Theo, who runs the pizzeria, except his family arrived from Greece two generations ago."

"A Greek cooking Italian food?" Tony sounded skeptical.

"Our Swedish palates think he makes a pretty good

thin-crust pizza in his wood-fire oven, not to mention fabulous Greek flat bread. I guess you could always put Sven's Swedish meatballs into a tomato-based sauce and that would give you Bolognese." His horrified expression made her laugh. "Or not."

"My *nonna* thinks I've moved to the ends of the earth so she's sent me her treasured lasagna recipe. I have strict instructions not to share it with anyone except my firstborn."

He laughed, a warm, rolling sound that gathered her in and hugged her, and then he said, "The way things are going I might be forced to make it."

I'll cook it for you. "So you can cook?"

His mouth tweaked up on one side. "I learned out of necessity."

She stirred her drink. "Bachelors have to, I guess."

"I'm divorced, Nicole."

His matter-of-fact words seemed devoid of any residual pain about the end of his marriage, which was in stark contrast to her own experience. "I'm sorry."

His dark eyes stared into hers. "No need for sorry. Getting divorced was the best decision Loretta and I ever made. Together we were both miserable and we should never have got married in the first place."

"So why did you?"

He shrugged. "We'd been dating for a few years, all our friends were getting married and we blindly followed without discussing a few basic life goals first."

She thought about her own premarital counseling. "Even when you do, things can change."

"Sure, but when one of you wants children and the other doesn't, it's a pretty fundamental difference."

He was so great with Max she couldn't imagine he'd

been the one not wanting children but she had to ask. "And where do you sit on the issue of children?"

His entire face creased into a wide smile and something flared in his eyes that made her breath catch.

"I was the one who wanted them."

An internal sigh rolled through her. She'd always wanted another child but Bradley had asked her to wait. And wait. "Did you always want to live in a small town too?"

"I never really thought about it. Hackensack's big compared with Whitetail but in a lot of ways it's very similar with everyone up in everyone else's business. It took me a while to realize things would be better if one of us was out of there. Given Loretta's busy building her accounting firm and recently married her business partner, it was always going to be me who left. This job came up and I took it."

She thought about the past eighteen months where she'd lurched from anger at Bradley's bombshell to grief and then back to anger again, how trapped she felt and how at times depression had cloaked her. "You seem so together about it all."

His lips quirked up into a wry expression. "Now I am, but believe me, when it happened, I was a mess. No one ever gets married thinking it's going to end."

She kept silent but she understood all about that.

His fingers thrummed the table. "Divorce puts you in this weird place where you have to watch the other person getting on with their life while you're floundering with yours. At least death's final—" His face paled under his tan. "Shit, Nicole…" His hand quickly covered hers, squeezing it tightly. "I didn't mean… Oh hell… Shit, sorry."

He looked so remorseful, so upset and yet caring that guilt whipped her in much the same way it did when the town was being solicitous toward her. They thought they were sharing her loss. Only their grief and hers were not remotely the same thing.

She hated that Tony was feeling bad when there was no reason for him to feel that way at all. As much as she loved and craved the touch of his hand and the wonderful things it was doing to her, she knew she was accepting it under false pretenses. It was time for her to be totally up front and tell him the truth about Bradley.

"Nicole," John Ackerman's voice boomed out as he marched determinedly toward them.

Not ready to deal with disapproving looks from John, she hastily withdrew her hand and thrust it into her lap seconds before he appeared at the table.

"We need to talk about the chocolate order for Sunday's wedding," John said, completely ignoring the fact she was dining with Tony.

An irritated breeze blew through her. "Can't it wait until we've eaten?"

John shook his head. "No. The supplier's got a problem and we have to make some decisions now or the bride's handmade chocolates will be store-bought and Whitetail Weddings will get a reputation for not delivering. You know we can't risk that."

Despairing that John was right, she rose regretfully to her feet as disappointment pummeled her. "I'm sorry, Tony. Perhaps we could—"

"We'll be gone for the night," John interrupted, "and I'm sure the chief understands about sacrifice for the greater good."

Tony stood up, his expression neutral but his eyes

had narrowed into tense slits. "If it's that important, John, I'll leave you both to get the job done. Good night, Nicole."

The relaxed and easy rapport they'd shared froze like the lake in winter and then cracked, making the distance between them wider than ever before.

She wanted to snatch back what they'd had, keep it warm, dry and alive, but she could see in his eyes it had died. Trying hard not to bite her lip, she gave him a mouthed *I'm sorry*, a nod goodbye and trudged after John, exiting the restaurant with resentment and disappointment curdling her gut. Why had John chosen that precise moment to interrupt their evening when it had been going so well?

Tonight had been all about Tony seeing her as a woman—not a widow, or Max's mom, or the town's hairdresser and wedding planner, but a desirable woman who was really attracted to him. None of that had happened or if it had, it had been cut short so fast she wasn't sure he'd even noticed her missing wedding band.

John opened the door for her and she stepped through, stopping abruptly as the thought struck her. She knew what she had to do. "John, I just have to text Max good-night."

John smiled. "Of course. Say good-night to him from his uncle John."

She gave a sharp nod and brought up a new message, attached the number and tapped out, *Erin, book me in for those photos ASAP. Nic x*

ERIN HAD FALLEN into bed at midnight, exhausted after a long wedding shoot. She'd been vaguely aware of Luke getting into bed a little while later and pulling her close. His warmth and the security of his arms wrapped around her had sent her into a deep and delicious sleep. Now coolness pooled at her lower back and she stretched out her arm, feeling for the heat bank that was Luke. She touched an empty space. Rolling over, she squinted into the dark and could just make out his bulk sitting on the edge of the bed.

"Luke?"

"Shh, go back to sleep." He kissed her forehead and tucked the quilt around her.

She finally managed to focus on the clock. 3:10. "Where are you going?"

"To deliver a calf."

She turned on the light and threw off the quilt. "Can I come?"

Surprise flitted across his face. "Ah, sure, if you want but I'm warning you, it's messy and bloody."

She rolled her eyes. "I think I can cope. Besides, we can shower together after."

He grinned at her with the wicked twinkle she loved so much. "Definitely come then."

Maggie-May and Mac looked up expectantly and Erin stifled a smile. "Exactly how did these dogs end up sleeping at the foot of the bed?"

"That mutt of yours is leading Mac astray," Luke said without heat and threw her hoodie and jeans at her.

They took the four-wheeler as the cottage wasn't as conveniently positioned to the barn as the farm house and five minutes later she was surrounded by pregnant cows and the sound of low mooing. While Luke put the laboring cow in the headlock, she asked, "Do you have to help every cow?"

He shook his head. "No. Ninety percent do it all on

their own. This is Essie's first calf and she's been in labor too long so I'm going to give her a helping hand."

Erin saw the chains he'd put down next to a bucket of soapy water. "Chains?" The word came out on a squeak as her girly parts flinched on behalf of the cow.

"Bovine obstetrics is fairly basic." He washed the cow's rear and then pulled on a long glove that went the length of his arm. "I'm going to sleeve her and check the lie of the calf first."

"Can I take photos?"

"Sure."

He covered the glove in lubricant and talked to the cow in a soothing tone before holding the tail up high and inserting his arm up to his shoulder. His brow creased in concentration and he staggered slightly as the cow moved back against him.

"Problem?"

"No. The calf's in the right position but just like humans, sometimes the first birth is longer and harder than subsequent ones. The calf's not overly big so that's a good thing." As he removed his hand, two hooves appeared and then slipped back inside. His gaze hooked hers, filled with questions and overlaid with doubt. "How's your brute strength?"

"Pretty good. I lift weights in the gym and lug heavy photographic equipment, why?"

"I need your help to pull out the calf."

The whole idea of the chains slightly horrified her but if Luke needed her help she was up for the task. "O-kay."

He didn't mention her queasiness but set about slipping the chains around the calf's fetlocks. His every action said this was a man who was confident in his work and knew exactly what he was doing. She recorded it all in a series of shots.

"Time to put down the camera." He handed her the triangular handles of the obstetric chains. "This is going to be hard because there's nothing to brace yourself against so spread your feet wide and bend your knees so you can get some traction."

"When do I pull?"

"When I say. See how there's one leg out farther than the other? This means elbow lock."

That didn't sound good. "Cows have elbows? Who knew."

"You're going to pull on the affected limb while I push the calf back to unlock it." His hand was back in the cow, checking the position. "Erin, pull now."

"On it." She hauled back, feeling like her shoulders were going to pop out of their sockets and she could only imagine what it must feel like for the cow. She really wasn't certain she was achieving much at all and it made her gym work seem vanilla and safe.

"Stop pulling. Good work, the legs are now even."

Panting like she'd run a marathon, every muscle in her arms threatened to explode from lack of oxygen but she was excited that she'd been able to help. "This is a good thing, right?"

"Yep. It's all straightforward from here. I'll take over now." He dropped to his haunches, his arm muscles straining, and he pulled.

More of the legs appeared and suddenly she could see the calf's head and lolling tongue. The cow stopped straining and the calf retreated slightly.

Relieved of her job, she grabbed her camera, keen to record the moment the calf was born.

"Not. Long. Now." Luke paused in his efforts. The black-and-white body of the calf was half out of the vagina and he quickly inserted his hand inside the cow again.

She bit her lip. "Should it just hang like that?"

"It's fine. Humans do this too although not from this height."

"That's more information than I needed to know."

He laughed. "That's such a city thing to say. This is animal husbandry. Okay, get ready with that camera 'cause this calf's coming out."

He gave one last mighty pull and a gush of fluid squirted everywhere. The next moment, the calf was on the straw with the remains of the amniotic sac clinging to its rump and its white patches stained pink with blood. Its huge brown eyes blinked as if to say *how did I get here?*

A lump formed in Erin's throat. It was the most amazing thing she'd ever seen.

Luke quickly rubbed the calf's belly, wiped its mouth and then lifted the top rear leg to check the sex. "Score. We have another milker. Welcome to the world, young lady."

Erin was torn between just watching him and photographing the event and her camera hung from her hand. For the first time in a long time she experienced something special through her own eyes, rather than through the lens of a camera. "That was incredible."

Luke's smile was wide, genuine and filled with happiness. "Yeah, it is."

He stripped off his glove, grabbed her hand and as they moved back out of the way, the cow started to lick her calf clean. They sat down on baled hay to watch.

"She might have had a tough first birth but she knows what to do," Luke said proudly, as if the cow and the calf were related to him. "Watching the first few minutes of life of a new calf is one part of the job that never gets old."

She thought about his grumpy moments. "So what does get old?"

He shrugged. "Most everything."

She felt inexplicably sad for him. She loved being a photographer and she couldn't imagine spending her days doing something she wasn't passionate about. "So why are you farming if it doesn't float your boat?"

He slowly stripped a piece of hay into thin lengths. "That's the question I've been asking myself for months."

"Did something change?"

He tossed the straw away and sighed. "This is going to sound crazy…"

"Try me. It probably won't sound crazy at all." She elbowed him gently in the ribs. "And you know me, I'll tell you if it is."

He gave a wry smile but kept his gaze fixed on the calf, watching it struggle to rise to her feet only to fall back when its wobbly legs let her down. "As a kid I dreamed of taking over, and farming is all I can ever remember wanting to do. During the two years I worked alongside Dad as part of the handover process, I was quietly going crazy as he blocked every suggestion I made. I found myself counting down the days until he retired and I was the boss and could run things my way. The moment he and Mom left for Arizona, I started implementing changes."

She thought about the photo she'd taken of him holding soil in his hand and staring across the fields. "That makes sense. You wanted to put the Luke Anderson stamp on the farm just like I put the Erin Davis touch on my photos."

He ran his hand through his hair. "All I've done is make the parlor more efficient so milking is faster and I'm working on a higher fat content in the milk by experimenting with different feed."

All I've done? "I know nothing about farming but they sound like improvements. What else do you want to try?"

He huffed out a breath. "That's the thing. Dad was a good farmer. When he took over from my grandfather, the farm was a lot smaller than it is now. He basically doubled the size of it in twenty years, making it one of the most successful farms in the district."

"Are you saying there's nothing else you need to do?"

"It ticks over pretty good. Some seasons are better than others and the price of milk goes up and down but yeah…"

Under the artificial lights of the barn, she saw the aura of discontent she'd glimpsed at the picnic and the haggardness of stress. She wondered about this intelligent, hardworking man. "So you've inherited a well-run, profitable farm?"

"Yep."

"And it's making you miserable?" She tried hard to keep the incredulity out of her voice.

His blue eyes filled with bewildered pain. "I told you it was crazy."

She thought about how much she craved to have an established and solid business, and part of her wanted to say, *Do you know how lucky you are?* Only she could see in the lines around his eyes and the set of his mouth that he knew he was fortunate indeed and that he was at war with that very thing. "Can you picture yourself doing anything other than farming?"

Luke heard the question, which was identical to the one he'd been asking himself for weeks. "No. That's what sucks because technically I'm doing what I want to do, only every day is like dragging myself through mud. I've got no clue what I'd do if I left the farm and me leaving impacts on the entire family. Keri wants us to sell up so she can take the money for her kids' college fund and she's putting the pressure on. Wade and Dad will do everything in their power to prevent a sale and will never talk to me again if I force the issue. Every time I try to have a sensible discussion with any of them it gets heated and ends with someone stomping off."

"I gathered something was going on. The picnic wasn't without some tension." She gave him a contemplative look. "How about we forget your family for the moment and take a look at you. When you think about your future, what do you see?"

His usually square shoulders slumped. "I alternate between the farm and a big black hole."

"What else can you farm here besides cows?"

"I can't destroy a successful dairy, Erin." He dropped her hand wondering why he'd even thought an urbanite might understand.

Her green eyes flashed at him. "I wasn't suggesting that you do but I think you need your own project."

She had no clue and didn't understand. "The farm *is* a full-time project."

"I'm aware of that but the way I understand it is that you've tweaked your father's farming techniques.

I don't think that's enough for you. Think about it. Your dad took over from his dad and doubled the size of the farm."

The idea of doing the same was like a millstone dragging at his neck. "We don't need to get any bigger."

Her hands turned palm up. "So diversify. Although the bulk of my business is wedding photos, I also do family portraits and some boudoir photography."

"Boudoir?" He pulled her close, happy to think about anything else but the farm and he buried his face in her hair. "Do you have photos of yourself?"

She planted her palms against his chest and raised her gaze to him. "Don't even think about getting off topic. We're talking about you."

His jaw got tight. "I think we're done now."

"Luke." She poked him in the chest with a manicured nail. "You need to find something in farming that lights a fire in your belly. A challenge. Something new that's totally yours."

Her words rained down on him, adding to the swirling mess of emotions that had become part of him. As much as he wanted to reject her suggestion out of hand, he couldn't. Was she close to the crux of his problem? He plowed his hand through his hair, not certain about anything. He ran an efficient and productive farm and as that was the goal of every farmer it should be making him ecstatic. If that wasn't enough to make him happy, then what the hell would it take?

The calf finally got her legs to work and she wobbled to her feet, looking around for her mother's udder and that first taste of colostrum, rich in all the good things she'd need before she could enjoy the sweet taste of creamy milk.

He pulled Erin to her feet. "Come on. We've got work to do. This calf needs to be put in her own hutch, given some oral antibiotics and then fed her mother's colostrum from a bottle. It's a busy first hour of a calf's life and there're lots more photos for you to take."

Hopeful expectation danced on Erin's cheeks. "Can I give her the bottle?"

"Sure, if you want to."

She continued to surprise him. He'd appreciated the fact she'd offered to get up in the middle of the night and that she hadn't blinked when he'd asked her to help with the delivery, but he'd expected her to have had enough by now. "You can milk Essie too if you like."

She shuddered. "I think I'll just stick to feeding the calf."

Laughing at her expected response, he pulled her into his arms. "Wimp."

"Slave driver."

He lowered his mouth to hers because as much fun as it was teasing her, kissing her was so much better. He loved the way she relaxed against him the moment his lips touched hers.

Essie mooed and he reluctantly pulled back from Erin and got back to work. Together they herded the calf into her hutch before he returned to milk Essie. "I guess you know that Nicole's requested a hay wagon for this damn wedding."

"It will make great photos," she said from behind her camera.

He'd known she'd say that. "The wagon hasn't been used for a while so I'm hitching it up to make sure everything works. It's bad enough the wedding is taking place here. No way in hell am I risking a Bridezilla meltdown."

Erin lowered her camera with a long, weary sigh. "She's not Bridezilla."

Luke was starting to think Erin had tunnel vision when it came to Connie Littlejohn. He was pretty certain Nicole had the bride's number because she'd taken to sending him one email a day with bullet-point questions, which always started with, *Sorry, Luke, but...* He forwarded them straight to Wade. If Wade wanted this wedding to take place on the farm so badly then he could deal with the headache that was Miz Littlejohn.

However, Luke had agreed in a curt conversation with his brother to sort out the wagon. "Wade wants to give the kids a bonfire so I thought you and I could drive them there on the wagon and test it at the same time."

She tilted her head, watching him closely, and he could see the cogs of her mind at work. As he waited for her to reply, a sudden rush of anxiety filled his gut with acid. He instantly tried to shake off the ridiculous feelings. What the hell was there to be anxious about? It was a hayride and it made no difference if she came along or not.

You'll be disappointed if she doesn't come.

He refused to acknowledge that. What he shared with Erin was what he shared with all women—causal, easy and fun with no strings or expectations. The farm tied him down enough without adding in the complications of a serious relationship.

Her eyes danced and enthusiasm raced across her cheeks. "That sounds like fun."

The tightness in his gut relaxed.

That shocked him even more.

FIFTEEN

FROM HER POSITION on the hay wagon, Erin stared up into the clear night sky and listened to the rhythmic *clip clop* of the horse's hooves against the farm road. They were on their way to meet Wade, Keri and Phil at the bonfire. Up front, Luke was using an app on his phone and pointing out the different constellations to Grace and Ethan. A few minutes prior, Luke had been alternating between kissing her in the shadows and showing her the stars, taking advantage of a few quiet moments while the kids and the dogs raced ahead chasing fireflies.

All too soon, the dogs and kids had tired of that game and had scrambled back up onto the wagon demanding attention.

Luke had squeezed her hand and instantly gone from attentive lover to responsible yet fun uncle, leaving her with the dogs. She scratched behind their ears, fairly certain that Luke's invitation for her to join in the hayride was to use her as a buffer with his siblings, although she doubted the adults would argue in front of the children.

She felt for all of them. Luke's restlessness affected more than just himself and she was certain that added to his dilemma. Not that he'd mentioned it since the night in the barn. He wasn't a big talker but she hoped he could find a way forward and rediscover the joy and purpose in his life.

Everyone needed a purpose and unlike Luke, she had it in spades, along with added contentment flowing through her veins. She couldn't remember being this relaxed in a very long time. She had money going into her bank account, happy clients and enough work coming in so she wasn't stressing about where the next job was coming from. Things were on track with Connie's wedding.

And then there's Luke.

She smiled to herself. Luke was like extra frosting on the cake that was Whitetail. He was the unexpected bonus and she gave thanks every night, usually around the time he was doing delicious things to her that made her scream out his name. She planned to make the most of him in the few weeks she had left because once she returned to Minneapolis, her focus would be back on building the business. Who was she kidding? Her focus was on the business here, it was just that Luke had landed in her lap.

"Wow, look at that fire," Grace squealed.

"That's so awesome," Ethan breathed out in wonder.

The dogs sat up and Erin followed. Massive flames soared into the dark, a dancing mess of yellow, orange and red with occasional flashes of blue.

"What are you burning in that thing?"

"Junk from the old barn," Luke said. "We do a bonfire every year as part of a cleanup. Whoa." He pulled back on the reins and the wagon rolled to a stop. "Okay, kids, down you get. Grandma and Grandpa have got marshmallows."

"Yay!" The children and dogs jumped off and raced toward the fire.

"Your parents are here?" She couldn't hide the shock

from her voice as unease rocketed through her. It was one thing to meet his siblings but meeting his parents was a very different thing entirely.

"They got back late this afternoon," he said matter-of-factly, as if introducing a lover to his parents happened every day. "You don't need to worry. We Andersons keep our arguments out of the public arena and Dad and I will manage to be civil." He lifted her down off the wagon and slid his palm into hers.

Arguing wasn't what she was worried about. "Maybe I should go back to the cottage."

"Are you feeling sick?"

His concern wrapped around her like a blanket and she shook her head. "No, but this is a family thing and—"

"No, it isn't. Employees and guests are always invited to the bonfire and you're both. Keith and Lindsay are here and I invited Nicole and Max, plus a bunch of other people from town. Besides, you can't leave before you've tasted my bonfire specialty."

She met his eyes that twinkled in the firelight. "What's that?"

"Damper. I learned to make it in Australia."

"Damper?" She slid her hand up into his hair, the need to touch him strong. "You're not tempting me one little bit. It sounds like mold."

"It's like cake." He lowered his head and ran his tongue slowly and decadently around the curve of her ear. "You won't be able to get enough of it."

A shiver ran through her, reminding her just how addictive he was to her. It should bother her that he knew every erogenous zone on her body and how to use it to his advantage, but as he kissed her and pleasure swirled through her, all her concerns floated away because he was right. She could never get enough of him.

"Where's your uncle?" Wade's voice floated above the crack and pop of the fire. "He's supposed to be cooking."

Luke broke the kiss. "Go talk with Lindsay and Keith and I'll catch up with you later when the damper's on the fire."

She did as he suggested and Keith and Lindsay introduced her to Melissa who ran the Northern Lights dress shop.

Erin sipped on a wine cooler that Keith had opened for her. "Do many of the brides buy their dresses through you?"

"Some do. I'm slowly building up my wedding dress stock but I can't compete with the big bridal houses in the cities."

"Can you offer more personalized service?"

"We try. When a bride comes to Whitetail for a wedding tour, Nicole and I take the preliminary meeting. We give them a tour of the town in a horse and carriage and then, after a glass of champagne, I usually encourage them to try on some dresses. It sets the mood and they can picture themselves as a bride when they're in a dress."

"Now that's a great idea." Erin's brain started popping. "Do you take a photo of them in the frocks?"

"No."

"It might help you build the wedding dress side of the business if you did. For less than a hundred dollars you can buy a Polaroid camera. This way you can take a photo of the bride looking happy in one of your dresses and send it home with them. They'll look at the photo, think about the lovely day they had and the seeds are sewn for them to buy the dress from you."

"That's a great idea and not just for selling wedding dresses but for selling the town." Melissa's expression was pure respect. "Nicole said you were good."

She let the buzz of the compliment flow through her. She loved this part of the business—dreaming up new and different ways to stand out in a crowded marketplace. "It may not work but it's worth a shot, right?"

"I need all those ideas and more," Melissa said with a wistful sigh. "I love fashion and I love Whitetail but it's never easy being in retail in a small town. Actually, it's not easy being a single woman either." She glanced around at the crowd and her eyes lingered on Luke who was lifting Max Lindquist up onto the hay wagon. "That man would make gorgeous babies and be a terrific dad, too, but no one's been able to land him."

A proprietary streak of green spun through Erin at the way Melissa was openly ogling him. "You make him sound like a fish. Luke's not interested in being a one-woman man so you'd be wise to look elsewhere."

Melissa's mouth thinned. "Are you warning me off?"

The thought that she might be horrified her. She hadn't realized she'd sounded harsh and she softened her tone. "No, not at all. It's just if you're looking for a man to make babies with I think you'd be wasting your time with Luke."

Melissa's shoulders slumped. "You're right. I know you're right and I don't have time to waste on a man who won't commit. My ovaries are shriveling as we speak."

Erin gave Melissa's arm a supportive squeeze. Although she didn't want to get married and risk the heartache it brought along with the loss of financial independence, she appreciated that most women wanted the full catastrophe of marriage, mortgage and babies. "Is Whitetail short on men?"

"Just ones that want to commit." She drained her wine cooler. "I need another one. You?"

"No, thanks."

Melissa got chatting at the bar table and Erin took a walk watching the different groups clustered around the fire. Lindsay was deep in conversation with Luke, probably something to do with farming. He winked at her as she walked past and yet still managed to look like he was paying attention to everything Lindsay was saying.

Nicole was chatting with Keri about the joys and challenges of raising boys, and Brett, Wade and Luke's father were a bit farther over, their heads close together and their expressions serious. Erin had a moment of feeling alone in a crowd and was about to go and join Keri and Nicole when someone called her name. She turned around to see a woman walking toward her who was an older version of Keri.

"Hello, Erin. I'm Martha Anderson and I think I'm the last person in the family to meet you."

Despite Martha's smile, Erin wasn't certain if she was in trouble or not. She returned the smile. "Did you enjoy your visit to Janesville?"

"We did, thank you. I talk to my sister a lot on the telephone but we don't often get to sit down together." Martha gave her an inquiring look. "Do you have a sister?"

She shook her head. "I've a younger brother, although I imagine that's not quite the same thing. Jesse isn't big into talking."

"Most men aren't," Maratha said with feeling. "Keri tells me you're busy with the Whitetail wedding business and helping out Wade."

Erin relaxed now she was on familiar ground. "I am. It's been great. I like to keep busy and all the couples have been lovely to work with."

Martha nodded and the firelight cast shadows on her face. "So you and Luke are…?"

Having a lot of sex.

"…spending a lot of time together it seems," Martha said.

There was no point in denying it but Erin hesitated a moment, uncertain as to the direction the conversation was going to take. She girded herself for disapproval. "We are."

Censure didn't come. Instead, Martha beamed. "I'm glad. He needs some fun in his life."

Erin blinked. Had Luke's mother just said she approved of a casual, summer fling? "Um, I like to think we all need some fun and happiness in our lives."

"Wise girl." Martha patted her hand. "Keeping it light is definitely the way to go with Luke."

Confusion trickled through her at the older woman's words. Was she being warned off or being congratulated? She scanned Martha's face and examined her tone but she couldn't detect any sarcasm.

"Now that Vern and I live in Arizona, I consider the house we bought there to be our home and not the farmhouse."

"Ah, that's great." She didn't know what else to say. This conversation was like being flipped into a parallel universe because although Martha looked like an ordinary person this chat was decidedly odd.

"In fact," Martha continued, "the farmhouse needs a renovation. It's been twenty years since the last upgrade and it would be a fun project. I wouldn't mind any changes Luke made."

Erin laughed. "I think Wade got all the interior design skills, don't you?"

Martha fixed her with a long look. "I think Luke just needs a reason to become interested." She dropped her gaze and sipped her drink. "Do you have your own place?"

"I rent an apartment in Minneapolis. Once my business is more established I hope to buy. Like you said, renovations would be fun."

A flash of firelight showed surprise on Martha's face. "With all the wedding photography work you're getting in town, I would have thought you'd be planning on moving your business to Whitetail."

"I'm committed through September but after that I'm not certain. It depends a lot on other things."

Martha nodded. "Like Luke making a commitment to you."

A hot flash raced across her skin followed quickly by a cool shiver. "That wasn't what I meant."

Martha gave her a knowing look. "It's okay, Erin. I watch *Dr. Phil* and I know what young women are up against these days trying to get men to commit."

"Mrs. Anderson—"

"Call me, Martha, dear." She leaned in, her expression intense. "Luke's thirty and ready to settle down. He just doesn't know it yet. All he needs is a strong woman in his life to show him what he's missing out on. Come to supper soon."

"Hey, Erin, Mom." Luke strolled up to them, the firelight dancing like platinum in his hair and the shadows making him sexier than ever. He held a plate filled with clumps of what looked like scones or biscuits and all were smeared with jam. "Try the damper."

Erin had never been so pleased to see Luke in her life. The conversation with his mother was totally freaking her out. Weren't mothers of sons supposed to stand as an obstacle between their son and the woman of his choice? And she wasn't even Luke's long-term choice and he certainly wasn't hers.

Her hand shot out toward the crumbly mess. "It looks great," she said despite the fact it looked totally gross, but if her mouth was full of food, Martha couldn't ask her any more questions. She picked up the largest piece and in one fell swoop shoved all of it in her mouth.

TWO NIGHTS LATER, Luke was watching Erin develop photos in the red gloom of the darkroom he'd helped her create in a storage space next to the farm office. "Are you nearly done?"

"Almost." Her head was bent over a tray, and she was intently studying a piece of developing paper.

He pulled her hair to the side and pressed his lips to her neck, loving the taste of her skin. Then he ran the tip of his tongue slowly and deliberately inside her ear.

She shuddered against him and then turned around, hooking her hands behind his neck and kissing him the way he loved best—hard, deep and scorching hot. Hell, he loved all the ways she kissed, even butterfly kisses on his chest.

The timer beeped loudly and she pulled away abruptly. He couldn't stop his audible groan of disappointment.

"If you distract me like that, we'll be here even longer." She kissed him on the nose as if he was a little boy who needed placating. "Five more minutes, I promise."

"I'm holding you to that." He snuggled in behind her in the small space and peered over her shoulder. Black-and-white pictures of his family were appearing on the paper.

She used a pair of tongs to pick up each photo and then rinsed it underwater. The next step involved running a squeegee over it before pegging it on a line to dry next to the others.

Luke studied all of them. "I like this last one best."

"Why?" She quickly transferred another piece of developing paper into the stop bath and agitated it.

"Maybe the way the kids are snuggled in to Phil and Keri."

"And?"

He studied the photo again. "I guess the long shot of the farm behind us. Dad will love it."

"What about this one?" She dried the excess water off a print he hadn't noticed was developing and pegged it up.

It was a photo of him squatting down with his hand filled with the black earth of the farm and he was gazing off toward the thick grove of white ash, yellow birches and basswoods that divided the lake pasture from the lake. His favorite part of the farm. It didn't matter how many different ways he looked at the photo, his connection to the land was unmistakable. He looked at peace, as if he knew exactly what he wanted out of his life.

He stared at Erin, irritation rippling through him at the lie the photo portrayed. "So how did you doctor this to make me look like that?"

"I didn't change a thing. That's you and your land."

She kissed him gently on the cheek and her field-green eyes bored into him. "You just have to work out what you want to do."

"I know exactly what I want to do and it has nothing to do with the farm." He kissed her and gently guided her backward until her back was resting against the wall. Lifting her up, he wrapped her legs around his waist and gazed at her. Her eyes flashed with excitement and she wriggled against him, sending his blood rushing to his groin.

She ran her finger softly down his cheek. "Had I known that me developing photos was such a turn-on for you, I would have done it more often."

"Sweetheart, you're a turn-on every moment of every day." And he lost himself in her mouth and then her body until the peace he craved settled over him once more.

TONY ADDRESSED THE town meeting, making sure he covered every point on his list. "I've spoken with the Gundersons and the lumber's being sprayed with water until it can be removed. The issue with the pagers is ongoing and we're trialing a cell phone notification service for all volunteers. Meanwhile, the emergency siren at the station and in the main street will always sound as it's done for years before we had the—" he raised his fingers in quotation marks "'—help of technology.'"

He paused, expecting a few wry smiles and sounds of agreement but got nothing. He pressed on. "The problem of people burning is a frustrating one for the department. I want to remind everyone that it's illegal to burn on your property without a permit."

A rumble of discontent shot around the room and he

felt the wave of animosity hit him. Again. Ever since the night at the supper club he'd experienced unexpected moments just like this. Small slights—the wrong grocery order, the lack of an invitation to a social function the rest of his team were attending and less friendly greetings as he walked around town. Today, at practice, his volunteer brigade had been sloppy and there'd been times when he'd swore they were deliberately misconstruing his instructions. And now this reaction from the meeting. The atmosphere of the room was a far cry from his enthusiastic welcome weeks ago. "Are there any questions?"

"It's the summer people you need to be telling about the permits, not us," a discontented voice called out from the back.

Tony took in a fortifying breath because the town wasn't immune from law breakers. "Brent, I hear you and I've been working with the vacationers but we got five calls on the burnout by the mill last week because it didn't have a permit and no one was expecting it."

"You don't have any dive and rescue experience, do you, Chief?"

What the hell, Eric? One of his best volunteers had just broken rank and was publically undermining him. Tony had been totally up front about his deficit in water rescue when he'd applied for the job and it hadn't concerned the town board then. "That's correct. However, I'm enrolled for my dive certificate and rescue training." He smiled, trying to lighten the mood. "I can't actually pass the under-ice rescue until winter comes."

Another dissatisfied rumble vibrated around the room, followed by the scraping of chairs and general shuffling. Mrs. Norell wasn't smiling and unlike his first meeting, Nicole wasn't even present. No other hands had gone up so he decided to wrap it up. "Thanks very much for your time and if I can just remind you all that smoke detectors save lives. Please check your batteries."

John Ackerman declared the meeting closed and everyone drifted into the reception room. Tony made his own coffee from the urn and selected his own cake rather than being forced to choose from a myriad platters being pressed against him by the local ladies. All around him people were clustered in closed groups and eye contact was only being made when absolutely necessary.

He walked over to Ella Norell. "I defrosted that potluck casserole you made me, Ella, and I enjoyed it for supper last night."

"That's good to know, Chief."

"It's a big meeting today. I would have thought Nicole would be here."

Ella pursed her lips. "You know, Chief, Melissa and Emily are single."

"I'm well aware of that, Ella." He tried not to sigh. She and the other older women in the town had been pushing him toward Emily and Melissa from day one. It wasn't that he didn't like them, it was just he didn't like them enough.

Ella's pale blue gaze hooked his with a punch. "Nicole's been through a lot."

He pushed down a rising frustration. "It's hard to live in this town and not know that."

She pursed her lips in disapproval. "She's grieving for her dead husband. Bradley was a wonderful man who sacrificed his life for our freedom and we'll do anything to protect her from harm."

"I'm hardly a mass murderer."

The set of the older woman's mouth said she wasn't so sure.

He raked his hand through his hair, desperately seeking some calm. He needed to remember that he now lived in a small town and as such he was an outsider until proven otherwise. At least now he knew the reason behind the change in the town's attitude.

"I have no intention of hurting her, Ella, and although it's none of your or the town's business, she isn't interested in me other than as a friend and a mentor for Max. So I'd appreciate the gossip mill knowing this so everyone stops treating me like a social pariah and cuts me some slack and allows me to do my job."

Ella's smile returned, tinged with equal parts guilt and relief. "I'll let them know. I'm sorry, it's just…"

"You're protecting your own. I get it." He sighed again. "How long does it take until a newcomer belongs here?"

"Twenty years." She patted his arm sympathetically. "Less if you marry a local. Ask Melissa out on a date."

He put down his coffee cup and strode back to the station, changed into his gym clothes and pulled on the boxing gloves. As his hands and legs hit the punching bag, he didn't know what hurt more—the fact the town didn't trust him to care for Nicole or the fact it was moot because Nicole didn't care for him.

When exhaustion had numbed his mind, he showered at the station and then drove home. He opened a beer and started sorting his mail into bills to be paid, advertising flyers and personal. A heavy and large plain

envelope with *do not bend* handwritten on the front
didn't easily identify itself as personal or business. He
turned it over to see who it was from but there was no
return address. Intrigued, he reached for a knife and
carefully sliced it open.

His fingers touched photo paper and he pulled out
some black-and-white photos. Spreading them across
the table, he blinked. His eyes and his brain argued.
What the—?

*Nicole's huge eyes stared straight at him, as her hair
cascaded across a pillow and her hand rested against
her chin as if to say I'm here and I'm waiting for you.*
His blood beat hard and his fingers trembled as he slid
the photo aside to reveal the next one. She was sitting
cross-legged on a bed with her bare shoulders and back
facing the camera. A rug spooled from under her arms
and draped itself sensually around her hips and lower
back. It revealed less skin than a bikini but it was the
way it said *there's so much more* that made it the sexi-
est thing he'd ever seen.

He realized there was one more photo. This time
she was lying on her front wearing her black-rimmed
glasses, a gray-and-black lace bra and panties. Her legs
were raised behind her and her ankles were crossed,
showing off sexy, black high heels. He groaned as his
erection strained against his trousers.

He grabbed his phone and somehow he managed to
get his fingers to cooperate on the touch screen.

Send Max to your parents. I'm coming over. Now.

SIXTEEN

NICOLE CHECKED HER hair and makeup in the mirror and nervously bit her lip. Tony's text had come in twenty minutes ago and he'd be here soon. Ever hopeful that he would make contact with her when he'd received the photos, she'd arranged for Max to have a sleepover with her parents just in case. Excitement and nerves fluttered, giving her a heady feeling like the bubbles of champagne.

The doorbell pealed. She smoothed down her hair. "This is it, Nic."

Pulling open the door, she smiled. "Hi, Tony."

Wearing a tight expression, he strode past her into her sitting room and turned around, waving the photos at her. "What the hell are these?"

Stunned, she closed the door. This wasn't the reaction she'd been expecting. Rifts of panic immediately flattened her excitement. Had she misjudged him? "Don't you like them?"

"Liking has nothing to do with it." Anguish crossed his face. "Do you have any idea what the town would do to me if they saw these? And you mailed them." His voice rose in disbelief. "What if they'd split open and Henry had seen them or anyone else in the postal service? What then? Damn it, Nicole, I have to work with these people and they froze me out because I went on a hike and had supper with you. They'd hang, draw and quarter me based on these."

Her growing frustration with the town spilled over. "It's none of their business. We're adults and I had those photos taken for you not them."

He slammed them down on the table and she jumped, her stomach curdling. This wasn't going anywhere close to the way she'd imagined it in her head over the past few days. She'd been nervous about the photo shoot but Erin had been so great with helping her relax that she'd ended up having fun. For the first time in far too long, she'd felt like a desirable, sexy woman and she was really proud of the photos. But now, faced with the anger and confusion in Tony's eyes, she was second-guessing everything.

He plowed his hand through his inky-black curls. "What I don't understand—" his voice was low and controlled "—is why you sent these to me when you're still in love with your dead husband?"

She shook her head so hard that her hair whipped against her mouth and she rushed to reassure him. "I'm not. Surely these photos tell you that. How could you even think I was after looking at them?"

His dark eyes filled with something akin to sadness. "I don't know what to think. Everyone in town believes he's your one great love and, hell, you're still wearing your wedding ring."

Her hand shot out and she waved it in front of him as if he was blind. "I took off the ring two weeks ago. I invited you to the supper club." She couldn't stop her voice from developing a wild and crazy tone. "How could you not pick up on those signals?"

His head jerked back as if she'd struck him. "Maybe

because you made it very clear to me that you only want to be friends. Maybe because the town's constantly telling me about how great you and Bradley were together and how you're still grieving." He gave a strangled laugh. "Not to mention the polite threats and passive aggression I get from everyone whenever I even glance in your direction."

A spurt of hope that she hadn't got it all wrong filled her. "Do you want to glance in my direction?"

Again, he ran his hand through his hair. "Nicole…"

She stared straight at him, needing to know. "Do you?"

His hands fell to his side. "Of course I do."

She smiled and reached out her hand, gladness filling her to overflowing. "So we both want the same thing. Let's just ignore everybody else."

"Are you serious?" This time his voice held an edge. "That's impossible when it affects my job."

The army is my life. This job is everything to me. Bradley's words slammed into her, stealing her breath. Was she being set aside yet again for a man's career?

"Nicole, my entire team is made up of volunteers. I can't do my job in Whitetail if people don't respect me and we won't even have a fire department if people refuse to work with me."

The tremble of anger and fear started at her toes and she wrapped her arms around herself trying to stop the shaking. "So you're going to let other people's opinions rule your life? It's none of their business. They don't know…" She'd held the truth so close to her chest for so long she didn't know how to articulate it.

"Know what?" The anger and hurt in his eyes faded

and the caring warmth she'd grown to love shone brightly. "You need to tell me exactly what's going on."

She'd never told anyone, not even her parents. Could she do it? She bit her lip again and swallowed hard.

Tony watched her silently, his entire body attentive and on alert.

"A…" The word sounded hoarse and she cleared her throat. "A week before Bradley died he sent me an email telling me he no longer loved me, that he hadn't loved me for quite some time and that he wanted a divorce. He said he'd outgrown Whitetail and he'd outgrown me."

"Had you seen it coming?"

She laced her fingers tightly in front of her and shook her head. "Put it this way, despite the fact he'd signed up for a second tour of duty and that he'd seemed distracted and sometimes distant on his last leave, I had no clue he wanted a divorce."

Sympathy flared in his eyes. "That would have been tough but don't be hard on yourself. We never see what we don't want to know."

And she hadn't wanted to acknowledge the changes in Bradley. For the months preceding his last leave and during his time back in Whitetail, she'd found excuses for his behavior and she'd clung to them tightly. "Opening that final email was like detonating a bomb."

She remembered vividly the chaos of emotions that had swamped her that week. How the memories still had the capacity to swamp her when she least expected. "I was in shock. I was ashamed that I was no longer enough for him, that he loved the military more than me and I was utterly furious with him for ending our marriage in such an impersonal way."

She sucked in a breath, willing herself to keep going

now she'd started. "I replied to his email, telling him I refused to accept the end of our marriage until he came home, faced our families and friends, and spoke the words out loud. Until he looked his little boy in the eye and told him he was not coming back to live in our house and until I could scream at him and call him all the names I'd hurled at a computer screen." Her left hand gripped her right, crushing her fingers. "Only he never made it back."

"Was it suicide?"

The quietly asked question hung heavily between them and she shook her head emphatically. "No, Bradley might not have loved me anymore but he loved life. He loved his life in the forces and it had become his new family. He died trying to save a fellow soldier and Max has his medal."

Understanding slowly dawned, crossing Tony's face before disappearing into his ash-colored stubble. "You haven't told anyone about Bradley's email, have you?"

"No." She closed her eyes for the briefest moment as pain burned tightly in her chest. "Do you have any idea what it's like to be expected to play the grieving widow when so often I just want to scream that he betrayed me?"

Two deep lines carved in above his nose. "So why don't you?"

"How can I?" She threw up her hands as the black, choking cloud that was everything to do with her feelings for Bradley tried to suffocate her. "I'm stuck, can't you see? To the town and to Max, he's a hero. How can I tell them that he took a coward's way out to end our marriage? They won't be able to even recognize that behavior as Bradley's." Her voice broke. "I'm still so furious with him for putting me in this position."

"Maybe he didn't put you in this position. Maybe you put yourself there."

The quietly spoken words burned her. "No! He left me living a lie with no way to reveal the truth to a town that misses him more than I do. They think they share my grief but they don't."

"Just tell them."

"Are you deaf? I've just explained why I can't tell them."

He nodded slowly and closed the gap between them until his chest skimmed hers and their hips touched. "I hear you."

His heat rolled into her, lighting the fuse on every particle of unmet need that had pulsed in her from the moment she'd met him. Her breathing quickened and she caught the heady scent of his soap and spicy cologne—a potent combination of clean and hot—that surged into her nostrils. His dark gaze tugged and pulled at hers and she willingly threw herself into the inky depths, desperate to be there.

His palms slid along her cheeks, the touch firm but gentle and without a word he tilted her head. She sighed, anticipation singing. This was what she'd wanted for so long. Waited for and dreamed about for weeks and now it was about to happen. Her fingertips traced the line of his jaw and then his mouth covered hers. Hot, wet and intoxicating.

The tip of his tongue trailed along her lips. Sparks of desire—pure and heady—flared and her blood pumped hot need around her body, leaving no place untouched.

His lips closed over her lower lip, suckling her, and then his tongue slipped inside.

Silver spots rained behind her eyes. His touch and taste infused her with everything she knew about him—his warmth, his caring and generosity, and all of it overlaid with a potent sex appeal that made her knees buckle. She gripped his shoulders for support not wanting anything to break the kiss.

The wondrous pressure of his mouth against hers danced through her and she let the river of sensations carry her along, taking her on the journey she ached for. She savored every strand of bliss, every delicious tingle and let it all soak into her body and her mind, so it took her a moment to realize the intensity of the kiss had changed. Like mist clearing, she became aware that although his lips were still pressed against hers, they weren't moving.

He lifted his head. "Nicole…"

No. Cool air zipped between them and she grabbed his hand, wanting to be the woman in the photos. The woman who knew what she wanted and wasn't afraid to take it. She turned toward the bedroom and started walking. Her arm stretched out behind her and then pulled hard at her shoulder.

He hadn't taken a step to follow her.

Confused, she swung back to him. "My bedroom's down the hallway."

"This isn't a good idea."

She realized with a thud that he would be uncomfortable having sex with her in her marital bed and she couldn't believe she'd been so stupid not to think of that. "So we go to your house."

Torment flared in his eyes for a moment and then

he extricated his hand from hers. "Nicole, I want you. God knows I've wanted you from the moment I met you. That day in the salon when you were washing my hair, every part of me wanted to pull you onto my lap and feel you close around me."

She smiled at him, remembering. "I came so close to kissing you that day, which is why I sent you the photos. I'm that woman. I want this."

He scrubbed his face with his hands. "I know you do."

She didn't understand why they were standing here having this conversation when they could be burning up the sheets. "Max is at my parents' house. We're both consenting adults, so I can't see a problem."

He met her gaze full on. "Bradley is part of the problem."

She blinked. "How can he be? He's dead and no longer part of my life."

"The town doesn't think so."

"We're not back at this again." Abject disappointment fizzed with disbelief that he was letting other people rule his life. "I can't believe you're so threatened by a dead man."

A steely glint of silver sparked in his dark eyes. "I'm not threatened by him. He will always be Max's father and I respect that. The other part of the problem is you."

She wanted to stamp her foot. "No. I. Am. Not. You're the one making this way more complicated than it needs to be."

He sighed. "Nicole, I want a future with you. In Whitetail…"

Her heart flipped in her chest.

"...but that can't happen until you declare yourself free of Bradley."

"But I am free of him." Blood pounded so loudly in her ears it almost deafened her. "I've told you I am. I've just shown you that I am."

"I'm not the only person who needs to know." His soft words carried the deceptive smoothness of a sharp knife that delivered a deep, clean cut. "I've been divorced, Nicole. I've walked the path of pain and anger, disappointment and grief, and I've found peace with that part of my life. You're not there yet and if we try to be together before you've done all that, we'll fail. I've already had one failed marriage and I refuse to have another. I'm not prepared to put me, Max or you through that sort of pain."

She stared at him. "You have no clue about me or about this town. I don't need to say anything to anyone. In fact, you're the one who needs to take charge here with your team. Everything you're saying is just an excuse because the reality is that you're putting your job and the town ahead of me."

He suddenly looked inexplicably weary and he slowly opened his hands palm up as if to say *if that's what you believe.* "Good night, Nicole."

God, he wasn't even going to deny it. The truth hit her like a truck. Well, she wasn't going to allow herself to be second best ever again. Tears burned the backs of her eyes and she willed them to stay and not spill. "Goodbye, Tony."

His head gave the smallest of nods and then he silently let himself out.

As the door clicked shut, she lost her battle with holding back her tears. They splashed down her face hot and angry before becoming cold and sad until finally they ran dry. All that was left was a vast and empty feeling sitting heavy in her chest. A space that echoed loudly with her past and was drowning out her future.

Was she pathologically attracted to men who were defined by their jobs? Who put their careers first? She took the soggy mess of tissues into the kitchen and dropped them in the trash. Opening the fridge, she pulled out some cheese curds and poured herself a glass of wine. She drank it fast, feeling the hit against her empty stomach and grabbing on to the spreading warmth that followed.

She bit into a fresh cheese curd, hearing and feeling the squeak against her tongue and savoring the freshness of the comfort food. She ate more and then alternated between the wine and the cheese. There was nothing wrong with her, she reminded herself sharply. This was Tony Lascio's loss and if he'd just walked away from an opportunity and he wasn't prepared to fight for her then she didn't need to spend any more time thinking about him.

Certainly not the way his thick hair curled at his nape. Or how his dark eyes seemed to absorb her every time he looked at her.

She gulped some more wine.

No, she was not thinking about him one more second when all he could think about was his job. Bradley's focus on work had come later in their relationship, after he'd joined up when work in Whitetail had been harder to find. Always happy to be a laborer and not ever having had clear work plans before signing up, he'd embraced the routine and the camaraderie the forces offered and had left her behind.

I want this more than I want you. The words she worked so hard to expunge from her memory taunted her. At least this time, with Tony, she'd recognized the signs up front and saved herself more heartache.

Despite not wanting to relive the evening, her mind was stuck on rewind. *I can't do my job in Whitetail if people don't respect me.*

He was trying to pin the problem on her where it didn't belong, only the moment that thought pinged into her head she suddenly remembered how many times John had ignored him at the coffee cart. The picture of Tina being curt and rude at the supper club loomed large and real. At the time, she'd attributed that behavior to Tina being Tina but the image triggered a flood of small slights, all of which poured into her mind. She pressed her thumbs hard into her temples. He wasn't imagining it—the town was protecting her.

Nicole, I want a future with you.

The wine in her stomach sloshed against the cheese. Nausea rolled in its wake.

Tony had said those words to her but she'd lost sight of them in the quagmire that was the death throes of her marriage. Was Tony right after all? Was she stuck?

Maybe he didn't put you in this position. Maybe you put yourself there.

The stark reality of what she'd done whipped her.

After Bradley had died, she'd let the truth about her marriage take on a warped reality to protect her pride and to protect Max and the town. At the time it had seemed the right thing to do but now it was as if Tony had pointed a bright flashlight onto all of it and illuminated a total mess.

For the very first time she could see that she, not Bradley, was her own worst enemy. Exactly how to help herself was less clear.

"This is so cool, Uncle Luke," Grace said, her expression serious as she shook a sealed baggie full of ice.

"It's my turn now," Ethan said, pulling on gloves and reaching for the bag.

Luke and the children were in the farmhouse kitchen surrounded by sticky maple syrup they'd tapped from the maple grove, milk from the dairy and cream from his Amish neighbor. The only items that hadn't come fresh off a farm were pecans and vanilla essence.

Luke crossed his fingers and rechecked the recipe he'd found on the internet. "I hope it's going to work."

He'd been tempted to involve his mother as his cooking skills weren't fabulous but he figured he was capable of heating ingredients and stirring. Besides, if it was an absolute disaster, doing it this way made it look like he was just being a good uncle and involving the kids in an activity. No one would realize he was exploring an idea that had taken hold of him a few days after Erin had given him that photo.

It had kept calling him back to look at it, the black-and-white tones showing no mercy on his emotions. Every time he studied the photo, he got the same tug on his soul that the farm always inflicted and he knew it would be impossible to walk away from it.

You just need to work out what you want to do with the farm. You need your own project.

The night Essie's calf was born and Erin had said those words, he'd rejected the suggestion out of hand. It was only after seeing the photograph that her words had kept coming back to him like the rhythmic beating of a tribal drum. They refused to leave so here he was, experimenting with making ice cream.

"My arms are getting tired." Ethan passed the bag to Luke.

He checked the clock as he shook the bag. "Not much longer and we'll be eating maple syrup and pecan ice cream." He'd also put a batch in the freezer just in case the shake-in-ice method failed.

"Yum!" Grace licked her lips.

"Mom, look at us," Ethan called out to Keri as she entered the kitchen with his grandparents, having just got back from town.

Martha's eyes popped at the scene and Vernon shot Luke a questioning look while Keri burst into laughter.

"What are you guys doing other than making a big ol' mess?" Keri asked.

"I'm teaching your kids that everything in ice cream comes off of a farm." Luke passed the bag to Grace for a final shake.

"We tapped maple syrup and milked a cow too." Ethan ran his finger through the trickle of syrup on the counter and then licked it clean.

Vernon nodded his head in approval. "All food comes from farms, Eth. When I was a boy my grandma gave me the job of turning her ice cream churn and my reward was that I always got the first scoop."

"I'll get out the careful cups then," Martha said, using her expression for the good china in the cabinet. "Homemade ice cream deserves the best."

Five minutes later they were all seated around the large farmhouse table, dipping small spoons into the ice cream.

Keri sighed as she finished her last mouthful. "Good job, kids. That's the creamiest ice cream I've tasted in a long time."

"Can we have more?" they chorused.

Martha looked at the small but now empty bag. "We'll have to make some more but this time we can use the ice cream maker."

"We have an ice cream maker?" Luke asked, surprised and pleased.

"Yes, Luke, we do." His mother smiled. "I used to make ice cream all the time when you were little but I guess over the years it's moved farther back in the cupboard."

Vernon's forehead was creased in concentration. "This is our milk?"

"Our Holstein milk and Josef's cream," Luke clarified.

"Ah." His father's eyes lit up. "Jersey butterfat. You can taste it."

Luke nodded. "It's good, right?"

"The texture's perfect. You can't get better than Jersey for butterfat."

His father gave him a smile of old—one that had been missing from the moment Luke had mentioned the possibility of giving up the farm. "I'd pull back on the maple syrup, though, son."

"Our syrup's obviously stronger than the shop stuff the recipe suggested." Luke was enjoying the shared understanding with his father. He'd forgotten that despite their occasional clashes about how some things should be done on the farm, most other times they'd talk long and hard about all sorts of things.

"We've been spoiled," Vern said. "Your great-great-grandfather planted the first maple trees a hundred and forty years ago and every generation's added some more from the seeds. They've always yielded quality syrup and I've always thought we should do more with it but the cows kept me busy enough." He checked his watch and stood up. "Talking cows, we should make a start."

They all rose and Keri and the children scooted off to find Phil with the promise they'd wash up the supper dishes. Martha started collecting the empty ice cream bowls. "Luke, I'm going to invite Erin to supper before Keri and Phil leave and your father and I drive back to Arizona for his next golf tournament."

He waited for the usual chagrin that bubbled inside him every time his mother waded into his life, but it didn't come. If agreeing to this avoided a lecture about settling down from his mother then it wasn't even a price to pay because spending time with Erin was no hardship at all. "Sure, why not. Just not Thursday because the radar's showing sunny weather and I'm going to cut the hay in the middle pasture."

"You've got plenty of time, Martha," his father said, reaching for his hat. "I withdrew from that tournament."

His mother's hand faulted on a dish. "You did? You didn't mention it to me."

His father's face showed no emotion other than a slight tick of a muscle in his cheek. "I'm telling you now."

His mother marched behind the counter and flicked on the faucet, jerkily squirting liquid detergent into the water. "Did it occur to you that I might have commitments in Arizona?"

His father sighed. "Bridge is not a commitment, Martha. Neither is golf."

His mother slammed the green container down on the counter. "Well it's a commitment to me."

"I'm off to the parlor," Luke said, feeling like an inadvertent voyeur in his parents' marriage. He grabbed his hat and made a hasty exit.

Martha punched down the faucet and the silence in the room swirled heavily in the air between her and her husband. She noticed a corner of the wallpaper peeling back where it met the tiles above the stove. This kitchen had heard so many of their conversations over the years and not all of them had been congenial, but this was the first time she felt like a massive chasm had opened up between them. That they were no longer walking the same life path.

"Mart—" Vern's face softened "—you can play bridge here in Whitetail. You know the farm has to come first."

A hot breeze blew through her, sparking a resentment that almost knocked her over. "The farm has always come first, Vern, but I'm not prepared to put it first anymore."

His pale blue eyes held a steely resolve. "You don't have a choice. Our retirement income is tied up in this."

"Of course I have a choice." She'd never liked being told what to do and she started scrubbing the first piece of china with more force that the gold rim required. "We both have a choice and I'm making mine. I refuse to spend another winter in Wisconsin. Come September first, I'm driving back to Arizona with or without you."

He strode to the screen door. "You best prepare for a solo journey, then."

The door banged shut into the latch with an ominous finality. She took in a deep breath. What had got into her? She knew better than to issue Vern with an ultimatum—she'd learned that in the first year of their marriage all those years ago. The man had stubborn as one of his chromosomes.

But the thought of spending another winter in Wisconsin was more than she could bear. Her mind raced, frantically flipping through options and searching for a solution. Her hands stalled in the suds. Her "get Luke settled" plans needed to kick up a gear.

Erin Davis was exactly who Luke needed as a life partner. With Erin here on the farm with Luke, she could get her husband back. She just needed Erin's cell phone number. Drying her hands, she picked up the kitchen phone with its long cord and dialed Wade.

SEVENTEEN

"SO ARE THERE any questions about the Littlejohn wedding?" Nicole asked the town meeting, playing for time.

"Why did the damn Littlejohn wedding need a town meeting anyway?" Luke asked Erin not so sotto voce from the front row.

Luke was right. Strictly speaking, this wedding didn't need a full town meeting, just one for the main stakeholders, but Nicole had called it anyway. As her eyes scanned the open doors and her mind willed Tony to walk through them, she heard Erin and Wade's unison response of, "Shh."

She leaned back into the microphone. "The bride has very particular instructions and I want to make sure everyone's on board. This wedding is bigger than Bridey Callahan's, which launched Weddings That Wow and everyone needs to view it as the next level in what we can offer brides. Erin, we've allowed extra time for the photography but the bride must leave Lakeview Farm by five."

"I'm more than happy for her to leave earlier than that," Luke said as he leaned back in his chair.

Erin elbowed him in the ribs.

John stood up with an indulgent smile. "I think you've covered everything, Nicole, and then some. So if there are no other items, I'll call this meet—"

"There's one more thing." Sweat broke out on Nicole's palms and she could feel her glasses slipping.

"Nicole, dear, I know this is a big wedding," called out Ella Norell, "but truly you've been over everything three times and everyone's ready for coffee."

"Did you make cream puffs?" Al asked hopefully.

"Sorry, Al, but the Littlejohn cake has taken me longer than I expected. The bride kept changing her mind."

"Now, there's a surprise." Luke rolled his eyes at Erin, which she ignored.

There was some movement at the very back of the room and she instantly knew that Tony had arrived.

Do it now. She opened her mouth to speak.

A chair scraped against the floor. "Nicole, can you hurry up, I have a date," Melissa said.

All heads snapped toward the dress shop owner.

"Oh for heaven's sake," Melissa said indignantly. "It isn't like I never have a date."

"Actually, it's been five months, dear," Ella said, pointedly looking toward the back of the hall. "So is it anyone we know? Someone *new* to town?"

No way in hell. Nicole wrenched back control of the meeting. "Sit down, Melissa."

The brisk tone in her voice stunned her friend, whose behind hit the chair abruptly. Everyone was now back facing her and she gripped the lectern to steady herself.

"I wanted to thank everyone here for the support you've given Max and me."

Murmurs of sympathy fluttered across the room but she kept her gaze fixed on the enormous clock set high on the wall and concentrated on saying what she needed to say.

"Bradley grew up here and he'll always be part of

this town. No one will ever forget his winning touchdown at the homecoming game in his senior year, which gave Whitetail its first win against Hayward in eight long years."

A ripple of nodding heads and smiles lit up the room with an energy that only a happy, shared memory can.

Her fingertips numbed. "Everyone here knows that Bradley wasn't afraid of hard work but being a farm hand or a barman didn't make him happy. When he joined the military he left Whitetail a husband and a father, but the transformation to the man he became took place while serving his country in a rocky and barren land so very different from here. It was there that he found his true calling."

She paused for a breath and heard Erin say quietly to Luke, "This sounds like a eulogy."

And in so many ways it was. It was the one she hadn't been capable of giving at Bradley's funeral—in fact she hadn't spoken at all, leaving everything to the town.

"Being a soldier opened him up to a new world and over time he came to see that his home was no longer here. He'd spoken of not returning to live in Whitetail."

This time the eddies of noise in the room were of surprise. Her gaze sought out Tony who sat perfectly still, his broad shoulders square and tight, but his dark eyes were fixed on her.

Her mouth dried and her tongue seemed to swell up to twice its size as she mustered the courage to say what needed to be said. To take a leap of faith into the unknown and to burst the complex bubble she'd placed herself in. It was time to tell the truth.

"Bradley was committed to the military and he'd

become a career soldier. Even if he hadn't died, our lives—his, Max's and mine—would have changed so much as not to be recognizable."

She could see questions on people's faces but she wasn't here to destroy their faith in the Bradley they wanted and needed to remember. She was here to take control of her future. "I want to continue to live my life in Whitetail with you all, just as I've always done. I want Max to learn your stories about his father and not just the ones where he made the touchdown or was a war hero. Max also needs to hear the stories about when his father was fallible."

"If you want, I'll tell Max how he put the tractor into reverse by mistake and flattened half a field of squash," Keith called out with a grin.

"Thanks." She threw him a grateful smile. "Me living here also means I need you all to accept that I've reached a point where I want to date again. I don't know what the future holds but what I do know is this. If everyone here wants me to be happy again, and I know you do, then the one thing you can all do is not give anyone I date a hard time, no matter what happens between us."

Tony's mouth opened and then closed. John's face showed a battle of emotions, including grief for his dead nephew and pain that she was moving forward. Empathy filled her. "John, me dating doesn't change the fact Max is a Lindquist and an Ackerman. Him having contact with that part of his family will always be important."

Ella Norell stood up, her pink hair bright under the lights and her face solemn. "We only wanted to protect you from being hurt again, dear."

She nodded. "I know and I let you do it but I've learned life is a series of bumps and getting hurt is part of it."

She was no longer the naive twenty-year-old who'd married her high school sweetheart, and Tony had weathered his own relationship breakdown. Both of them were seasoned marriage veterans without any illusions, but with a great deal of hope.

She looked directly at him. His swarthy and handsome face was filled with one big question.

She licked her lips. "Tony Lascio?"

Fifty heads of all shapes and sizes turned as one toward the back of the room.

He stood up, his chair scraping loudly on the floor. "Yes?"

"Today I baked my very first lasagna."

A slow smile spread across his cheeks and his curls danced wildly.

Ask him. "Will you share it with me?"

He strode down the center of the hall and bounded up onto the raised platform until he was standing so close to her she could feel the erratic beating of his heart. A beat that matched her own. Silently, he pulled her into his arms and kissed her swiftly but thoroughly.

As the bliss of the kiss wove through her, she lost her place in time and space and the next minute her feet left the floor. Now she was cradled in his arms with her cheek resting against his shirt and basking in the glow of heat and caring radiating from his eyes. "I'm thinking this means yes to the lasagna?"

He nodded. "And to everything that follows."

Her entire body relaxed inside and out.

He moved sideways, clearing her of the lectern, and

spoke into the microphone, his voice deep and author-
itative. "I'm depending on you all not to set anything
on fire tonight."

"You got it, Chief," yelled one of the junior firefighters.

As he carried her out of the hall, the noise of the
crowd flowed over them—some murmurings of surprise, some of resigned support, along with genuine
woots and cheers. She'd taken the first step in her new
life and it felt like freedom.

TONY LAY IN his bed with Nicole's legs tangled in his and
her white-blond hair spread across his chest like a veil.
Despite the reassuring press of her weight against him,
he still couldn't quite believe that his day had ended in
this most amazing but unexpected way. She'd put herself out there for him, demanded her place with him,
and his heart was fuller than it had ever been.

He pressed a kiss into her hair. "That was some
speech you made."

She raised her head, her brown eyes still slightly
glazed from her orgasm, and gave him a wry smile.
"You were right. I needed to take control and tell the
town what I wanted."

"And you did it in a way that protected their memory
of your husband."

"My ex-husband," she said firmly, her emphasis on
the ex. "I'm thinking some people might guess, though."

He shrugged. "That doesn't matter, let them wonder. You made it clear it wasn't open for discussion."

She propped up on one elbow and her fingers traced
circles on his sternum. "I hope I made it clear to everyone that you and I are not open for discussion either."

"Baby, given what happened at the end of the meeting, we're *all* that they're talking about right now. In the Udder Bar, at Sven's and in kitchens all over town. Hell, I bet there'll be a pop quiz at the coffee club in the morning."

She laughed and kissed him. "I bet out of everyone, though, we're having the most fun."

Remembering how generous a lover she'd been, he felt his body stirring again, pressing hard against her thigh. Her eyes instantly darkened. God, she was beautiful and he wanted to make love to her forever.

Her hand started to move down his body but he wrapped his palm around her wrist, halting the progression. There were things that needed to be said first. Checks that they were both on the same page. "Nicole, I meant what I said the other day. I want a future with you. With you and Max."

Her love and honesty circled him. "I know you do. That's what today was all about. I want it too."

"We should probably go slowly for all our sakes, right?"

Her eyebrows hit her hairline. "Tony, we just had sex. I think the trail of discarded clothes between here and the sitting room is evidence we overtook slow at your front door."

He grinned at her. "I meant going slow for Max. I promise to respect his father's memory but I want to be his stepdad. He'll need some time to get used to the idea of us as a couple and all of us being a family so I was thinking, picnics and outings and stuff like that. He was telling me his soccer team needs a coach. I could do that."

Nicole blinked rapidly, trying not to cry because every self-help book on the planet probably advised a woman not to become a blubbering mess in front of a new lover. Only Tony was so much more than a lover. He was her friend and her future partner. "Max will love it."

"How would you feel—" he suddenly looked uncertain "—at some point in the future, about a brother or sister for Max?"

Her tears of happiness breached and fell, hitting his shoulder. "I love it."

"And I love you."

He kissed her tears, flicking them off her cheeks with his tongue, and her body caught the wave of a different kind of happiness.

He wrapped his arms around her and rolled her under him. Her breasts ached for his touch and her nipples hardened, brushing his chest. She gasped as his hot mouth closed around the sensitive bud, and she bucked against him, sending delicious shocks of pleasure into her. But it wasn't enough. Need had her wet, slick and ready, and her muscles twitched to feel him pressed hard and deep inside her.

Her legs wrapped around his waist and her hands tugged at his hips, pulling him forward and guiding her into him. A long, blissful sigh left her lips.

He gave a deep, throaty laugh and hooked her gaze. "Baby, this is only the beginning."

As he moved inside her, she matched his rhythm and they drove each other upward, higher and higher until they flung themselves out into a shared future filled with optimism and trust.

ERIN STRODE ALONG Main Street waving to people she knew as she took a call from Connie. "You know, I'm not sure Mac is the sort of dog who needs a white bow on his collar," she said, already able to see and hear Luke's reaction to *that* suggestion. Before Connie could counter she added, "My Maggie-May, however, would be darling in bows if your flower girl wants to walk her down the red carpet aisle."

"I wanted a farm dog, Erin," Connie said tartly.

Erin stood a bit taller. "Maggie-May bailed up a raccoon last night, preventing it from getting into the barn with the cows, so she's a farm dog now." Even Luke had said Maggie-May had earned her stripes.

"I'll think about it." Connie didn't sound convinced.

When the bride hung up, Erin pocketed her phone and kept walking. She had a list of errands a mile long, including talking to Al about driving the hay wagon for Connie. As she neared the market, she made a mental note to collect the ice cream she'd ordered on her way back. With John's help, she'd been sourcing all sorts of different-flavored ice creams for Luke, who adored the cold, sweet stuff but was unusually fussy about what constituted good ice cream. It had become her mission to find a brand that totally wowed him. So far she was falling short but she was determined to succeed.

A text came through and she hesitated to look. For the past three days her father had been texting around this time of day. She knew she should reply and tell him she didn't want to see him but the tiny seed of hope she could never quite squash that he'd changed was holding her back from typing the words. Her phone beeped again and she pulled it out of her pocket.

Erin, Vern and I would love it if you came to supper tonight at the farmhouse. 7pm? Martha Anderson.

Her mouth dried. She could ignore a casual "you

must come over sometime" like she had at the bonfire party but this was an invitation with a specific date and time. Did Luke know his mother was trying to push them together? She needed to check with him before she replied to Martha because in her book, casual and fun didn't include a sit-down meal with the parents. She hit speed-dial but it went straight to voice mail.

As she listened to Luke's deep voice and was composing a message in her head ready to deliver as soon as the beep sounded, she heard her name being called. She spun around and her phone slipped from her instantly numb fingers.

"Dad?" The word came out faint as she rescued her phone from the sidewalk. A jagged crack spread diagonally across the screen.

"I'm sorry, darling, I didn't mean to startle you."

Her father's brow creased in concern under an expensive haircut. "Of course I'll pay for your phone to be repaired."

She swallowed against a tight throat, remembering all the promises he'd ever made her and how less than half had come to fruition. "Wh…why are you in White-tail?"

If he was taken aback by her direct question he didn't show it. Instead his face creased in a smile and his apple-green tailored shirt made his eyes a keener and deeper color. "I'm here to find you. We've been estranged too long and I want to apologize and start over. It's time, don't you think?"

A throbbing pain pulsed in her temple. Was it ever time after that sort of betrayal?

Yes. No. Maybe. "To apologize for what, exactly?"

His head dropped for a moment and then he raised it,

giving her a long look, regret clear in his gaze. "Sadly I lost the chance to make it up to your mother but if you allow me, I can make it up to you and your brother."

He's changed, Erin. Jesse's words from a few weeks ago echoed in her head, begging to be believed. The stable part of her childhood called out to her, urging her to accept the olive branch but the memories of the bad times burned strong. "I don't know, Dad, I—"

"I've stayed away because I thought that was what you wanted but you not being in my life's left a huge hole in my heart. I want to try and fix us. Please let me try." His hand hovered between them and the charming, charismatic man who'd always stormed through her life looked oddly out of his depth. She couldn't ever remember a time he'd hadn't been confident.

Something inside her softened slightly. "I guess I should let you try."

"Thank you, Poppet," he said, invoking his childhood name for her and then he unexpectedly pulled her into a bear hug.

She stiffened as his arms held her firmly. She didn't know what to say or what to feel with so many unspoken issues lying between them.

He let her go. "You look lovely as ever. How's the photography business?"

"It's going well."

"Have you bought yourself that studio you always said you wanted?"

"Not yet." She thought about the injections of funds into her account from the Whitetail weddings. "I'm getting close to a lease though."

He smiled. "That's wonderful. Come have coffee

with your dear old dad and fill me in on your life. Are you in love?"

"Erin!" Luke crossed the street, his smile wide for her but his face filled with questions. His gaze kept moving between herself and her father as if saying, *Who's this guy?* He waited expectantly to be introduced.

She swallowed a groan. She wasn't ready to introduce her father to Luke but unlucky timing gave her no choice. Plastering on a smile, she said, "Luke Anderson, I'd like you to meet my father, Tom Davis."

Luke's eyes widened a fraction but only someone who knew him well would have noticed. He extended his hand. "Welcome to Whitetail, Tom."

Her father returned the steady handshake. "Thank you. It looks like a pretty place to spend some time."

Erin really didn't want the two men to be deepening their conversation beyond the basic pleasantries. "Sorry, Luke, but Dad and I have an appointment to fix my phone screen."

If he was surprised at that, he didn't show it. "No problem. I just wanted to check that you're coming to the farmhouse for supper tonight." He turned to Tom. "You're most welcome to come too. My mother's cooking is legendary in the county."

Panic scuttled through her veins. Why couldn't Luke be channeling the aberration of the horrible man she'd met on her first day in Whitetail instead of Mr. Exceptional Manners and Hospitality? The idea of sitting down at the Andersons' table with Martha clearly match-making was bad enough without adding her father into the mix. "I don't think—"

"I'd love to come," Tom said smoothly. "What a lovely invitation, Erin. Aren't we fortunate?"

Her mouth dried like water in a hot wind and her throat was so tight that no words could pass. She sent a pleading look to Luke but his attention was absolutely focused on Tom as he gave him directions to Lakeview Farm.

It was a done deal. Her summer fling had suddenly become mired by family, which was wrong on so many levels she couldn't even begin to count.

WEATHER-WISE IT WAS a perfect evening. The blue of the lake shimmered against the lush green of the corn and the now ripe and flowering sunflowers were turning their massive heads to the early evening sun. Luke smiled and took in a deep breath—the sweet and earthy scent of the farm filling his nostrils and mingling with the slightly tangy aroma of the citronella flares Phil had been instructed to light by Keri. She had a pathological hatred of mosquitoes, probably because for some reason they found her far tastier than anyone else in the family.

"It was a good idea to eat al fresco tonight, Mom." He surveyed the empty plates on the long table that had been unearthed from the back of the farmhouse shed to do its duty again after a long absence.

"It's a beautiful view, Luke, and it seems a shame not to enjoy it."

"I do enjoy it."

"Not that I've noticed," she muttered as she returned inside.

He accepted the hit. He totally understood that his parents wanted their retirement back and as soon as he received the final set of figures from his accountant, he would call a meeting with everyone and discuss his ideas. He scanned the garden, looking for Erin. The kids, full of ice cream, were romping with Mac and Maggie-May. The fluffy, white dog was doing a fair job working with Mac to round them up and going by the shrieks of delight the kids were loving it as much as the dogs. Farther over, Erin was talking to Keri but everything about her was tense. Just as it had been all evening.

At one point during the meal, he'd swung his arm casually around her shoulders but it had been like resting on a rocky ridge. She'd quickly leaned forward, the action pushing his arm onto the back of the chair. He'd wanted to pull her onto his lap, tickle her and make her laugh like he did when they were alone but she'd dodged every one of his attempted displays of public affection. He was putting all of her unusual behavior down to the unexpected arrival of her father. Even now, as she listened to Keri, he could see her gaze shifting toward Tom, just as it had over supper.

Her father was chatting with Vern over by the post-and-rail fence. One booted foot rested casually on the bottom rail and along with his jeans and a button-down shirt, he could have almost passed for a farmer at a social gathering. The longneck in his hand completed the picture. From the moment he'd arrived, he'd taken a great deal of interest in the farm and he'd even put some milking cups onto cows' udders during the evening milking. Given what Erin had told him about Tom, Luke was reserving judgment but from what he'd observed so far, the man did genuinely seem to want to reestablish his relationship with his daughter.

Luke could understand that. This summer had taught him that there was a hell of a lot more energy consumed by strained family bonds than by companionable ones.

The dogs interrupted his musings by belting up to

him excitedly and demanding a scratch behind the ears. By the time he'd done that, Erin and Keri had vanished and Tom was walking over and offering him a beer.

He accepted it. "Thanks."

The older man smiled. "It's been a great evening. I can see why Erin's so happy here."

"Lakeview's one of the prettiest farms in the county so it has a lot of photographic appeal."

"I'm sure there's more to it than just aesthetics of the countryside. A warm bed helps a lot too." He winked and clinked his beer bottle against Luke's.

An uncomfortable feeling slithered along his spine. Last time he'd checked, fathers didn't make jokes about sex with the man their daughter was sleeping with, and he didn't plan to let the conversation continue down that road. "She's done an entire series of trees in the grove near the lake. You should get her to show you some of her photos."

"I'll do that." He took a swig of his beer and extended his arm out toward the horizon. "I was just talking to your father about all of this. It's a pretty big operation you've got going on. There's a profit in milk, is there?" he asked casually.

"We're doing okay. We've had some good years and my father was pretty financially savvy, which helps a lot, but it's my job to build on that."

"So I gather the bank's not on your back?"

"Nope."

"Good for you." Tom smiled. "Still, diversification is the key to financial security. Must be a concern to you that all your income is dependent on milk prices."

Luke thought about the gelling plan in his mind. "You have a point."

Tom nodded and focused on the view. "Are you thinking of diversifying?"

"It's crossed my mind."

Tom slipped one hand into his pocket and rocked back on his heels as if he and Luke chewed the fat all the time. "I know a surefire investment plan with guaranteed returns of twenty percent."

The number slugged Luke in the chest. "That seems too good to be true."

Tom's eyes filled with a shared understanding. "That's what I thought but I've been benefiting from the generous dividends for the last few months. Not that I'm sharing it around, mind you, but I want Erin to get the advantage from this too. Seeing as the two of you are keeping company, I'm prepared to extend the offer and share it with you and your family."

Every cell in Luke's body went on alert and it took everything he had to hide it. *My father calls himself an entrepreneur.* He didn't want to jump to conclusions too early, given the guy had gone to the effort of finding his daughter after a few years apart. "Have you talked to Erin about this?"

"Not yet. Unlike you, she lacks the big picture business sense. She's squirrelly with money rather than letting it work for her." He gave Luke a conspiratorial smile. "I thought perhaps together we can make her see that this investment is her future. As her dad, all I want for her is to get her long-awaited studio and the returns would pay her lease. After all, you and I are on the same page, aren't we? We just want to make her happy."

Luke gripped the beer bottle hard as a cold rage took seat in his gut. Tom was a chameleon—the clothes, the interest in the farm, getting his hands dirty milking—

all of it had been to warm Luke up for this. Using him to scam his daughter out of her savings.

You might be wrong. Go slowly. "How much are we talking, Tom?"

"To make it really worthwhile?"

"Yeah. Would a hundred thousand do it?"

Lights of excitement glittered in the depths of Tom's eyes. "That will certainly get Erin her studio."

Luke's finger wanted to close around Tom's throat. "If I had a spare hundred thousand, Tom, I'd be buying the studio for her." He leaned forward, using his height to intimidate, and he dropped his voice low so there was no chance of anyone overhearing. "So this is why you're here? To rip us off? To fleece your daughter of her savings?"

For the briefest moment, a flare of fear pierced Tom's sanguine demeanor. "Luke..." He shook his head as if Luke was a child who needed reassuring. "I'm her father and like all fathers, I just want the best for her."

"The hell you do." The urge to protect Erin from this man, from the world, from everything bad, took hold of him with such ferocity of feeling that it almost knocked him off his feet. "She's told me how you love the thrill of a fast buck and I don't know what this too-good-to-be-true investment is all about but there are two things I'm certain of—the company will have your name on it somewhere and I won't allow you to destroy everything Erin's working so hard for."

Tom's eyes narrowed as if sizing him up and then he shrugged as if they'd only been discussing the poor performance of the local baseball team. "You're her latest boyfriend, Luke, but you know she's planning on returning to Minneapolis, right? Going on her track record, you won't be around much longer whereas I'm her father. Who do you think she's going to take advice from?"

The man who loves her.

Me.

The thought exploded in his brain, shattering years of belief that he didn't want love, marriage and the whole damn thing of children, dogs and a pet alpaca. He hadn't wanted it with other women, but with every fiber of his being he wanted all of it with Erin. Erin who'd exposed what was lacking in his life and had opened his eyes to what his life could be. Made him see what he really wanted.

He loved her. He wanted to spend the rest of his life with her, loving her, protecting her and making her happy.

And it started right now. "Tom," he said with the steel of a man protecting his family, "I'm going to walk you up to Erin where you will make your apologies, tell her you're sorry but you've been called back to whatever swamp you came out of and then you are going to drive back down my driveway, leave my property and never come back."

As if realizing he'd explored an avenue of revenue to its cul-de-sac, Tom did exactly that with all the charm and grace he was known for.

ERIN WATCHED THE dust settle on the farm road as her father's car disappeared from view and she realized that Luke was clutching her hand so tightly that he was crushing her fingers. "Hey, ease up."

He glanced down at her, his jaw tight, and then he smiled. "Sorry. Are you okay?"

She really didn't know. Her father had left almost as quickly as he'd arrived, appearing from nowhere and now apparently returning there. The time they'd spent together today had been enjoyable but she'd been on edge the whole time. Now relief tangoed with disappointment, sending unsettling feelings whizzing along her veins. She didn't know what to think.

Think happy. "Luke, can we take a walk to the sunflower field?"

"Sure." He whistled Mac.

The border collie raced over to him and Maggie-May followed, her shorter legs working overtime to keep up with the bigger dog.

"I don't have Maggie-May's leash."

"You'll behave, won't you, MM." He bent down and scooped her dog up into his arms.

Maggie-May, who looked tiny against his broad chest, didn't bark or struggle at being summarily wrenched away from Mac, and neither did she growl. Instead she tried to lick Luke's face.

Erin laughed, struck by the image. "Have you been taking dog-whispering lessons from your dad?"

Luke grinned, his eyes bright and full of life. "She and I have an understanding."

A rush of something she couldn't name filled her. God, she was going to miss him when she left but she wasn't going to think about that. She rose up on her toes and kissed him until Maggie-May tried to get in on the act too.

Luke released her dog and they strolled down to the sunflower field and clambered up the rails and sat on the fence. The white canopy for the wedding service had been erected earlier in the day and tomorrow the chairs and green carpet would be set out. Sunflowers would be tied with green ribbon to decorate the chairs, which lined the aisle. She could barely believe they were less than forty-eight hours away from the big day.

She leaned into Luke. "Do you have your phone? I want to check the forecast."

He passed the device over with an indulgent smile. "It wouldn't dare rain on Connie Littlejohn. She wouldn't allow it."

She thought of everything she had riding on this wedding shoot. "It has to be perfect, Luke."

He slipped his arm around her just as the sun dropped below the tall flowers and fingers of fire red and orange spread across the sky. Pressing a kiss into her hair, he said, "It already is."

EIGHTEEN

"HERE YOU GO, Dad." Luke had made coffee in the office and he handed his father a mug. They were taking a break after having spent an hour with the vet doing a herd check. The results were pleasing with many cows ready to be impregnated.

"Did you remember my sugar?"

Luke laughed. "Amazingly, it hadn't gone hard." When his mother made the coffee it was always served with thick cream but never sugar and his father had always hidden a jar of the sweet stuff in the office.

"A good seal keeps out the air and the ants," his father joked. "I'll start on the AI for you as soon as I've drunk this."

A strand of guilt wound through Luke. When his father had arrived back on the farm, he'd immediately taken on the milking but as the weeks passed Vern had taken on more and more work. Luke had let it happen without comment, not prepared to discuss it with his father because he'd known if he did it would lead directly to Vern saying, "I need a decision." That in turn would lead to an argument.

"I'm fine to do it, Dad. Why don't you and Mom take the boat out on the lake?"

"Are you telling me you don't want me to do it?" The reflections in his father's direct gaze matched the firm set of his mouth.

"No, it's just I don't think you working almost full-time on the farm is what Mom thinks is a vacation. I couldn't help notice that you and Mom seem a bit…"

"Leave your mother and me out of this." His father stared silently into the old mug that Luke had given him one Father's Day years and years ago. Finally, a long sigh rumbled out of him. "She wants me to play golf."

"I thought you liked it."

"I did when I played it a few weeks a year during the summer."

Luke thought about the phone calls from his father over the past year. "But not three times a week?"

"Hell, no."

Luke studied the tension on Vern's face and a slow realization dawned. His workaholic father hadn't adapted to retirement in quite the way he thought he'd done. "So despite some of the crap you've been dishing out to me, you working on the farm these few weeks isn't all about you getting prepared in case I walk away, is it?"

His father shifted in his chair but had the decency to meet his gaze. "Not exactly, no."

Luke felt some of the weight in his chest lightening. "Why didn't you tell me you missed the farm?"

His shoulders slumped. "Because of your mother. Because in the six months before I left I recognized your eagerness to take over and your frustrations that I was still running the show. They were identical to mine when I was your age."

Luke didn't understand. "But Grandpa died before he could hand the farm over to you."

"I know and truth be told, I doubt he ever planned to hand over the farm to me. Like his father before him and back down the line of Anderson men, he would have chosen to die with his boots on if that truck hadn't taken him first."

"I didn't realize."

Vern shrugged. "You were young when it happened but I have to tell you, the three years before your grandpa died were tough. I felt hog-tied. I was thirty years old with three kids and I was still working for my father, not with him. I even investigated making cheese."

Luke remembered his mother's comment about the cheese tours and stared at him in astonishment. "I can't imagine you making cheese."

His father's mouth curved into a wry smile. "That's how desperate I'd got. Making cheese would have made me my own boss and I'd no longer have Dad looking over my shoulder all the time and clicking his tongue at me."

Luke was trying to absorb it all. "That's why you retired? To give me free rein of the farm?"

He nodded. "That and your mother. She was desperate to go to Arizona and if I couldn't farm anymore then I needed to be a hell of a long way away from the place."

"Shit, Dad."

"Yeah." He drained his mug.

Incredulity filled him. His father had left the farm earlier than he'd wanted to allow Luke the opportunity to work it his way. No wonder Vern had been so furious with him when he'd said he wasn't happy. His unhappiness and lack of direction had been the ultimate betrayal of a sacrifice Luke hadn't even known his father had made.

He wanted to honor what his father had done for him

and he pulled up a spreadsheet on the computer. "Dad, can you take a look at this and give me your thoughts?"

Vern pulled his glasses out of his top pocket, slid them up his nose and peered at the screen.

ON THE MORNING of the Littlejohn wedding, Erin had risen well before the milkers and while they worked, she'd held her breath, watching the dawn crawl bright and clear over the horizon. Then she'd breathed out. The farm, bright, shiny and clean after a light shower of rain at midnight, glowed as if it knew it was on show today. The corn leaves shone glossy green, the sunflowers positively beamed, the stream that run under the covered bridge gurgled and sparkled and the B and B in its Victorian splendor waited expectantly for the bridal party to arrive.

All of that had been hours ago and now Erin was waiting for the all-important text that would fire her into action. Everyone else was doing their allotted jobs, with Martha, Keri and Phil all helping Wade out in various ways and Vern looking after the farm. Even Luke had got involved. At breakfast, she'd almost choked on her toast when he'd said, "Do you want me to lug your gear around for you today? Hold the flash, stuff like that?"

She hadn't been able to hide her disbelief. "You've been adamant from the start you've wanted nothing to do with this wedding and now you're offering to be my assistant?"

He grinned sheepishly. "If it's going to help you take your best shot ever for that award thing, then I can handle crazy Connie Littlejohn for a few hours."

She'd been so stunned she hadn't even called him on the fact that Connie wasn't crazy. He understood how important the Memmy was to her and he wanted to help. The lump in her throat had blocked all words so she'd wrapped her arms around his neck and kissed him.

Holding her tightly, he'd kissed her back and then brushing her hair behind her ear, he'd said, "I've got champagne chilling and tonight, after you've taken your last photo, and the newlyweds are enjoying their reception, you and I are going to enjoy ourselves."

She'd nibbled her bottom lip. She'd been waiting so long for this day and now it was here strands of anxiety ran through her. "When I've seen the rushes and found *the* photo, then we can celebrate."

He'd kissed her on the nose. "Oh, we'll be celebrating all right."

Now, as she stood staring out the cottage window, she appreciated his belief in her photographic skills and every time she thought about his offer to help and his plans to celebrate the shot, the lump in her throat returned. She'd been on her own for so long, pushing forward with her business plans, that she'd forgotten what support was like.

You'll miss him.

As her phone beeped, she shoved the thought down deep. *Bridal party has arrived. You're on. Wade.*

She ran over to the B and B and as she opened the door she heard Connie's voice floating down the stairs. "Is that the *only* champagne you've got?"

"It was the one your fiancé ordered," Wade replied calmly.

"Honestly, I only gave Toby *one* job to do for this entire wedding and he couldn't even get that right. I want…" Connie named another brand.

Recognizing bridal nerves, Erin ran up the stairs and

passed Wade coming down. "Do you have the champagne she wants?"

He gave her a reassuring smile. "I've got one bottle, which will be plenty because the rest of the wedding party is fine with the one Toby ordered."

She gave his arm a squeeze. "Thanks. Is Nicole here?"

"She was, but Connie insisted she go to the sunflower field and text her a photo of the setup."

Surprise slugged her. "But I sent her one this morning."

Wade shrugged. "I guess she wants reassurance." Continuing up the stairs, Erin arrived at the honeymoon suite, which Connie was using as her dressing room. With her makeup complete, her thick, black hair swept up high on her head and a tiara in her hair, the bride looked utterly regal.

"Connie, you look amazing. Aren't we lucky with the perfect weather?"

"It wouldn't dare rain," she said, sipping the champagne with a grimace. "Where have you been? I expected you to be here to meet me."

Erin let the disapproval flow over her. "We thought it best to give you a few minutes to settle into the room and open the champagne." Turning, she introduced herself to the maid of honor and one of the six bridesmaids. The two women were busy enjoying Wade's canapés and she assumed the other bridesmaids were dressing in another room down the hall.

A harried woman rushed into the room with a large white dress bag slung over her arm. "Darling, it's time to start getting dressed."

"No, it's not, Mom," Connie said sharply. "I gave

you the schedule. I'm having photos in my underwear first and then getting dressed."

As Connie slipped off her silk robe, Sarah, the overly pale maid of honor with jet-black hair, said, "Toby's going to die when he sees you in that corset."

"That's if he can get her out of it," muttered Zoe, Connie's younger sister.

"Shut up, Zoe," Connie said tightly.

Sarah threw Zoe a scared and pleading look as if to say, "Don't go there."

"Why?" Zoe asked, her chin tilting sharply. "All I'm doing is telling the truth. Everyone knows he got so smashed at the bachelor party that he couldn't walk a straight line let alone operate his fingers to unlace a corset. And last night at the rehearsal dinner—"

"I. Said. Shut. Up!" Connie's mouth was a jagged line of red lipstick.

"Now, girls…" Their mother's ineffectual voice trailed off.

Recognizing the signs of a stressed bride and the undercurrents of family tensions, Erin swung into action. "If everyone can just give me five minutes alone with the bride that would be fantastic. Please go check that the other bridesmaids are dressed and ready for photos. I'll call you back when she's ready to put on the dress."

A minute later the room was quiet and Erin guided Connie over to the window. "Look at that view, Connie. Breathe it in and feel the peace of it filling you. This is your day and it's going to be perfect."

"Of course it's going to be perfect," Connie snapped. "That's what I'm paying you and everyone else for."

The words slapped Erin. Okay, so the view wasn't the key to relaxing this bride. Time to try for another angle. "Let's get started then, shall we, and take some photos to knock Toby's socks off?" She laughed. "Or should I say his pants?"

Connie wasn't the least bit nervous or embarrassed about being photographed in her lingerie; in fact she had some definite ideas, which Erin thought at times bordered on slutty but if that's what the client wanted she took them. She also encouraged and took a few more tasteful shots. By the time the attendants returned, the bride was laughing and smiling.

"Now for the dress." Erin loved capturing the moment a bride first sees herself in the mirror wearing the dress that represents so much. That moment of "wow" when a thousand strands of girlhood dreams unite.

Connie stepped into the dress and Sarah and Zoe carefully pulled it up to her waist before sliding it up her arms to sit just off the shoulders. Mrs. Littlejohn sniffed and Erin caught the emotional shot of a mother watching her daughter transform into a bride.

Connie's dress was exquisite. Layer upon layer of lace flowed from a tight-fitting bodice of ruche chiffon and her narrow waist was circled with a yellow sash—the exact brilliant yellow of the sunflowers that would surround her when she made the commitment to the man she loved. While two of the other bridesmaids fitted the veil, Erin raised her camera in preparation for when Connie turned around and faced the antique cheval mirror.

As Zoe smoothed down the wedding dress, Connie grabbed her sister's wrist and jerked it up to her face. "What's this? I told you and the manicurist that everyone's nails had to be gold."

Her sister shrugged. "I thought this color worked better for me."

Connie pinched the back of Zoe's hand.

"Ouch!" The young woman rubbed it against her thigh.

"You bitch." Connie turned on her, fury blazing from her eyes. "You did this on purpose, didn't you? You can't stand not being the center of attention for one day. Well, newsflash. Today isn't about you. I'm the bride and it's all about me. I won't let you, anyone or anything ruin it. Get out."

Zoe's expression was a mash of emotions including relief.

"Now, darling, don't be like that," Mrs. Littlejohn said, looking desperately at Erin. "Perhaps the wedding planner can find some gold polish for us and Zoe can paint her nails now."

"I can certainly ask," Erin said, pulling out her phone and desperately hoping Nicole had some at the salon.

"Didn't you hear me?" Connie shrieked, totally ignoring her mother. Her eyes bulged and a hot red flush raced along her skin, staining her décolletage to her jaw. Raising a shaking hand, she pointed straight at Zoe. "I've got five other bridesmaids who do exactly what I tell them and I don't need you!"

Zoe's shoulders squared. "Good, because I don't want to have to watch you make Toby miserable."

"Zoe, shhh," her mother pleaded.

"You're just jealous," Connie said tartly. "You always wanted him but he's never even looked at you and why would he?"

Oh God. Erin was used to dealing with mother-daughter tensions but this was a whole new realm of bride drama. Connie was melting down fast and taking happy bride photos with her. Erin frantically wished Nicole was here to help.

Zoe's cheeks flamed so red it was as if Connie had slapped them and Erin saw the moment the bridesmaid decided to go for broke.

"Toby—"

"Zoe." Erin clapped her hands so hard it sounded like a gunshot. Crossing her fingers she said, "Please wait for me in the hall. I'll be two minutes."

The bridesmaid surprisingly spun on her heel and left the room. Erin grabbed the new champagne bottle Wade had delivered and she poured Connie a full glass before thrusting it into her hand. "You look absolutely incredible, Connie, and I want to photograph that— not your stress. You've always said you want amazing photos and they're going to happen. Right now, all you have to do is enjoy your favorite champagne. Let the bubbles float on your tongue and picture yourself in the sunflower field. I promise you, I'll sort out the rest."

"She's right, princess," Mrs. Littlejohn said, her voice trembling. "We all want your day to be perfect and we're going to make it happen."

While the mother of the bride was soothing her daughter, Erin said very quietly to the other bridesmaids, "Go tell Connie how amazing she is and how she's the most beautiful bride you've ever seen in your life. Do you understand?"

They nodded mutely and sculled champagne.

Erin pulled open the door and grabbed Zoe's hand. Fortunately, the young woman acquiesced and walked with her down the passage to the room where the groomsmen were dressing. Erin knocked and then opened the door. Seven men gave her a welcoming nod. It was uncanny how they all had the exact same hair color and she realized with a belated jolt that the bridesmaids did too. She thought about the hissy fit Connie had just thrown over nail polish and asked Zoe, "Is Sarah a natural brunette?"

Zoe let out a tight laugh. "With that skin and those eyes, what do you think? Connie told her if she wanted to be her maid of honor she had to dye her hair."

Before Erin could fully absorb that bit of information, the groom, who was holding a longneck of beer, gave Zoe a long and furtive look before glancing away. A moment later he set his beer down and approached his soon-to-be sister-in-law. His forehead was a sheen of nervous sweat. "You look lovely. How's Connie?"

Their exchanged glances turned Erin's mouth dry. No, she was imagining things. She was letting her own nerves about taking a career-defining photo give free rein to her imagination. Still an internal voice yelled *act now*.

Before the bridesmaid could open her mouth, Erin said firmly, "Toby, your bride is utterly beautiful and she's going to take your breath away. Now, it's time for photos. If we can just get a photo of your mom pinning the boutonniere onto your lapel…"

An hour later, Zoe had gold nails, the groom was bolstered by both beer and his groomsmen and the bride was one of the most stunning women Erin had ever photographed. Connie was holding her father's arm and waiting to walk down the green carpet aisle to join her soon-to-be husband. Erin took the photo that would define the last moments of Connie Littlejohn's life as a single woman.

The music started and Erin snapped the cute flower girl walking a beribboned Maggie-May down the aisle. Under the canopy, as per Connie's instructions, Mac lay uneasily at the groom's feet casting confused glances at Luke.

Luke, dressed all in black and looking like an insanely handsome country music singer, bent his head until it was at the level of Erin's ear. "The groom looks like he's scared of dogs."

Erin was pretty certain the groom was scared of something but she'd swear it wasn't the dog. The service started and she aimed her camera, her attention completely focused on the bride and groom as well as trying to be as unobtrusive as possible so as not to interfere with what should be an intimate and emotional service. As with every wedding, she was so busy that she always felt the formalities went quickly but today it seemed even faster and a touch impersonal. Everything looked perfect so she couldn't quite put her finger on exactly what was different but there was a lack of something.

The groom kissed the bride and then together they walked back down the long, green carpet toward their hay wagon. The plan was that they would be showered in rice and then be taken on a short wagon ride. While they were catching their breath and spending some special and private minutes together as a married couple, Nicole and the Andersons would guide the guests onto the waiting buses. As soon as the last bus had exited the property, Connie and Toby would return to the field for the photo session.

"They make a striking couple," Erin said to Luke, who had her camera bag slung over his shoulder and her tripod in his hand ready to move.

He raised his brows. "That's one way of putting it."

She frowned, uneasy that she couldn't just brush away the comment. "What does that mean?"

"Nothing. They have white teeth, an even gait, good muscle tone and—"

"They're not cows!"

He grinned. "If they were, she'd be described as having a prominent udder. They can't be real, right?"

She thumped him playfully in the arm. "You're supposed to be carrying the gear not eyeing the bride."

He stole a kiss. "Sweetheart, I've only got eyes for you."

A fraction of her heart turned to mush, which scared her, and she swung her mind back to the job at hand. "Come on. I want to meet them as they turn back into the gate from the farm road." Summoning the rest of the bridal party, she led twelve people down the field.

While they were waiting for the happy couple to return, Erin thoroughly enjoyed taking the photos of all the attendants. Now that the ceremony was over, everyone was relaxed and ready to kick back and have fun. Wade helped by providing more food and drinks, all laid out beautifully on a silver platter, which rested on a white cloth-covered table. He'd even arranged a vase of sunflowers. She photographed the setup knowing it would add beautifully to the couple's album.

As she worked, Luke was surprisingly intuitive about what she needed and when, as he dexterously switched cameras and lenses. At one point she looked up to see him taking a photo of her taking a photo of the wedding party line dancing. She laughed and blew him a kiss.

Her phone vibrated in her pocket. She fished it out and read the text from Nicole. "Okay, everyone," she called the group together. "Connie and Toby are about to arrive."

The relaxed mood vanished. Zoe's brown eyes took on a hue of brittle, burned toffee. Sarah anxiously asked if her hair and makeup were still okay and the rest of the party stared at their feet. *No. No. No.* She needed happy for sensational photos. "Luke, call Mac and Maggie-May."

His expression questioned her but he let out a piercing whistle and the dogs appeared, racing around the group wildly and making everyone smile.

That's more like it.

The wagon rumbled into the field and Al called, "Whoa," bringing the horse to a halt. He jumped down and offered his hand to steady the tuxedo-clad Toby off the wagon.

The groom landed awkwardly before turning and putting his arms up to lift Connie down.

Erin was right there next to the wagon, camera ready, waiting for the moment Toby's hands circled Connie's waist. Waiting for the second their eyes locked in a long, deep stare that excluded the world—the look that only a couple deeply in love can share. Toby moved. Erin watched. Finally, her finger pressed the shutter despite the argument her brain was having with her retinas that the image wasn't quite what she wanted.

Toby's hands were on his bride's waist but his gaze was centered over her left shoulder looking directly at her sister.

"Be careful of my dress," Connie instructed. "Don't tear it or stand on it when you set me down."

Toby's hands fell away. "Do you want me to lift you down or not?"

Connie huffed. "I would if I didn't think you might drop me."

"If you were so worried about it then why the hell did you want a wagon ride?"

"How about he hands you down," Luke suggested, moving in with the box he'd pulled off the wagon.

"That's not the photo I want," Connie snapped.

Erin saw Luke's eyes blaze and panic engulfed her. *Please, Luke, don't say anything.*

Silently, Luke took a step back.

"And it's always about what Connie wants," Toby muttered as he roughly lifted her up and unceremoniously dumped her next to him. "Satisfied?"

Erin snapped out of her momentary panic and aimed to take back control with distraction. "Using the dogs to round you up in the middle of the sunflowers will make a fabulous photo."

Toby sighed.

Connie's golden forefinger poked at her groom's starched shirt. "You agreed to everything I've suggested about the wedding so don't go all whiney on me now. My wedding photos are going to get me into *US Bride* and I won't let you ruin them."

"And there you have it." Toby threw up his hands. "I'm just a convenient prop in *your* wedding."

An uneasy twitter of laughter rose from the group, breaking the tension between the couple.

"Daddy did tell you that it's all about the bride." Connie smiled, kissing her groom on the cheek.

Toby looked at Erin, his mouth tight. "Let's get this over with then."

Erin moved quickly before another disaster struck and skillfully maneuvered everyone into position. They did a conga line through the flowers. The couple held up a pitchfork and replicated American Gothic, and they played with the dogs. With each shot, Erin felt she was getting closer and closer to *the one*.

"What's next?" Luke asked as he replaced the black-and-white film.

"Peekaboo."

He scrunched up his face. "You know, I wouldn't ask this couple to do that one."

She remembered the time she'd asked him to do it and how he'd caught her in his arms and kissed her for the very first time. "Trust me, Luke. This will give me the defining photo."

Luke frowned but he didn't say anything more.

"Toby," Erin said, "you've been fantastic and there's just one more shot left. Can you step into the sunflowers and pop out like you're playing peekaboo?"

He stared at her nonplussed.

"Maybe think of it as hide and seek. You can catch Connie and twirl her around. It'll be fun."

He shook his head. "No."

"Toby, it's one photo," Connie said firmly.

"I've done all the others but I'm not doing that one."

Erin read the intransigence on Toby's face and heard it in his voice. She needed to tread carefully. "Okay. How about you just hold Connie close and rest your forehead on hers? Gaze into her eyes so we can all share the love you have for each other." She waited for him to move.

"No."

She needed this photo. "I'm happy to try something else. Do you have an idea of something you'd like to try?"

"You know what?" Toby pulled roughly at his bow tie as if it was choking him. "I'm done."

"You're done when I say we're done," Connie spat.

Erin could feel things slipping away from her and she knew she hadn't captured the moment between the couple that would win her the Memmy. "How about hand in hand walking down the field?"

"No, you don't understand. I'm totally done." He turned to Connie, his face haggard but a light of relief glowed in his eyes. "It's over, Con. We were over six months ago and I tried to tell you but like with everything you refused to hear."

Connie stared at him, her mouth moving but there was no sound coming out.

He ran his hand through his hair. "And I was too weak to push it but I'm pushing it now. Tomorrow morning, I'm applying for an annulment."

Erin's blood dropped to her feet. It was like watching a trucking rig careening out of control and heading straight toward a crowd, and being totally powerless to prevent the crippling carnage.

"Does anyone have a paper sack?" Sarah asked anxiously as Connie's breathing quickened and her face drained of color.

"You prick!" Connie finally screamed at full throttle before lunging for him. "You fucking bastard, I'm going to kill you."

Luke moved quickly, wrapping his arms around the flailing bride, working hard to keep her separate from Toby. Panting, he said to the groom, "If you're walking, pal, go now and go fast."

"Let go of me," Connie yelled, trying to kick Luke.

Toby hesitated half a beat, spun on his heel and marched toward the gate, dust rising from his heels.

Zoe hauled her long dress up to her knees, kicked off

her high heels and starting running. "Wait! I'm coming with you."

Toby paused and extended his hand. Zoe caught it and they both kept walking.

The rest of the bridal party stared in disbelief, their gazes shifting between the retreating couple and the screeching bride, all of them too shocked to speak.

Right on cue, the two limousines that were to have taken the bridal party back into Whitetail arrived and Nicole hopped out with a confused smile. "Is everything okay?"

Erin vomited.

NINETEEN

THE AIR IN the cottage was filled with a fraught anxiety, which had hit Luke in the chest the moment he'd stepped inside. He'd watched Erin click through every photo she'd taken at the ill-fated wedding at least five times and he knew she'd been at it much longer than that.

He ran his hand across her hair before letting it rest on her shoulder. "Erin, it's nine o'clock and time to stop."

It had been a memorable five hours for all the wrong reasons. The Littlejohns had helicoptered in their physician who'd sedated the hysterical bride. Mrs. Littlejohn had suffered an angina attack on hearing the news that the groom had run off with her other daughter and both Connie and her mother had been evacuated to the Twin Cities. With no room on the helicopter, the bride's father had wanted blood. Luke felt for him but at the same time, he didn't like the look in his eyes so for the safety of the Andersons and the townsfolk, Luke wanted him off the farm and out of Whitetail as soon as possible. Wade had understood and together they'd driven him to the tiny tri-county airport so he could charter a plane to return him to Saint Paul.

Nicole had been amazing, organizing the stunned wedding party into town with a minimum of fuss so they could join the other guests. The reception had gone ahead, in as much as the food was served because everyone was from out of town and hungry. Wade told him that Ella Norell had taken the much-anticipated cake to the town hall where all the Whitetailians involved in the wedding had gathered to eat cake and debrief. Every-one except Erin. She'd refused both Nicole's invitation and Wade's cajoling. Luke had stayed with her until he had to go mix the cow feed and distribute it in the barn. Now he was back and she was still at the computer.

Her hair stuck up in jagged spikes as if she'd pulled it up at the roots. "I think there's one I could use."

"One what?"

She stared at him, her eyes dilated and slightly wild. "Photo. For the Memmy."

"Erin," he spoke softly. "They're getting an annul-ment."

She shrugged his hand away. "I know that but they got married and I've poured hours of work into this shoot. I've been editing this one. What do you think?"

He stared at the photo. The sunflowers, so bright and cheery, almost leaped off the screen and it was impossible not to smile at the hope they inspired. In contrast, the bride looked like a bored model and the groom looked utterly miserable.

"Not even the 'Erin Davis touch' is going to make this work."

"I make people look happy," she ground out. "It's what I do."

He frowned. "You do when the conditions are right, but you can't create a moment that doesn't even exist."

She shook her head. "No, you're wrong. It's so much more than that." She dropped her head in her hands. "I can't believe he left her."

Luke could—Connie Littlejohn was obnoxious and

Erin had pinned so much on the shoot that she'd totally missed seeing that. "Come here." He pulled her to her feet and kissed her, hugging her hard and wishing he could absorb her disappointment. He moved her toward the bed and they lay down together.

"I wanted this so much, Luke. This was supposed to be my moment, my chance to shine and show the world that I take great wedding photos."

"You do take great photos. You just had the wrong bride and groom. Connie was all about the wedding, not the marriage, and the only emotional well available to tap was pain and anger. Don't beat yourself up."

Her entire body slumped against his. "Do you know anyone madly in love who wants to get married this coming week while the sunflowers are perfect?"

He let her hair slide through his fingers and smiled. The failed wedding had undermined his plan to propose to Erin over champagne after she'd found her perfect photo, but she'd just given him the perfect segue. "I might."

She sat up fast, her face alive with hope and enthusiasm. "Who? Do they have a photographer? Do you have their number?"

His heart expanded again. God, he loved her so much. Loved her zest for life, her "can do" attitude and the way she bounced back from disappointment. He couldn't help grinning. "Yes, I know them. No, they don't have a photographer but I do have their number."

"Can you call them, please? Set up an appointment?"

He traced her cheek with his finger. "No need."

Two frown marks scored the bridge of her nose. "I don't understand."

He rolled off the bed and kneeled down beside it before picking up her hand. "I love you, Erin. Marry me?"

Her eyes widened into a fathomless green sea. "Be serious, Luke. This is my future."

"I know it is," he said gravely. "Yours and mine."

Her face paled and she raised her free hand to touch his face. "Oh my God, you're really serious."

"I am." He pulled her closer. "You marched into my life and made me realize I've not only been lonely but I've been trying to fit myself into a business that doesn't totally fit me."

"Luke, I—"

"Please." He put his forefinger gently against her mouth, wanting to tell her everything. "I've got so much more I need to say. That night you helped deliver Essie's calf, you said I needed my own project. I didn't want to hear it but now I know you're right. I need the challenge and the excitement of something new to get me up in the morning, to keep me focused and enthusiastic, so I'm starting a new venture for me, for you, for us. I've got a meeting with the bank on Wednesday and we're going into the gourmet ice cream business."

She sat perfectly still. "I'm a photographer, Luke."

His eagerness spilled over. "I know and I want one of your photos of the farm to be the signature look for Lakeview Farm ice cream. Maybe that one you took of the cows through the trees?"

She stared at him and he scanned her face seeking delight on her cheeks for the idea, looking for the zest roving across her mouth for the project, and for her love for him glowing in her eyes. He found nothing. It was like looking at an expressionless plaster cast.

Blinking, as if she was coming back to him from a

very long way away, she asked faintly, "What sort of loan are you talking about?"

He sat back on the bed facing her. "Substantial. It's an investment in our future and I'm taking a two-pronged approach. There's the refrigeration plant for the ice creamery as well as establishing a Jersey cow herd." The buzz he got whenever he thought about the new venture fizzed in his veins and he squeezed her hand. "Initially, we'll be supplementing our milk with milk from the Amish farm down the road. Jersey milk's high in butterfat, which makes the creamiest ice cream."

Incredulity spun across her cheeks. "You're going into *debt* to make ice cream?"

He shrugged against a tiny ripple of exasperation that she wasn't as excited as he was. "There's a definite gap in the Midwest market right now for pure, simple, old-fashioned creamy ice cream straight off the farm." He grinned at her. "And who knows? Maybe in the future we can expand beyond the Midwest and take on those two guys from Vermont."

"If you invest in a luxury item you're likely to end up losing everything."

Exasperation morphed into chagrin. "It's not de-signer clothing or diamond-studded watches. I've stud-ied the market and done the math, Erin. This isn't a whim. Even in tough economic times, people buy ice cream because it's an affordable luxury."

She shook her head as her fingers pulled at the quilt on the bed. "It's too much of a risk."

The words penetrated his excitement as if amplified by her total lack of enthusiasm and a chill settled over him. "What is? The ice cream venture or marrying me?"

Her eyes filled with misery. "Both."

The softly spoken word was like the wet, black mud of the marshland, and it sucked him down, trying to bury his soul. He refused to let it. He could still convince her.

"I'm sorry, Luke." Her eyes implored him to understand. "I can't be with you with that insurmountable level of debt."

"It's not insurmountable debt," he said firmly, "and it's called a business loan."

She stiffened. "Don't lecture me when I know far more about debt than you do. How can you take the security of what you've got here and gamble it on a crazy idea that can risk you losing the farm?"

"Gamble it?" He couldn't believe what he was hearing given the nights he'd been turning figures while she'd been editing photos. "Shit, Erin, this isn't a gamble. This is a solid plan."

"And that's exactly what my father would say." Her fingers pulled at the quilt. "Can't you see?"

He could see all too well and at that moment he hated Tom, and he'd never really hated anyone in his life. He sucked in a steadying breath and tried to keep his voice even. "I can't see how it is anything like your father. I can give you a spreadsheet with real costings, projected earnings from the farm and the ice creamery, plus loan repayments and how they'll be serviced along with a buffer if things are slower to take off. It's a calculated risk on the low side of failure."

"Figures lie, Luke." The harshness in her voice thundered into him. "You can make them work any way you need them to."

I'm not the con man your father is. The words teetered on his lips but with a shock of clarity, he realized that hurling them at her would serve no purpose, nor would they change her mind. Tom was a charlatan but he was still Erin's father and familial ties ran deep and could surface at any time. Disparaging her father to defend himself and the business was not the path to take to make her change her mind. She feared financial risk and given what had happened to her, he could understand it but this situation, their situation, was totally different.

He'd rely on the simple truth. "Erin, I love you and together we can make this work."

She shook her head so hard her hair swung wide. "You don't love me. You're confusing loneliness with love. I filled a void in your life with a summer fling, is all. You can fill loneliness with anyone."

The black bog surged forward, its thick, sticky mass sticking to his heart with a message he refused to accept. He would change her mind. He'd show her that they truly belonged together because contemplating the opposite was far too terrifying. "Before I met you, Erin, marriage had never even crossed my radar, but with you it makes so much sense."

His hands cupped her cheeks and he sought her gaze. "I want to share my life with yours and I promise you, the ice creamery will not bankrupt us. Trust me. Know implicitly that I will never do anything or let anything hurt you."

Luke's words burned through Erin like the sizzle of a brand. Identical words used by her father called up the past so strongly it made her gasp. How often had he made her a promise that he then broke moments, hours or days later, hurting her deeply?

Jumping off the bed, she pointed to the screen where a slideshow of photos moved across the screen showing

Connie and Toby making their vows. "They pledged to love each other, made promises, invoked trust and it lasted less than two hours!"

His lake-blue eyes darkened like water under the clouds of an approaching storm. "You can't seriously be comparing us to them?"

"Why not?" Her heart pounded and her head hurt. "They've known each other longer than we have."

"Connie Littlejohn is a raving loon." He ran his hand through his hair as if dragging at his patience. "I know how much security means to you, Erin, and I'm not asking you to invest any of your savings into the farm. Just invest in me."

The panic that had been rising in her from the moment he'd first proposed overflowed and flooded her. Agitation vibrated every part of her. "I can't marry you, Luke," she said, begging him to understand. "It wouldn't work. We'd argue over money and make each other miserable."

He flinched as if she'd slapped him. "I don't believe that for a moment."

She spoke from her heart. "It's what I know to be true and nothing you can say will make me change my mind."

Luke's face crumpled for a brief moment, only to immediately harden. She saw the angry man—the one she'd first met all those weeks ago—return and she ached that she was the cause.

"So if you're not marrying me, what will you do?"

She bit her lip at the harshness in his voice. "What I've always done. Make people happy."

His bark of a laugh rained scorn all over her. "You don't make people happy, Erin. If they're happy to begin with you work with them and relax them so they can get past their nerves. Then you find the truth of their happiness and photograph it. If they're not, well, today is a case in point."

His words struck hard and she flicked the mouse onto a different folder and displayed a photo she'd taken of him and his siblings. "Look at that. You were hardly a cohesive family the day I took it."

"Sure, we had the issue of the future of the farm but we came together for our parents, to give them a photo of us all together. You captured the love that lives in each of us for Mom and Dad." He gave a pitying sigh. "You're a good photographer, Erin, but if the love for our parents didn't exist there's no way on earth you could have photographed it.

"I think you've confused the happiness you experience from photography with the clients. You need to believe you make people happy because it makes you feel needed and safe."

His words tore at her. It was as if he was emotionally undressing her and she fought back, wanting it to stop. "That's so far from the truth to be ludicrous."

"Is it?" His gaze zeroed in on her with laser-sharp precision. "You love developing your own photos even though you could send them to a lab."

The muted sounds of her parents arguing rumbled in the back of her mind and she blocked them out. "You know what, Luke? As a therapist you make a good farmer."

The insult rolled off his tense shoulders. "Taking calculated risks is a part of life, Erin, but you've run from that. You're hiding behind a lens and watching other people live their lives instead of living your own because you're scared."

His words hailed down on her, inflicting the sharp and burning pain of ice on skin. "My life is just fine, thank you very much. Just because I don't want to live with massive debt hanging over my head doesn't mean I'm hiding. I like my life just fine this way."

His eyes, now as hard as flint, seared her and his body sparked with anger. "And how's this life working out for you? You work two jobs just to meet the high city overheads so one day you can get that incredibly expensive studio that will continue to drain your resources? Working so hard you don't have a social life?"

She wanted to put her hands over her ears to block out his voice.

He wasn't finished. "You can't stand here and tell me you haven't had fun this summer, that being involved in the Whitetail wedding business hasn't earned you almost as much money as you earned last year from photography. What about the fact you've come to love the farm and enjoy being a part of my family? All of that has to be better than what you had before."

His ruthless deconstruction of her life, reducing it to a series of disconnected parts, torched her temper. "I came here to work and earn money, is all. I didn't ask for the rest. I didn't want to be part of your family and I surely didn't need your mother pushing me at you as if the two of us had no say in the matter."

"My mother has nothing to do with this." Exasperation ricocheted around them. "I'm my own man and I agreed to the supper invitation because I wanted you to be there."

She didn't want to hear any of it. "My life's in Minneapolis, Luke, not on this farm."

She threw up her arms as ridiculous tears—ones she didn't want to shed—stung the backs of her eyes. "We had a deal, Luke. Sex and fun for the summer and now you've gone and broken it." She hated the way her voice quavered and she blew out a breath. "I don't love you and I don't want to marry you. I don't want to marry *anyone*."

His entire body jerked as if her words were shrapnel straight to the chest. "Fine." He bit off the word with a snap. "You go on believing all of that, but you know what? I totally get not taking stupid risks but not taking any at all? That turns safe into catatonic. A life worth living involves taking some chances so go be safe and enjoy watching your life from the sidelines."

He crossed the room, wrenched open the slider and stepped out onto the deck into the night. She heard the click-clack of dogs' paws on the wood.

"Mac, come. Maggie-May, stay," Luke's curt voice instructed.

As Mac and Luke walked away, she heard disappointment in the high-pitched whine of her dog. She steeled her heart but part of it tore anyway. She'd just hurt a really good man and there was no way to feel good or proud about that. Scooping up Maggie-May, who'd trotted into the room seeking solace, she buried her face in her dog's short, white fur and let the tears flow.

Damn it, Luke. You of all people were not supposed to fall in love.

MARTHA SAT ON the rustic hickory glider, which their Amish neighbors had gifted them three years ago, and sighed. The farm had never looked prettier but apart from the animals and the crops, nothing and no one was particularly happy—not her, not Vernon and especially not Luke. It had been two weeks since the infamous wedding that had changed so many things.

Things she couldn't change or fix and her heart ached in many different ways. She sighed again and picked up the book she'd let fall into her lap. She'd only read a couple of pages when she heard footsteps. She glanced up to see Vern rocking back and forth, balancing his weight on the top porch step.

The constant movement was a sure sign he had something on his mind and he held a bunch of freshly picked cornflowers in his hand. The brilliant blue color came close to matching his eyes.

"I thought you might enjoy these." He extended the flowers toward her.

She recognized his olive branch or at least a request to talk in peace. Since she'd stated her ultimatum of returning to Arizona with or without Vern, things had been tense between them and their conversations hadn't drifted far from the time supper was being served and other general scheduling. Now she wanted the distance to close and the nights of lying stiffly side by side without touching to stop.

Patting the seat next to her she said, "How's Luke?"

Vern sighed and sat next to her. "Working like there's no tomorrow. Right now he's settling the new Jersey cows he bought at the dairy sale into the barn. At least he's got the new business setup to keep him busy."

Martha stared out across the garden toward the barns and a pang cramped her heart. "You know, I really liked Erin, but to do this to our boy…"

"There's no crime in not returning love, Mart." The

chair moved back and forth, soothing in its rhythm, and then Vern rested the flowers in her lap. "There is, though, in hiding the truth."

Her head whipped around at this unexpectedly deep maxim. It wasn't that Vern wasn't capable of deep, emotional thought, it was just he didn't often voice it. A reply rose to her lips but she cut it off, experience having taught her not to break his train of thought.

The lines around his eyes were tight. "I haven't been honest with you."

A flicker of unease stopped her breath. "About what?"

"I'm not happy."

Nausea clogged her throat and a flash of panic pooled sweat on her top lip. She was no naive bride and she knew marriages could falter at any time. She'd thought their shared thirty-six years, weathering the ups and downs, had soldered them together so they could enjoy their "third age."

Don't you dare do this to me now. Fear sparked anger and her fingers started shredding the bright blue flowers. "Since when has one argument been the basis of wanting a divorce?"

Confusion haunted his eyes. "What the hell are you talking about?"

Her heart pounded. "You not being happy."

"What's that got to do with a divorce?" He sounded utterly bewildered.

"I don't know." Petals scattered. "You tell me."

Vern removed the flowers from her lap and set them aside in safety before picking up her hand. Tracing her wedding band he said, "I don't want a divorce, Mart.

I've loved you from the moment you threw yourself onto me on the state fair roller coaster."

She tried to sound huffy. "I did not throw myself at you. That ride was scary and I just—"

"Either way…" he smiled—the special smile he reserved for her "…that kiss made me yours for life." He leaned in and pressed his lips against hers.

Despite the familiarity of his mouth on hers and all those years together, he could still spark a tingle at the apex of her thighs and she sighed. Leaning her head against his shoulder she said, "So what's making you unhappy?"

"I don't want to play golf three times a week."

She relaxed and wondered why she'd let a week of toxic thoughts unsettle her so much. "So don't. You can take up bocce—that looks like fun."

A long sigh shuddered out of him. "I don't want to play bocce but most importantly, I don't want to retire. I want to move back to the farm."

Her head shot off his shoulder so fast that the glider chair lurched unsteadily. "No."

"Hear me out, Martha," he said firmly. "I know the last two years we spent here you were tired, sick of the long, cold winters and dreaming of any place warm. Luke was champing at the bit to take over and I wanted both of you to be happy." His eyes clouded. "I've tried retirement, but I've missed this place like an amputee misses a limb."

His heartfelt words slid through her like the ache of an old wound. "But you never said?"

He shrugged. "You were so happy and I know that over the years there were times you missed out some because the farm always came first. I owed you Arizona."

"Oh, Vern." She heard his love for her and his pain. She hated the fact that neither one of them could be as happy as the other in the same place. "Do you truly hate Arizona?"

"No." He hooked her gaze. "Do you truly hate the farm?"

She thought about the past few weeks spent with her children and grandchildren and despite the friction over the future of the farm, she'd loved spending time with them all together in the same place. "This summer has been mostly enjoyable."

"Good." He gave her a wry smile. "So does that mean the truck isn't driving off without me in forty-eight hours?"

She gave him a shrewd look, knowing he was calling her on her threat. "Maybe, but it also doesn't mean I want to move back here permanently."

"I know that and I'm not asking you to do it."

He'd surprised her again. "So, I'm gathering you've come up with a plan?"

"I have." He winked at her. "Long, lonely nights make a man think."

She raised her brows. "And here I was thinking you were mostly spending them snoring."

He tilted his head so it touched hers. "Summer in Arizona is way too hot."

"Winter in Wisconsin is way too cold."

"Exactly. Winter here will be Luke's quiet time and we'll spend it in Arizona playing golf. We'll spend summer and fall here. He can't make this ice creamery work without help and I'll go crazy not working at all. That said, I don't expect you to get back into the harness when you're here. Heck, you can do even less than you did this summer if you want."

"Actually, I quite enjoyed helping Wade with the B and B, playing with the grandkids and feeding everyone," she admitted without reluctance. "I just don't want to do it three hundred and sixty-five days of the year."

He patted her hand. "Noted."

Under the warmth of his love and consideration for her, the logistics started to firm up in her head. "How does this affect the family trust?"

"Luke wants the farm so the transfer goes ahead as planned. He's insisting on paying me extra when I'm physically working here but I'm thinking we can afford to invest it back into the farm, at least at the start to help him out some." He put his arm around her waist. "So is it official? Are we semi-retired?"

She looked up into his eyes where weeks of strain had drained away and the twinkle she loved so much was back. "Almost. I want to hammer in some start and end dates. Come November first we are most definitely in Arizona."

"That late?" He grinned. "I'm two weeks ahead of you there."

She thought about the harvest calendar. "What about the soybeans?"

"They'll be in and if it's an unexpectedly long season, Luke can manage the last crop. Besides, if I'm only playing golf during the winter, I have to keep my average up."

She laughed and laid her head back on his shoulder. "Then I guess we're semi-retired."

"I guess we are." He kissed her again. "This calls for a celebration, don't you think?"

She recognized the look in his eye and smiled.

"Ooh, what are we celebrating?" Keri's voice sounded behind them.

She heard the run of the children's feet and the heavier tread of the men and realized the entire family had arrived back for supper. "There are fewer interruptions in Arizona," she said quietly to Vern, trying not to laugh at the resigned disappointment on his face.

Luke saw his parents exchange a knowing look—one of many he'd witnessed over the years. He'd often wondered about the secret code they seemed to share and now he got it. He'd had it with Erin, or at least he thought he'd had it with her.

These past two weeks had been beyond tough. With his emotions swinging like an erratic pendulum, he had moments where his anger at Erin for not giving them a chance consumed him. The anger would then vanish as fast as it arrived and all he'd feel was an emptiness that pervaded him like the chill of a Wisconsin winter. He missed her like— God, there was no analogy. He just missed her. Desperately. He didn't know what he hated more—the fact she didn't love him enough to try for a future together or, despite the crushing reality that she didn't love him, he still missed her so very much.

Don't look at me like that. He scratched Mac behind the ears as the dog gave him a doleful stare. The border collie had been fretting since Erin and Maggie-May had left.

If she can't love us then she's not worth missing.

The mantra he'd taken up chanting under his breath since Erin had left called up the whoosh of hot anger. He welcomed it because it was easier to feel the heat of fury in his veins than deal with the cold, desolate and empty space in his soul.

Vern stood up. "We're celebrating the fact we milk cows, make ice cream and maple syrup, that we're part of local tourism and the Whitetail wedding business."

Wade grimaced. "We didn't do so well with our first wedding."

"Nonsense," Vern said with paternal pride. "We did just fine. The farm looked beautiful and you and your mother created delicious food. It isn't our fault the bride was a nut job. But back to Keri's question, we're celebrating the diversity and changing needs of the family farm. Long may she be prosperous."

Keri wrinkled her nose. "Dad, everything you've listed only involves Luke and Wade."

"You're a shareholder, Keri," Luke reiterated calmly what he'd said to her more than once just recently. "More importantly you're part of the family. Ideally, I hope you take your farm dividends, no matter how large or small, and invest them into the kids' college fund. But, if you do want to sell your share—" he visualized his financial spreadsheet "—I can't buy you out immediately but by the time Grace and Ethan are in high school I should be able to make you an offer."

Keri glanced at Phil who nodded encouragingly at her. "Thanks, Luke, I appreciate the thought behind the offer but Phil and I have been talking about it and we want to be able to bring the kids up here and have them feel like they belong on the farm."

Wade gave Luke a jubilant grin as if to say *I told you so.* His hosting of the family in one of his vacation cabins had paid off.

Keri caught the grin and gave a wry smile. "I mean

why should Grace and Ethan miss out on the character-building opportunity of getting up at 4:00 a.m. in their vacation time to milk cows?"

Vern snorted. "I think your memory's a bit faulty on that score. Can anyone remember Keri doing that?"

Wade laughed. "I remember the bitching, whining and moaning."

Keri moved fast, wrapping her older brother in a headlock.

The children cheered on their mother and uncle while Phil rolled his eyes and turned to his mother-in-law. "So, Martha, is there anything I can do to help with supper?"

She smiled at him. "Phil, I'm sure it's your and my night off." She jerked her thumb toward her two eldest children who were still horsing around. "Those two can serve us."

Keri and Wade immediately started arguing good-naturedly over who was doing what in the final stages of the meal preparation. As everyone started drifting into the house, Luke leaned back on the porch post and the irony of the situation sucked the breath right out of his lungs.

The family farm was now safe. His family was at peace again in a way that only five strong-minded adults can be—a way that worked for them—and everyone was looking forward to new directions. It should have been perfect. A few weeks ago he would have considered having his mojo back and his family on board with his plans nirvana.

Now he knew it didn't come close.

But it was going to have to do.

When he'd offered Erin everything, he'd put his heart

on the line for the first time in his adult life. She'd returned it battered and had trampled all over his plans, not wanting to be part of any of them. Not wanting his love.

The dull ache that had become part of him throbbed. Love either existed or it didn't. Futures couldn't be built on a one-sided dream nor could they happen where there was no trust that together they could build something great. If he could wave a wand and have what he wanted most in the world it would be Erin loving him and being an enthusiastic partner in his life, as he would be in hers.

But magic wands didn't exist.

He heard the low mooing coming from the barn, reminding him of his new Jersey cows. Unlike Erin, he could see something great. He could taste it and with hard work, sound business planning and a little bit of luck, he'd build something he was proud of. He could do this and by hell, he would.

He pushed off the porch railing with a clarity of purpose for his life. He was done with Erin and like the excruciating rip of a bandage coming off of hair-covered skin, he let go of her and visualized his future.

The sting lingered on his heart.

TWENTY

IT WAS PAST eleven and Erin was staring at her appointment board. She wasn't going to have to move a single thing around to accommodate a bride who wanted to discuss the idea of photos in the Cowles Conservatory and the sculpture park.

There's work in Whitetail.

So not going there.

Over the past two months, Nicole had been doing everything in her power to get Erin to consider moving to Whitetail permanently. She'd even visited Erin in Minneapolis during a short break with Tony and Max.

"Erin, we worked so well together, you must come back. Please."

"We need you." Tony had smiled encouragingly before putting his one arm around Nicole and the other around Max. "Besides, we need you there to take our wedding photos."

"Can your dog come?" Max had asked hopefully as Maggie-May licked his face.

Although her bank account would love the work, Erin didn't think she could be that mercenary. Whitetail meant steady employment but it also meant meeting Luke at town meetings, in the bakery and at social functions. She'd been back to shoot one wedding where he had been a guest. He'd left before dessert was served and she knew it was because of her. He didn't deserve

to have to dodge her all over a town he'd called home
for thirty years. She owed him that at least. So, she
was back in Minneapolis again, touting for business
and sticking to her original plan. There was nothing
wrong with that. A slow and steady growth was better than expanding too fast, too soon and losing everything. At least she didn't have huge debt and she could
sleep at night.

You are so not sleeping at night.

True, but it wasn't due to debt.

Male voices outside her door jerked her out of her
thoughts and Maggie-May gave a halfhearted bark.
Apart from being excited with Max, she'd been mostly
listless since coming home. Erin had been worried
enough to take her precious to the vet, but the young
woman had given Maggie-May a clean bill of health
and suggested plenty of exercise. Erin knew what the
problem was but she doubted the vet believed in a broken heart. Maggie-May was going to have to toughen
up and get over it.

What? Just like you are?

The scratch of Jesse's key in the lock knocked the uncomfortable thoughts aside. Although she'd been back
home for weeks, Jesse was still living with her and as
much as she grumbled at him about his appalling inac-
curacy in using the laundry hamper as the hoop and his
dirty clothing as the ball, she appreciated having him
around. He filled and overflowed the way-too-quiet
spaces in her life and she needed that.

Soon after her return from Whitetail, acquaintances
had frequently asked, "Didn't the quiet of the country
make you crazy?" At first she'd tried to explain that
what with the moos of the cows, the calls of the loons,

the hum of the tractor and the gentle wash of the lake water against the beach, it wasn't quiet at all. But their question was always rhetorical so instead of telling them that in Whitetail people stopped by just to chat and that in many ways her days were a lot less quiet than here, she just smiled and nodded. At first she'd made a flip comment about being glad she was back close to decent coffee half a block away, but she'd soon dropped that line because Luke had always made good coffee and talking about it reminded her of him.

She didn't need or want reminding of Luke. Her cold and empty bed did that every single night.

You've turned safe into catatonic. Luke's voice taunted her and she blocked it out with, *He didn't understand me. Remember, no regrets.*

"Look who I found at the club," Jesse said as he put his guitar down by the door and dropped his keys into the bowl.

Her father stepped into the apartment with a smile and wide, open arms. "Erin."

A shock of surprise detonated inside her. Although she'd had the occasional text and phone call, she hadn't seen him since he'd driven away from the farm. Thoughts of the farm gave life to the hollow feeling inside of her and she suddenly had an overwhelming need for human contact. Without thinking, she walked into his arms for a quick hug. He smelled of expensive cologne just as he'd always done. "Why didn't you tell me you were coming?"

"He came to hear the band," Jesse offered by way of explanation as he opened the fridge and pulled out some beers. "You want one, sis?"

She shook her head. She was having enough trouble sleeping and alcohol always made it worse. "No, thanks."

Her father accepted the beer and they all sat around her small table. "You're looking good, Poppet."

Was her father just trying to cheer her up? With dark rings under her eyes that no concealer could totally mask, she knew she looked like hell. "Thanks, Dad."

"Jesse tells me that you won a photography competition." His eyes held hurt, which briefly flickered with something else, but before she could catch it, it faded.

"I thought you would have told me about it," he continued, "seeing as I visited the sunflower field where it all took place."

Unexpected guilt fluttered through her and she tried without success to block it. "Sorry. I didn't actually win the competition. I won a section but not the grand overall prize and it wasn't with a sunflower photo." She bit the inside of her mouth so that the memory of what came after the failed wedding didn't swamp her. Despite knowing she'd done the right thing for both of them, Luke's pain-filled face had a habit of reappearing in her mind. "The photo was one I took of an older couple in their strawberry field."

"Show Dad the photo," Jesse said encouragingly. "What's awesome is that the bride must be forty but the way the guy's looking at her, all you can see is how totally hot he thinks she is."

"Jesse!" Erin gave him a gentle shove on the shoulder. "Please don't turn my wedding photos into porn. The art of the shot is in the fact that the bride's bare feet are pressed into the soil of the strawberry field."

He looked at her utterly dumfounded at the criticism

in her voice. "You're wrong, you know. It won because of the look on that guy's face."

Luke's voice surfaced uninvited. *You find the truth of their happiness and photograph it.*

She didn't know what she did anymore.

His father grinned at his son. "From my position, forty is the new twenty." He turned to Erin. "Don't be ashamed of not winning overall."

"I'm not." A bristle of irritation raised its head—not just at her father but at herself. She'd been battling for two months to find the same joy in her work that she'd always found, but since the Littlejohn wedding she'd doubted her artistic eye. It was Nicole who'd asked her permission to enter that particular photo of Lindsay and Keith into the small competition run by a Midwest weddings website in the hope it would raise the profile of Whitetail Weddings That Wow. Erin thought the photo had no chance and that the fee was a waste of Nicole's money but the judges had loved it. Now it seemed even Jesse could see something in the photo she'd missed. It reinforced a nagging and persistent voice that she had no clue what she was doing anymore. That perhaps she'd never had a clue.

"Did you get a plaque to dust?" her father asked.

"She got cash and a new camera," Jessie said, rising to pick up the plaque to show his father.

Tom smiled. "It all helps to build your nest egg, eh?"

"It does." She thought about how much working in Whitetail had done that.

Jesse's phone rang. "Sorry, it's Lenny about the tour next week." He excused himself to take the call.

A silence stretched out between them. "What did you think of the band, Dad?"

"He'll grow up one day, I guess."

Again the bristling sensation sent a crop of goose bumps across her skin. Did her father have the right to criticize when he'd been absent for years? "Jesse works hard at his music."

"But does he work smart?" Her father spun a cardboard coaster. "You know that working two jobs often isn't enough to pay the bills."

She thought about the years on the move where her mother had been working while her father had been working at chasing the next big thing. "Yeah, you taught me that."

He nodded as if not realizing she hadn't given him a compliment. "I also taught you to make your money work for you but you're still not doing that, are you?"

"I'm investing in my account in the bank."

"That's a step forward I suppose." He grinned at her. "At least it's no longer under the floorboards." He squeezed her hand. "I'm glad you're back in town, Erin. I was worried about that guy you were seeing— "

That guy? "Luke?"

"Yeah, Luke." Tom nodded thoughtfully. "I think breaking it off with him was a good idea."

The offer of parental support warmed her. "Thanks, Dad. I do too." *Liar.* She immediately needed some reassurance to counter the screaming denial in her head that kept gaining volume. "Why was it a good idea?"

Tom scratched his chin. "Just a feeling I had. He was telling me about the farm and the sort of debt that's involved in a huge operation like that."

"And he's extending the debt for a new business." Just thinking about it made her shiver.

"Is he now? Well, that makes a lot of things clearer." He leaned back and finished his beer.

She studied his expression. "What do you mean? Clearer?"

Tom shrugged. "I said to him that I wanted to help you out with getting enough money together to lease a studio. At that point he told me to get off his property."

That doesn't sound like Luke. "I don't understand. Why would he do that?"

Tom picked up her hands with fatherly affection. "I'm sorry I have to spell it out to you but he had other plans for your money. He didn't want me around insisting that you get your studio."

Had she heard right? "You want to help me with the studio?"

He smiled widely. "Of course I do."

Hope soared out of the ashes of the past. After all the years of not being there and constantly letting her down, her father had come to her offering to help. He'd really meant what he'd said in Whitetail.

"If having your own studio is what you want," Tom continued, "then that's what I want for you too." He gave her a long look. "I only want for you to be happy."

"Thanks, Dad." Excitement spun in her belly. "There's the perfect space down in the Northrup King building. I can show you tomorrow and I'm only a few thousand short but if you go guarantor for the lease—"

"Hang on a bit, Poppet." He laughed. "Don't get ahead of yourself. I want to help, I really do, but it won't be a cash handout. You've always been so independent and I know you wouldn't want that either."

She wanted to yell, *I'm so tired and worn down by*

everything that I'd love a cash gift, but she made herself keep listening.

"I can advise you on how your money can work for you. I know you prefer the bank and if you move some of it into a high-interest account, then that's a start. I also have some money in a company which is giving good returns right now. It's as safe as the bank but with better returns. Of course the less you invest the less you get back but I promise you, you'll either be working in your studio by the end of the year or the end of next." He smiled. "It's totally up to you."

I promise you. The well-worn words that had always fallen so easily from his mouth burned her like acid and opened her eyes. She studied her father as if really seeing him for the very first time tonight. The collar on his designer shirt was worn, the expensive cut of his hair was growing out and his eyes held the hard glitter of an addict close to getting his hit. In his case, money. *You fool.* She withdrew her hands from under his, pressing the palms hard onto the table so she didn't hit him or face-palm herself. "Are you involved in another start-up company, Dad?"

He shook his head almost too heartily. "No. I've been importing cardboard boxes from China for the last two years."

She wanted desperately to believe him. "Is this investment in cardboard boxes?"

"Diversity is the key, Erin, and your money will be invested in a variety of companies, all of which will return your money to you and more. Like I've always said, work smart not hard."

With the skill of a politician, he'd dodged a straight question and given a vague answer intended to reassure. "What's the name of the investment group, Dad?"

"Rochester Holdings."

She immediately typed the name into the internet browser on her phone.

"When did you get so skeptical, Poppet?" He plucked the phone from her fingers and tilted her chin. "Look at me. I'm here to help you. If I didn't care about you I would have let Luke take all your money for his money pit of a farm."

The words bombarded her. Pulling at her complex feelings for her father and her need to believe he had her best interests at heart, and tugging at the mess that was her now dead relationship with Luke.

I know how much security means to you, Erin, and I'm not asking you to invest any of your savings into the farm.

It was as if Luke had just entered the room, striding forward in his work boots to insert himself between her and her father.

Guarding her.

Loving her.

Her head jerked away from her father's hand. "Do you love me, Dad?"

His head moved slightly back and forth as if the question was ridiculous. "Do you really need to ask?"

"No. I know you do in your own way, only it's not the right way." With her heart bleeding, she stumbled to her feet sending her chair falling backward. "You love my money more than me and damn it, Dad, there isn't even all that much of it. Despite everything you've just told me, I know in my heart of hearts that you need the cash for another start-up or to pay off a debt collector. I can't believe I was blind to the signs but then again, you're a smooth operator." Her voice rose. "Using Luke against me was the bull's-eye on my emotional weak spot, only this time you've miscalculated."

"Erin—"

"What's going on?" Jesse came back into the room, his phone still in his hand. "Why are you yelling?"

"Your sister's having an emotional meltdown," Tom said calmly. "It's understandable, really, given everything she's been through lately."

"How do you even know what I've been through?" she shouted as everything fell more securely into place. "I've never told you a thing about what happened when I left Whitetail and yet here you are using it to get money."

"Oh, shit." Jesse paled. "I'm sorry, Erin. I told him you'd broken up with Luke." His eyes suddenly blazed with anger and hurt and he turned on his father. "So that's why you've been coming to the club and grilling me on Erin. It's got nothing to do with fatherly concern or wanting to make things up to her, has it?"

Tom took a step forward with his hands up. "You've got it all wrong, son. I've been coming to the bar to reconnect with you."

"You rat bastard." Jesse's right hand formed into a fist.

Erin moved between them. Things were bad enough without adding a fistfight. "Scamming your daughter is as low as a father can possibly go, don't you think, Dad? Leave now and get some help."

Jesse moved to the door and yanked it open. "Erin's right, you need help. Remember to tell the therapist that you used your son as an unwitting accomplice so it goes on your rap sheet."

"Kids, you've got it all wrong," Tom said, desperation clinging to every word.

"No, we haven't." Jesse's voice tumbled over Erin's and he reached for her hand in a show of support.

Tom hesitated a moment, glancing between the two of them and then his body seemed to slump and he looked every minute of his fifty-five years. "I know you've got no reason to believe a single word I say, Erin, but that farmer of yours did ask me to leave his farm, only it wasn't for the reason I said."

Anger, disbelief and a thousand other emotions piled in on top of each other, making her question everything. "Then why did he ask you to leave?"

He sought her gaze. "To protect your money."

The memory of watching her father leave the farm with Luke's hand gripping hers so tightly that he crushed her fingers was as clear to her as if it was happening right this very moment.

Trust me. I will never do anything or let anything hurt you.

For the first time she truly believed them. Luke had done something that her father wasn't capable of doing. His love for her had instinctively protected her, whereas her father's love was warped by his addiction. "Dad, you've got a gambling addiction."

Tom shook his head. "That's a bit harsh, Erin."

Sadness trickled through her for all of them. "It's the truth, Dad. It's cost us Mom and our life as a family."

"I love you both."

She gripped Jesse's hand. "You do in your own way but you love the thrill of the chase and the dream of the big bucks more. All I'm asking you to do is admit that and get some help."

"I'll think about it." He lingered for a moment but when neither of his children moved, he said, "Goodbye."

Erin nodded, closing the door behind him and then she leaned her forehead onto the wood, relief slow to come to her.

"Do you think he'll really go get help?" Jesse asked.

She raised her head, glimpsing the pain of betrayal in her younger brother's eyes. "I have no idea but I do know one thing."

"What's that?"

"Don't have any expectations or any illusions that he truly means it. Trust me, it's so much easier that way. And safer."

The pain of the truth made him flinch. "I'm so sorry, Erin. I would never have told him any of that stuff about you and Luke except that I thought he'd changed."

"Both of us hoped for that." She hugged him, wanting to make him feel better, just like she'd always done when he was a little boy. She'd always been the one who'd defended her mother and brother against her father. Always been the one trying to make things better and to keep them happy even when she was desperate for someone to defend and protect her.

Luke defended you. He protected you.

Her body started shaking and she sucked in a deep breath to steady herself. Luke had put her first and she'd let the past blind her to it. Her breath turned into a gulp and great racking sobs tore out of her, as if being hauled from her toes. Luke loved her enough to both defend her from her father and yet protect her feelings at the same time. What other reason was there for him not telling her what her father had done? Anyone else would have told her what a bastard Tom had been.

"Erin?" Jesse's hand patted her shuddering back. "Um, are you okay?"

"Yes, no, I'm not sure," she wailed into his shoulder. "I think I've messed up the best thing that's ever happened to me."

Jesse shoved a box of tissues into her hands. "Is this about Luke looking out for you?"

She gave a shuddering gasp of breath and wiped her eyes, surprised at her brother's intuition. "I told him I didn't love him."

Surprise crossed his cheeks. "Yeah, you told me you didn't love him so why are you crying?"

"Because I l...lo...love him," she stammered out between rafts of tears.

"You told him you didn't love him but actually you do?" Jesse looked and sounded utterly bamboozled. "I thought girls were supposed to know all this stuff and it was guys who were clueless."

She accepted the criticism. "I didn't know then."

"Does he love you?"

She sniffed. "He proposed to me."

"Jeez." He squeezed her shoulders so she had to look at him. "Do you miss him?"

She wiped her face on her sleeve. "Every single moment."

Jesse huffed out a breath. "Then go see him."

"It's not that easy. It's really complicated."

"It doesn't have to be," Jesse said pragmatically, picking up her car keys. "I'll drive you."

She swiped the keys back off him. "You've had beer."

"Then you drive but I'm coming with you because I want to shake this guy's hand."

She thought about the hurt on Luke's face the last time she'd seen him, how she'd stomped on his dreams for them both and her heart spasmed so hard it stole her breath. "That's if he'll let us."

"LUKE!"

Wade's yell and the blast of cold air made Luke glance up from his accounts to see his brother standing at the farm office door. "Come in and close the door."

Panting heavily, Wade stepped inside, madly waving a magazine in the air. "Remember that journalist who came and did a piece on 'fall in the northwoods' and he reviewed the B and B?"

Luke rolled his eyes. "I'd hardly have forgotten it given you suggested I might want to groom the cows so they looked good for the photos."

"You do it for the state fair," Wade quipped. "Anyway, he just sent me the advance copy."

Luke put out his hand. "So I'm figuring they gave you a great review."

Wade handed over the magazine. "I got a highly recommended."

"Good for you." He was proud of his brother. Wade worked hard, knew hospitality and he had the happy knack of reading what people wanted out of their long weekend or vacation. He started scanning the article but Wade's wide forefinger almost punched it out of his hands. "Look, here."

"I'm trying." Luke spun away from him so he could keep reading uninterrupted.

Unable to wait, Wade excitedly pulled the magazine back. "*American Road Magazine* describes your ice cream as—" he cleared his throat "—pure, old-fashioned decadence. How awesome is that?" He thumped him on the back enthusiastically.

Luke couldn't quite take it in. To get publicity like this in the second month of production was almost unbelievable. "You served him Lakeview Farm ice cream?"

Wade beamed. "Yep. I gave him a generous scoop of your vanilla bean buzz to complement my best cherry pie and he loved it. I was thinking when you get the farm ice cream shop up and running next summer, I might offer a selection of pies to sell along with your cones."

Luke stood up and grabbed his coat and scarf. "Good idea. Come on up to the house and we'll celebrate our good reviews."

Wade hesitated. "Ah, Luke…"

You need to get out more. Luke finished Wade's unspoken sentence in his head. He knew he needed to get out more and for the past few weeks he'd been planning on going into town to have a meal at the Udder Bar and get back into circulation. Tonight was as good a night as any. "What about a drink at the Udder Bar?"

"I think you should do that and any other night I'd join you but—" Wade shot him a sheepish smile "—I've got a date."

Surprise rocked him. "Where did you meet him?"

"He was in the wedding party for the Littlejohn wedding."

"He's not related to the crazy bride, is he?" Luke half joked.

Wade laughed. "No need to panic. He's a friend of the groom."

He was pleased for Wade because it had been a long time since he'd dated. "I hope it's a good night for you."

Wade's shoulders rose and fell in an awkward fashion. "Actually, it's our fourth date and his name's Steve."

"Fourth date?" Luke got the unhappy feeling that his brother's uncharacteristic lack of disclosure had something to do with him.

Wade's eyes filled with sympathy. "The reason I haven't mentioned Steve is because there'd be nothing worse than listening to me rattle on about how great he is when it's not that long since Erin left."

The feelings of loss he'd worked so hard to keep at bay started to rise and he shoved them down fast. "Damn it, Wade, I'm not one of your fragile English teacups. I can cope with other people being part of a couple. Just go enjoy your date."

Without waiting for a reply, he strode toward the house with Mac at his side and focused on the nip in the fall air biting into his skin. For weeks he'd been telling himself he was fine. Coping. Moving forward, but a few words from Wade had him battling to regain his equilibrium.

He needed to get back out in the world. He pulled out his phone, intending to call Lindsay and Keith to see if they wanted to meet him for a drink, when Mac suddenly took off, barking wildly and racing toward the house.

Luke squinted into the dusky gloom. He heard a high-pitched yapping and then he made out the bulky shape of an old station wagon.

Erin was back.

Delight and hope sprouted inside him like the corn flourishing in early spring sunshine and nurturing rain.

I don't love you, Luke.

Everything shriveled and withered under the frosty assault of her betrayal.

Harnessing a protective anger, he sprinted across

the yard, took the porch steps two at a time and yanked open the screen door. Without stopping to remove his hat or boots, he strode into the kitchen. Maggie-May threw herself at him with enthusiastic delirium, bouncing against his legs and barking manically.

He picked her up and deposited her outside with Mac before turning back to face Erin.

She sat at the kitchen table with a container of Lakeview Farm ice cream in front of her and two spoons. Her face was thinner, huge smudges of black tainted the delicate skin under her eyes, and her normally glossy hair lacked shine. She looked miserable and he wanted to gather her into his arms and take care of her.

I can never marry you. My life's in Minneapolis.

He steeled his heart.

"What the hell are you doing in my house?"

TWENTY-ONE

"Most people call first."

Erin swallowed against the lump in her throat as Luke stood in the middle of the room. With his feet wide apart and his hands on his hips, he stared at her with more loathing than the first time she'd gate-crashed his kitchen. He looked as handsome as ever but the lines around his eyes seemed deeper. Any plans of throwing herself into his arms and begging for forgiveness were stalled by the torment on his face and in his eyes. By the pain she'd put there. All of it kept her in her chair. She knew that coming back this way to see him was a risk, but she'd learned a lot last night and it was a risk she needed to take. She had no other choice.

She tried to stay strong against his anger, which buffeted her like wild winter winds, and she pulled up every ounce of calm she had in her. "If I'd called ahead you would have refused to talk to me, let alone agreed to see me."

"You got that right." He stalked to the fridge like a panther preparing to rip into its prey and dispensed a large glass of water. "It's what I plan to do now. Take your dog and leave."

The antipathy in his eyes churned her stomach and shattered her hope. "Luke, I'm so sorry for the way we—"

"Not interested in rehashing that particular evening,

Erin, or any version of it." He pointed across the room. "The door's that way."

His resolute stance along with his unambiguous words made his message resoundingly clear. He wanted her gone. Now. Five minutes ago. A ripple of unease tore through her that he might want her gone so badly that he'd pick her up and dump her outside on her ass.

I will never do anything or let anything hurt you.

His words, which had sounded so reassuring in her head on the drive over, quailed under his unforgiving expression.

Don't count on it. He said all that before you broke his heart.

She tried to keep her fear contained—fear that she'd hurt him too much and it was all too late to make amends—and instead held on to her wish that somewhere deep down under all that pain, he still loved her. Flipping off the lid of the ice cream carton, she dug in a spoon and tasted the contents. The creamy taste sent her taste buds into overdrive and left them in a begging frenzy desperate to taste more. It was beyond any ice cream she'd ever tasted.

His eyes narrowed and his voice dropped to a low growl. "Erin, asking you to leave wasn't an invitation to stay and eat ice cream."

She sought his eyes and sent up a prayer that he'd remember. "I know, but I'm not leaving until I've said my piece and I need ice cream to do it."

He stood perfectly still for a moment before releasing a deep sigh and then he moved around the counter and kicked out a chair. As he sat down opposite her, his body language was anything but conciliatory. "Start so you can finish and leave."

Panic that he wasn't going to actually hear what she had to say dove into her, flailing about like a drowning man and stalling her words.

His blue eyes flashed. "I mean it, Erin."

She knew he did and she blurted out, "My father stopped by to visit me last night."

A muscle ticked in his jaw but he stayed silent.

She pushed on, trying to keep her dread at bay that this was all going to end badly for both of them. There was no sign in Luke of the man who loved her and his absence was all her fault. "To cut a long story short, he wanted to invest my studio money."

His eyes narrowed. "And?"

"I said no."

"Good for you." He crossed his arms. "Is that it?"

She shook her head. "No, it's just the start." The harsh look in his eyes and the tautness of the anger on his face upended the speech she'd been rehearsing on the long drive from Minneapolis and she went straight to the truth. "He made me realize that I love you."

Apart from the blink of his eyes, no other part of his body reacted to her declaration.

Her heart tripped over itself and despair flooded her. *It's too late. It's too late, it's too late…*

He leaned back in his chair, his demeanor one of boredom. "Do you want me to send in the band? Throw a ticker-tape parade?"

Is that what she'd expected? Bells and whistles? Woots of joy and him twirling her around in his arms at her admission of love?

Deep down, yes you did.

She knew he was hurting and that it was all her fault but a surge of frustration lanced her that he couldn't see this was an offer of a new starting point for them. "Actually, I thought we might be able to have an adult conversation about it."

"An adult conversation?" His voice cracked. "Are you freaking kidding me?"

"Well, what else do you want me to say, Luke?"

"I don't know."

His weary words rained over her and she bit her lip at the hopelessness that took massive bites of her heart and soul. She was too late to fix this.

You have to fight for him.

"I'm so sorry, Luke. I never wanted to hurt you. I was scared witless when you told me you loved me. It wasn't part of the plan and I never expected it. The idea of marriage terrified me not because of who you are but because of what might happen to change us. I couldn't face us destroying each other like my parents destroyed their lives."

"I never saw it that way, Erin." Sadness scored his face. "Plenty of marriages work if both partners want it enough."

Recognizing the truth, she sucked in her lips and hauled in a breath. "You were right when you said I wasn't prepared to risk anything. I told myself that walking away from you was the price I had to pay for my overall security. I'd held on so long to the ideal that financial security offered me everything I needed to keep me safe, that I totally believed it. I didn't realize that by losing you I lost everything else."

The catch in Erin's voice and the utter misery on her face almost undid Luke and he had to hold tight to his hurt to protect himself. As much as he wanted to lean across the table and grab her hands, he really didn't know if she'd truly changed. There were things he needed to know before he'd put his heart on the line all over again. "What do you mean you lost everything? You still have your savings?"

"I have the money but nothing else." Her hands opened, palm up. "For years I've used my camera as a barrier between my life and the world. I was absorbing the happiness of others through my camera lens, because it offered me a detached safety from my unsteady world. To be totally honest, I craved it. It all came tumbling down with Connie's wedding. I didn't want to accept it had all been an illusion of safety."

She tugged at her hair. "Since I left Whitetail, I've lost the joy I always found in my job and I'm second-guessing every frame I take. I can't even see the good stuff in my previous work." Her face filled with pleading. "I need you."

His heart gave a traitorous leap. He'd dreamed of hearing her speak those words but now that they floated between them, they weren't enough. "Erin, I'm not your new safety zone. You can't depend on me for your creative spark."

Her eyes implored. "One part of me knows that but is it so wrong that my happiness is connected to you and that it flows into my work? Isn't that love?" She pointed to the quickly softening ice cream. "You were lonely when I first met you and you'd lost your passion for your work. Will you deny that I was part of your returning happiness?"

Her words hit home. She'd been integral in him finding the joy in his life. "No, but—" he plowed his hands through his hair "—the things you feared still exist. Life with me isn't going to be a safe cocoon. No marriage is immune from tough times and when you add in the inherent risk that is farming, I can't give you an absolute guarantee that we won't have some hard times."

"I'm prepared for that."

"Are you really?" He'd vowed never to revisit that night but he let his guard down enough to speak the truth. "Do you have any idea what it was like watching you walk away from me? I'm not sure I can trust you not to do it again."

"Luke." Her voice wobbled over his name and her green eyes seared him with their honesty and pain. "I'm asking you to trust me and believe that I will never hurt you like that again."

His heart wanted to trust what he saw in her eyes—her regret for hurting him so much—but his brain was saying no. "I'm not sure words are enough."

"I know actions speak louder than words. Last night my father used words that masqueraded as love and caring to try and steal my money. As appalling as that is, I have to thank him for it because it put everything into perspective."

A rush of intense fury at Tom dueled with a surge of protection for her. "I wish I'd been there to kick his ass."

"You were there."

Her softly spoken words made no sense. "I don't understand."

"I heard your voice saying to me, 'I'm not asking you to invest any of your savings, just invest in me.' Luke, you've only ever loved me for me. You only want good things for me, for us. I'm sorry it took me so long to realize that you're the best thing that has ever happened to me."

Her love for him shone in her eyes and the tips of her

fingers touched his. Her heat, love and entreaty rolled into him, calling at him, appealing to him to give her a second chance. To give them both a second chance at a future together.

She bit her lip. "As much as I didn't want to see it, you've shown me I can't wrap myself up in a bubble of sterile safety and control everything from there…" She gave a resigned smile. "What did you call it?"

He flinched for her, knowing how hard it was to be emotionally honest. "A catatonic life, but I was angry, Erin—"

"No." She shook her head. "I needed to hear it. I'm just sorry it's taken this long to really understand it. You also showed me that without a calculated risk my life will be one of lost potential. I'm done with being 'catatonic.'

"Luke, I want you. I want Mac and the cows. I want the ice cream business and the mortgage and all the calculated risks. I promise you, I'll be here for the bad times and I want to celebrate the good. I want it all and I want it with you." Her hand moved so her fingers interlaced with his. "Luke, will you marry me?"

Her honesty and sincerity spun around him like the joy of sunshine after rain, and his heart soared. She loved him and the last pieces of the rickety barricade he'd erected around his heart fell away.

Erin held her breath. She'd laid everything out on the line including her heart, just like Luke had done two months ago. Apprehension and dread raced in opposite directions up and down her veins, slowing time down to a standstill. The agony of waiting for him to speak ramped up her own culpability when she'd summarily rejected his love for her at the end of the summer.

The multihued facets of color in his blue-on-blue eyes sparkled like a kaleidoscope. "You really want to marry me?"

She breathed in jerkily. "I really, really do."

"You want to take the biggest risk of your life with me?"

She held his gaze. "It's not a risk, Luke. It's living my life with potential."

Still holding her hands, he stood up and she did too. They walked sideways down the table until there was nothing between them but air. Her heart beat crazily. Did this mean yes?

He stared at her so intently that she could barely shift air in and out of her lungs and the crows of doubt assailed her.

"Thank God." He pulled her into his arms and holding her tightly against him, he kissed her hard as if she might suddenly vanish. His mouth melded to hers, making her whole again and when he finally pulled away, he gazed down at her intently. "You taste like maple syrup delight."

She started to laugh and relief flowed through her, making her shake. He loved her. They had a future together. Leaning into him she savored the feel of the solid muscle underneath his shirt and what it represented— love and a life lived to the fullest.

"Erin?"

"Hmm."

"I'm starting a desensitization program right now. You need to start associating eating our ice cream with happy occasions." He pulled them down onto a chair and settled her on his lap before picking up a spoon, scooping ice cream and feeding her.

Resting against him and after three glorious mouthfuls of the wickedly delicious ice cream, she said, "This ice cream is definitely celebration stuff. Let it be noted that the day you agreed to marry me we toasted with magical maple syrup ice cream. Which flavor will we have at the wedding?"

He grinned at her. "Vanilla Bean Buzz because it goes with every occasion. At the moment the choice isn't huge but slow and steady expansion is the way to go." His smile turned serious. "Erin, the farm is a business that pays me a salary and most of the time it pays dividends to everyone in the family, which go up and down depending on the season. The mortgage is against the business, not against personal savings. I want to sit down and explain it all to you tomorrow so you fully understand how it all operates."

Her heart swelled at the new partnership that he was offering her. "My photography books are not quite as complicated but I'll go through them with you too. I've only just got to the point of being able to draw a salary."

"It will grow," he said confidently. "Lindsay was really thrilled that one of their wedding photos won some prize."

She looked up at him in surprise. "You know about that?"

"This is Whitetail, remember. Nicole and Lindsay told everyone who'd listen and despite everything that had gone down between us, I was really proud of you." He brushed her hair behind her ear. "I still am. So, are you going to become Whitetail's resident photographer for weddings, christenings and every other occasion? You've already got the darkroom here and the option of a studio in town."

For the first time since she'd left Whitetail she got a buzz of excitement for her work. It was totally different from the past but it was equally exhilarating. She kissed him. "I think I will be that person."

"That's what I was hoping you'd say."

His love surrounded her in warmth and security. "How do you feel, though, about me working many weekends of the year?"

"Probably much the same as you feel about me milking cows most days of the week, but the boss here is pretty flexible." He grinned. "We'll get Brett to milk on Wednesdays and make that our weekend. I was wondering…"

She recognized the scheming in his eyes. "What?"

"Do you think you could get a few wedding gigs in warm places during winter so we could turn them into mini-vacations? One thing I've learned from my parents is that escaping off the farm now and then is a very good idea."

She laughed. "I hear Hawaii and Mexico are popular wedding destinations so I'll add that to my five-year expansion plan for the business, shall I?"

He pressed his hand against her belly and his lips against her neck. "Talking expansion and five-year plans, how do you feel about a seventh generation of Andersons running around the farm?"

A wave of wonder washed through her. "It totally thrills me and terrifies me all at the same time."

He nodded with a soft smile. "Me too, but totally worth the risk."

She knew family was a big part of Luke's life and she wanted to have everything out on the table between them. "The thing is, Luke, we both know my father, and I have no clue if we'll ever be able to trust him."

Empathy shone in his eyes. "My folks will be on the farm for half the year in their own house, and they'll be falling over themselves to be grandparents."

She thought about her wonderful brother who was sitting in a motel in Whitetail waiting for her. "I can provide a bachelor uncle with Jesse."

"Perfect. We might just need a bachelor uncle because Uncle Wade may not be a bachelor by then."

"Really?" She sat up straight. "That's lovely for Wade. Who's the guy and—"

Luke raised his brows. "Do you think we can we talk about Wade's love life later and concentrate on our own for now?"

"What a good idea." She wrapped her arms around his neck and kissed him, reveling in his touch and taste and everything that was quintessentially Luke. "I've missed you so much."

"Welcome back." He kissed her, infusing her with his love and support and she opened herself up to it all, knowing without a doubt she was finally home.

US Bride

WHO PHOTOGRAPHS THE *bride when the bride is a wedding photographer? Everyone! When Erin Davis married her dairyman, Luke Anderson, the couple exchanged vows in the middle of a shimmering golden canola field and all the guests took photos with cameras provided by the bride.*

"Everyone had so much fun and although we did have one professional photographer on hand for the

signature shots, my favorite photo of the day was taken by my brother, Jesse," Erin said. *"He's got an amazing eye."*

The wedding was a family affair. The bride wore a straight white sheath overlaid with antique lace and her bouquet was filled with peonies and fragrant old-world roses. Her brother gave her away and she wore her mother's pearl necklace. The farmhouse garden was the perfect setting for the reception and long trestle tables curved through the trees. Pretty field flowers displayed in jam jars along with tea candles were dotted along the center of the tables, adding to the rustic feel of the wedding. The table settings said love, being a mish-mash of fine china from the groom's family with some pieces dating back over a hundred years.

The groom's brother catered the event and Lakeview Farm ice cream and cherry pie were served for dessert. When Luke Anderson was asked why the couple's pets were not part of the ceremony, he replied drily, "They're dogs." He was later seen holding the Maltese–Shih Tzu terrier cross under one of his suited arms.

Nicole Lindquist, Whitetail's soon-to-be-married wedding planner and the couple's maid of honor, said, "The farm is a magical place for a wedding and may be available for other weddings pending a successful interview with the Andersons."

The couple is honeymooning in warm and sunny Fiji.

* * * * *